Dead Again

Holly Copella

To Lori Bilinsky,

Thank you for taking such
wonderful care of "the big guy"!

ACKNOWLEDGMENTS

Copella Books: First Paperback Edition 2022
Cover Artist: Daniela Owergoor
Dani-owergoor.deviantart.com
Model by Holly Copella
Model: Maverick; Aka: Batman
Printed by KDP, an Amazon.com Company

PUBLISHER'S NOTE

CHAPTER 1

A brilliant flash of lightning lit up the dark April sky and was immediately followed by loudly rumbling thunder. The light rain soon turned heavy and drenching. A young woman in her early twenties, wearing nothing but a soaking wet, oversized t-shirt, ran barefoot across the field while clutching her bleeding shoulder. A large portion of her shirt was now stained pink from the rain washing the blood past her hand. Sage Remington was an attractive twenty-two-year-old woman with emerald green eyes and long dark hair that now stuck to her drenched body. She was panting heavily, partly from her sprint but mostly from the severity of her injury. Her once beautiful face was contorted in pain, and her skin was pale from blood loss. Despite her bare feet being dirty and sore, she couldn't afford to stop. She continued running through the pouring rain until she reached an apple orchard.

Sage stopped only a moment and looked around. The large apple orchard spanned many acres with hundreds of tall trees. The full strawberry moon was partially visible despite heavy cloud cover, casting creepy shadows off the trees. She'd be exposed to her attacker if she continued through the orchard. Although she couldn't see it, she knew the road was just beyond the apple farm. She had to keep moving, and she needed to cross the orchard if she wanted to reach the road. Sage no longer heard the frightening sound of her attacker behind her, but that didn't mean she was alone. As the pouring rain eased, the clouds parted, exposing more of the rare strawberry moon. Sage caught her breath only a moment, then looked at the stained shirt beyond her hand. She pulled her hand away from her shoulder wound for only a moment. Blood continued to run from the deep puncture. She gasped and again clutched the wound.

Sage wasn't sure how much blood she had lost, but she had to find help soon. She gathered her strength and bolted across the apple orchard. What was a beautiful orchard during the day was amazingly frightening in the dark. The thunder continued to crack loudly, just about rumbling the ground beneath her feet. A nearby flash of lightning struck one of the trees, and Sage could almost feel the energy in the air. Although the sod was mostly soft and wet, she could still feel hard protrusions, possibly roots or broken branches from the trees, bruising the soles of her feet. She had to ignore the pain if she wanted to survive. As she continued to run almost sluggishly now, she could see the dark road up ahead. There was no guarantee anyone would be on the back road this time of night, but she had to risk it. The road was her only remaining lifeline.

As she neared the road, she saw headlights from an approaching jeep. She had to stop that jeep! Sage heard movement behind her, but she couldn't look back. It would be the end if she lost even a second on the approaching vehicle. Sage ran out into the road several yards in front of the swiftly moving jeep and raised her hands in the air despite the pain it caused her injured shoulder. She screamed even though the driver would never hear her. The jeep slammed on its brakes and skidded loudly across the wet road. Sage saw the headlights getting closer as the sound of the tires squealed. She considered diving out of the vehicle's path for a second, but she needed the driver to stop no matter what. The jeep came to a screeching stop only inches before hitting her.

Sage released the breath she'd been holding and slowly lowered her arms, clutching her bleeding shoulder again. She weakly clung to the front of the jeep and hurried for the passenger side as the driver's side door opened. She panted while waving to the driver.

"We have to go," she gasped, feeling her legs becoming almost too heavy to move.

She no sooner heaved herself into the passenger side when the jeep sped off down the road.

§

Two months later. The small town of Great Bend was bustling with activity at the end of another work week. The remote farming community was filled with friendly people who looked out for one another. Many shops and small homes lined the clean streets while massive ranches and farms surrounded the town. Many older historical buildings were located in Town Square and along the main drag. Not far from the center of town was an old, beautifully detailed building, one of Main Street's more imposing structures. Large glass windows in front revealed a grand bookstore. There were shelves of vintage books within the antique shop, looking more like a historical library. There was also a selection of new books. Toward the back of the shop was a sitting area with desks and antique furniture, inviting patrons to browse and relax.

The modern section of books occupied the back of the building, which was not far from an old door marked 'private'. The employee's only door led up the stairs to the store owner's living quarters. Near the back of the shop, Sage sat on the floor and unpacked some newly arrived books before closing up for the evening. After her harrowing ordeal just two months earlier, Sage appeared fully recovered and in fine spirits. The bookstore owner, Sage's older sister, stood nearby and reorganized one of the shelves. Sage's sister, Tobias 'Toby' Remington, was a beautiful, twenty-six-year-old woman with wavy medium brown hair that hung down just below her shoulders. She stood roughly five-foot-five with a mildly petite frame. Her emerald green eyes that sparkled beyond dark lashes were almost identical to Sage's eyes. There was little doubt the two women were related. Sage removed the last book from the cart and drifted out a moment while staring at the book's decorative gold trim.

Toby eyed her sister, saw the look on her face, and seemed almost concerned. "You okay?" she asked.

Sage jolted back to reality and smiled at her sister. "Yeah, I'm fine," she replied and felt somewhat embarrassed. "Just thinking about *things*."

Toby seemed to tense at the comment and shifted uncomfortably. "Don't go there, okay?" she remarked sympathetically.

"I can't help it," Sage replied with a soft, frustrated groan as she stood. "It's been over two months, and it still seems like some horrible dream that I can't shake." She shook her head. "I lost two weeks somewhere, and I just want those two weeks of my memory back."

"Maybe it's best that you don't remember," Toby insisted while raising a brow.

"Some psycho killed our mother, and I possibly witnessed the entire thing," Sage informed Toby with frustration. "If I could just remember what happened, maybe they could find the guy."

Toby approached Sage and leaned against the bookshelf alongside her. She affectionately placed her hand on her sister's shoulder.

"I want nothing more than to find the guy who attacked you and killed Mom," Toby gently announced, then compassionately stared into her sister's eyes. "But your memory loss wasn't because of a head injury, so you intentionally blocked it out. You spent almost a week in that hospital in the city listed as a Jane Doe after the attack." Toby held her breath and tensed. "I even assumed you were dead too until you showed up at my door here in Great Bend two months ago."

"It's kind of frightening," Sage remarked, shuttering slightly. "My last memory was right before I went to bed in my apartment in Colfax. Then, two weeks later, I wake up in some hospital halfway between here and Colfax." She shook her head. "Two whole weeks just erased from existence."

Toby affectionately rubbed Sage's shoulder. "I know it's scary not remembering what happened during those two weeks, but maybe not remembering Mom's death and your attack is a bit of a blessing." Toby held her breath while staring into her sister's eyes. "I'm just happy to have you back. You're the only family I have left."

Sage hugged Toby in a warm embrace and then released her just as quickly. The last two months had been extremely emotional, and she hadn't felt like herself since the attack. She heard what her sister was saying, but she had a difficult time believing her memory loss was for the best. No matter what trauma it brought, she needed to know what was buried deep inside her subconscious. She must have seen the killer, but her mind refused to let her remember. The old-fashioned bell above the door dinged, signaling customers despite being almost closing time.

"I'll check on that," Sage announced and turned away from her sister.

Obviously, she was avoiding the difficult conversation with Toby about everything that had happened, but she hated being a burden. At times, Sage felt defective. Losing those two weeks of memory was more painful than recovering from her physical injury. Sage headed to the front of the store and saw a man almost ten years older than herself enter. Sage managed to smile at Toby's on-again-off-again boyfriend. Leo was a taller, physically fit man with more than his share of charisma. The handsome, thirty-year-old man had slightly longer dark hair and incredibly dark eyes. Despite his charm and good looks, he wasn't Sage's favorite person in the world.

"Hey, Leo," Sage announced with false pleasantries for the man she secretly loathed. "Toby's in the romantic fiction section."

"Thanks, Sage," Leo announced a little too pleasantly while offering his usual, charming smile, then continued past.

Sage rolled her eyes and sneered her distaste. She was almost certain Leo knew how she felt about him, but they continued to pretend everything was okay for Toby's sake. Honestly, it was none of Sage's business, and she was determined to stay out of her sister's relationship. Toby had been dating Leo for over a year now, but the way he waltzed in and out of her sister's life was enough to piss off Sage. She just wished her sister held a grudge the way she did. The bell above the door again rang, catching Sage's attention. A man and woman around Sage's age entered and grinned enthusiastically at their friend. Her two new friends, Henry and Shelly, were a brother and sister that lived in Great Bend for more than a year. Sage had met them shortly after moving to the small town after her 'accident' in Colfax.

Henry was a good-looking man in his early to mid-twenties with medium brown hair that was slightly longer yet perfectly styled for that classic boy band look. He had just enough facial stubble for something almost resembling a beard. Henry stood close to six-foot-tall with broad shoulders and a slim build. His sister, Shelly, was a vision of the girl-next-door with shoulder-length, dirty blonde hair and a lean, petite frame. The woman in her early twenties stood a lanky five-foot-seven. She actually looked much younger than her age, appearing more like an older teenager, which was sometimes a disadvantage while out at bars. Sage smiled happily and approached her two friends, although she was a little surprised to see them at the shop.

"I thought we were meeting at the diner?" Sage asked while giving them a curious look. "Has there been a change of plans?"

"We thought we'd just eat at the tavern tonight," Henry informed her.

Sage made a face and almost groaned her disapproval. "You want to spend another evening at the tavern?" she moaned. "Friday, no less?"

"Told you so," Shelly muttered to her brother.

"What else is there to do on a Friday night?" Henry replied and eyed both women. "They're having country line dancing tonight. It could be fun."

"Could be," Sage replied, then raised a cocky brow, "but I doubt it." She eyed him almost suspiciously. "I hope you aren't planning on entering another unsanctioned poker game in the back room."

"No, I learned my lesson," Henry just about pouted with a slight look of defeat. "I'm not ready to play cards anytime soon with those characters again."

"And no playing pool with the Morgan boys either," Shelly scolded. "You know those boys eat their young."

Henry appeared further embarrassed and frowned. "No, I learned that lesson the hard way too."

Shelly eyed Sage and raised her brows. "Did you know he lost two hundred dollars to those boys last Saturday night?" she asked.

Sage's eyes widened in horror. She then shot a look at Henry. "Two hundred?" She shook her head and frowned. "You were warned about those Morgan boys. No one messes with a Morgan boy."

"I know," Henry replied with a sigh, resembling a whipped pup. "It won't happen again."

Shelly finally tore her eyes away from her brother and glanced at her friend with renewed hope. "So, can you leave now?"

"Maybe we should ask Toby to come along," Sage suggested.

Sage internally cringed at the thought of Toby spending another weekend sitting on the couch with Leo doing nothing. It was depressing.

"Toby doesn't want to go to the tavern," Toby called out from the back of the shop. "Go on. Get out of here!"

Sage tensed slightly, then smiled with embarrassment. "She has freakishly good hearing."

CHAPTER 2

$\mathbf{D}$espite the early hour, the tavern was already alive with activity. The tavern was a two-story building that looked more like a large house with a massive wrap-around porch. The enormous stone parking lot was filled with dozens of vehicles, mostly pickup trucks. There wasn't much else surrounding the tavern, as it was positioned on the edge of town, keeping bar traffic away from the residential areas. Inside the tavern, there was hardwood flooring throughout and a large bar that took up the back wall while dozens of tables filled the room. An open section in front of the jukebox also constituted a makeshift dancefloor. Toward the back was the secluded pool parlor with two pool tables and some pub seating. The parlor was partitioned off to provide some much-needed privacy for both pool players and the bar patrons. The pool parlor sometimes got rowdy and often led to profanity from its players.

Although most patrons didn't actually start dancing until they had a few drinks, country music filled the tavern. It was close to dinnertime, and most locals had something to eat before a night of heavy drinking and dancing. Sage, Shelly, and Henry secured a table in the middle of the room and were almost immediately greeted by the already tired-looking waitress, Kennedy. Despite being in her mid-forties, Kennedy was a stunning vision of beauty with alabaster skin and a slim but curvy body. Her dirty blonde hair was straight and just about shoulder-length. Kennedy often looked tired this past year, having gone through a messy divorce, which had been well-broadcasted around town. Yet, despite appearing beaten down and overworked, Kennedy attempted to remain cheerful while working.

"A pitcher of beer and one iced tea?" Kennedy asked with a pleasant smile.

"You've got a great memory," Henry announced.

"Well, I've been working here my entire life. Or at least it seems that way," Kennedy announced, then smiled and pointed her pen at Henry. "And a plate of French fries."

"You know me too well," Henry announced. "I'm going to marry you one day."

Kennedy snorted a laugh. "No offense, but I already have one ex-husband," she replied while remaining pleasant. "The last thing I need is a future ex-husband."

While Henry and Shelly argued about what songs they should play on the jukebox, Sage glanced across the crowded room. Nearly every table was already filled. Friday and Saturday nights were usually packed, and more patrons would continue filling the place as the evening progressed. Although she'd only been in town two months, this was Sage's fourth weekend at the tavern. It was almost sad that she already knew all the regulars. There were the regular regulars, those who were there almost every night of the week. They were the bar jockeys, as Shelly would call them. And then there were the weekend regulars. There was an unauthorized poker game in the back room on Friday nights, and the Friday night poker crowd was already trickling in.

Almost everyone within the tavern dressed casually in faded blue jeans, boots, and flannel shirts. Anyone wearing khakis, polo shirts, and loafers would stand out like a sore thumb. The patrons were all locals, mostly farmers and ranchers. Sage recognized two poker regulars already sitting at the bar, waiting for their game to begin later that evening. The two men were

Fat Matt, a nickname he gave himself, and Slim. Fat Matt wasn't nearly as heavy as his nickname suggested, being only about fifty pounds overweight. The man in his forties was about average height with unkempt brown hair that was slightly longer and wavy with mutton chop sideburns, although the rest of his face was mostly clean-shaven. On the other hand, Slim was about as thin as a man could get without being malnourished. He, too, was in his forties. He stood a lanky six-foot-tall with a mop-top of light brown hair in a sixties hairstyle. Slim remained clean-cut and seemed to care a little more than Fat Matt regarding his clothing.

Although the duo was somewhat loud, they seemed to mind their own business, for the most part. Both men were friends with the bartender, who also happened to be the tavern owner. The tavern owner and bartender, Dusty, was in his early fifties. Standing close to six-foot-tall, Dusty sported what was considered a 'dad-bod'. He had short, ginger hair that he kept hidden beneath his signature, beaten-up baseball cap and a short, thin ginger beard. Dusty was a little lax with gambling in the tavern, but it didn't seem to be hurting anyone, so no one really complained. As Sage scanned the barroom, she felt an odd wave of depression pass over her. Every night at the tavern was exactly the same. It was painfully predictable and almost boring. Maybe that's why Toby never wanted to come along.

§

Sage, Shelly, and Henry were just finishing their dinner as more locals poured in. It was going to be exceptionally crowded tonight. When Henry's cellphone dinged, he removed it from his pants pocket and briefly eyed it.

"What is it?" Shelly asked. "Some sort of alert?"

"Yeah, they're calling for a pretty wicked thunderstorm tonight," he informed her. "But it should clear out by the time we're ready to leave."

Sage squirmed slightly in her seat and subconsciously rubbed her chilled arms. Shelly glanced at Sage and gave her an odd look.

"Something wrong?" Shelly asked.

Sage managed a tiny smile and shrugged. "I get a little freaked during thunderstorms, that's all," she informed them.

"Why's that?" Henry asked.

Shelly glared at her brother and kicked him under the table. He yelped and jumped before eyeing her.

"What was that for?" he demanded.

Shelly silently scolded him and shot looks at Sage.

Henry tensed as if realizing his blunder. "Oh, that's right," he remarked timidly. "Sorry."

"It's okay," Sage replied and managed a tiny smile. "It's not as if I remember anything from that night. Just that there was a massive storm."

"Still," Henry announced and shifted uncomfortably, "I should have remembered that."

"Cities are dangerous places," Sage replied almost timidly, then attempted to shrug it off. "After my mother was killed, moving in with Toby was the only sensible decision. At least it got me out of the city."

"Well, if you were looking for boring, you came to the right place," Henry informed her.

"Memory loss is such a mystery to me," Shelly remarked and shook her head while leaning on the table. "I mean, some people forget hours, some days, some even forget years. Did you just lose that one night?"

"Actually, about two weeks surrounding the attack are a complete blank," Sage informed him. "And then there are patches of missing information here and there. My poor sister. I sometimes talk about her daughter--"

"She has a daughter?" Shelly asked with surprise.

"No," Sage replied with a tiny, uneasy laugh. "That's the problem. I sometimes refer to my niece, and then I remember that she doesn't have children. And she's constantly reminding me of things that I should know, but I don't." Sage shrugged. "Thankfully, she's understanding and patient with me about all of it."

Henry continued to study her and shook his head. "Not even bits and pieces of those weeks?"

"No, nothing," Sage replied as she managed a tiny smile. "Except for thunderstorms. Apparently, there was a horrible thunderstorm. Toby tells me I never had a problem with them before the attack."

"Well, it's only been two months," Henry countered. "You could still get your memory back."

"Maybe it's best that I didn't," Sage insisted and again shivered. "Who knows what I witnessed and what I went through. Some things are best left in the dark where they belong."

"If you remembered what he looked like, maybe they could catch the guy," Shelly remarked.

"I think about that all the time," Sage replied and was momentarily lost in her own thoughts.

The tavern door opened, and a whirlwind of activity seemed to fill the crowded bar with the arriving patrons. The mood of the tavern immediately changed as tensions mounted. Sage didn't even have to look up to know it was the Four Horsemen of the Apocalypse arriving. That was the nickname given to the four Morgan brothers. The tavern's worst nightmare arrived in their typical whirlwind of hellfire and brimstone. The four unruly men entered with their usual laughter, loudness, and profanity. Even though everyone knew it was them, most still looked anyway. Despite being about fifty years old, the eldest brother, Jackson Morgan, was a physically imposing figure. Standing nearly six-foot-three, Jackson was built somewhere between athletic and muscular from years of hard, physical labor on his cattle ranch. His dark hair, peppered with gray, was kept moderately short, and his beard was nearly fifty percent gray. Jackson would be what most women would consider a 'silver fox'. Unfortunately, his arrogance and offensive personality overshadowed his rugged good looks. He had a bad reputation, and he seemed almost a little too proud of it.

Creed Morgan was the second oldest brother, being forty-seven years old. He was quite possibly the most serious of the four and didn't seem to talk nearly as much. Creed stood close to six-foot-tall with a mildly athletic body, and his dark hair was kept short and neat with only minimal signs of graying. He remained clean-shaven, giving his handsome face a somewhat younger appearance. Dean Morgan was the second to youngest of the four, being forty-five years old, and despite being middle-aged, he was still considered handsome by just about any woman's standards. He stood over six-foot-tall with an impressive athletic build. His medium brown hair was kept mostly short, with some graying at the temples. Definitely more rugged than his younger brother; he sported that authentic rancher appeal. He was also the most ill-mannered of the four and nearly twice as vocal as Jackson.

Lance Morgan was the youngest of the four brothers, being forty-three years old. He was tall, nearly six-foot-three, and had a lanky to athletic build. His slightly longer, medium brown hair was thick and straight, while he sported a sparse beard that looked more like a five o'clock shadow. Despite being over forty, he still had a baby face, making him look much younger. Although not nearly as quiet as Creed, he wasn't as vocal as Dean or Jackson. The four brothers lost their mother when they were little, and their father died about five years later when they were teenagers, which left Jackson to care for his three younger brothers.

Without looking as if they were looking, Sage, Shelly, and Henry kept an eye on the four brothers, as did most everyone else in the tavern. A few of Jackson's poker buddies at the bar seemed happy to see him and greeted him. Jackson and his brothers crossed the room in a rowdy whirlwind to their usual table near the back. Despite the large crowds on Friday night, their table was always left vacant for their arrival. Dean winked at one of the younger waitresses, who sneered back at him, which only seemed to amuse him. It didn't help any that the bar owner, Dusty, was good friends with Jackson. Whenever the boys got into trouble, Dusty defended them. Being the tavern was the only game in town as far as barrooms went; it didn't hurt his business any. Despite their tarnished reputation, there seemed to be certain lines the Morgan boys didn't cross. They didn't hit on other men's women, they didn't pick fights with anyone who wasn't looking for one, and anyone who minded their own business was left alone.

The last rule didn't apply to single women, at least not where Dean and Lance were concerned. The two younger brothers would flirt with single women, but once it was established the woman in question wasn't interested, which they usually weren't, they'd back off. It was a rule Jackson strictly enforced. Not only did the eldest Morgan boy's rules apply to his brothers, but he also ruled other patrons with the same iron fist. Although Sage had only seen the eldest brother three or four times since she moved to Great Bend, she already knew most of the stories, which were almost certainly true. Despite Jackson's abrasive and threatening personality, he was surprisingly in control of his emotions.

Sage had never seen Jackson 'go off' on anyone, but she had heard about it. Mostly everyone knew to stay on Jackson's good side. He was unquestionably accepted as the alpha male not just at the tavern but around town as well. Feared yet respected. You didn't want to get on Jackson's radar.

CHAPTER 3

Nearly an hour later, Sage found herself casting looks at Jackson seated at his table, being he was directly in her line of sight. Naturally, something about the man commanded her attention, but she couldn't quite explain her fascination with him. Despite being undeniably handsome, she certainly wasn't attracted to Jackson Morgan, considering he was easily twice her age. Still, she felt a strange connection from the first moment she laid eyes on him. Almost as if she knew him, but that was impossible. Jackson lived in Great Bend his entire life, and she had never been to his hometown before two months ago. There were times she felt as if he were watching her as well, but she was certain he wasn't. There was nothing shy about Jackson. If he wanted to talk to her, he would. Unlike his two younger brothers, Jackson showed little to no interest in the women at the tavern. All four brothers remained single, and, at their age, it was likely they'd stay that way.

"I know it's just me," Shelly announced, bringing Sage back into reality. She then raised a curious brow. "You weren't checking out Jackson Morgan, were you?"

"What?" Sage just about gasped and immediately fidgeted. "No, of course not."

"Good," Shelly replied and sighed with relief. "Never mind that he has more than twenty-five years on you, but it is, after all, Jackson. And, it goes without saying that all of the Morgan boys are off-limits. The last thing you want or need is to get on their radar."

"I wouldn't even consider it," Sage replied without hesitation. Although, she felt compelled to sneak another peek at Jackson as he finished his dinner, then quickly looked back at Shelly and shifted in her chair. "It's just, well, I get this really weird feeling of déjà vu whenever I see him. Which is weird because, obviously, I've never met the guy before."

"Obviously," Shelly replied.

"It's just, well, every time I see him, I have this strange urge to talk to him, and I don't know why," Sage informed her friend, then cocked her head. "I couldn't possibly know him, right? I mean, there's no way."

"A million to one shot," Shelly insisted without hesitation. "We've only lived here maybe a year or so ourselves, but I can tell you those boys have never left the area. They have that big cattle ranch to run. That's where they spend most of their time. I doubt they've ever even gone anywhere on vacation in their lives."

"Memory gaps or not, Toby swears I've never been in this town before two months ago," Sage insisted. "Still--" She again glanced at the rowdy table. "I keep thinking I should talk to him and be certain."

"And say what?" Henry asked with a slightly humored look, now paying attention to the conversation. "Have we met before? He'll laugh in your face."

"Or worse," Shelly muttered and cringed. "He'll think you're trying to pick him up."

"Yeah, that would be worse," Henry remarked and glanced at the Morgan table. "He's such a cocky, arrogant bastard. You may very well be the most beautiful woman in this place, and he'd probably still laugh at you and think you're beneath him."

Sage hesitated and glanced at Henry with a curious look. "Wait," she suddenly remarked, then cocked her head. "Did you just say that I'm the most beautiful woman in here?"

"Yeah, I heard that too," Shelly remarked and slyly eyed her brother for clarification.

Henry immediately shifted in his chair and appeared embarrassed. "I said you *could* be," he replied. "I was just making a point."

"No," Shelly announced while grinning. "He definitely said you *were* the most beautiful woman in here."

"And on that note," Henry announced and stood, "I'm going to play pool before the Morgan boys finish their dinner and take over the pool parlor."

"And when they show up, you leave," Shelly informed him with a commanding look to match.

"Yes, Mother," he muttered, then walked away.

Shelly groaned and shook her head. "Brothers," she scoffed, "be happy you don't have any. I don't recommend them."

Sage chuckled at the comment.

"I'm going to hit the lady's room before the hoedown starts," Shelly teased as she stood. "You coming?"

"No, I'm good, thanks."

"I'll be right back," Shelly insisted before crossing the crowded room for the back hallway that eventually led to the bathroom.

Sage sank into her thoughts. She again cast a look across the room at Jackson. She felt the need to settle her curiosity once and for all, but Henry was right. What would she say? Despite arguing with herself over the entire situation, she was already on her feet and walking across the tavern toward the Morgan table. Sage screamed at herself in protest. She had no idea what was driving her to do something so insane as to talk to Jackson Morgan willingly. She was still wrestling with herself on the conversation and what she'd say when she almost reached their table. The four men were talking and laughing, clearly annoying everyone around them, but no one dared say anything because, well, they were the Morgan boys. The self-professed womanizer of the brothers, Dean, was the first to notice Sage as she got closer. He must have realized that she was clearly heading for their table, and he immediately roused his best smile.

Whatever he said to his brothers, it caused them to shift their attention, and they were now all staring at her. The way all four looked at her was enough to send shockwaves of fear through her. Dean and Lance were studying her with what could only be considered bedroom eyes, while Creed seemed slightly bewildered that the young woman was actually approaching their table. Jackson, on the other hand, appeared indifferent as he casually swirled the whiskey around in his glass. Sage was internally screaming at herself for willingly flying directly into their radar. She'd never spoken with any of the Morgan boys until now. Not even a polite 'hello'. It was possibly the most frightening moment of her life; well, that she remembered.

Unfortunately, she was at their table now, and all four were already looking at her. If she turned tail and ran, she'd lose any credibility with them and look like a frightened deer in headlights. Sage paused before their table, summoned all her courage, and met Jackson's gaze. When their eyes locked, Sage felt her heart pounding almost painfully within her chest. It was quite possible she'd have a heart attack and die on the spot. Jackson's usual devious grin seemed to vanish as he stared back at her, his curiosity getting the better of him.

"Something I can do for you, darling?" he asked in his usual overly confident and somewhat cocky tone, almost certainly mocking her.

She heard the slow song playing on the jukebox and went with it. "Would you care to dance?"

Jackson's arrogance diminished completely as he stared at her with what could only be described as astonishment. He then cocked his head as his arrogance and cheap grin quickly returned.

"Are you drunk?" Jackson asked with a chuckle.

His three brothers snickered in response.

Dean practically shot up from his chair. "I'd love to dance," he announced a little too eagerly.

Jackson didn't take his eyes off Sage while holding a finger up to his brother, then indicated for him to sit without words. Dean frowned with disappointment and sank back into his chair. Jackson's command over his brothers was not exaggerated.

Sage stood her ground and maintained her pride despite feeling like she was selling her soul to Satan. "Only pleasantly buzzed," she replied, matching his sarcasm with her own.

Jackson smirked, let out a throaty laugh without taking his eyes off her, and again cocked his head. "How old are you?"

"Twenty-two," Sage replied.

The look on Jackson's face was priceless. He looked back at his brothers and withheld his laugh. "Hell, I need a calculator to do *that* math." His three brothers chuckled in response. Jackson again looked back at Sage with that arrogant smile. "I'm *almost* old enough to be your granddaddy." There was another round of laughter from the table at her expense. Jackson then turned less intimidating. "Head back to the kiddy table and ease up on the rum and coke, darling. You'll thank me for it in the morning. Your reputation will take a serious hit just for being seen talking to us."

All four again chuckled at the insult now directed at themselves. Sage didn't flinch or back down despite internally screaming at herself. Instead, her eyes remained locked on his, and she immediately spoke without thinking.

"Is it really my reputation that you're worried about?" Sage asked and raised a cocky brow. "Or is it yours?"

All four stopped laughing at the comment, possibly surprised at the boldness of the young woman.

Jackson eyed his brothers and indicated Sage with a slight nod. "Did she just threaten me?"

"No," Creed replied with little emotion. "I'm pretty sure she called you a coward."

Jackson leaned back in his chair and seemed to consider the comment. "Huh?" he huffed, then downed his entire glass of whiskey in one large swallow.

As he slid his chair out with a little added vigor, Sage twitched by the aggressiveness of the action but refused to back down. Jackson kept his eyes on her as he slowly stood, towering over her. Sage couldn't deny his height and build were even more impressive up close, but she wasn't going to let him bully her. The arrogant look on his face was hard to read.

"Get those cameras ready, boys," Jackson announced without taking his eyes off Sage and grinned. "This is a Kodak moment."

Jackson suavely held out his elbow to her. "Shall we?"

Sage could feel her heart pounding in her chest at the prospect of actually touching the infamous man. She lightly linked onto his arm and allowed him to escort her to the dancefloor. A hush immediately fell across the entire room at the sight of Jackson escorting Sage across the room. Whispers turned into a low murmur at the couple. Shelly returned from the bathroom just in time to witness Sage and Jackson about to share a dance, compelling her to stop in her tracks. Jackson turned to face Sage, now wearing a hard-to-read grin.

"Tongues will be wagging tomorrow," Jackson informed her. "Willingly dancing with the devil."

Before Sage could suffer in the awkwardness of the moment, Jackson placed his right arm around her waist and roughly pulled her against him, startling her. The force of the action was enough to make her gasp. As he held her hand in his against his shoulder, Sage apprehensively placed her free hand on his other shoulder while her heart now pounded at the situation she'd put herself into. Jackson's smirk was almost enough to send her running in fear, and that he kept his eyes locked on hers was mildly frightening. He then gracefully glided them across the floor, surprising her with his ability to slow dance.

"Well," he announced while withholding his chuckle. "This isn't so bad. Of course, now all the sorority girls will want to dance with me." He nodded toward his table across the barroom. Sage glanced where he indicated. "Smile for the camera, darling."

Sage saw all three of Jackson's brothers grinning while taking pictures and videos with their cellphones. Of course, they weren't the only ones. Others within the tavern were taking pictures and videos as well. Jackson chuckled and somehow managed to move in even closer, dancing cheek-to-cheek. At least she didn't have to look him in the eyes now. Despite that the man was mostly shower fresh, Sage detected the faint scent of horses and possibly cattle on him.

"Was it a dare?" he whispered close to her ear, his warm breath sending a small chill through her body. "You should know, Sage. I get a ten percent cut of all bets of a hundred dollars or more."

She was surprised that he knew her name and attempted to pull back and look at him, but he maintained their closeness, making it impossible. Finally, Sage gave up and tried to relax.

"You know my name?" she asked, although it was more of a statement.

"I know everyone and everything," he informed her. "You might say I have my finger on the pulse of this town. I know everything that happens. I'm the ultimate busybody." He chuckled warmly in her ear. "Now, thanks to you, I'm officially a dirty old man too." He was silent only a moment. "Was it a bet? Your little friend, Shelly, lay down a few bills that you wouldn't do it?"

She resisted the urge to shutter at his warm breath in her ear. "Sorry to disappoint you," Sage announced. "It wasn't a bet or a dare."

He chuckled in his throat close to her ear. Jackson's low chuckle sent chills down her spine. "Why am I not buying that you just wanted to dance with me?"

"I was curious about something," she announced, forcing herself to say what she'd been thinking from the moment she'd first laid eyes on him. "And I didn't want to ask you in front of your brothers."

"Well, I can't blame you there," he replied, then snickered. "They're pretty immature, despite that each of them is old enough to be your daddy. What's been bothering you, and what does it have to do with me?"

Sage held her breath a moment before getting directly to the point. "Have we met before?"

Jackson pulled back just far enough to meet her gaze and raised a curious brow. He suddenly snorted a laugh, then grinned before returning his cheek to hers.

"Are you hitting on me, little girl?" Jackson asked as he chuckled into her ear. "You've got quite the set of lady balls on you."

Sage felt his beard scratch against her face. She was almost certain she felt his nose as well, and it was entirely possible he was smelling her hair.

"I think I'd remember if we had," he informed her. "Don't take this the wrong way, but you're not the kind of girl a man would forget. Even one old enough to be your daddy." He had a good laugh at her expense. "I'm fairly certain you'd remember me too. If you hadn't noticed, I'm kind of *unforgettable*."

"Have you ever been to Colfax?" she boldly asked, not wanting to waste this opportunity.

"Colfax?" he remarked and again laughed. "That's two hours from here. I'm a cattle rancher, darling. I have no business in the big city."

"Colfax isn't a big city," she corrected.

"It is compared to here," he replied before turning serious. "No, I've never been to Colfax. Never in my entire life. And, in case you're wondering, I've never fathered any illegitimate children either." He again snickered. "So you're one hundred percent *not* my daughter."

"That's good to know," she casually replied. "It makes what's poking me in my hip a little less awkward."

Jackson chuckled with added humor close to her ear and allowed his lips to brush against her face. "I may be almost old enough to be your granddaddy, darling, but I'm far from dead."

"It would have been sometime in April," she insisted, redirecting his attention.

"What would have been in April?"

"That I possibly met you," she replied.

Jackson groaned and nuzzled her hair with his face. "We've never met," he assured her, now turning insistent. "April is the stormy season. I'm far too busy birthing calves and keeping my cattle from washing downstream to be running off to the city stalking young co-eds."

"Then why do you look at me that way?"

Jackson pulled back just far enough to meet her gaze, then pulled her sharply against him, allowing his pelvis to dig into her hip. He raised a cocky brow.

"Does that answer your question?" he asked.

Sage didn't even react to the sensation or the action despite feeling her cheeks become hot and red. Instead, she continued staring into his eyes while they slow danced, refusing to back down.

"Joke all you want," she announced and shook her head. "I know what I feel."

"Yeah, I know what you feel, too," Jackson informed her with some humor, then cocked his head and again turned serious. "You don't ruffle easily, do you? Honestly, you kind of scare me." His grin increased. "I *definitely* like that."

"I'm being serious."

"So am I," he joked while studying her, his grin never faltering. "Why don't you cut to the chase, darling, and tell me exactly what it is you want?"

"We already went over that," she informed him.

"Why are you so adamant about us having met before?" he finally asked, seeming almost frustrated. "Even if we had, what does it matter?"

Sage held her breath a moment, then frowned at the prospect of confiding her trauma to this man. "Two months ago, I almost died," she replied. "I can't remember anything before and after the incident. I lost two weeks of my life as well as assorted other details. I suppose I'm grasping for anything that remotely feels familiar."

"And this incident happened in Colfax?" he asked, almost sounding interested.

"Yes," she replied.

Jackson held his breath and sighed. "I wish I could help you, darling," he announced with actual sincerity. "I honestly do. The only place I've been during the entire month of April was on my ranch and the occasional trip to town." He stared into her eyes and seemed to smile more naturally. "I'd remember you if we'd met. That's the God's honest truth." He again moved in close while they finished the slow dance, his face partially buried against her neck. As the song ended, he whispered in her ear, "Big finish."

To her surprise, he gracefully dipped her as the song ended. He held her partway to the floor a moment, then pulled her back up and into his arms, meeting her gaze.

"This was nice," he informed her with some humor. "I forgot how soft, warm, and fleshy women could be."

Jackson pulled away, raised her hand he held to his lips, and warmly kissed it. Sage couldn't deny the action made her heart race. Despite the show he seemed to put on for others, she wasn't expecting him to be quite so charming. Jackson didn't release her hand as he escorted her back to her table. Once she was safely at her table with Shelly, he moved in and warmly kissed her cheek. Jackson then smiled and offered a somewhat playful grin.

"If you need anything," he informed her while raising his brows, "anything at all, you let me know."

Word around town was 'never get on a Morgan boy's bad side'. Although, there was an unspoken other side to that. If you got in good with a Morgan boy, you were set. Jackson then released her hand and walked away. He didn't bother stopping at his table, where his brothers now applauded and cheered at him. Jackson casually continued past, gave his brothers the middle finger, and headed into the back for his usual poker game. Sage felt half the eyes within the tavern now on her as she pulled out her chair.

"You're insane," Shelly shamed Sage while shaking her head. "I can't believe you'd go out of your way and get on their radar like that."

Sage sank into her seat and eyed her friend. "I did what I had to do," she assured her.

"And?"

"And nothing," Sage replied with a defeated sigh. "He's never been to Colfax, and he insists he'd remember if we'd ever met."

"Well, at least that's over with," Shelly announced. "I just hope we can go back to ignoring the Morgan boys. Once you open Pandora's Box, you can't close it."

Sage thought about Shelly's words, and she couldn't deny what she did came with that risk. She initiated contact with a Morgan boy, which left the door wide open.

CHAPTER 4

An hour later, Sage sat at the table by herself and watched Shelly line dancing with some of the other patrons. Sage wasn't really into line dancing, but she enjoyed watching others. The tavern was now full of town folk enjoying their Friday night and celebrating the end of a long work week. Shelly had a good time line dancing with the others and attempted to get Sage to join in several times, but she stayed firm and refused. After watching her friend dance for a while, Sage glanced toward the back pool hall and was surprised when she saw Henry playing pool with Creed Morgan. Sage shook her head while frowning her disapproval at Shelly's brother. Henry just didn't learn his lesson. He possibly felt he could beat them tonight.

Knowing Creed, he probably gave Henry a false sense of security, but he'd eventually mop the floor with Shelly's brother. Sage couldn't believe Henry allowed himself to be conned, yet again, by a Morgan boy. It wasn't long before things started to heat up in the pool hall, and Sage decided to check on Henry. Someone had to keep an eye on him. As she approached the back room, Dean and Lance kept the crowd at bay, not letting anyone enter the pool parlor. Sage heard a commotion and attempted to force her way past the two Morgan boys. Dean seemed somewhat amused by her hostility and playfully grabbed her around the waist, holding her back. Lance scolded his brother with a look.

"Dean, let her go," Lance muttered.

Dean appeared annoyed but released Sage, who then bolted into the back room just in time to witness a Bowie knife falling to the floor between Henry and Creed. Creed punched Henry across the face and hit him twice in the gut. Sage ran for them with horror on her face.

"Let him go!" she cried out.

"This doesn't concern you," Creed shouted back in anger and punched Henry again, knocking him against the pool table.

When Creed grabbed Henry by the shirt collar and pulled him back up, Sage snatched the knife from the floor and lunged for them, brandishing the knife.

"I said, leave him alone!"

Creed eyed the knife in her hand, released Henry, and stepped toward her while showing little to no emotion. "Or what?" he demanded. "Are you going to stab me?"

Sage clutched the knife without taking her eyes off Creed and the stern way he looked at her. She was suddenly grabbed around the waist from behind, and a hand clamped down on her right wrist.

"Drop the knife, Sage," Jackson announced close to her ear.

There was no mistaking Jackson's voice and the seriousness of his command. Sage refused to drop the knife while struggling in vain against Jackson, who could easily overpower her. His hand tightened on her wrist while forcibly shaking her hand, compelling her to drop the knife. Once the knife fell to the floor, Sage struggled against Jackson, who held her firmly from behind, with an arm over her shoulders and one around her waist, refusing to release her.

"He's going to kill him," Sage snarled in anger, now clutching Jackson's arm across her shoulders with both hands, attempting to free herself.

"Doubtful," Jackson casually replied without releasing her.

Creed again grabbed Henry by the shirt collar and coiled back for another blow.

"That's enough, Creed," Jackson boldly announced without releasing Sage. "You've made your point."

Creed sneered his annoyance with his older brother and reluctantly released Henry, who seemed moderately dazed and thoroughly pissed.

Henry straightened while glaring at Creed, then sneered at Jackson. "I'm going to get even with you and your brothers," he launched.

"Yeah, yeah. I've heard that before. Get out of here," Jackson groaned, sounding almost bored. "Don't come back until you learn how to play nice with the other boys."

Henry turned and left the back room without even acknowledging Sage being held by Jackson. Sage was shocked that Henry didn't even barter for them to unhand her. How could her friend do that to her? It was as if he didn't even care. Dean and Lance turned and watched Henry head from the parlor and out the front door. Both had strange looks on their faces before looking back and raising their brows.

"Well, if that isn't a kick in the ass," Dean muttered, then eyed Jackson while indicating Sage, who was still held captive. "Just left her here at our mercy."

"You need better friends, Sage," Jackson informed her, speaking over her shoulder.

"Let me go," she snarled in anger.

"Mind your manners, darling," Jackson announced with little emotion. "*You* were the one threatening my brother with a knife, and I don't take too kindly to that."

"He was going to kill Henry," Sage snapped in response while squirming against his arms around her from behind while he held her snug against him.

"Actually," Creed announced with little emotion, "he pulled the knife on me. I was just defending myself. I take being threatened a little personally."

Sage suddenly tensed and attempted to understand what had just happened. She eyed Dean and Lance, who shared the same look, indicating that's what actually happened. Sage had a hard time believing Henry pulled a knife on Creed and not the other way around.

"Things aren't always as they seem," Jackson informed her while keeping her firmly against him and refusing to release her. "I think you owe Creed an apology."

"Your brother is lying," Sage scoffed and again fought in vain against Jackson's grip on her.

"Creed doesn't lie," Jackson informed her. "At least, not to me." He placed his mouth close to her ear. "What's more believable? Creed lying to his older brother, who practically raised him? Or the man you barely know, who left you with four mildly questionable characters? Does he even care what happens to you?"

Sage wanted to answer that Henry did care about her, but the sting of him leaving the pool hall and the tavern without attempting to help her spoke louder than words.

"Having a little trouble answering that?" Jackson remarked near her ear. "How about this one? Do you honestly believe I'd hurt you?"

Sage relaxed her body against his and no longer fought the arm around her neck. Jackson loosened his grip around her neck and shoulder but didn't release her.

"Would you like to apologize to Creed now?" Jackson announced in a gentler tone.

Sage lifted her eyes and met Creed's gaze.

Creed avoided looking at her. "It's not necessary, Jackson," he announced while frowning. "It wasn't her fault. She didn't know what happened."

"Not the point, Creed," Jackson replied. "We need to maintain a level of respect with one another. That also includes attractive young women. Having a pretty face doesn't give her a free pass. That's not how a fair and honest system works."

Although Sage wasn't happy with Jackson manhandling her, he made a valid point. She didn't see what had happened, and, although she doubted Henry pulled the knife, it was entirely possible he started the fight.

"I'm sorry, Creed," Sage announced somewhat timidly, taking the high road. "I may have been mistaken."

Creed nodded but didn't respond. Jackson lowered his arms, releasing Sage. She took a quick step away from him and avoided looking at him. Dean picked up the discarded Bowie knife, studied it a moment, and then snorted a laugh while turning the handle so Sage could see it. It contained Henry's initials. Sage held her breath and tensed.

"Go get yourselves a couple of drinks," Jackson announced to his brothers. "I'll be along. Sage and I need to have a little talk."

Dean, Lance, and Creed left the pool area, leaving Sage alone with Jackson. Sage tensed and met Jackson's gaze as he leaned against the nearby pool table. Why did she feel as if she had been sent to the principal's office? Jackson wasn't the law in town, yet everyone, herself included, seemed to submit to him and his authority.

"You may not want to hear it, Sage," Jackson announced while folding his arms across his chest, "but Henry is bad news."

"He's Shelly's brother," Sage insisted in his defense.

Jackson cocked his head. "Well, your friend Shelly isn't much better," he informed her.

"You don't even know Shelly," Sage insisted.

"Neither do you," he countered, then shrugged. "I know her well enough. I can sniff out bad apples. Shelly's a bad apple, and that brother of hers is rotten to the core."

"I've heard plenty of bad things about you and your brothers as well," Sage insisted as she folded her arms across her chest matter-of-factly. "I guess being a bad apple is a matter of perspective."

"My brothers and I have faults," he corrected and didn't seem fazed by her insult. "This town has weak deputies and a corrupt sheriff. My brothers and I do our best to keep the town safe. We rein in the madness, which makes us a little unpopular."

"That makes you vigilantes and bullies," Sage corrected him.

Jackson shrugged. "Titles are unimportant," he casually replied. "We do what needs to be done. Twenty years ago, a young woman such as yourself would have feared walking into this place alone. My status as a bully, as you call me, makes this town a safer place for everyone."

Sage stared at him a moment while attempting to refute everything he'd said, but he wasn't wrong. Her eyes then strayed to the black braided leather bracelet he wore on his left wrist above his watch. An engraved golden pendant was woven into the leather. Sage stared at the golden pendant a moment and felt a cold shiver run down her spine. A brief image flashed through her mind. She could see rain pouring down on the stormy night as a brilliant flash of lightning lit the black sky. At that moment, thunder cracked loud and long just outside the tavern, snapping Sage out of her traumatic flashback. She suddenly jumped at the terrifying sound and looked around, revealing her fears. Jackson gave her a strange look and straightened.

"It's just thunder," he informed her, then appeared almost amused. "Christ, you're spookier than the cattle."

Sage attempted to relax while looking around as she listened to the storm picking up strength outside. She insecurely folded her arms across her chest and rubbed her chilled arms.

"I don't like thunderstorms," she timidly informed him while slipping into her own thoughts and shivered.

"The *incident?*" he asked in a more serious tone.

Sage nervously nodded while looking around the empty pool room. She subconsciously continued rubbing her arms while looking mildly frightened. Her eyes again strayed to the leather bracelet he wore. She stared at the pendant a moment longer. Images of the charm flashed through her mind like a tidal wave of emotion and unfounded fear. She'd seen that pendant before, and it wasn't a coincidence. There was another loud crack of thunder that seemed to roll across the sky outside and just about rattled the entire room. Sage gasped and jumped as if death had placed its cold hand upon her. Her overreaction startled Jackson

"Hey, hey," Jackson announced with some surprise and moved closer to her. "It's okay. Relax."

The thunder again cracked loudly. Sage cried out and saw an image flash of the dark sky that night, brightened by the lightning, and a glimpse of the strawberry moon. Rain was pouring down, and she could almost feel it drenching her body, soaking and chilling her. When Sage opened her eyes, she was in Jackson's arms, clinging to his waist and chest while practically climbing up his body in fear. Her entire body was shivering, and she couldn't control it.

"You're okay, Sage," Jackson whispered into her ear while stroking her hair and caressing her back. "It's just a storm. It's not going to hurt you, I promise."

"I'm sorry," she whispered into his chest while clutching his shirt.

Sage subconsciously dug her fingernails into his chest. Jackson cringed as he gently pried her fingernails from his skin and held her hand in his to keep her from scratching him.

"I don't usually let a woman dig her fingernails into me until the third date," he teased with a tiny chuckle.

Sage felt his lips graze her temple near her hairline. The action had a calming effect, and she finally stopped shivering while remaining glued to his body. Sage wished she could force herself to release him, but she couldn't loosen her grip around him. She controlled her breathing to match his and let the warmth of his body and the feeling of his heart beating relax her.

"Maybe I should take you home," Jackson remarked while gently caressing her back in a comforting manner.

"I'm really sorry," she replied timidly. "Shelly can take me home."

When Jackson's three brothers entered the pool parlor, they eyed the scene and snickered.

"Fuck off," Jackson snarled at his brothers.

As Sage attempted to release Jackson, her body again shivered uncontrollably. Jackson immediately pulled her back against him, allowing the shivering to cease.

"You're fine where you are," he insisted in a soft, reassuring tone. "I doubt the storm will last much longer." He hesitated a moment. "Incidentally, what do you do when I'm not around during a thunderstorm?"

"Curl into a ball in the corner and rock back and forth like a mental patient," she replied.

"I had a dog that used to do that during thunderstorms," he remarked with some humor. "Big, tough German shepherd turned into a lap dog during storms." Jackson ran his finger just behind her ear in a mild scratching motion. "He'd sit on my lap, and I'd rub the back of his ear to calm him."

Sage lifted her head just enough to meet his moderately mocking smile.

He met her gaze and grinned while continuing to scratch her behind the ear. "Is it working?" he joked.

"Actually, yes."

"How about that," he remarked, then laughed. "Maybe you should try sitting on my lap too."

Despite the snickers coming from his brothers, Sage couldn't deny she entertained the thought while listening to the rumbling outside and feeling calm for the first time. At times, the panic attacks were so severe that she had difficulty catching her breath, and she'd start hyperventilating. Jackson gave her something to focus on, and she feared releasing him.

While looking around, Shelly entered the pool area and spoke to Jackson's brothers. "Has anyone seen my friend--?" She abruptly stopped and stared at Sage.

Jackson grinned with his usual arrogance and waved at Sage's stunned friend.

"What's going on here?" Shelly just about demanded.

"Found a cure for Sage's fear of thunderstorms," Jackson cheerfully announced while resuming stroking her hair.

Shelly eyed Sage, who refused to release Jackson, and raised a cocky brow. "He's not serious."

Sage shrugged while keeping one arm around Jackson's waist and her head against his chest. "It's actually working quite well," she replied.

"Doing wonders for me too," Jackson announced.

Despite his perverted response, Sage didn't flinch. Nothing he said or did was going to peel her body from his.

"Gross," Shelly muttered, then eyed Sage demandingly. "The storm is almost over. I should have enough time to finish my drink; then we can leave, okay?"

"Okay," Sage replied.

Shelly shook her head and left the pool area.

Jackson tightened his arm around Sage and held her against him. "I don't know about you," he announced, "but I had fun tonight."

Sage briefly eyed the leather bracelet on his wrist as his hand stroked her hair. She'd been thinking about the pendant from the moment she'd laid eyes on it and had that flashback. The gold pendant had to mean something.

"What's with the bracelet?" she gently asked while keeping her head against his chest.

Jackson didn't even bother looking at the leather bracelet he wore. "Parting gift from a lovely young woman," he informed her. "Has some sentimental value."

"Girlfriend?"

Jackson grinned and strained to look at her, although she refused to lift her head from his chest. "Jealous?"

Sage groaned her annoyance at the question.

Jackson chuckled and continued to stroke her back and hair. "I'm sorry. That was rude." There was a brief pause. "Despite that you're far too young for me," he announced with increasing humor, "that doesn't mean I won't be thinking about you the next time I'm in the shower."

"That's pleasant," she remarked with a slight groan.

Jackson hid his slightly embarrassed smile. "I mean it, though, Sage," he replied. "I really did enjoy tonight. Maybe giving up on the entire female population was a decision made in haste."

The last of the thunderstorm seemed to have passed, leaving just the pouring rain on the roof.

Sage finally lifted her head, met his gaze, and offered a timid, embarrassed smile. "You're not so bad, Jackson."

"Well, that's one opinion," he joked.

Sage placed her hand on his face and gently caressed his beard. "Thank you," she whispered, then stretched upward and warmly kissed him, surprising him. She broke off the kiss before he had a chance to respond.

He met her gaze and grinned somewhat deviously. "I'm a little hard of hearing," he announced and lowered his mouth to hers. "Do you mind repeating that?"

"Goodnight, Jackson," Sage replied and finally pried herself away from him.

Jackson was reluctant to release her but eventually gave in. "So I'll see you during the next thunderstorm then?"

She eyed the cheap grin on his face, hid her smile, and left the back room. As Sage walked out, she could hear Jackson's three brothers teasing him with rounds of 'cradle robber' and 'sugar daddy'.

Jackson's response was simple. "Fuck you."

CHAPTER 5

Sage's bedroom in her sister's apartment was nicely appointed with a large throw rug over the hardwood flooring alongside the bed. Her double bed was an antique, as was the rest of the bedroom set. Toby enjoyed antique furniture as well as vintage books. Sage's bedroom had two windows that provided a nice cross breeze on warm summer nights and a ceiling fan that helped circulate the air. Despite the gentle, cool breeze coming through the windows, Sage tossed and turned half the night. Her dreams were filled with visions of Jackson's leather bracelet with the gold pendant. She hated to admit there were also sporadic erotic dreams involving Jackson mixed in. In her dreams, she welcomed his sexual advances with matching enthusiasm.

Sage woke at five in the morning and couldn't get her mind off the pendant and Jackson. She finally sat up in bed and clutched her knees to her chest. The charm meant something, but what? She needed to get her hands on that bracelet, but she certainly couldn't ask Jackson to simply give it to her. Sage would need to find a way to borrow his bracelet and figure out what it meant and why she had a vision when she saw it. She needed to come up with a plan to get that bracelet without Jackson's knowledge, just in case he had something to do with what happened to her and her mother two months ago. One thought kept plaguing her mind. What if Jackson had been the one who attacked her and killed her mother? After her vivid dreams of Jackson seducing her, Sage gave up on sleeping anymore. She didn't need those thoughts stuck in her head more than they already were. She took a long hot shower and puttered quietly around the kitchen so she wouldn't wake her sister.

In addition to the two bedrooms, Toby's apartment had a nicely appointed kitchen and a living room that was also furnished with antiques. Toby's living room had fancy Victorian sofas, a velvet fainting couch, and two smaller chairs. The only thing it didn't have was a television. Each of the bedrooms had televisions, but there wasn't one in the living room. After making a cup of tea, Sage curled on the sofa with her thoughts. Despite the early hour, her sister's bedroom door opened, alerting Sage. She feared she had somehow woken her sister even though she had tried to be quiet. Instead of her sister, when she looked across the living room, she saw a shirtless Leo in just his pants, padding across the floor to the bathroom.

Sage internally cringed. Apparently, Leo and Toby were 'on' again. She didn't know what it was about that man that annoyed her so much. It was one of those conversations she would have enjoyed having with her mother. Toby made bad decisions when it came to matters of the heart. She knew there was one particular guy that broke her sister's heart, but she somehow couldn't remember him. Sage somehow thought it involved a pregnancy, which may have explained why she often thought her sister had a baby. It seemed as if a lot of her lost memories involved men, which may or may not have meant anything. After Leo finished in the bathroom, he was about to head back to Toby's bedroom when he spotted Sage on the sofa. He changed direction and approached, collapsing in the closer chair not far from her.

Leo looked exhausted yet wore that cheap grin that seemed to scream, 'I banged your sister last night'. Sage wanted to like the guy, but she just couldn't stop her feelings of contempt for him.

"How was the tavern last night?" Leo asked, seeming genuinely interested.

"Nothing to write home about," Sage replied as politely as she could manage. "Henry got into a fight with Creed Morgan."

Leo snorted a laugh and shook his head. "I'm guessing that didn't work out too well for him," he remarked.

"His face was almost as bruised as his ego," she casually replied.

"Considering he's lived here a year or more," Leo announced. "You'd think he'd learn to avoid those boys by now. Unfortunately, there's something not quite right with him."

Sage couldn't stop thinking about Henry abandoning her and leaving her at the mercy of all four Morgan boys. Although it didn't end tragically, that whole scene still stung. It certainly made her rethink how she felt about Henry.

"Well, you may be right about that," Sage replied with a defeated sigh. "I like Shelly, but I'm a little soured on Henry right now."

"I'm kind of glad to hear," Leo informed her while leaning back in the chair. "You can do better, that's for sure."

Sage cast a quick sideways glance at Leo. The irony would be lost on him. "Henry's just a friend," she reminded him, then frowned. "Thank God."

"That's a relief," Leo replied while staring at her.

Sage eyed her sister's boyfriend where he sat bare-chested, manspreading in the antique chair. She finally realized part of what she despised about the man. Whenever she was alone with him, he sat with his legs spread apart and his hand resting close to his crotch. It was a simple action, but she felt it was on purpose. Was he deliberately drawing attention to his crotch whenever he was alone with her? She was sure she was mistaken. Although--? He did act more masculine around her.

Was it a subliminal act of domination? Some animalistic instinct?

"A strong-willed woman like you needs an alpha male," Leo announced, then snorted a laugh. "Not a little scavenger like Henry. He can't handle a woman like you."

Now that was an odd thing to say. Sage was getting a very clear picture of why she didn't like Leo. Something told her he was possibly referring to himself. The thought made her a little nauseous. She suddenly wanted to burst his bubble and knock down his 'alpha male' ego.

"Well," Sage announced with a moderately humored smile and snorted a laugh. "There's only one alpha male in this town, and I'm pretty sure Jackson Morgan is a little too old for me."

Leo immediately shifted, closing his legs and sitting up straight in the chair. "Jackson Morgan?" he just about gasped, taking offense to the comment. "He's a hick cowboy with delusions of grandeur."

Sage was mildly amused at how easily she ruffled Leo's fragile ego. She should have felt bad, but she liked watching him squirm.

"Oh, no," Sage insisted while shaking her head. "I assure you, there are no delusions there. He's a natural-born leader. And after our slow dance together last night, I have nothing but respect for the guy."

"You're insane," Leo just about shouted while shooting up from his chair. "How can you even think something like that about that man?"

Leo's raw emotion was clearly an indication that he was threatened by Jackson Morgan, and it was satisfyingly amusing. Toby appeared from the bedroom in her short satin nightgown, looking exhausted.

"What's going on out here?" Toby practically demanded while eyeing both.

Leo looked back at Toby with some surprise, then immediately forced a smile. "Nothing, we were just talking," he replied and joined her by the bedroom door. "Sorry if we woke you."

As Leo and Toby disappeared into her bedroom, Sage couldn't help but smile. A true alpha male wouldn't feel threatened by the mere mention of another.

§

Sage left the bookstore early that morning, leaving her sister to open the shop alone. She needed to pay a visit to the Morgan ranch, and it couldn't wait. Being they were cattle ranchers, they'd be up early and possibly out of the house by seven or eight. It was a calculated risk, but she had to take it. As Sage headed for her car, Henry appeared out of nowhere and greeted her halfway. She jumped in surprise when she saw him and slowed her approach. She had kind of hoped he'd give her more time to get over her anger before he showed up.

"Hey, Sage," he announced almost sheepishly. "I wanted to apologize for last night."

"Oh?" she demanded while folding her arms across her chest. "You mean when I came to your rescue, and you abandoned me, leaving me at the mercy of all four Morgan boys?"

Henry fidgeted and looked down at the ground with shame. "I was angry and embarrassed. I wasn't thinking straight," he replied timidly. "But I knew they wouldn't do anything in the crowded tavern."

"Oh, you did, did you?" she launched back in anger.

"I'm sorry for what happened," Henry insisted and frowned. "Shelly told me what Jackson did after I'd left."

Sage eyed him and was somewhat surprised by the comment. "What Jackson *did*?"

"Harassing you and putting his hands all over you," Henry replied remorsefully. "I'm really sorry about that. I'll make it up to you, I promise."

"Jackson didn't put his hands all over me," she snapped back. "I freaked out because of the thunderstorm, and he kept me calm. Ironic, I go out with my two best friends, and the town bully is the only one looking out for me."

"You're not honestly defending the guy, are you?" Henry demanded. "You know the kind of man he is, right? He's a narcissistic bully and the most feared man in town. You saw how his brothers beat the crap out of me."

"No, Creed beat the crap out of you," Sage launched back while raising an arrogant brow. "Because you pulled a knife on him."

"He cheated at pool," Henry insisted defensively.

"So that justifies pulling a knife on the man?" she countered.

"Why are you defending them?"

"I'm not defending them; I'm calling out your role in what happened last night," Sage informed him. "You left me there to fend for myself, four on one. If Jackson was the monster everyone claims he is, I would have been in serious trouble, but that didn't stop you from running out on me. Thankfully, he's not a monster."

"He is," Henry corrected. "You're just not seeing it. You're not seeing it because he's sizing you up as his next conquest. Of course, he's going to be nice to you. He wants to defile you."

"And I suppose he's doing that by pretending to be a gentleman, huh?" Sage snapped. "He had plenty of opportunities to make a move, but he didn't."

Henry shifted uncomfortably. "Can we at least talk about this?"

"There's nothing to talk about," Sage informed him. "If you'll excuse me, I have someplace I have to be."

CHAPTER 6

Sage drove up the long, never-ending dirt driveway to the Morgan ranch. Her plan wasn't perfect, but she couldn't exactly walk up to the ranch, forcing her to improvise if someone saw her driving up. The ranch's driveway was a quarter of a mile long and offered plenty of seclusion from the quiet back road. When the ranch came into view, Sage saw a large horse barn with enough stalls for twenty horses, a paddock, and many horse pastures enclosed with tall, wooden fences. The house was about fifty yards from the barn. The large, two-story plantation-style home had many windows and an enormous, wrap-around porch. For an impressive home, it was void of any landscaping. The Morgan cattle ranch consisted of more than a thousand acres of woods and pastureland and seemed to be completely secluded from the rest of the world.

Sage pulled up to the house, got out of the car, and looked around. She didn't see any sign of the Morgan boys or any of their ranch hands. The place was eerily quiet, making Sage feel somewhat anxious about her task. She was no longer sure how she intended to pull this off. Did she honestly think she was just going to walk into their house, slip into Jackson's bedroom, providing she could even figure out which was his, and hope he left the bracelet conveniently lying on the dresser? As she walked closer to the porch, she realized she needed an alternate plan. She was doubting her own willingness to simply walk into their house uninvited. When she heard the sound of a horse approaching along with the creaking of saddle leather, Sage stopped just before the porch and anxiously turned. Jackson rode his large horse across the dirt driveway and up to the house at a leisurely canter.

Jackson's horse, Raven, was a tall, muscular, blue roan stallion that stood an imposing sixteen hands. His blue roan coat looked almost steel gray or bluish in color, while his head, mane, tail, and legs were jet-black. Jackson slowed the horse and then stopped near her. Sage took in a sweeping eyeful of Jackson, looking cowboy authentic from his severely beaten, black Stetson hat to his worn cowboy boots. He wore a strange grin when he saw her and pushed his hat back on his head.

"Sage, what a pleasant surprise," he announced and added a throaty, devious chuckle. "There aren't any thunderstorms in the forecast, so to what do I owe the honor?"

Sage couldn't take her eyes off the older man. Despite having almost thirty years on her, she couldn't deny he made a stunning cowboy. Her heart pounded in agreement as she relived a few of her racier dreams from last night, then immediately shamed herself for her thoughts.

"Well, look at you," she announced while attempting to hide her nervous smile, although failing. "Straight out of a Clint Eastwood movie."

"I assume you mean that as a compliment," he announced with a chuckle while casually leaning forward on the saddle horn, completing the entire authentic cowboy package. "You come to play cowgirl with us?"

Sage's eyes strayed to the braided leather bracelet before returning to meet his gaze. So much for sneaking in and stealing it. It would seem he never took it off, although she was positive he'd take it off while in the shower, being it was leather. A lot of good that would do her.

"Honestly, I don't know why I came here," she informed him, knowing how stupid that sounded. "I ran into Henry this morning, and I started out angry, then I felt a little embarrassed about last night." She managed a tiny smile and waved him off. "You're busy. I shouldn't be bothering you. I shouldn't have stopped by unannounced."

"The best medicine for anxiety is putting your ass in a saddle," he informed her, then patted the horse's neck. "Riding a horse, working the cattle, and the fresh air--" He shook his head while maintaining his grin. "Cures just about everything. I'll saddle a horse for you. It'll be fun."

For a moment, she wasn't sure if he was serious. As Sage studied his somewhat devious grin, she could see something kinder behind the smile. She wasn't sure what was happening, but he was being suspiciously nice.

"I don't want to put you to any trouble."

"No trouble at all," he announced and chuckled. "We could use a cowgirl in our posse."

§

Sage rode a smaller, black and white pinto gelding alongside Jackson on his horse. The black and white gelding was approximately fifteen hands and built somewhat stocky. The horse's large white spots looked like massive clouds on its body. Three of the horse's four legs were white, while its mane and tail were mostly black. Although she had some prior riding experience, Jackson gave her pointers and even fixed her with an old Stetson hat that smelled of a thousand steer. It was a lengthy, pleasant ride at a slow trot along large, rolling pastures that were lush and green. Once they reached the herd as well as Jackson's brothers and a few ranch hands, Sage had almost forgotten the rest of the world even existed. The massive pasture, where hundreds of steer grazed, stretched as far as the eye could see with woods on both sides and many streams throughout.

As they crossed the large pasture, Sage saw Jackson's three brothers sitting on their horses and staring at them with somewhat stunned expressions. As Sage and Jackson approached them, the three brothers had a quick conversation, undoubtedly about her. Dean and Lance were grinning like schoolboys while Creed maintained his serious demeanor. Creed seemed to scold both younger brothers just before Jackson and Sage stopped their horses before them.

"Where'd you pick up the stray?" Dean was the first to ask while sizing up Sage with a mildly lustful look.

Jackson's glare was cold and menacing. "Sage is riding with us this morning," he informed his brothers in possibly the gruffest tone she had ever heard from the eldest brother. "If I hear one rude or disrespectful comment from any of you, I'll put my boot up your asses. Are we clear?"

Dean immediately wiped the smile from his face, and all three brothers nodded respectfully while tipping their hats to Sage. Their rapid transformation was shocking. As his three brothers scattered and did their job keeping the cattle from straying, Jackson glanced at Sage and grinned.

"They're used to it being the boys' club out here," Jackson remarked. "Sometimes, they forget their manners. I blame the fresh air."

"If I was easily offended, I wouldn't have agreed to come along," she informed him with a humored smile. "Being considered one of the boys means taking the good with the bad."

"That's nice of you to say because my threats only go so far with this bunch," he replied with a humored smile. "The moment the novelty of a cowgirl wears off, they'll be back to business as usual, which often involves a lot of crude and colorful language."

"So basically Friday night at the tavern," she remarked with a humored smile.

Jackson hid his embarrassed smile. "You've got me there," he replied.

After Sage was introduced to the rest of the ranch hands, Jackson gave her a crash course in cattle and the job of a wrangler. His ranching knowledge made him seem like the smartest man in the world. She was almost astounded at the level of patience he had with her, considering his 'bad guy' reputation. Surprisingly, his brothers and the four other ranch hands seemed to accept her without question once the initial surprise wore off. They seemed almost too polite. While he rounded up a few stray steer with Creed, Jackson left her with Gus and Marv, two of their ranch hands. Gus was a tall, strapping man in his mid-forties, with sandy brown hair hiding beneath his dark brown cowboy hat. He was as authentic a cowboy as they came. He looked unshaven for a day or two, as a man of his profession might. He rode a mid-sized palomino gelding with a rope hanging off the side of the saddle, and his trench coat rolled up behind the seat.

Marv was a little younger than Gus, being in his early forties. He wore his unkempt, sandy blonde hair beneath his black cowboy hat. Marv was slightly larger and more muscular than Gus. His handsome looks were somewhat rugged, yet he had a baby face. He rode a taller, light gray gelding with the same equipment as Gus had on his saddle. Sage watched Jackson and Creed gallop their horses across the pasture, chasing after stray steer. She hadn't realized how sexy a cowboy actually was until that moment. It was a rugged job for rugged men. Even more impressive was the way Jackson interacted with his horse, seeming to work as one with some sort of mysterious bond.

"I must say," Gus announced while grinning at Sage, interrupting her thoughts. "Usually, when Jackson picks up strays, they have horns and tails."

Marv chuckled at Sage's expense. "He's never picked up any stray ladies before," he joked.

"Are you going to be our new wrangler?" Gus pressed with some enthusiasm. "A lady wrangler would add a little class to this not-so-classy testosterone party."

"I'm pretty sure he's not offering me a job," Sage replied while hiding her smile. "Honestly, I came here to apologize for last night at the tavern, and next thing I know, I'm sitting on a horse."

Both men stared at her for a moment as if attempting to process her comment.

"I have a lot more questions now than I did a minute ago," Gus remarked, then grinned. "Usually, it's Jackson who needs to do the apologizing to the ladies. I don't think anyone's ever come out of their way to apologize to him. Especially a woman."

"I just want to know what you need to apologize for," Marv announced a little too eagerly.

"Don't be rude, Marv," Gus huffed and slapped him with his hat. "Jackson will skin you if you're rude to his lady friend."

When he said 'lady friend', why did it sound a lot like girlfriend? Sage heard it, but she wasn't going to correct them. That would be up to Jackson to set his men straight. Lance and Dean rode up to them and stopped alongside Sage. All five were now watching Jackson and Creed round-up strays. Sage was aware that the two brothers were secretly casting looks at her, evident by the tiny grins on their faces.

"So, Sage," Dean chirped somewhat enthusiastically and was immediately met with a groan from Lance. "What brings you all the way out here? You just happen to be in the neighborhood?"

Sage glanced at Dean and the huge, suggestive grin on his face. Lance groaned and rubbed his eyes. Apparently, Dean lacked a filter and enjoyed making people uncomfortable.

Sage maintained her smile despite that she was internally squirming. "I was feeling a little embarrassed about last night," she replied.

"Which part?" Dean teased, now humored. "Slow dancing with Jackson or cuddling with him in the pool parlor?"

"Dean," Lance scolded under his breath.

Marv and Gus were now looking at Sage with surprise and equally broad grins, anticipating her response.

Sage shifted uncomfortably on her horse but maintained her smile. "The latter," she replied. "Thunderstorms freak me out ever since my *accident*."

"Must have been one hell of an accident if cuddling with Jackson comforts you," Marv remarked with a chuckle.

"Marv," Gus scolded.

"Obviously, Jackson didn't mind," Dean remarked to Gus, then indicated Sage. "I mean, would you?"

"Keep it up," Lance warned them while shaking his head. "If you scare her away, Jackson's going to kill both of you."

"Christ, Lance," Dean moaned and removed his canteen from the saddle horn. "*She* asked *Jackson* to dance. Obviously, she's not easily frightened." He took a swig from his canteen before eyeing Sage, raised his brows, and offered her the container.

Sage was thirsty but suspiciously eyed the canteen. "What's in it?" she asked.

Dean chuckled at the question. "Water," he replied with some humor.

Sage accepted the canteen and took a drink. Dean then removed a flask from his inner jacket pocket and extended it to her.

"If you're looking for whiskey, I have that too," Dean announced while grinning.

Sage eyed the flask and shook her head while returning the canteen. "A little early for me, thanks."

"Young, attractive, and *not* an alcoholic," Dean remarked while shaking his head. "There has to be *something* wrong with you that you're out here with us."

Gus and Lance both groaned at that one while Marv just snickered.

"Did you just break up with a boyfriend?" Dean then asked almost suspiciously.

"That's an odd question," Sage remarked with some surprise.

Dean shrugged it off. "Jackson attracts a certain type," he replied.

Jackson spotted them across the field and galloped toward them with purpose. Creed soon followed. Gus and Marv immediately gasped and took off.

Lance groaned and shook his head. "Great," he muttered, then spun his horse and took off as well.

Sage was curious about what had just happened that the three men took off. Dean didn't seem bothered as Jackson rode up to them and abruptly stopped his tall horse near his brother. The look on Jackson's face sent a chill down Sage's spine.

"Don't you have work to do?" Jackson snarled at his brother.

"Just entertaining your girlfriend," Dean replied with a cheap grin on his face.

"Get back to work," Jackson growled while silently killing his brother with his eyes.

Dean muttered something under his breath that sounded a lot like 'go fuck yourself' before turning his horse and riding after his younger brother. Creed stopped several yards behind Jackson and eyed the situation. He didn't even speak as he took off after his brothers.

Jackson's expression immediately softened as he looked at Sage. "Sorry about Dean," he announced. "He wasn't taken out back behind the woodshed enough growing up, and it shows. I'll punch him in the mouth later."

"That's not necessary, Jackson," Sage remarked, taking it as a joke, but she was secretly concerned he was serious. "I wasn't offended by anything he said."

Jackson seemed to relax and even managed a smile. "As long as you say so," he replied.

CHAPTER 7

Almost four hours in the saddle later, the moment Sage dreaded all morning had finally arrived, and she couldn't put it off any longer. When she started squirming in her saddle and casting looks around the large field, Jackson eyed her and grinned almost knowingly.

"Looking for the little cowgirl's room?" Jackson asked with a chuckle.

"Is it that obvious?" she asked while hiding her somewhat embarrassed smile.

"Laws of nature," he replied, then nodded to the nearby tree line. "Pick a tree. Just watch out for snakes."

Sage groaned, not looking forward to the experience. "Thanks."

Jackson removed a roll of toilet paper from the saddlebag and handed it to her. "Might come in handy," he teased.

Sage eyed him, groaned, and snatched the roll of toilet paper. "What about the horse?"

"Oh, there's a good chance he's going to watch," Jackson remarked while grinning.

"I meant, so he doesn't run away," she scoffed.

Jackson chuckled at the comment. "He's not going to run away," he replied. "He's going to be more interested in what you're doing." He then winked. "He's kind of nosy."

"You're enjoying this, aren't you?" she remarked.

Jackson maintained his grin and shrugged. "A little," he replied. "We don't get much entertainment out here. We take what we can get."

Sage did her best to ignore the comment and rode the horse to the nearest tree line. She left the reins around the saddle horn, swiftly dismounted, and hid behind a larger tree. She made sure to look for snakes before attempting the awkwardness of squatting behind the tree. When she was just about finished, she looked up and saw the horse's large nose directly in front of her face. Jackson hadn't been wrong. The horse did appear curious.

"Pervert," she muttered to the horse, feeling subconscious.

Sage finished, pulled herself together, and mounted the horse with minimal effort. As she rode back, Jackson and his three brothers were all sitting on their horses facing her, wearing matching grins and looking like a tribute to Bonanza. All four then applauded.

"Congratulations," Dean announced. "You're officially a cowgirl."

"Wow," Sage announced as she stopped near them and just about tossed the roll of toilet paper to Jackson. "You boys really are low on entertainment."

"And that's lunch," Jackson informed her and his brothers.

"Already?" Sage asked and looked at her watch. She was stunned to see it was almost noon. She didn't know where the time had gone.

"Ready to head back?" Jackson asked.

Sage glared at him and raised a curious brow. "If you had said we were heading back, I could have waited until we returned," she insisted.

Jackson chuckled. "Where's the fun in that?" he teased.

"Trust us," Creed remarked, then grinned. "You wouldn't want to ride back on a full bladder."

"Why's that?" Sage asked.

"We're taking the express line," Dean informed her, then winked.

"Think you can handle a sprint back to the farm?" Jackson asked slyly.

"I think so," she replied.

"Stay behind Lance," Jackson informed her. "I'll bring up the rear in case you run into trouble." He grinned and met her gaze. "Are you ready?"

Sage had a bad feeling but nodded anyway. Dean, Lance, and Creed let out a war cry of sorts and sent their horses into a gallop across the field. Sage didn't even have to touch her horse. When it saw the other horses running, it happily ran after them. Jackson let out a whistle and chased after her, bringing up the rear. Galloping across the field was exhilarating and like nothing Sage had ever experienced before. Jackson maneuvered his horse alongside hers and coached her while leisurely galloping alongside her.

"You okay?" Jackson asked while grinning at her.

She smiled and nodded. "Yeah, this is amazing."

"I'm glad you think so because we're picking up the pace once we hit that dirt road."

Sage looked at Jackson with some surprise. She thought they were going fast as it was. As promised, once the horses hit the dirt road, they picked up the pace and went into a full run. Jackson remained glued to her side to keep her out of trouble. When they reached the stream not far from the ranch, Jackson's brothers slowed to a trot and then into a walk to cross the stream. Once they crossed the stream, Jackson again rode alongside Sage at a leisurely pace.

"Did you like that?" he asked.

"Yeah, it was a lot of fun," Sage informed him, then patted her horse.

"Was from my point of view, too," Jackson announced while grinning. "Nothing quite like a woman's ass slapping leather to brighten a man's day."

Sage eyed his devious grin, hid her smile, and shook her head. "You're almost as big of a pervert as the horse," she remarked.

"Enjoy the little things, darling," he announced with humor, then clasped her free hand resting on her thigh and quickly but warmly kissed the back of it. Jackson met her gaze as if gauging her reaction.

Sage couldn't resist smiling and gently squeezed his hand, still holding hers.

§

Jackson kept ahold of Sage's hand as they rode at a leisurely walk the rest of the way back to the ranch. Sage glanced at Jackson several times while listening to him talk about the ranch's history, which had been in his family for generations. She was consciously aware of his thumb gently caressing her hand the entire time. It wasn't until they stopped in front of the barn that she remembered how much older Jackson was than herself. Jackson dismounted near her and was already alongside her horse as she dismounted, placing his hands on her waist and guiding her safely to the ground. When she turned, she realized how close he was standing.

"You are staying for lunch, aren't you?" he asked.

Sage was suddenly reminded of her reason for showing up at the ranch in the first place. She needed to stay for lunch. She needed to stay long enough to figure out how to get her hands on his bracelet.

"I'd love to," she replied.

Jackson looked at his brothers. "Take care of the horses," he instructed the men. "I'll get lunch started."

Jackson's hand found its way to the small of Sage's back, and he remained close to her as he guided her toward the house.

"I hope to God you're not a vegetarian," Jackson announced loud enough for his brothers to hear, sending them into a round of laughter.

Jackson opened the front door and allowed Sage to enter first. As she entered the large, plantation-style home, she immediately marveled at the well-maintained structure. The hallway foyer combination had several pairs of work boots and cowboy boots scattered about. The hardwood floor had some muddy footprints and dust while lacking any sort of sheen to it, but it wasn't as bad as she imagined it would be. The old carved wood staircase was elegant and stately, with an old-fashioned carpet running up the middle. The carpet runner on the steps was moderately dirty with a few stray dust bunnies, but all things considered, it could have been worse.

"Excuse the mess," Jackson announced with mild embarrassment as he attempted to kick some dirty boots across the foyer. "It's the maid's day off."

Jackson removed his hat and jacket, placing them on a wall-mounted rack near the door. Sage removed her borrowed hat as well and placed it alongside his. He then took off his dirty cowboy boots and left them near the rest. Sage was about to remove her shoes when he stopped her.

"The floors are kind of dirty," he informed her. "You might want to keep your shoes on. They're not nearly as dirty as mine."

Sage followed his recommendation. Although there appeared to be a layer of dust on some of the antique furniture and various items were scattered about, the home wasn't nearly as dirty as she thought it would be, considering there were four bachelors living there. Jackson led her down the hall to the kitchen. The kitchen was dated but with an elegant charm. The massive stove was quite possibly an antique yet functional and mostly clean. In the middle of the sizeable kitchen, there was an old, thick wooden table with enough seating for six, and the cupboards and countertops appeared to be hand-carved from decades past. It was evident that someone in the Morgan family had been quite the carpenter many generations ago.

Jackson attempted to tidy up, somewhat embarrassed by the kitchen's state. It was obvious no one had cleaned up after breakfast that morning and possibly not even from dinner the night before. Despite having a dishwasher, many dirty dishes were scattered around the counter. The home needed a good straightening, but, for bachelors, it wasn't all that bad. As Jackson washed up in the kitchen sink, he again made it a point to apologize for the mess.

"I used to run a tighter ship," he informed her and once again resumed straightening. "Creed's pretty clean, but Dean and Lance live like pigs."

"I lived in a dorm room with three other girls," Sage remarked. "We shared a bathroom. Believe me; I've seen worse."

Jackson laughed, but he was obviously still worrying about the mess. As sage washed her hands in the kitchen sink, she watched Jackson wipe the counter to make a clean spot to prepare lunch.

"Can I help with anything?" she asked while drying her hands on the same dishtowel he had used.

"No, I've been doing this a long time," he informed her, then smiled with humor. "I was Mr. Mom since Junior High."

As Jackson retrieved items from the refrigerator, Sage rinsed the dirty dishes and placed them in the dishwasher while listening to him talk.

"My, uh, father was the last of a dying breed of men," he informed her while hiding his smile. "He didn't believe men should concern themselves with cooking or cleaning of any kind." Jackson placed a wrapped slab of beef on a cutting board and removed several spices from the cupboard. "When my mother died, it was pretty much a free-for-all around here. I was fifteen, Creed was twelve, Dean only ten, and poor Lance was just eight. We pretty much lived on canned food and whatever meat my father threw on the grill. My brothers were turning into feral dogs, in my opinion."

While Sage loaded the dishwasher, she watched Jackson cut the beef into thick filets and then added seasoning. Once he had the beef prepared, he chopped fresh vegetables like a master chef as he continued to tell his story.

"About a year after our mother died, my father brought a nice woman home," he informed her as he smirked and shook his head. "She whipped this house into shape." He then chuckled and raised a humored brow. "She whipped the four of us boys into shape. I did everything in my power to keep that relationship going for my father, but, unfortunately, he resorted back to his old ways. No real surprise that she got fed up and left, but at least she was around long enough to teach me how to run a house properly. Good thing too. When my father died three years later, I had to play mom and dad to those three demons."

Sage leaned her back against the counter and watched him prepare something resembling a gourmet lunch. She couldn't deny she was impressed with how easy he made it look. On the other hand, his story made her feel a little sorry for him. He didn't really have much of a childhood and was forced to grow up fast.

"None of you ever married?" she finally asked, although she already knew the answer from gossip around town.

Jackson cast a quick glance at her and hid his smile. "I suppose none of us are equipped for marriage," he replied. "If Lance couldn't manage to settle down, there wasn't much hope for the rest of us." Despite that he smiled, Sage could see the turmoil on his face. "Four boys. You'd think one of us would have popped out a kid or two to continue the Morgan legacy. This ranch has been in our family for generations, and the four of us couldn't even do the one thing men are supposed to be so damned good at." He snorted a laugh. "Jesus, you'd think Dean would at least have one illegitimate child running around out there." He shook his head. "The boy is such a disappointment."

They heard someone clearing their throat. Jackson looked across the kitchen and then wiped his hands on the nearby dishtowel. Sage saw Creed in the kitchen doorway.

"If you'll excuse me," Jackson announced. "My not-so-subtle brother is attempting to get my attention."

Jackson joined Creed just outside the kitchen in the hallway. Sage couldn't hear their conversation, but she assumed it had something to do with her. She wondered if they were upset that Jackson invited her to stay. Both men soon returned to the kitchen.

"Creed is going to finish lunch prep while I take a quick shower," Jackson informed her.

Sage felt her heartbeat suddenly quicken. If he was taking a shower, that would mean he'd be removing the bracelet. It might be her only opportunity to snatch it. Sage watched Jackson head up the back stairs. Unfortunately, Creed was summoned to entertain her.

"Everything okay?" Sage asked.

"Yes, of course," Creed replied and finished dicing onions for the fried potatoes. "Why do you ask?"

"Doesn't he have to go back out after lunch?" she then asked.

"No," Creed replied without looking at her. "Jackson takes care of the bills, purchasing, and bookkeeping. So he doesn't need to go back out."

Sage eyed Creed's profile, but he didn't look at her.

"Is this your subtle way of keeping me from playing cowgirl the rest of the afternoon?" she asked and leaned against the counter again.

Creed glanced at her and seemed slightly surprised by the comment. He tensed but quickly covered. "Of course not," he replied. "Jackson's a slave driver, and we prefer when he stays home in the afternoon."

"You're a terrible liar," Sage remarked.

Creed frowned, then eyed her. "Men are far easier to con than women," he announced while turning to face her. "We don't need him out there. His time would be better spent here." He then hesitated and raised his brows. "Entertaining company."

"Oh, I see," Sage replied and smiled with some embarrassment. "You want to give Jackson and me some privacy for a few hours."

Creed stared at her as if attempting to read her. "Answering that feels like a trap."

"Okay," Sage announced bluntly. "Whatever the two of you think is happening here, that's not what's happening here. I'm not *that* kind of girl."

"What kind of girl?" Creed asked, appearing serious.

"The casual sex kind of girl," she replied.

Creed seemed slightly surprised and fidgeted. "Is that what this looks like to you?" he asked. "With Dean, I'd understand. Jackson's a little more *reserved*." He then hesitated and considered the comment. "Actually, a lot more reserved."

"Now, I'm really confused," Sage remarked and studied the mildly embarrassed man. "How about putting the guessing games aside and being straight with me?"

Creed frowned and shifted uncomfortably. "None of us has seen Jackson this happy in a long time," he informed her. "He's spent most of his life being mother or father to us. We just want to see him happy. The guy hasn't called me a dickhead once today. It's kind of refreshing. Sure, everyone knows he's too old for you, including Jackson, but that doesn't mean you can't be friends."

"No, of course, it doesn't," Sage replied. "Just as long as he realizes that."

"He does," Creed announced. "Trust me; having Jackson as a surrogate big brother in this town has its perks."

"You can stop trying to sell it," she informed him and patted his shoulder. "I'm enjoying his company too. I should wash up. Which way is the bathroom?"

"There's one in the hallway to the right," he informed her.

Sage nodded and left the kitchen. Once she was out of Creed's sight, she hurried up the main stairs.

CHAPTER 8

Sage crept along the second floor hallway and listened for a running shower. She hesitated before a partially open bedroom door, then pushed it open a little further and peeked inside. Jackson's room was massive compared to her bedroom in her sister's apartment. There was a throw rug over the hardwood floor, a small bay window, a private bathroom, and a closet with double louver doors. The tall bed was hand-carved out of tree trunks and had a massively rustic appeal. The tall dresser, bureau, and two nightstands were also hand-carved. There were old, framed photos on the walls and a large, fancy wood and glass gun cabinet along the wall closest to the bed. The decorative, handmade quilt over the bed was probably over one hundred years old. Sage took a moment to look around the room and saw the braided leather bracelet on the dresser directly across the room from the bathroom.

She listened to the running shower a moment, held her breath as her heart pounded, and then decided to slip into the room. She hurried to the dresser and picked up the bracelet intending to put it in her pocket, but the moment she touched it, a flash of images hit her all at once. They came so fast and hard that she couldn't even make them all out. When the images stopped flashing, she could barely catch her breath, and her heart was pounding.

"Sage?"

Sage looked into the mirror and saw Jackson standing just outside the open bathroom doorway. She spun around, feeling slightly lightheaded from the intense flashbacks, and stared at the partially wet man wearing just a towel wrapped around his waist.

"What are you doing?" he asked and seemed slightly puzzled.

Sage stared at Jackson's barely covered and amazingly toned, wet body glistening from his shower as his light coating of chest hair dripped water down his toned abs. Being a rancher, most of his muscle mass came from working hard every day and not from some fancy gym. The towel draped around his waist allowed a generous view of his unrestricted man parts protruding against the thin material. He may have been more than twice her age, but he certainly didn't look it. All she saw was a vision of manliness.

"I'm, uh, sorry," she announced and fumbled to replace the bracelet on the dresser behind her without him noticing. "The door was open. I, uh, would have thought the door would be closed if you were--"

Her eyes again strayed across Jackson's body and the towel he held wrapped around his waist. Whatever he may have been thinking, the outline beneath the towel was now further pronounced than it had been a moment ago. Sage snapped out of her erotic thoughts and turned almost defensive due to her embarrassment.

"Who leaves their door open when they're in the shower?" she just about demanded.

Jackson smiled and snorted a laugh, not the least bit shy by her presence. "A man living with his three brothers," he lightly teased, then turned playful. "What brought you up here? And does it require pants?"

At least he still had a sense of humor, but it was wasted on her at the moment. After the dizzying effects of the flashbacks, the rush of getting caught in Jackson's bedroom, and the rapidly expanding bulge beyond his thin, wet towel, she didn't quite know how to recover.

"I, uh--"

She didn't seem to be thinking straight, now unable to get her mind or her eyes off his barely clothed body. Jackson cautiously approached without taking his eyes off hers and loosened his grip on the towel, allowing it to slide further down to his hips.

"If you don't say something," he gently announced, "I'm going to go with my first instinct, and, to be honest, it's pretty indecent."

"I shouldn't be here," she timidly replied, although unable to look away.

"No, you shouldn't be," he remarked in a soft tone, then grinned, "but I'm not complaining."

Sage tensed, returning to reality, and managed a tiny smile. "Maybe you should put some clothes on."

Jackson's grin turned playful. "Maybe you should take some off."

Sage felt her cheeks become flushed with embarrassment, but she maintained her smile. "I'll, uh, see you downstairs." She turned and headed for the open bedroom door.

"Are you sure?" he asked. "You can see *more* of me up here."

She looked back and saw him let the towel slide further down his hips. Sage hid her smile, shook her head, and quickly looked away.

"You're terrible."

"I've been called worse."

Sage hurried from the room, shutting the door behind her. She remained by the door a moment and held her breath. Sage wasn't sure what had just happened, but she felt as if she'd been struck by lightning. Perhaps cupid's cruel arrow. She knew that the age gap alone was way too much, but it had been a long time since she'd connected with someone that fast. What was the harm in enjoying the company of a much older man anyway? He admitted he wasn't marriage material at his age. Why couldn't they just have fun together? Was that really so wrong?

"Either walk away or come back inside," Jackson called to her from the bedroom.

Sage jumped with surprise, then smiled with embarrassment that he somehow knew she was still outside his door. As she hurried away from the bedroom, she heard several creaks of the old floorboards beneath her feet. He probably knew she hadn't left when he didn't hear the floorboards creaking.

CHAPTER 9

Shortly after finishing possibly one of the best grilled steaks of her life, Sage sat at the patio table with Jackson and his three brothers. In addition to the newer gas grill on the stone block patio, there was hand-carved furniture from decades past and more chairs set up around a stone fire pit. The house didn't have a lot of landscaping, but the furnishings were incredible. The Morgan boys were pretty rough around the edges, although evident they would have benefited from at least one woman in their lives, but Sage could kind of understand them. Even though a woman at the ranch would have balanced out some of their destructive behavior, it was possibly too late for any of them to settle into a committed relationship at this stage of their lives.

Jackson had remained somewhat close and cozy with Sage throughout the meal, and it seemed as if he was attempting to gauge her reaction by maintaining subtle contact. In a way, he was behaving a bit like a teenage boy trying to figure out if a girl liked him before asking her to the dance. It was actually quite endearing. Less endearing was his three younger brothers watching their older brother's subtle flirting and grinning like horny teenagers. As Sage periodically caught the light scent of a musky aftershave wafting from Jackson, she was consciously aware of his effort to impress her. Meanwhile, she was reminded that her own clothes smelled strongly of cattle and horses. When Creed looked at his watch and sighed, Dean and Lance just about sprang to their feet and collected as many of the dirty dishes as possible.

"We should get back to work," Creed announced not so subtly and grinned knowingly at Sage. "You two have a nice visit."

Jackson didn't even seem fazed as all three vanished into the house like a cyclone. He looked past Sage at his fleeing brothers, then resumed his original position with his arm over the back of her chair, although still not on her shoulder.

"Subtle, huh?" Jackson teased as his finger lightly brushed against her shoulder from the back of her chair. "They mean well."

Now that they were alone, Sage was conscious of his finger grazing her shoulder and his subtle flirting. She felt a slight pang of uncertainty tingling within her without his brothers around as a buffer. Would he ramp up the flirting now that they were alone and come on strong? Was it possible he was just playing up the 'good guy' angle until he got her alone? There had to be a reason that so many in town feared the Morgan boys. Maybe she should be afraid too. She needed to somehow break up the cozy little scene on the back patio and redirect Jackson. Sage sat up straight and partially turned on her chair, facing him.

"I should probably help you clean up from lunch before I go," she insisted.

"It's fine," he informed her with a casual wave. "I'll clean up later." Jackson met her gaze and appeared slightly curious. "Are you suddenly in a hurry to leave?" His grin increased. "Does it make you nervous being alone with me?"

"Maybe a little," she replied.

"Don't trust me?" he joked.

"It's not you that I'm worried about."

Jackson stared at her a moment, then sat forward as well, placing his left hand on her leg just above her knee. "Can't stop thinking about me in a towel, huh?" he announced with some humor.

"I'm a bit *conflicted*," she replied.

The playful look vanished from his face and was replaced with something more serious. "Conflicted?" he remarked. "As in, 'he's too old for me, but maybe I don't care' sort of conflicted?"

Sage held her breath and avoided looking at him. "Something like that," she replied almost timidly.

"Wait," he announced and kept his eyes locked on her despite that she wouldn't meet his gaze. "Are you suggesting I actually have a shot here?"

Jackson's hand seemed to tighten on her leg, and she could almost feel the energy surging through him. She gently removed his hand from her leg, hesitated, and then held his hand. She eyed the leather bracelet but avoided looking at the pendant. She didn't need any more flashbacks clouding her judgment right now.

"I feel like things are spiraling out of control," she insisted, finally meeting his gaze. "I'm worried that if I say or do the wrong thing, you're going to pounce, and that makes it difficult for me to think straight."

Jackson hid his smile and seemed almost embarrassed to meet her gaze. "No one's rushing you into doing anything, Sage," he announced gently. "To be honest, holding you last night was probably the closest I've gotten to getting laid in a long time."

Sage eyed him with some surprise. "Really?"

Jackson managed a tiny smile despite the awkwardness of the admission. "Years ago, I fucked up, and I never quite forgave myself," he informed her. "After that, I made repelling women an art form. I made sure they didn't like me, and they were more than happy to oblige."

"I'm not sure what that says about me," Sage remarked with a tiny laugh.

"You got through," he insisted and again placed his hand on her leg. "I promise; I'm not pressuring you into anything. I'd really just love to hold you." He smiled with some embarrassment. "Even if it's just as a friend." His smile then turned into a grin. "Obviously, a mildly dirty, perverted friend, but the world's not perfect."

Sage caressed the hand on her leg while maintaining their gaze. "I like that you're so open and honest with me. Most guys aren't like that."

"I'm too old to play games," he informed her. "As you get older, your priorities change. You appreciate things a little more, but you also realize your mistakes."

"Such as?"

"I was so busy punishing myself for my mistakes that I didn't realize how it affected my brothers."

"I don't understand."

"When I pushed women out of my life, I set off a chain reaction with my brothers," he replied. "I led by example, letting heartache defeat me, and I pulled them down with me."

"You honestly believe that?"

Jackson nodded. "When we got home last night, the three of them had a lot of fun at my expense," he explained. "The entire evening was kind of amusing. The whole young, beautiful woman paying attention to the older, surly man." He managed a tiny chuckle, then turned serious. "But when you showed up here at the ranch--" Jackson sighed and shook his head. "I'll admit; I was a little stunned, and so were my brothers. The change in them was almost shocking. Stay of execution kind of shocking. I haven't seen those boys that enthusiastic in a long time."

"So you think if they see you in a relationship, it'll motivate them to seek out their own?"

"It might push them along," Jackson replied. "Better late than never."

Sage looked at his hand that was gently caressing her leg and subconsciously stroked his hand. She lifted her eyes and met his gaze.

"I like you, Jackson," she announced. "I didn't think it was possible, but I do." She held her breath a moment. "And I'd like to have you as my mildly dirty, perverted friend."

Jackson suddenly grinned with delight. "Yeah?"

"I don't mind if you embellish our relationship to your brothers or anyone else, for that matter," she informed him. "I know you have a reputation to protect."

Jackson snorted a laugh. "My bad boy reputation?" he joked. "You think I'd be embarrassed if others found out my girlfriend doesn't put out?" His smile mocked her. "Honestly, that's none of anyone's business."

"I thought you were my mildly dirty, perverted friend," she remarked and cocked her head. "When did I become your girlfriend?"

"Are either of us dating other people?" he asked.

"No, not that I'm aware."

His grin increased. "Did you kiss me?"

Sage's eyes narrowed while glaring at him

Jackson chuckled and raised his brows. "Sounds like you're my girlfriend to me." He appeared curious. "What do you intend to tell your sister about me?"

She stared at him a long moment, then fidgeted slightly. "I guess I can't exactly tell her you're my perverted guy friend, huh?"

"Boyfriend sounds better."

"It does, I suppose." Her mind reeled a moment while staring into his eyes. "Perhaps a symbolic gesture of some sort."

Jackson's smile increased as he leaned closer to her. "I'm listening."

"Well, if nothing else, you're consistent," she remarked and gently pushed him back. "I was thinking symbolic in the physical sense."

Jackson chuckled, somewhat amused. "Like my football jersey or class ring?" he asked while maintaining his grin. "So all the other sorority girls will know we're going steady?"

"Well, no, not like that," she insisted, then seemed to fumble over herself a moment. "Just, well, something close to you that you could maybe give me to wear."

Jackson's playful mood suddenly turned serious as he stared at her. "Did you just break up with a boyfriend?" he asked demandingly.

"What?" she asked with surprise at the question.

He seemed to consider it only a moment, then resumed smiling. "It's not important," Jackson replied while waving off his original question. He again turned playful. "I don't have any Morgan Ranch sweatshirts, if that's what you're thinking. Although, I could put the ranch brand on your hindquarters as I do with the horses and cattle." Jackson smiled and winked.

"Now you're mocking me," Sage remarked while squinting at him.

"No, I was actually serious," he replied and again smiled. "I have an official stamper in my office." When her look didn't change, he laughed and again caressed her legs with both hands. "I'm sorry. I'll stop talking now."

"Just something symbolic," she informed him, then indicated his bracelet. "Like your bracelet. You always wear that."

Jackson glanced at the bracelet and seemed to tense. He subconsciously touched the bracelet and appeared to be stranded in his own thoughts.

"That would be majorly symbolic," he muttered and seemed reluctant to take his hand off the bracelet.

"Then it should be that," she delicately insisted. Sage could feel her entire body twitching inside.

"But in the wrong sense," he informed her. "It belonged to another woman. It represents my worst fuck up. Giving it to you feels disrespectful to you."

"Sounds like you really need to let go of it," Sage informed him, then turned almost commanding. "Yep, it has to be the bracelet."

Jackson remained uncomfortable while Sage almost felt bad for putting him in that predicament, but she needed the bracelet from him.

"It's not the honor you think it is," he informed her, then sighed and removed the bracelet, "but I'm giving it to you in good faith." He placed the bracelet around her left wrist, took her hand in his, and held his breath. "Okay. We're officially going steady."

Sage felt relief flood her entire body. Finally, she'd gotten what she came for without having to steal it. Sage placed her free hand on his face, warmly caressed his beard, and smiled.

"Thank you," she replied. "This means a lot to me." She then leaned forward and kissed him warmly on the lips, pulling back before he had a chance to respond. Sage sprang to her feet and held her hand out to him. "How about you give me a tour of the house? Tell me about some of those old pictures on the walls."

Jackson grinned, accepted her hand, and sprang to his feet. "I'd love to," he replied.

He placed his free arm around her waist and pulled her against him without warning. Sage let out a startled gasp, braced her palms against his chest, and stared helplessly into his eyes. She was instantly reminded of all the rumors about Jackson and his brothers. Since she'd met him, he'd seemed too nice, not at all as she had expected. It was only a matter of time before the real Morgan surfaced.

"That's twice now that you've kissed me," he remarked while grinning slyly. "When is it my turn?"

Sage could feel her heart pounding at his aggressive nature. He was moderately intimidating, and it frightened her a little. She didn't know what he was capable of doing. Sage nervously placed her hand on his face and gently caressed his beard.

"You're an intimidating man, Jackson," she delicately informed him.

He seemed surprised by the comment and released her. "I wasn't trying to scare you," he insisted and suddenly seemed self-conscious. "I thought--" He hesitated and smiled with some embarrassment. "I'm sorry. Maybe it's best if I let you set the pace." He then laughed uncomfortably. "Hey, but at least I now know what you mean by things spiraling out of control."

Sage shifted nervously, then met his gaze. "I'm sorry, Jackson," she announced timidly. "It's not your fault."

"I've got a reputation that would scare a heathen," he announced. "Believe me; I get it."

CHAPTER 10

Sage joined Jackson in his study, which had a large, hand-carved desk with a marble top, a wall of built-in bookcases, and an older leather sofa along the wall near the door. There were many old framed photos on the walls of his family and the ranch dating back to when the original house was built in the early eighteen hundreds. His stories were engaging and entertaining, and he told them with passion and enthusiasm. Sage found herself studying Jackson's profile while he told each story as if he'd witnessed it firsthand. Jackson was an encyclopedia of knowledge on the ranch's history, and he was more than willing to discuss his family and, most importantly, his horse.

"Raven is nineteen now, and his successor is only a month old," Jackson announced. "That old boy and I have been through a lot together. Trained him from a colt."

Sage had to smile at the fondness he openly displayed for his horse. "The way you talk about your horse reminds me of the way guys would talk about their cars," she remarked with some humor.

Jackson hid his embarrassed smile. "Well, a cowboy has a special bond with his horse," he informed her. "Not having a girlfriend to occupy my time left that much more time for my horse. He's very special to me." He managed a tiny, uneasy chuckle. "I guess it's a little hard for you to understand."

"Understand what?" she asked while raising her brow. "That your horse is your partner and your best friend?" Sage shook her head. "No, I absolutely understand that."

"Does this actually interest you?" he asked with some humor. "Me talking about my unhealthy love for my horse?"

"I think it's fascinating," she informed him. "You're very passionate about the things in your life. Most guys I've known aren't passionate about anything except going out with friends and having a good time."

"Well," Jackson announced cheerfully. "I *am* an older guy. Honestly, if it weren't for the unauthorized poker game in the back room at the tavern, I'd probably never go out. I'm actually pretty boring."

"I disagree," she replied. "You carved out your own little piece of paradise here. Everything you need to be happy is right here."

"Well, almost everything," he remarked. "This place definitely needs a woman's touch." He then offered a mildly devious grin. "So do I."

"And he's back," she announced with a tiny laugh.

"Well, that's bound to happen when you smile at me the way you do," he announced and inched his way closer to her, where she stood near the desk. Jackson reached out for her, not making any sudden movements, and gently brushed the hair from her face. "I'd really like to kiss you."

Sage affectionately caressed his chest without taking her eyes off him as her heart pounded at the mere comment. "I'd like that," she whispered.

Jackson gently pulled her into his arms in an apparent attempt to keep his aggressiveness in check. He placed his hand to her face, lightly caressed her chin with his thumb, and then lowered his mouth to hers. As she shut her eyes, she couldn't deny her heart was pounding with anticipation. He lightly brushed his lips past hers, sending tiny shockwaves tingling through her body. Jackson then warmly kissed her in the most sensual manner, making full contact while manipulating his tongue past her lips. It was possibly the most erotic, sensual kiss she'd ever received. Jackson broke off the kiss and met her moderately dazed gaze while attempting to curb his grin.

"Well, I'm officially *not* impotent," he remarked.

"I'm glad to hear," Sage replied somewhat timidly as she hid her smile.

Jackson eyed her with some surprise, then suddenly chuckled. "That's encouraging," he announced. "Maybe I should consider changing my bedsheets."

Sage's mind was racing at the comment and what he was suggesting after her moderately encouraging comment. The thought of being in Jackson's bed scared her to death, but she also didn't want to go cold on him. She just needed to get out the door with the bracelet.

"That might be something to consider for next time," she remarked.

It didn't come out exactly as she had planned, and the increased grin on his face suggested he took it in the dirtiest possible manner. She was able to pull away from him just enough that she could no longer feel his enthusiasm pressing against her.

"Okay, then," he replied and winked at her. "I'll put on clean sheets for your next visit." Jackson immediately reeled in the free space between them, securing his arms around her and once again pressing against her. "How about coming over for dinner tonight?"

Sage let a nervous laugh escape while placing her hand on his chest in a half-assed attempt to put some space between them. She wasn't moving him, and he didn't take the hint.

"My sister and I have plans," she informed him and scrambled for something to say. "Why don't I give you my cellphone number, and you can call me?"

"Fair enough," he replied and finally released her.

Sage tensed while watching him approach the nearby desk. He removed a pen and a notepad and then returned to her. Jackson handed her the pen and notepad and crowded her while she jotted down her cellphone number. His closeness was enough to make her tremble slightly while writing. Unfortunately, her plan was somewhat flawed. Sage had to give him her actual number because he knew where to find her, and she didn't want to do anything to piss off Jackson Morgan. Avoiding him once she left his ranch would be the tricky part. She handed him the pen and notepad, which he accepted and tossed onto the desk so he wouldn't have to move away from her.

"I should probably get going," Sage informed him. "I was gone longer than I should have been. Toby will be looking for me."

"I'll walk you to your car," he announced a little too cheerfully.

§

Jackson was practically glued to Sage's side as he walked with her from the house where she had originally parked her car. He paused with her just before the driver's side door and opened it for her. Sage wanted to bolt into the safety of the car, but she'd already set the tone for some sort of goodbye kiss. If she didn't kiss him, it'd seem suspicious. She'd worry about damage control after she was away from him.

"Thank you for a lovely afternoon," she announced warmly while meeting his gaze.

"I enjoyed the company," he replied while grinning.

Sage felt somewhat anxious about the goodbye kiss, unsure how she wanted to handle it. As she placed her hand on his shoulder and stretched upward to give him a quick goodbye kiss, he leaned down and met her halfway with his own ideas. His hand slipped behind her neck, and he kissed her deep and long. Sage returned the kiss while lowering herself in an attempt to keep it brief, but Jackson followed her without breaking off the kiss. His free arm slipped around her waist, and he eagerly pulled her against him while adding some aggression to the kiss. It was enough to quicken her pulse and make her gasp with surprise. Her gasp seemed to encourage him, prolonging the kiss and its intensity while he simultaneously backed her against the car, pinning her against it with his body.

Sage returned the kiss just enough to appease him before breaking it off. She smiled with some embarrassment and again attempted to put some distance between them, but it was impossible with the way he had her pinned against the car.

"Okay," she announced pleasantly but firmly. "Down, boy."

Jackson smiled and groaned. "I'm looking forward to next time," he insisted cheerfully. "I'll call you."

Sage smiled and nodded, then escaped into the safety of her car. As she pulled away, she glanced at Jackson through her rearview mirror. He remained standing in the driveway with his hands in his pockets and watched her leave. She felt bad about her deception, but she did what she had to do. Sage needed answers, and the bracelet seemed to hold them.

CHAPTER 11

Sage sat in her bedroom within her sister's apartment the following afternoon and gazed at the bracelet around her wrist. She stared at it all evening yesterday and most of this morning, but there weren't any flashes or memories. She tried taking it off and holding it up. Nothing. Her frustration grew. It was bad enough she wasn't having any luck with flashes from her past, but she kept seeing that image of Jackson standing in the driveway, watching her leave like a dog being dumped alongside the road. Judging by the unknown number on her cellphone, Jackson had already called her once yesterday evening and once this morning. She would only be able to avoid him for so long before she'd have to talk to him. Sage knew she couldn't risk pissing him off. Jackson could make her life a living hell. Because she willfully and purposely led him on, she'd have no one to blame but herself.

It was possible she'd need to move back to Colfax just to get out of the mess she'd gotten herself into, but Toby might be made to suffer. There was no telling the extent of Jackson's wrath. Sage fell backward onto her bed and stared at the ceiling, feeling alone and miserable. She'd gotten her hopes up, thinking Jackson's bracelet held the answers to her memory loss. Yesterday's flashback was almost enough to drive her insane. She might have seen the killer. If she could only remember that night, she could identify him. She needed closure for her mother's murder. Sage was certain the bracelet held the answers, but now that she had acquired it, she got nothing from it. She struggled to solve the riddle. What caused the flashbacks? It was definitely the bracelet. When she picked it up in Jackson's bedroom, the flashback was so intense, that it nearly knocked her off her feet. Her next thought was somewhat concerning. What if it only happened while Jackson was present?

Sage sat up and eyed her cellphone with one new voicemail. It was undoubtedly Jackson. How badly did she want answers? Bad enough to risk going back to Jackson's ranch? The man desperately needed to get laid, and with her behavior yesterday afternoon, another visit would fire him up. He'd now be anticipating something more intimate. She again had to ask herself how badly she wanted answers. Unfortunately, the answer was pretty simple. In order to find her mother's killer, she was willing to do whatever it took. Sage finally picked up her cellphone and pressed Jackson's number without listening to the voicemail he'd left. The call was answered on the second ring.

"Hey, Sage," Jackson announced from the other end, without even saying 'hello' or asking who it was. "You got my message."

"Jackson," she replied while fidgeting and jumped off her bed, feeling the need to pace. "I saw I missed your call earlier. Sorry, I didn't actually listen to the voicemail. What's up?" Sage cringed at her senseless nervous talk.

"Just checking in," he remarked pleasantly. "Maybe lock down a date for dinner one day this week."

Sage felt every muscle in her body tense. She could easily pick a day later in the week, which would give her more time to come up with a better excuse, but it would also keep her from getting any answers regarding the flashbacks. She needed to meet with Jackson if she wanted answers, and she couldn't put it off. It couldn't wait.

"I'll have to talk to Toby about my work schedule for the rest of the week," she informed him. "But I'm sure we could do breakfast at the diner tomorrow morning."

"Mornings can be pretty crazy around here," he replied without hesitation. "If you came to the ranch for breakfast, it would make my life easier."

Morning or evening at the ranch, the end result was still the same. "What time do you do breakfast in the morning?" she asked. "Must be early."

"Around six in the morning," he replied with a tiny laugh. "I didn't mean you should be here that early. We could do a late breakfast. You know, normal breakfast for normal people. I don't need to go out with my brothers. I'll just plan to do work around the house."

"Sounds like I'd be complicating things for you," she remarked and immediately cringed. She was quickly running out of excuses.

"It'd be easier if you just came over for dinner," Jackson informed her. "But I'll gladly rearrange my schedule if you want to do breakfast."

He wasn't going to give up. Unfortunately, Sage was internally struggling with her emotions again and allowed too much time to pass without responding.

"I hope I'm not pressuring you into coming over," Jackson remarked from the other end, then hesitated. "I just--I'd like to see you, that's all."

Sage once again saw that image of him standing in the driveway like an abandoned dog, watching her drive away, hoping she'd turn around and come back for him. She'd given a lonely man a false sense of hope for female companionship, but what made it worse was that man was Jackson Morgan. She didn't even want to imagine what his wrath would be like if she disappointed him.

"I suppose Toby will let me start work a little later tomorrow," she replied. "But I can't stay long."

"I understand," Jackson replied cheerfully. "How about nine o'clock?"

Sage cringed as her heart pounded. "Okay, I'll be there at nine tomorrow morning."

"Great," he announced, coming back to life. "I'll see you tomorrow morning."

"I'll see you then," she replied, then disconnected the call, groaned, and fell back onto the bed. She eyed the bracelet on her wrist and frowned. "You better be worth it."

§

Sage helped her sister in the bookstore later that afternoon. A new shipment of older books arrived, and Sage needed to sort them and place them in the appropriate section in chronological order. Her sister's love for old, weird books was nothing short of perplexing. Sage stared at one of the books and wondered why her sister would handpick such a strange book. She leafed through it several times and still couldn't make heads or tails of it. Finally, giving up, she headed toward the front of the store. Leo stood in front of the desk and kissed Toby across the counter. Since they'd gotten back together, it was going to be non-stop make-up sex. It seemed as if that was the only thing the two didn't argue about. Sage gently cleared her throat so they'd realize she was there. Leo and Toby broke off the kiss and attempted to act innocent.

"I'll see you tonight," Leo announced, then waved to Sage and headed out the front door.

"Coming over again tonight, huh?" Sage remarked and leaned on the counter across from her sister. "I guess the two of you have officially kissed and made up."

Toby hid her smile and avoided looking at her sister. "I know you don't particularly care for Leo--" she began somewhat delicately.

"We're okay, honestly," Sage interrupted and managed a pleasant smile. "As long as you're happy in your relationship, I'm happy."

"Yeah, sure," Toby remarked and smirked. "I don't believe that for a minute. You don't have to worry about Leo. He's fun to be with, but I don't intend to marry the guy."

"Really?"

Toby shrugged. "He's really great in bed," she announced. "Right now, that's all I can commit to."

"You're okay with sex for the sake of sex?" Sage asked, honestly surprised that her sister felt that way. She always remembered her being more commitment-minded and somewhat prudish.

"A lot of things changed since Mom died," Toby explained almost delicately. "Almost losing you as well made me want to enjoy each day. So I just want to take things one day at a time for now. I have plenty of time to worry about all that other stuff." Toby then frowned. "Since Mom died, it's been hard to focus on anything past tomorrow."

"I can understand that," Sage replied and thought about her own situation.

There was no denying she was attracted to Jackson, but his age would be a major hurdle for anything beyond a fling. What Toby said made sense, though. She needed to live each day right now. Giving in to Jackson's sexual desires was something she had to do if she wanted answers about the bracelet and the flashbacks that seemed to be playing hide and seek with her. If Toby could do it for fun, Sage could do it for answers. When the bell above the door rang, both looked at the main entrance. Sheriff Baxter and Deputy Milton entered the shop. Sheriff Baxter was a large, overweight man in his mid-fifties. Obviously, he'd spent many years sleeping in his patrol car rather than doing actual police work. His short, light brown hair was kept in a military buzz, and his face was clean-shaven. His uniform was somewhat wrinkled and seemed almost too tight around his mid-section, putting pressure on the fatigued buttons.

Deputy Milton was an African-American man in his mid to late forties. Unlike the sheriff, Deputy Milton seemed physically fit. He was fairly handsome with a bald head and a meticulously clean-shaven face. Appearances aside, it was difficult to take either man seriously, and most didn't. They couldn't find an 'X' marking the spot between the two of them. Their positions were mostly symbolic these days. Sniffing out free coffee and pastries while spending most of their afternoons sleeping at their desks and in their cars. Handing out parking tickets was about all they were good for. When they did any actual police work, it was usually handed down from Jackson, who was almost certainly pulling their strings. For a brief moment, Sage wondered if Jackson had sent his lackeys to check on her when she didn't return his earlier phone calls.

"Sheriff Baxter," Toby announced somewhat cheerfully. "What can I do for you?"

"Good afternoon, ladies," Sheriff Baxter announced politely, although he seemed almost disinterested. "We've had multiple complaints of dogs barking early this morning."

"We don't own any dogs," Toby informed the sheriff.

"No, not complaints against you," the sheriff insisted. "Complaints from dog owners."

Sage and Toby were equally baffled.

Sheriff Baxter cleared his throat and attempted to explain. "Dozens of dogs in and around Main Street started carrying on early this morning. It's possible something got them all going. Occasionally, we get the stray mountain lion or coyote venturing into town. We're just checking with everyone in the general proximity to see if you heard or saw anything early this morning."

"Possibly around three or four this morning," Deputy Milton added.

"I thought I heard dogs barking," Toby informed them, then shook her head. "But I didn't think much of it and went back to sleep."

"I heard them too," Sage remarked while eyeing both officers. "Some cats were rustling around in the alley around that time. I had my window open, so I heard them pretty clearly. Knocked over a few garbage cans, but they do that a lot in the middle of the night."

Toby eyed Sage and appeared curious. "It's strange you should say that," she remarked to her sister. "I haven't seen any stray cats lately, which is odd considering the deli next door is always putting food out in the alley for them."

Sheriff Baxter drew a deep breath and offered a tiny smile. "I'm sure it's nothing," he informed them. "Dogs around town always seem a little more wired in the summertime, especially when it's almost full moon."

"Strawberry moon," Deputy Milton muttered while shaking his head. "Every June, during the strawberry moon, every dog in town thinks he's Elvis Presley."

"Full moon isn't for another week or so," Toby informed both officers.

"Great," Sheriff Baxter announced with a false smile. "That means we get to enjoy dogs barking and complaints of the boogeyman for another week or more." He then tipped his hat. "You, ladies, have a nice evening."

Toby and Sage watched the sheriff and his deputy leave the shop. They exchanged strange looks.

"Did you find any of that odd?" Toby asked while folding her arms across her chest.

"Which part?" Sage then asked. "The sheriff actually investigating something? Or their concern over a few dogs barking in the night?"

"Both, actually," Toby muttered. "The only time those boys do any actual police work is when there's food involved or Jackson Morgan lights a fire under their asses."

Sage cast a sideways glance at her sister. "Why would Jackson Morgan care about dogs barking in town?" she asked. "He lives far from town on that secluded ranch of his."

"That's why it's odd," Toby insisted. "Those two certainly didn't decide on their own to investigate something as trivial as dogs barking, and Jackson usually holds their leashes."

Sage sank into thought. What would any of that have to do with Jackson? It didn't make any sense.

CHAPTER 12

Sage barely slept that night. She couldn't get her breakfast date with Jackson out of her head. Considering how sexually aggressive he was during her last visit, he'd probably be a hundred times worse tomorrow with what was going through his head. She felt a dull ache throughout her entire body from the moment she got up, and it intensified while she was in the shower. The more she thought about her morning with Jackson, the more intensely her body reacted. She actually only needed a few minutes in Jackson's company to see if the bracelet prompted any flashbacks. Sage could easily have done that at the diner or any other public place, but Jackson wasn't having any of that. She knew *why* he was insistent that she come to his ranch.

Although she would do her best to keep it from going that far, she prepared herself emotionally and mentally for the reality of her predicament. She needed to put her morals aside and do what she had to do to appease him. When she carefully and thoroughly shaved her legs and nether region, she knew she'd already made up her mind about how far she was willing to go for answers. She couldn't deny she was sexually attracted to him, despite his years over her, but she kept coming back to the bigger mental stumbling block. He was Jackson Morgan! He was imposing and intimidating, rattling everyone with his mere presence, and here she was shaving her houchi for him! In what world was this normal?

§

A few minutes before nine, Sage pulled up to Jackson's plantation-style house and parked her car. She sat behind the wheel and stared at the large, quiet house for a moment, working up the courage to do what she needed to do. She groaned and aggressively ran her trembling fingers through her hair. It was harder than she thought, but she had a backup plan just in case she chickened out. Sage removed a travel bottle of tequila and drank the entire contents. Despite how bad it tasted and how much it burned, she managed to choke it down. She needed to dull her senses and relax enough to push through whatever happened this morning. As she got out of the car, she immediately felt the alcohol tingling in her toes. It actually felt quite pleasant and would relax her enough to get her through what she had to do.

As Sage walked onto the porch and paused before the door, she felt a tiny nervous pang, but the tequila dulled it just enough that she was able to brush it aside. Sage knocked on the front door and waited only a minute before Jackson opened it. His intense, sly grin was almost more than she could handle.

"Sage," he announced cheerfully, "I'm happy you could stop by this morning."

Jackson then stood aside while extending his hand for her to enter. Sage immediately felt uncomfortable. Even the tequila couldn't suppress the feeling of pimping herself out to this man. Instead of money, she was bartering for information. If she crossed the threshold, she knew there was no turning back. Sage made peace with it and stepped through the doorway. As Jackson shut the door behind her, Sage immediately noticed the spotless hallway. Everything was put away, the floor was mopped, and there wasn't a speck of dust.

The smell of pine cleaner and lemon wood polish was an assault on her senses.

Jackson clasped her hand in his and affectionately kissed it, then offered a pleasant smile. "I thought we'd have breakfast in the dining room," he informed her as he guided her down the hallway while lightly clinging to her hand. "Honestly, I'd forgotten we even had a dining room."

Sage looked around as they walked along the hall toward the kitchen, conscious of the way he gently caressed her hand in his.

"You cleaned?"

"It was long overdue," he announced as if it were no big deal. "I'd let the boys slip in their house chores for far too long." His grin increased while eyeing her. "Twenty loads of laundry and three cans of furniture polish later; the place is finally up to code."

Honestly, she would have loved to see the four of them cleaning the house. In her version, they were singing pirate songs. She was certain it was a sight to behold. They entered the old, large dining room. The table, chairs, and china hutch were all hand-carved and many decades old, like the rest of the furniture in the house. The dining room table contained numerous covered serving platters and carafes of beverages. Jackson suavely pulled out the heavy chair for Sage, then uncovered the serving platters containing an amazing breakfast spread. Sage was once again impressed by his cooking expertise. He'd prepared some sort of scrambled egg hash, bacon, sausage links, hash browns, and French toast. There were carafes of orange juice, tomato juice, coffee, and hot water for tea to drink. Alongside the carafes was a bottle of tequila and a bottle of champagne.

"Help yourself to breakfast," Jackson insisted as he approached the beverages. "I didn't know what you wanted to drink, so I prepared coffee, tea, juice, and champagne from the wine cellar for mimosas and mixers for tequila sunrise."

Sage eyed the bottle of tequila and felt her body tense slightly. "Would you think less of me if I wanted the tequila sunrise?"

Jackson chuckled while hiding his smile. "Not at all," he announced. "I like your spirit of adventure." He poured orange juice and tequila into two champagne flutes and then joined her at the table.

"You really went out of your way," she insisted while helping herself to a sampling of everything.

"Yes and no," he informed her. "I do this every Sunday for the boys. Sunday brunch is a Morgan family tradition dating back to my great-grandparents. The only thing missing from this particular Sunday brunch is it's not Sunday, and there's no steak. Dean and Lance scarfed that down this morning. I should have made our platters before the boys came to breakfast."

"Well, you've done a wonderful job," she announced and held her glass up to him. "I'm impressed."

Jackson grinned and clinked his glass to hers. She then took a large swallow from the champagne flute, hoping he'd gone heavy on the tequila. Thankfully, it was plenty strong. Sage made a face and shivered.

"Too strong?" he asked with some humor. "If you can't stay, I may have to limit you to one."

"Yes, it's very strong," she replied, giggling. "But it's also very good."

"I'm glad you like it," Jackson announced cheerfully.

Sage initially wasn't hungry due to her increased anxiety, but the added tequila helped reduce her stress, and the food was beyond amazing.

"You certainly know how to cook," Sage remarked and pointed at the egg dish. "This is fantastic."

"The secret is tabasco sauce," he informed her, then winked. "We're a spicy family. We go through tabasco and hot sauce by gallon jugs."

Sage giggled and held up her champagne flute. "I think the secret is tequila."

He chuckled and again clinked his glass to hers. "I'll drink to that," Jackson replied as he finished the rest of his drink. "Unfortunately, we also go through a lot of tequila." He hesitated and frowned. "Whiskey too."

Sage drank the contents of her glass as well and then returned to her breakfast. Jackson got up and fixed himself another drink while eyeing her.

"Would you like another? Or just orange juice?" he asked in a slightly docile tone while attempting to gauge her mood.

Sage considered the question and smiled, enjoying her tequila buzz. "One more," she replied. "Then that's it."

"Nothing quite like a Sunday brunch buzz on a Monday morning," he remarked while grinning as he fixed a drink for each of them. Jackson set her glass near her plate, then raised his brow. "You may want to call your sister and tell her you'll be an hour late. I'm not letting you drive until your head is clear."

"It's okay. I told her I'd be in around noon," she informed him without thinking.

Sage immediately remembered she didn't intend to tell him that. He was supposed to think she needed to leave early so she could make a hasty getaway. She said it, and it was too late to walk it back.

"I'm happy to hear," Jackson remarked cheerfully, then managed a tiny chuckle. "I'll be honest; I was worried you were avoiding spending time with me." He shrugged while picking at his food. "A guy my age seeking attention from a beautiful young woman brings its own insecurities." He met her gaze. "And I suspect I came on a little strong Saturday afternoon. I was a little concerned that I may have frightened you." He again looked down at his plate. "Maybe even embarrassed myself a little."

When his eyes flicked upward, he met her gaze. Sage maintained her moderately buzzed smile.

"I won't deny you did come on a little strong," she informed him. "And it did make me a little apprehensive." Her grin then increased as she held up her glass. "But a little tequila seems to be taking the edge off."

Jackson chuckled and held up his glass. "I hear that. I had three of these before you got here," he informed her and seemed amused and possibly a little buzzed himself.

Sage laughed, now almost giddy. "I did a double shot in the car out front," she admitted.

Both laughed and again clinked glasses.

"Great minds--" he announced proudly, then sipped his drink. He set his glass down and leaned a little closer, now seeming serious. "If I say or do anything to make you uncomfortable, just tell me. I don't want you to feel intimidated or bullied into something just because I'm sexually repressed." He picked up her hand, raised it to his lips, and suavely kissed the back of it without taking his eyes off hers. "I'll happily take whatever you offer without pressure."

"You are devilishly charming, you know that?" she remarked while grinning.

His grin increased. "Oh, I know it," Jackson replied, kissed her hand again, and then released it.

CHAPTER 13

After they finished breakfast, Sage helped Jackson put the leftovers away and load the dishwasher. She couldn't get over how immaculate the kitchen was compared to yesterday. Once they were finished, they took their drinks, the carafe of orange juice, and the half-empty bottle of tequila onto the front porch, where they sat on the large swing and watched the mother horses and their foals frolic. Sage wasn't sure how many times Jackson had refilled their glasses, but she was sure they were now on their fourth or fifth drink.

"The baby horses are so cute," she remarked as they both watched them prance alongside their mothers.

"All legs." He then pointed to the pasture. "You see that little black colt?" Jackson asked.

"Aren't they all black?" she asked.

Jackson chuckled and shook his head. "No," he replied. "I think you need glasses. The one next to the black horse."

"The tall leggy fella," she replied.

"Yeah," Jackson announced, then smiled proudly. "That's Raven III."

"That's a cool name," she remarked. "What's Raventhree?"

He again chuckled. "Not Raventhree," Jackson insisted. "Raven III. Raven, the third."

"What happened to Ravens one and two?" she asked, now confused.

"Raven I is out to pasture with his girlfriend, Karma," he replied. "He's a very old man, even older than me. He's thirty-five years old. That's late nineties in human years." Jackson pointed further up the field to two horses grazing. "And Raven II is my current cowpony partner that you'd already met. By the time Raven III is ready to work the cows, Raven II will be ready to retire." He looked at her and smiled. "I'm sentimental about my horses. I hand-picked each mare for my boys." Jackson leaned closer to her and suggestively raised his brows with a humorous look. "If my brothers knew how much I paid for that new broodmare, they'd kill me." He leaned back on the swing seat and stared proudly at the horses. "I'm a *very* sentimental old prick."

"How much did you pay for the mare?" she asked while cleverly raising her brows.

"Too much," he replied without looking back at her.

"Mid-five figures?"

Jackson grinned and sipped his drink.

"Upper five figures?" she just about gasped.

Jackson chuckled while nodding. "Karma cost almost that much as well, and that was twenty-three years ago." He then raised his brows. "When I get my horse laid, he gets nothing but the best." Jackson maintained his grin. "I like letting them pasture breed. On Sunday mornings, I turn my boy loose with the un-bred mares and let him have at it. Some days, it's like Woodstock out there. Everyone needs some lovin'. Even us old guys."

"My God," Sage remarked and snorted a laugh. "You're a hopeless romantic."

"After Raven II gets some mare booty on Sunday afternoon, he's completely chill on Monday morning," Jackson remarked.

"Okay, you're a dirty, hopeless romantic," she corrected, then laughed.

Jackson laughed with her, then placed his hand on her thigh and warmly caressed it. "Take the good with the bad, I suppose." He finally looked at her and maintained his grin. "I like having you here. Living with three bachelor brothers is about as fun as it sounds. Dean and Lance are pretty much feral, and Creed is far too serious for my liking." He then frowned and shook his head. "Those boys need good women in their lives. Straighten them out. Make them into good men. I get tired of playing mother and father to them." He held his breath a moment and fumbled with his watch. "What time is it anyway? Do you have time for one more drink?"

"I think it's almost noon," she informed him.

Jackson looked at her and appeared disappointed. "Do you have to leave?" He then squinted at her. "You're in no condition to drive. You have to call your sister and tell her you need the rest of the day off to sober up."

She met his gaze and smiled almost slyly. "If I'm going to call her for the rest of the day off, I may as well continue drinking."

His grin increased. "You want to stay and get silly with me?"

Sage stared at him for a long moment as the alcohol worked its magic. Her hand affectionately caressed his thigh close to his crotch, immediately catching his attention.

"Maybe the horses can watch you get lucky for a change," she informed him.

Jackson suddenly groaned and laughed. "Oh, that is an offer I can't refuse."

Creed, Dean, and Lance loped along the driveway and approached the barn as if perfectly timed. Sage and Jackson both frowned.

"Well, that certainly is bad timing," Jackson scoffed, then leaned over and kissed her. "I'll get rid of them."

She pulled her hand away from his leg and stopped him. "No, just give them lunch," she insisted. "They'll be gone within an hour."

"You might change your mind in an hour," he informed her.

She smiled and giggled. "I'll be a lot drunker in an hour."

"Here's hoping," he remarked, then stood and took a moment to adjust himself, catching her attention. "Fucking kids." He eyed her, saw where she was looking, and noticed her grin. Jackson groaned and hid his smile. "Keep drinking and thinking dirty thoughts."

CHAPTER 14

Sage woke later that afternoon to the warm sun shining on her. Although she could barely focus, she could tell she was outside in an open field. If memory served her correctly, she was sure she had ended up in the horse pasture. The sun was an hour away from setting, and her head was spinning. She clutched the sleeping bag to her naked body and slowly sat up. Sage immediately held her head and groaned. After a few seconds, she again opened her eyes and looked around. Jackson roamed the pasture in just his pants with the belt undone and picked up articles of clothing that appeared to be strewn everywhere while the horses watched him. Sage wasn't entirely sure what had happened. However, she remembered bits and pieces of the afternoon. Although she didn't remember how they got into the pasture, she knew there was some intense, sexually explicit activity that followed.

"Stay there, Sage," Jackson called to her, sounding almost irritated.

That couldn't be good. She then heard some faint laughter. Sage looked across the pasture toward the fence at least fifty yards from her. Dean and Lance leaned on the wooden fence, watching them with grins on their faces while Creed shamed them. Jackson approached Sage with an armful of clothes and dropped to his knees in front of her, blocking her view of his brothers as well as the other way around.

"Sorry about my brothers," Jackson muttered while handing her some of her clothes. "I intend to kill two of them as soon as you're dressed."

Sage managed to slip into her shirt while keeping mostly covered despite that Jackson remained in front of her, blocking his brothers' view. Even in her still mostly drunken state, she couldn't deny she was almost as subconscious about Jackson seeing her naked as she was his brothers. Despite that they'd obviously had a pretty intense afternoon, she didn't remember most of it, so being naked in front of him was a bit uncomfortable.

"How long have they been there?" Sage asked while quickly slipping into her underwear and keeping mostly covered within the sleeping bag.

"Not long," he replied. "Creed called my cellphone when they spotted us in the sleeping bag. They didn't start looking for us until after dinner." Jackson offered a tiny smile. "Don't worry. You were covered the entire time within the sleeping bag. They only saw my naked ass while I was looking for my pants."

Sage slipped into her pants and then moved out of the sleeping bag to close them. She looked around, having difficulty looking Jackson in the eyes while still feeling mostly drunk and somewhat unsteady.

"Have you seen my shoes?" Sage asked before hesitating and briefly met his gaze as her cheeks reddened. "And my bra?"

"I'll find your shoes," he insisted, then stood and scanned the nearby area. He looked back at her and cocked his head. "Were you wearing a bra?"

She raised a brow and glared at him. "Yes, I was wearing a bra."

Sage stood with some unsteadiness and lifted the sleeping bag to check beneath it. Her phone fell to the ground. She recovered her cellphone and slipped it into her pocket. She then found her socks but still no sign of her shoes. Jackson finally found both her shoes and approached.

"Still no sign of your bra," he informed her.

Sage sat on the sleeping bag and slipped into her socks and shoes while feeling her embarrassment increase. Jackson finished dressing as well while standing over her. He then looked down at her and the aggressive way she put on her shoes.

"Are you upset?" Jackson asked, now turning concerned as he kneeled on the sleeping bag before her.

"No, of course not," she replied while sitting on the sleeping bag a moment as her look strayed to the fence line. "Do they have to stand and stare?"

"They have no manners," Jackson informed her. "They're having fun at my expense, and they sometimes don't think about how it affects others."

"Well, I'm feeling embarrassed, drunk, and vulnerable right now, and they're not helping," she informed him.

"Consider it handled," he informed her, then whipped out his cellphone. He pressed a button and waited a moment.

Sage saw Creed place his cellphone to his ear.

"Creed," Jackson announced in a stern, gruff tone. "Lance and Dean are making Sage uncomfortable. Do something with them now. If they're still there when I reach the fence line, I'm castrating both of them."

Creed returned his phone to his pocket and immediately lunged for both men, shouting at them and shoving them with hostility. Sage could hear Creed's angry shouts as he just about chased both men back to the house. Once all three disappeared inside the house, Jackson smiled timidly at Sage, where he remained sitting in front of her.

"Better?"

Sage groaned with frustration and raked her fingers through her mussed hair. "I realize this is my own fault--" she remarked.

"No, I'll deal with them," Jackson insisted with a look resembling concern. "Don't let them get to you. I'll knock them back in line." He seemed to tense and held his breath. "Don't be mad. I'll make this right."

Sage finally looked into his eyes and seemed slightly surprised by his words. "I'm not mad," she remarked.

It was Jackson's turn to be surprised. "You're not?"

"No, of course not," Sage informed him, then groaned. "Just embarrassed that your brothers witnessed the 'aftermath' of our drunken rampage."

Jackson seemed to relax now and smiled more naturally. "Well, they didn't really witness anything," he replied. "They just saw us sleeping in a sleeping bag together."

Sage snorted a laugh and attempted to hide her embarrassment. "I'm sure they can pretty much guess what happened before that," she informed him.

"They can certainly guess," he remarked, then chuckled while shaking his head. "But even their wildest fantasies pale in comparison." His grin brightened. "You were so wild, at one point, I prayed to live just long enough to witness the grand finale."

She sharply eyed him. "I doubt I was the instigator," Sage insisted.

Jackson raised an arrogant brow. "The last time I was in the company of a woman, my age started with a three. Now, it starts with a five," he informed her. "And I'm pretty sure the only reaction I got out of her was 'are you finished yet?'." He considered the comment a moment, then frowned. "Come to think of it; I got that reaction from most of the women I've been with." He snorted a laugh and shook his head. "Pretty pathetic, huh?"

"If they weren't into it, why would they have sex with you?" Sage asked, now curious, then hoped she wouldn't regret asking that question.

"When you don't get out much, you take what you're offered," Jackson replied, despite being slightly uncomfortable about the admission. "Lance and Dean were somewhat popular in their twenties, and I was still somewhat tolerable at that time. I'd sometimes get the desperate third wheel. I was also somewhat popular with women after they broke up with their boyfriends."

Sage eyed him and started putting the pieces together. "Is that why you asked me if I'd recently broken up with a boyfriend?"

"Yeah, I was the ultimate ex-boyfriend repellant," he informed her. "Got me into a lot of fights initially, but you break a few noses and a couple of jaws, and it earns you a bit of a reputation." He shrugged. "After a while, I started feeling like a gigolo bodyguard. By the time I hit forty, I had avoided the barroom drama and turned to unsanctioned poker games in the back room. I didn't get fucked as much in the poker room, and I was paid in cash."

"You never had a girlfriend?" Sage asked while staring into his eyes.

"I was busy raising three brothers after our mother died when I was fifteen." He snorted a laugh. "And look around. This isn't exactly the sort of place you find and keep girlfriends. I was too busy running the ranch and raising my feral brothers in my twenties. I was already defeated and angry in my thirties. And in my forties, I stopped giving a shit and focused my energy on the ranch."

"I'm kind of surprised you let me in," she remarked without taking her eyes off him.

"Well, you intrigued me," he reported while grinning. "Jean busting hard-on aside, being in your company felt like redemption for everything bad I'd done and all the mistakes I'd made. Maybe it's just age talking, but it felt as if fate was giving me another chance." Jackson studied her a moment and maintained his timid smile. "Is fate giving me another chance? Do you intend to stick around?" He then cocked his head. "At least until after breakfast tomorrow morning?"

"Well, I'm still too drunk to drive," she announced with a sigh. "I should probably call my sister, so she doesn't worry, and I'll definitely need to take a shower." Sage then smiled warmly and gently placed her hand on his face. "But, yeah, I think I might enjoy a sleepover."

"Yeah?" he asked while attempting to hide his enthusiastic grin. "Well, then, okay."

He was quick to spring to his feet and extended his hand to her. She let him help her to her feet, being she felt unsteady and still mostly drunk. As he gathered the sleeping bag, one of the horses approached them, interested in what they were doing. Both eyed the curious horse that wore her lacy black bra over its head and ears. Obviously, someone had put it on the horse.

Jackson indicated the horse. "I swear," he announced. "I don't know how that got there." As the horse walked away, Jackson managed a nervous laugh. "I'll, uh, get that back for you." He then gave a nod. "You may also want to check your cellphone and delete some things on there. You were taking pictures at one point, and there's a good chance I used the video feature."

Sage eyed him with surprise and shock. "I hope you realize I'll be asking to check your phone as well," she remarked.

"Understandable," he announced and indicated the horse. "Give me a minute."

CHAPTER 15

Despite being approximately six hours since her last drink, Sage still felt the dizzying effects of the tequila and relied on Jackson to help her up the porch steps. How he seemed sober was beyond her. Sage was sure she was still drunk, although her head wasn't nearly as fuzzy as it had been. She clung almost insecurely to Jackson as they entered the brightly lit house. Dean and Lance were sitting in the living room and smiling like immature schoolboys.

"So, how was the date?" Dean asked, clearly mocking his brother.

Jackson glared at his two youngest brothers. "Not another word," he snarled while holding up a warning finger.

Dean maintained his grin but quickly minded his own business. Jackson kept his arm securely around Sage as he guided her into the kitchen, where they found Creed cleaning up from dinner. Creed glanced at them and attempted to keep from staring.

"I have some leftover dinner warming for you in the oven," Creed informed his brother. "And if you want to sleep in tomorrow morning, I can handle breakfast."

"Thanks, Creed," Jackson replied and pulled a chair out for Sage. "I'll take you up on that offer."

Creed smiled knowingly and seemed almost pleased. "Think nothing of it," his brother replied.

Sage half-collapsed into the chair and still felt mildly dizzy and mostly drunk. Creed grabbed some oven mitts and removed two plates from the oven. He set a plate on the table in front of Sage, then placed the second on the table for Jackson as he sat down alongside her. Creed served both glasses of iced tea and then excused himself, giving them some privacy. Sage picked at her meal. Although she wasn't exactly hungry, she forced herself to eat, knowing it would help counteract the alcohol in her system. She texted her sister somewhere along the way, although she barely remembered doing it. After eating half her meal, Sage pushed her plate away. The world wasn't spinning nearly as fast now, although she was still feeling the effects of the tequila. She cast a look at Jackson, who had finished his entire meal and now had his arm across the back of her chair. She hadn't even realized he was caressing her back with his thumb.

"I don't get it," she remarked while eyeing him. "You seem sober. Why do I still feel so drunk?"

Jackson chuckled at the question and grinned. "I assure you; I've had a lot more practice at drinking than you," he informed her. "How are you feeling?"

"Drunk and dizzy," she remarked, then giggled. "Not nearly as tired as I was, though."

"Might be a good time for you to take that shower," he responded. "If you still want to take one."

"I would if you don't mind," she replied.

Jackson chuckled lowly. "Of course, I don't mind," he announced. "I'm pretty sure we were both walking around barefoot in the horse's pasture. A shower is probably a good idea. I'll get you a towel and washcloth and find you a clean shirt to sleep in."

§

Sage had some difficulty tackling the stairs, but Jackson remained behind her to keep her steady. She didn't even remember entering his bedroom or the bathroom, but she definitely remembered taking a shower, and she was pretty sure she wasn't alone. She felt Jackson's soapy hands thoroughly washing her entire body while he was pressed against her from behind. She kept her eyes closed a lot of the time, which made her slightly dizzy, but she enjoyed the way his hands and body felt against her. As the hot streams of water sprayed over her, she braced her hands against the wall while Jackson remained behind her and warmly caressed her. The sensation was amazing, although she seemed to lose her footing several times. Jackson warmly kissed her neck and shoulder, then chuckled softly in her ear.

"This is an accident waiting to happen," he informed her. "We should probably get you dried off."

Sage barely remembered getting out of the shower, but she remembered them drying each other off, which was kind of erotic. Her head finally began to clear after they finished towel drying each other alongside his bed. Jackson tossed their towels aside, pulled her into his arms, and kissed her warmly yet somewhat aggressively. She immediately returned the kiss while eagerly caressing his slightly damp chest, then placed her arms around his neck. His warm and slightly damp, naked body felt good against hers. His hands slipped beneath her buttocks, and he easily lifted her up off her feet and to the bed without breaking off the kiss. She again felt somewhat dizzy from being taken off balance, but she didn't mind.

Unlike earlier in the pasture, where she matched his aggressive actions with her own drunken ones, in the nearly dark bedroom, she now felt relaxed and a little tired, easily letting Jackson take control. Rather than a wild romp, like earlier, Jackson made slow and passionate love to her, allowing her to enjoy every kiss and every caress. She forgot this was the man that so many in town feared for a brief moment. Sage caressed his beard while lightly kissing his neck.

"You feel so good," she cooed near his ear.

Jackson groaned, then warmly kissed her neck before pulling back just far enough to meet her gaze and smiled. "You're an amazing woman, Sage," he whispered, then kissed her warmly.

Sage returned the kiss while clinging to him.

§

Sage woke the following morning to sun poking through the part in Jackson's curtains. Jackson clung to her from behind and nuzzled her shoulder, which was possibly what woke her. When he felt her stir, he sighed and cuddled against her from behind with his naked body as his hand traveled her body, warmly caressing her breast.

"Did I molest you in my sleep?" he asked close to her ear with a low chuckle.

"I think so," she replied with a tiny laugh. "But I'm pretty sure I fell asleep halfway through."

"Well, considering I wasn't even awake for it, I suppose that's okay," he teased while fondling her. "Shouldn't you be beating me off with a baseball bat by now?" His hand moved from her breast and down her abdomen. "If you don't, I'll continue treating your body like my own personal amusement park."

Sage showed no resistance and groaned softly while guiding Jackson's hand, encouraging his behavior.

"The park is open," she informed him with a tiny giggle. "Play as much as you want."

Jackson groaned and kissed her shoulder. "One more time through the tunnel of love," he announced. "Then I should go to work."

"Roller coaster might be more fun," she announced with a sly smile.

Jackson groaned loudly and aggressively flipped her onto her back. Sage cried out with surprise, then laughed.

CHAPTER 16

By the time Sage and Jackson got up, it was late morning. Although his brothers had left hours earlier to start their day, Creed had left some breakfast for them. After breakfast, Sage left the Morgan ranch while Jackson saddled his horse and went about his day as well. Sage wasn't nearly as hungover as she thought she'd be, considering how drunk she had been the previous afternoon. Her sister was just opening the shop when Sage arrived. Toby gave her a strange look and appeared more than a little curious and possibly concerned about last night.

"What happened yesterday?" Toby asked as she followed Sage across the shop to the door marked 'private'.

"I texted you that I wouldn't be home," Sage reminded her. At least she thought she had texted her sister.

"A somewhat incoherent text," Toby muttered as they stopped by the apartment door.

Sage glanced at her sister but had difficulty looking her in the eyes. "I, uh, drank too much and decided to spend the night," she informed Toby, then indicated the door to the stairs. "I need to shower and change before work. I'll be back down in thirty minutes."

Toby nodded, then turned stern and almost motherly. "And then I want to know what happened," she insisted.

Sage nodded, although she wasn't looking forward to that particular conversation.

§

After a quick, hot shower and a cup of coffee, Sage returned to the store downstairs feeling refreshed and awake. Surprisingly, she felt good, almost too good. She couldn't deny she was a little saddle sore from her initial drunken romp with Jackson. She still had no idea what happened in the pasture, but she had several suspicious bruises on certain conspicuous parts of her body that told a pretty good tale. Thankfully, Toby was with a customer when Sage returned to the shop below. Her sister and the older woman talked about a book they'd both read, giving Sage time to think about what she'd tell her sister about Jackson and last night. Her phone dinged, indicating a new text message. Sage removed her phone and saw the message was from Jackson. She checked the message, which was simply a kissy face emoji.

Sage smiled and sent one back to him. She then remembered something Jackson said in the pasture and opened her photo files. She was a little surprised to see over a dozen new photos and one video file. Sage drew a deep breath, concerned about what she might find, and looked at the photos. Most were ones she had taken. There were several of Jackson wearing only his cowboy hat while sitting naked, bareback on his horse. Quite a few were of her and Jackson bundled in the sleeping bag while smiling for the camera, and a couple were of the horse wearing her bra on its head. Apart from Jackson naked on his horse, which didn't really reveal much, they weren't too bad. Sage hesitated before opening the video file and playing it.

To her horror, the graphic video was of them having sex doggie style, with Jackson filming from his point of view behind her. At the time, she knew he was filming it because she turned once to smile at the camera. Jackson then turned the camera on himself and grinned his own drunken smile. Sage immediately gasped and stopped the video. She backed out of the video without watching the rest and was about to hit 'delete' when she reconsidered.

"Sage," Toby announced, startling her.

Sage returned her camera to her pocket and faced Toby with her best innocent look. "Yeah?"

Toby folded her arms across her chest while eyeing her sister and raised her brow. "Want to tell me what happened yesterday?"

Sage shifted, now uncomfortable. Her sister's reaction wasn't going to be good, and she wasn't exactly sure how to approach the subject.

"I, uh, had a breakfast date," Sage remarked, attempting to sound casual, then shrugged. "It turned into a lunch date with a fair amount of tequila, and it just kind of snowballed from there. Neither of us was in any condition to drive, so I spent the night."

"That's not really like you," Toby remarked as she allowed her arms to fall to her sides. "To do that sort of thing on a first date."

"Well, it wasn't technically our first date," Sage replied somewhat insecurely. "More like our third, I suppose."

"So who is this mystery man?" Toby asked as the shop bell rang, indicating someone had entered.

"Customers first," Sage insisted, then took a step toward the main aisle. Sage refrained from groaning when she saw Leo and managed a tiny smile. "Hey, Leo."

Leo suddenly grinned while eyeing Sage. "Got drunk last night, huh?" he announced with a throaty chuckle. "Who's the lucky guy?"

Sage shot a look back at her sister. "You told him?"

Toby turned defensive. "I didn't have to tell him," she insisted. "He was here when you sent that drunken text last evening."

"So, who's this new guy?" Leo asked, unable to stop grinning.

Sage just groaned and walked away from her sister and Leo. She couldn't have that conversation right now and certainly not with Leo.

§

Apparently, Leo had nothing better to do all day than hang around the bookstore. It was possible he was just waiting for the name drop, but she wouldn't give him that satisfaction. Thankfully, Toby went about her business and didn't push the subject. But Leo, on the other hand, periodically popped up in the aisle where Sage was working and fished for a name. Leo could be immature at times. When Leo and Toby finally went to lunch, Sage was happy to be rid of him. It was close to one o'clock when she heard the bell above the door ding, signaling Toby and Leo's return from lunch. Sage briefly glanced toward the front of the store just to make sure. Leo and Toby approached the check-out counter. Toby appeared pissed about something, while Leo seemed annoyingly humored. It was possible Leo was about to be kicked to the curb again. Sage could only hope.

When the bell above the door rang again, Sage cast a look to the front counter, half expecting Leo to be gone, but she wasn't that lucky. She saw Toby and Leo both staring at the door with matching looks of surprise on their faces. Sage was now curious and stepped around the corner to see what caught their attention. Jackson entered the bookstore looking completely out of place. It was possible he'd never set foot in the bookstore before, and it showed. Sage couldn't take her eyes off the imposing man. Her heartbeat quickened, and she felt a dull ache deep inside her body. She suddenly couldn't stop thinking about their endless night of passion.

"Uh, Mr. Morgan," Toby announced, summoning her courage, then forced a smile at the infamous Morgan brother. "Can I help you find something?"

Jackson was about to speak when he saw Sage. As their eyes briefly met, Jackson's eyes lit up. He looked back at Toby and smiled.

"Already found it," he replied almost smugly. "Thanks."

Toby and Leo appeared equally surprised as Jackson approached Sage across the shop. He paused before her and placed his hands in his pockets while attempting to hide his schoolboy grin.

"I had some errands to run and thought I'd stop in and see you," Jackson said just loud enough for her to hear. "I hope it's okay that I dropped in unannounced."

"Yeah, of course," Sage replied, unable to hide her smile at the handsome, much older man.

"Is it weird that I'm here?" he asked as his smile faded. "I'll understand if you hadn't said anything to your sister."

"Well, I was looking for the right moment," Sage remarked, then frowned. "Preferably when her boyfriend wasn't hanging around, but he's making that difficult."

"It's okay," Jackson reassured her while maintaining his grin. "It's too soon. I get it; believe me. I just, well, I thought it would be nice to take a walk with you while I ran my errands."

"Actually, I'd like that," Sage replied.

Jackson smiled but appeared almost bashful at that moment. It was kind of endearing. "What do you want to tell your sister?"

Sage stared into his eyes, unable to control her smile. "Nothing," she replied.

"Nothing?"

Sage placed her hand to his face, stood on her tippy toes, and stretched up to meet him. Jackson breathed a sigh of relief and met her halfway, placing his lips against hers. They kissed warmly but passionately before breaking off the kiss. Sage then took his hand and led him across the shop to the front counter. Toby and Leo wore matching shocked looks at what they'd just witnessed.

"Toby; Leo," Sage announced while looking at both. "I'm sure you know Jackson Morgan. He's the man I've been seeing."

Neither could take their eyes off Jackson. Leo remained shocked while Toby attempted to be polite.

"Uh, well," Toby announced and even managed a tiny smile, although she clearly wasn't happy. "I didn't see that coming." She quickly glanced at Sage while fidgeting. "I'm, uh, not really sure what to say."

Jackson suddenly grinned and looked from Toby to Leo, who still stared at them, somewhat shocked. "Well, I suppose you could start by pointing out that I'm kind of old." He then looked back at Toby. "That my reputation proceeds me." He shrugged and grinned. "Crude, barbaric prick comes to mind."

Sage cast a look at Jackson, but he didn't look at her. Instead, he seemed almost amused by their reaction.

"Well, I wouldn't go that far," Toby remarked while forcing a tense smile.

"I get it," Jackson replied in a cheerful tone. "I'm aware of my reputation, and I understand your concerns about Sage being with someone, well, like me. Honestly, if it didn't worry you, I'd lose respect for you."

Leo was unable to comment or take his eyes off Jackson, but Toby seemed able to relax.

"I'm sure Sage and I will talk extensively about it later," Toby remarked. "But I don't personally know you, so I'll hold off passing judgment."

"Thank you," Jackson announced somewhat cheerfully. "I appreciate that. Is it okay if Sage leaves for about an hour to run errands with me?"

Toby managed a tiny smile and indicated the door. "Of course," she replied. "She's entitled to a lunch break."

"Be back in an hour," Sage announced to Toby, then left the shop with Jackson.

The moment they appeared outside the shop, Jackson grinned, lifted her hand, and warmly kissed it. They immediately received stares from just about everyone who was out and about that afternoon.

"That went better than I expected," Sage remarked as they walked, immediately noticing the stares they received.

"What could she say?" Jackson asked, then snorted a laugh. "I said it all for her." He cast a look at her and smiled with some insecurity. "Can you come over for dinner tonight? If your sister doesn't lock you in a closet, that is."

Sage grimaced and patted his arm. "Unfortunately, I'm working until closing," she informed him. "The shop is open until eight o'clock. Punishment for taking the entire day off yesterday."

"Your sister is a slave driver," Jackson huffed in a disapproving tone. He then appeared amused and chuckled. "Takes one to know one." Jackson looked at her while caressing her hand in his. "I suppose you'll be too tired to come over after work, huh?"

"It's not physically demanding work," she informed him with a tiny laugh. "But it wouldn't be worth it to come over for just a couple of hours. Of course, if you're suggesting a sleepover, that's different."

Jackson suddenly grinned and eyed her. "I am most definitely suggesting a sleepover."

"I'll need to leave first thing tomorrow morning," Sage informed him somewhat sternly. "I need to open the shop by nine."

"We have breakfast very early," he reminded her. "You can leave after that. That'll give me a chance to go out in the morning with the boys and make sure they're not having any fun."

"Sounds perfect," she replied.

Jackson stopped her on the sidewalk and spun her into his arms. "Yes, it does," he announced, then leaned down and kissed her warmly on the lips, prolonging the kiss.

When he broke off the kiss, Sage gazed into his eyes while smiling. "You're aware everyone is staring, right?"

"You're aware that I don't care, right?"

Sage laughed softly, placed her hand on his face, and leaned up to kiss him. He met her halfway and kissed her again with a little more passion. She pulled away when he tried to prolong it and patted his chest.

"Save something for tonight," she announced cheerfully.

"Don't worry," he informed her while grinning. "I have plenty saved for tonight."

Jackson led her down the sidewalk and stopped in front of the flower shop. He turned to face her and appeared almost playful.

"You know, it just occurred to me that I've never bought a woman flowers before," he informed her, then pulled her into the flower shop.

"Then we're even because I don't think a man has ever bought me flowers," she replied as they entered the shop.

"Well, then," he announced dramatically. "We need to go big or go home. I'm thinking a dozen red roses."

"Less is more," she informed him. "One red rose."

Jackson groaned while frowning. "I wanted my first time to be special," he informed her and offered a devious grin. "You're making me feel cheap."

"Oh, I didn't know you were going for special," she replied and smiled while cocking her head. "Fine." She pointed behind him. "I want that."

Jackson turned and looked where she pointed. He stared at the small rosebush, then eyed her suspiciously. "You want a whole bush?"

"Not special enough for you?" she mocked him as she gently ran her hands along his chest. "Plant me a rosebush in front of your house."

116

Jackson placed his arms around her and held her against him. "You want a rose bush?" he remarked, then grinned. "I'll plant you a rose bush, and then you can enjoy it for *years*."

"Kind of the idea," she replied and considered what she'd just said.

Jackson kissed her warmly on the lips and attempted to prolong it when they heard the florist.

"Mr. Morgan," the woman announced, sounding almost nervous. "Good afternoon."

Sage pulled away from Jackson with some embarrassment, and both looked at the older lady florist. The woman managed a smile, but it was apparent she was still stunned by what she had just witnessed.

"Good afternoon, Maggie," Jackson announced politely while maintaining his smile. "I'd like to buy one rose bush, and a single red rose for the lady."

CHAPTER 17

Once Jackson left, Sage was forced to have a rather awkward conversation with her sister. Thankfully, Leo wasn't part of the conversation. Toby was upset that Sage was seeing Jackson Morgan, but at least she didn't get angry and irrational. Sage just explained that they were enjoying each other's company and that it wasn't serious. That seemed to appease Toby, but it left Sage wondering what she was doing. Entering into an intimate relationship with Jackson started out as a fact-finding expedition, and now she looked forward to seeing him and being in his arms. Jackson, on the other hand, might have seen her as the answer to at least some of his problems. Hook up with a younger woman in the prime of her childbearing years and pop out a few kids to continue his legacy. What if that was his endgame? Maybe he was just playing a game with her to get what he wanted.

Sage couldn't relax on the short drive to Jackson's ranch a little after eight o'clock that evening. She kept thinking horrible thoughts and reminding herself who and what Jackson Morgan really was. He seemed so sincere, but was he? As she pulled up to the house, she saw the rose bush planted right out front to the left of the porch steps. It had a little red bow tied around it. Sage had to laugh when she saw it. Well, no matter what game he might be playing, she could still enjoy it while it lasted. Jackson stepped onto the porch to greet her as she got out of the car. He smiled and proudly indicated the rosebush. Sage hurried up the steps, and he immediately gathered her in his arms.

"I missed you," he announced into her ear while holding her.

"You just saw me a few hours ago."

"I can still miss you," he insisted while releasing her. Jackson then took her hand and led her into the house. "The feral dogs are still up. Dean bet me twenty bucks you wouldn't show."

"No wonder you're so happy to see me," she teased with added humor.

"Yeah, that's why," Jackson muttered, then chuckled deviously.

§

Sage woke in Jackson's bed before sunrise. Jackson was nestled against her from behind, clinging to her naked body like a security blanket. She affectionately caressed his arm around her and eyed the bracelet around her wrist. Sage sank into thought while studying the pendant. Whatever happened with the bracelet and the flashbacks those few times wasn't happening anymore. No matter what she did, she couldn't recreate whatever made them happen. It was possible she was never going to get the answers she was looking for. Jackson warmly caressed her beneath the sheet covering them. He groaned softly while pressing his morning enthusiasm against her, then warmly kissed her shoulder. She smiled while enjoying the sensation of his arousal against her and his beard lightly tickling her shoulder.

"Morning," Jackson announced softly into her bare shoulder.

She caressed his arm while his hand firmly traveled her naked body. "Morning."

"I love waking up to you in my arms," he whispered while his lips moved from her shoulder to her neck.

"I love the way you wake me up," she replied with a soft giggle.

Jackson groaned at the comment and firmly pressed himself against her. "You mean *that*?" he remarked with a devious chuckle.

"Yes, that."

"I'll take that as an invitation," he announced, then swiftly cast her onto her back and easily maneuvered himself on top of her.

Jackson kissed her warmly on the lips while working his way down her neck and to her chest. Sage shut her eyes and groaned softly while enjoying the sensation of his mouth and tongue on her skin and his firmly traveling hand. Given the hour, she knew he was pressed for time, forcing him to get right to the point. Sage clung to him as he had his way with her. She knew they had to keep it down, particularly at this hour when his brothers would be waking soon. Sage listened to the bed lightly creak in rhythm with his movements. Although the creaking wasn't all that loud, to her, it sounded deafening. When she heard someone moving around in the next bedroom, she became a little self-conscious. Sage tensed slightly as she heard someone else moving around in the hallway as well, hearing each floorboard as it creaked beneath their feet. His brothers moving around within their rooms and in the hallway didn't faze or deter Jackson.

The creaking of the bed got louder with Jackson's increased movements. He finally groaned loudly into her shoulder while breathing heavily and then became still. He'd given new meaning to the term 'quickie'. Sage couldn't say for certain, but she was pretty sure she heard Dean snickering in the hallway just outside the door. Jackson affectionately kissed her shoulder, then rolled off her with a loud sigh. As he remained motionless for a moment attempting to catch his breath, Sage continued listening to the movement within the hallway and in the next-door bedroom. Jackson came back to life and pulled her into his arms. He kissed her warmly on the forehead while holding her.

"I'm sorry about that," he whispered into the top of her head.

"Sorry for what?" she asked while clinging to him somewhat insecurely.

"I felt you tense the moment I heard my brothers moving around," Jackson remarked, then sighed with defeat. "I shouldn't have started something knowing they'd be getting up any minute. It was rude and selfish of me." He groaned while releasing her and again rolled onto his back. Jackson placed his arm over his eyes. "You're right. I am a bully."

Sage turned, moved against him, and placed her head on his chest while clinging to him. "We're all adults here," she informed him while gently running her fingers through his light coating of chest hair. "Your brothers know we're having sexual relations." She held her breath a moment before sighing with defeat. "Yes, I was a little uncomfortable, but I'll get used to it."

Jackson attempted to look at her. She turned her head and met his slightly humored gaze.

"You're actually okay with it?" he asked.

"No, but I will be," she replied, then smiled as she reached out and caressed his beard. "I'm not willing to forego sex-on-demand just because your brothers might hear us." She returned her head to his chest and nuzzled him. "I enjoy 'spontaneous'. And the two of us sleeping in my room at my sister's place is a non-starter."

Jackson snorted a laugh. "Your sister hates me that much, huh?"

"Toby strongly disapproves, but that's not really the issue," Sage remarked and again lifted her head, now meeting his gaze. "I'd jump on you with your bedroom door open before I'd give

Leo the satisfaction of knowing there was a man in my bedroom."

Jackson studied her a moment and raised his brow. "You really don't like Leo, do you?"

She groaned while rolling her eyes and buried her face into his chest. "Everything about him makes me uncomfortable," Sage muttered. "Yet I can't seem to put my finger on any one incident."

Jackson securely held her in his arms and kissed the top of her head. "I get it," he replied, then snorted a laugh. "Over the years, Dean has had a parade of women traipsing through his bedroom. The man whore. There was one repeat offender in particular that chaffed my ass. Beautiful woman and pleasant as can be." He groaned and shook his head. "I don't know why, but I just couldn't stand her."

"I feel stupid for even thinking it, let alone saying it aloud," Sage remarked while shuttering slightly. "But I sometimes feel like Leo is undressing me with his eyes. He's never actually made a pass at me, but he's always doing little things that make me uncomfortable."

Jackson lightly brushed her hair with his fingers, seeming unaffected by the comment. "I'm sure he's harmless," he remarked, then kissed her head. "Of course, I'll break his hand if he ever touches you."

Sage's eyes popped open at the comment as concern swept over her. She was again reminded of Jackson's reputation. Was he also jealous and possessive? Jackson looked at the bedside clock and groaned.

"Well, we have just enough time to take a quick shower for two before breakfast," he informed her while straining to look at her.

Sage lifted her head and met his gaze. "Our last shower together wasn't so quick," she reminded him.

"Sorry to disappoint you," he announced while grinning. "My turnaround time isn't nearly that good." His grin then increased. "Not that there won't be an honest effort, but I wouldn't be expecting much if I were you."

Sage laughed and kissed him quickly on the lips. "I'll start the shower."

CHAPTER 18

W hen Friday afternoon finally rolled around, Sage was actually looking forward to Friday night at the tavern. Since she had off Saturday morning, Jackson decided he'd take off the morning as well so they could spend the morning in bed after their night out. He would then work around the ranch, which meant she could spend the whole day alone with him while his brothers were out with the cattle. It sounded perfect, but she couldn't deny she was a little self-conscious about their first official night out together in public. When he stopped by Tuesday afternoon, their public appearance in town had been a bit uncomfortable, so she didn't expect Friday to be much better. Sage had spent an amazing week with Jackson, and it was nice being in a relationship again. She suddenly hesitated before one of the bookshelves in the back of the shop and sank into thought.

Was she actually referring to what she and Jackson had as a relationship? A moment of panic swept over her at the thought. Sage didn't even notice the ding of the door opening since Toby was working upfront and would handle any customers. When she heard someone approaching, she looked up and saw Shelly. Her friend didn't look happy, considering it was Friday. Sage knew some of that may have had to do with

Shelly's feelings over her friend dating Jackson. Sage roused her best smile despite Shelly's lack of one.

"Hey, Shelly," Sage announced cheerfully. "It's Friday. Why so glum?"

Shelly folded her arms across her chest and glared at Sage with a condescending look. "Are we still going out tonight?" she asked.

Sage was genuinely surprised by the question. "Of course, we are," she replied. "We always go out on Friday night."

"Considering your new guy friend--" Shelly remarked while maintaining her scowl.

There was a moment of silence between them as Sage attempted to understand the hostility she was getting from her friend.

"Well, yeah, Jackson's going to be there," Sage replied, then cocked her head. "Is that a problem?"

"So we're all going to sit at Morgan's head table?" Shelly asked. "You, me, Henry, and *them*?"

"I suppose so," Sage replied while studying her friend. "I mean, it's basically just for dinner. You know his brothers play pool after dinner."

Shelly relaxed a little and allowed her arms to fall to her sides. "I suppose it won't be that uncomfortable if it's just for dinner," she remarked. "Once Jackson goes into the back for poker, and his brothers retire to the pool parlor--"

"Well, Jackson isn't playing poker tonight," Sage informed her friend. "So it'll be the four of us after dinner."

Shelly again turned defensive and shook her head. "No, I can't do it," she announced as her hostility increased. "I can't spend an entire evening with Jackson Morgan."

Sage stared at her friend with surprise. "That's ridiculous," she scoffed and straightened proudly. "You act like he's some sort of monster."

"Well, he kind of is," Shelly snapped back.

"No, he's not," Sage scoffed, turning angry. "You're my friend. He's not going to say or do anything to offend you."

"I'm sorry, Sage," Shelly announced firmly. "You're either hanging out with him or us. It can't be both."

"Then I'm choosing him," Sage snapped back without a moment's hesitation, surprised she had to *choose* at all. "He's not the one being unreasonable."

"Unreasonable?" Shelly cried out. "It's Jackson Morgan! It's not even the guy's age that's the problem here!" Her eyes widened. "He's *Jackson Morgan!*"

"Yeah, I heard you the first time," Sage muttered while folding her arms across her chest. "If you change your mind tonight, you know where to find me."

Shelly huffed, then spun and stormed away. After she heard the ding above the door, Toby approached the back room, where Sage now leaned against the bookshelf while lost in her own thoughts.

"I'm sorry about Shelly," Toby remarked somewhat timidly.

Sage looked at her sister and straightened. "You know, I get that people have issues with Jackson and his brothers," she remarked, "but he's not as bad as people in this town think he is."

Toby shifted uncomfortably and rubbed her chilled arms. "Well, that's debatable," she remarked somewhat timidly.

Sage eyed her sister with a curious look. "What's that supposed to mean?" she asked.

Toby drew a deep breath while studying her sister. "Many years ago, I heard there was an incident at the tavern involving the Morgan boys, a couple of men, and a woman," she replied while remaining uncomfortable. "Sheriff Baxter was called in, but he didn't arrest anyone. Instead, he left everyone off with just a warning." Toby shuttered. "Early the next morning, two of the men involved in the fight with the Morgan boys were found severely beaten just outside their home. A witness claims to have seen Jackson's truck leaving that area at three in the morning."

Sage felt a cold chill run down her spine as her sister continued with the story.

"Sheriff Baxter went to the Morgan ranch to question Jackson," Toby continued, then met her sister's gaze. "No one knows what happened for certain, but Sheriff Baxter returned to his office with fresh bruises. Nothing was ever said, none of the Morgan boys were ever arrested, and that was the beginning of their hold on this town."

Sage remained tense without taking her eyes off Toby. "But no one knows for certain what happened?" she then asked.

"No," Toby replied. "The men who were beaten never filed a report, and they moved out of town a few days after the incident. There was plenty of gossip around town, but it was mostly crazy talk."

Sage couldn't deny the story bothered her a little, but Jackson didn't seem to be that man anymore. "I get that he has a reputation," she remarked somewhat timidly, "but I think age has mellowed him. I haven't seen anything to indicate he's any kind of threat."

"I trust you, Sage," Toby informed her sister. "I trust you to make good choices, and if you believe there's good in him, I'm willing to give Jackson the benefit of the doubt. Just forget about Shelly and have a good time."

Sage stared at her sister a moment with some surprise, then smiled. "Thanks, Toby."

§

Sage met Jackson and his brothers at the ranch where she left her car and then drove to the tavern with Jackson in his truck. Creed took his truck as well. The boys always took two vehicles, which had more to do with Dean thinking he'd find overnight company than anything else, although that didn't seem to happen as often now that he was middle-aged. As Jackson's truck pulled up to the tavern, Sage was initially excited. It was kind of their first official date. Jackson was insistent that she allow him to open the car door for her, which seemed kind of weird at first, but she had to admit, she sort of liked it. Seeing him acting all gentlemanly was an incredible turn-on. As Sage got out of Jackson's truck, she saw Creed's truck approach and pull up alongside them.

Dean and Lance jumped out of the truck in an explosion of energy. Even Creed was a little pumped for their evening out. Something suddenly clicked inside Sage as she watched Jackson's brothers while they loudly joked around outside their truck. She just now realized she was on the other side of the fence, and it scared her. Jackson took her hand in his, suavely kissed it, and proudly led her to the tavern porch. Creed, Dean, and Lance filed into the tavern behind them. The moment they entered, Sage noticed several eyes upon them and the commotion that Dean and Lance seemed to bring. As Jackson guided her toward their usual table, Sage noticed everyone was staring at them, her in particular. She could almost hear their whispers.

Creed found an extra chair that they pulled up to their table to accommodate Sage, seating her snug alongside Jackson. As Jackson pulled her chair out for her, Sage felt sick to her stomach. She felt as if she had joined a mob family lording over the frightened masses. Sage sat down and avoided looking around the tavern. She didn't want to see the way people were staring at her. As she listened to the Morgan boys carrying on as they always did, she remembered what it felt like being on the other side. Kennedy approached their table within seconds of them being seated and tensed when she saw Sage among them. Kennedy was probably wondering if the Morgan boys had abducted her.

"What can I get you, boys?" Kennedy asked, then hesitated and smiled. "And girls--"

"Ladies first," Jackson announced, then nudged Sage while placing his arm across the back of her chair.

"Uh, I'll have a double of Johnnie Walker Blue neat," Sage replied.

Jackson grinned and chuckled loudly. "That's my girl," he announced enthusiastically, then looked at Kennedy. "Make it two."

"My usual scotch on the rocks," Creed announced.

"Bring a pitcher and keep the shots coming," Dean announced loudly while nudging Lance, who also laughed.

Jackson leaned closer to Sage while allowing his arm to fall across her shoulder. "Everything okay?" he asked just loud enough for her to hear.

"Yeah, I'm fine," she replied even though she wasn't. "It's just; I don't know. It feels strange being here on this side of the room."

"Am I being too clingy for you?" he asked with sincerity.

Sage eyed him, then smiled and relaxed a little. "No, you're fine," she replied and touched his face.

Jackson suddenly grinned and lowered his mouth to hers. "I'm glad to hear," he announced as he kissed her warmly on the lips.

Sage returned the kiss while gently caressing his beard.

"Oh, give it a rest," Dean bellowed and pelted Jackson with peanuts.

"You're just jealous," Jackson launched back at his younger brother.

Dean took in a sweeping eyeful of Sage, then looked back at Jackson and nodded. "That's fair," he announced. "I'll give you that one."

Lance and Creed laughed as Kennedy brought their drinks. She barely set the shots down in front of Lance and Dean when they clinked their shot glasses together and downed them. Jackson held Sage against his side, allowing her to rest her head on his shoulder. She felt secure when he held her, and it made the situation around her a little less frightening. After they ordered dinner, Dusty took a moment to approach their table and eyed Jackson.

"What's this I hear?" Dusty demanded, sounding almost angry. "You're not playing poker with us tonight?"

Jackson smiled at the tavern owner and laughed while indicating Sage. "I got a better offer," he announced proudly. "Dusty, this is Sage."

Dusty smiled and politely extended his hand to her. "Toby's sister," he announced as they shook hands. "It's a pleasure, ma'am." Dusty then looked back at Jackson and shook his head. "Good luck keeping that one."

"Ah, she loves me," Jackson announced to his friend, then looked at Sage and winked.

Sage hid her smile and had to look away.

"Well," Dusty announced while chuckling. "She didn't deny it, so I guess you're good." He then drew a deep breath and sighed almost sadly. "Welp, I guess I'll break the news to the boys that you won't be playing with us tonight. It's gonna break their hearts."

Dusty turned back toward the bar where Fat Matt and Slim sat on their stools, eagerly watching the Morgan table.

"He's not playing!" Dusty cried out excitedly.

Fat Matt and Slim cheered loudly and clinked their beer mugs together. Jackson groaned and rolled his eyes.

"Some friends," Sage remarked to Jackson.

"In their defense, I do win a lot," Jackson teased.

CHAPTER 19

After finishing dinner and her double shot of whiskey, Sage was finally relaxed. Surprisingly, Jackson seemed to be nursing his first drink. Creed was still on his first glass of scotch as well. While among the general population, she never really noticed how much the Morgan boys drank. Lance and Dean often got drunk on Friday nights, but they also weren't the ones driving either. She just sort of assumed they were *all* three sheets to the wind.

Kennedy stopped by their table to clean up some of the dirty dishes and eyed Sage's empty whiskey glass. "Want a refill on that, dear?"

Jackson signaled for Kennedy to get Sage another. Sage eyed Jackson after Kennedy left the table.

"I thought you'd be on your second or third by now," she remarked.

Jackson snorted a laugh, then smiled at her. "It only takes one time putting my truck in a ditch for me to learn my lesson," he informed her.

"You put your truck in a ditch?" she asked with some surprise.

"Yeah, I got messed up one night after my prized mare lost her foal," he informed her, then drew a deep breath. "Fucked up my truck and got a concussion." Jackson sank into thought. "That entire week was a cluster fuck. Since then, I do all my heavy drinking at home." He hesitated, eyed her, and smiled.

"Besides, I need to get you home in one piece, but don't let me stop you from having a few." He chuckled and grinned somewhat deviously. "I don't mind if you want to get a little wasted. It brings your morals down to my level."

"If you're sleeping out under the stars tonight," Creed announced, interrupting them, "do it out behind the barn. Fewer spectators." He then nodded, indicating Lance and Dean, who weren't paying attention to their conversation.

Jackson eyed Sage and grinned suggestively. "He makes a valid point."

Sage rolled her eyes while hiding her smile. The sound of glass shattering was followed by men shouting. The room fell silent except for the music from the jukebox. Lance and Dean strained to see what was happening. Two men were about ready to fight just two tables over. Jackson groaned and abruptly slid his chair away from the table, screeching the legs against the floor. As he stood, the two men about to fight stopped and looked across the room at the way Jackson stared at them with his head cocked. As they released each other, the first man grabbed his jacket and left the bar. Jackson sighed, pulled his chair back to the table, and sat down. Dean and Lance frowned while returning to their seats.

"You're no fun," Dean scoffed at his brother.

"If you're so eager for me to beat the piss out of someone, come on over," Jackson gruffly remarked to his brother. "I'll happily slap the silly out of you."

Sage tensed at the threat. Now, they were the Morgan boys she remembered. Sage stared at Jackson, surprised by what she'd just heard and its seriousness.

Jackson looked at her and immediately turned defensive. "What?" he demanded, then indicated Dean across the table. "He started it!"

"I know exactly how you feel, Sage," Creed muttered to her. "Welcome to my world."

"Your boyfriend is a bully," Dean pouted to Sage and made what could only be described as 'puppy dog eyes'. "See how mean he is to me?"

Jackson turned angry and leaned closer to his brother across the table. "Don't play on her sympathies," he scoffed. "She's not Mom."

"Yeah? Well, you're not Dad," Dean snapped back.

"Obviously," Jackson snarled in response. "I wasn't nearly tough enough on you. Didn't beat you as much as I should have."

Dean looked at Sage while raising his brows and pointed at Jackson. "See?"

"Shouldn't you be playing pool by now?" Jackson growled at his brother.

"No," Dean replied cheerfully and grinned slyly. "Torturing you is much more fun." A slow song then played on the jukebox, and Dean immediately smiled at Sage. "Sage, want to dance?"

Jackson abruptly stood and extended his hand to Sage while glaring at Dean. "Get your own girlfriend," he snarled.

Sage placed her hand in Jackson's and allowed him to guide her to the dancefloor. He gracefully spun her into his arms and slow danced with her.

"Sorry about that," Jackson muttered. "In case you haven't noticed, we're a bit dysfunctional."

"Actually, you're just four brothers who see too much of one another," she informed him. "Of course, you're going to get on one another's nerves from time to time."

"You're far too understanding," he remarked with a chuckle. "We should have frightened you away after the third day."

Sage stared into his eyes, then smiled warmly as she caressed his beard. "Too late," she gently replied. "I'm crazy about you."

He stared into her eyes only a moment, then kissed her quickly but passionately. Jackson pulled back and softly groaned.

"I may never let you go," he announced while holding her close as they continued to dance.

"Does that mean you're putting out tonight?" she asked while giggling.

Jackson smiled and groaned. "Oh, definitely."

CHAPTER 20

Saturday, late morning. After taking a long, relaxing bath in Jackson's tub after breakfast, Sage set out to find the eldest brother. He was supposed to be spending the morning working on bills and other ranch business. So the office seemed the logical place to begin her search. Sage paused in the doorway to Jackson's office and saw him sitting behind his desk while paying bills. He wore his reading glasses while writing out a check from the company's checkbook ledger. Sage leaned against the doorframe and smiled. He looked cute in his dorky, black-rimmed reading glasses.

"You look like a sexy librarian," Sage remarked while grinning.

Jackson looked up, saw her, and immediately removed his glasses, possibly thinking they made him look even older. It wasn't as if she didn't know how old he was. He smiled while casting his glasses onto the desk and casually leaned back in his chair.

"How was your bath?" he announced with a slightly devious look.

"Lonely," she replied. "You should have joined me and kept me company."

Jackson chuckled. "I didn't know that was an option," he remarked while lightly scratching his bearded chin. "I'll remember it for next time, though."

Sage straightened and approached the desk. "Is there anything I can help you with?" she asked. "Relieve some of your burden."

"Well," he announced cheerfully. "Aren't you thoughtful?" Jackson stood and approached her while maintaining his grin. He swiftly pulled her into his arms as he kicked the door shut and met her gaze. "I think I can find something for you to do."

Without warning, he picked her up off her feet beneath her buttocks and just about tackled her to the nearby sofa, landing on top of her. He immediately kissed her neck while unbuttoning her shirt.

"Not what I had in mind," she informed him while holding back her humor.

"Too late," Jackson announced between kisses. "You offered."

Sage groaned, then laughed. "Fine," she replied with a fake dramatic sigh. "Just make it quick."

"I can do quick," he announced as he sat up and eagerly opened his belt. "I'm getting good at quick." He unzipped his pants and tackled her back onto the sofa while reaching for her pants. "Quick is fun with how kinky you are." He swiftly and forcibly pulled her pants down.

"You're the kinky one," she insisted while flopping back on the sofa.

"That's a conversation for another time," he announced, then twirled his finger. "Flip it over, you naughty girl. Assume the position."

Sage giggled and met his gaze. "Make me."

Jackson smiled and groaned. "Oh, you want to play that way, huh?"

As he lunged for her, Sage cried out and laughed.

"Jackson?" Creed was heard calling from the foyer as the front door shut. "Jackson, we need you. One of the guys got hurt!"

Jackson groaned, quickly moved off Sage, and pulled up his pants. Sage practically jumped up and did the same.

"I need to see what's happening," he muttered while closing his belt.

"Yes, of course," Sage replied. "Go. I hope it's nothing serious. I'll wait here."

Jackson nodded, then hesitated and kissed her quickly but passionately. "I'll be right back."

§

Whatever happened to Jackson's ranch hand was enough cause for him to take his truck to their location. The men had been too far from the house, and if the ranch hand required medical attention, he might not have been well enough to make the journey back by horse. Sage was alone at the house, and, for the moment, she remained in Jackson's study. She found an old photo album on the bookshelf and paged through it. One of the older photos caught her eye. She saw what looked like a medieval wine cellar, and the photo was quite old. She remembered Jackson commenting on getting the bottle of champagne from the wine cellar. Was the wine cellar in the photo actually in the house basement? Judging by the picture, it was nothing short of impressive. Sage set the photo album down and went on her quest for the basement to see for herself.

She approached what she assumed was the basement entrance within the hallway. Sage opened the door and felt inside the doorway for the light switch. The broad, wooden steps must have been replaced within the last decade. They certainly weren't steps from the 1800s. Sage walked down the stairs and looked around the basement. There was a large storage area to the right and a door to the left. Despite containing an impressive lock, the door wasn't locked. Sage opened the door to the darkened room and felt the inner wall for a light switch. The light came on and brightened the room. She was stunned to see the amazing wine cellar almost exactly as it had looked in the picture but with a few added cobwebs. Three of the walls had hand-carved racks that were filled with bottles of wine coated in thick dust. Sage marveled at the extensive and expensive wine cellar.

As she looked around, she noticed a door to the right. Sage approached the partially open door and pushed it open a little further. She found a light switch and looked inside the room. To her surprise, she saw what could only be described as an armory filled with all sorts of weapons. There were many locked wood with glass cases. Sage tensed a moment, then entered the room while somewhat awestruck. She saw a lot of rifles, shotguns, semiautomatic handguns, revolvers, crossbows, swords, and knives. All were contained behind glass. What appeared to be drawers beneath each case almost certainly held each weapon's corresponding ammunition. An old desk at the back of the room contained a disassembled rifle and cleaning supplies.

Sage wasn't sure what to make of the room. Was Jackson an avid gun collector? Did the weapons belong to one of his brothers or maybe his father? Although, without proper context, the room gave her the creeps, but it was a small town, and they lived in the deep country. It was possible most men had a collection of rifles and assorted weapons out here. She didn't want to jump to any conclusions. She walked deeper into the weapon's room and approached the desk. A large whiteboard on the back wall contained photos and newspaper articles. It reminded her of a detective's board. As she got closer, she discovered that was exactly what it was. Sage eyed several gruesome photos and immediately tensed.

The photos appeared to be crime scenes of murdered men and women. There had to be more than a dozen of them. Some looked to be actual crime scene photos that only the police would have access to. There were dates scribbled on the photos. Some were as recent as five years ago; others dated back twenty, thirty, and forty years. There were also police reports and newspaper articles posted everywhere. Sage could barely absorb the information she was seeing. Her heart was pounding, and her head was spinning. None of what she saw was registering. All the murders seemed to be the work of a serial killer. Was it the same killer from forty years ago as it was from five years ago?

The killer would have to be older than Jackson if that were the case. She noticed there weren't any murders newer than five years ago, which made her feel a little better. Perhaps the killer was found and stopped, but that didn't explain what Jackson was doing with all that information. Then, something else caught her eye. A small section of the board near the wall contained something very different. Sage approached the end of the board and scanned various articles from nearby towns. All had to do with ghost sightings. Now, she was really confused. Certainly, one didn't have anything to do with the other. She shivered at everything she'd just seen. It was terrifying, and she wished she hadn't been so nosy in the first place. Sage turned and looked at the desk containing the disassembled rifle spread out on a towel.

Alongside the rifle was an old, leather-bound journal with some photos sticking out. Sage bravely took a step closer to the desk and opened the journal without picking it up. She preferred not to disturb anything, afraid Jackson might notice if she had. Her heart suddenly skipped a beat at the photo within the pages of the journal. It was a picture of her and her sister at the tavern taken about two months ago when she first arrived in town. She knew the approximate time since it was one of the few times her sister went with her to the tavern. Sage picked up the picture with a trembling hand. Many people took pictures with their cellphones these days, but how many actually bothered to print them out? So why print one out of her? Sage was getting a bad feeling.

Had Jackson been stalking her? No, that wasn't possible. She caught him looking at her a few times, but she was positive he wasn't staring and certainly not stalking. In fact, when she approached him last Friday night, he did his best to chase her away. That wasn't stalker behavior. Maybe the creepy armory belonged to one of his brothers, but that didn't seem logical either. Why was there a picture of her? She eyed the journal. There was one way to find out, but she was almost afraid to read what was written on the pages. Sage held her breath and looked at the journal entry where she had found her photo. Whatever the journal said, it wasn't in English. She turned a few pages in the journal, but it was all written in a foreign language. The last entry was from two months ago on the page where she had found the photo. Sage felt as if her heart would pound out of her chest. It was beating so fast, that she was having a difficult time thinking straight. She had to think fast. Did she take the journal and make a run for it?

Perhaps she could find someone to translate it and make sense of it for her. If she did that, there was no going back. Jackson would find out. There was no telling what he would do. She could confess to finding the room and ask him about what she'd found. But, of course, she'd need to do that in a public place. His reaction could also spell doom for her, depending upon what was going on. It wasn't just herself she needed to worry about. She had her sister to consider. Anything she did would have consequences for her sister as well. Her third option was to walk away. Either pretend she didn't see anything within the room or run as far from the Morgan boys and their ranch as possible. Sage considered her options despite not thinking clearly. Despite wanting answers, she needed to choose option number three. Confronting Jackson was too risky for her and her sister.

Sage considered her options one more time and then fumbled with her cellphone. There was another option. She took a picture of the journal pages that included the last entry as well as the photo of herself. She replaced the photo in the journal, leaving it exactly as she found it, then turned to the whiteboard and took several pictures of everything on it as well. She'd review what she'd found later when she was alone. Once she had photo documentation of everything, she replaced her cellphone. One article, in particular, caught her eye. Sage stepped closer to the whiteboard and studied the article with the headline, 'Double homicide rocks Great Bend'. Something stuck out within the article. A name. Her mother's name. Sage scanned through the article and suddenly felt sick to her stomach.

According to the article, two people were found murdered in a home outside of town. Tobias Remington and her mother, Grace Remington, were found murdered in their home on Friday night around ten in the evening. Sage stared at the article and was unable to read any further. The article didn't make any sense. Sage's mother was killed in Colfax in the same attack that nearly claimed her own life. Her sister, Toby, was alive and well and had been nowhere near the incident. Why was the article saying Toby had been killed? Why was the article claiming it had happened in Great Bend when it happened in Colfax? Sage's heart was pounding, and her head was spinning. None of it made any sense.

CHAPTER 21

Jackson and Creed helped Marv hobble to the pickup truck parked alongside the dirt road within the ranch property. The sky was turning dark with an approaching late morning storm. As Marv collapsed within the passenger seat, Jackson shook his head at the man.

"You may have nine lives, but you're clumsy as hell, Marv," Jackson informed the man.

"It wasn't my fault," Marv protested. "The horse went crazy."

"Yeah, sure," Jackson remarked. "Blame it on the horse. We all get thrown. Difference is, the rest of us know how to take a fall." Jackson shut the truck door and then looked at the dark sky. He groaned and ran his fingers through his hair. "Ah, hell." Jackson eyed Lance. "Take Gene Kelly to the emergency room. I'll take your horse back to the ranch. Sage is alone."

"She's a big girl," Dean teased while grinning. "She's even old enough to vote."

"Yeah, funny," Jackson scoffed. "She has a tiny phobia about thunderstorms. I don't want her all alone at the house." Jackson mounted Lance's horse and then spun to face his brothers. "Take Mr. Graceful's horse back to the farm. I'll take the express line and meet you there when you get back. Don't lollygag. You don't want to be stuck out in that storm."

"Yes, Dad," Dean muttered.

Jackson spun the horse and sent it into a gallop in the direction of the ranch.

§

As Sage hurried from the house and stepped onto the porch, the sky was nearly black, and thunder rumbled loudly in the near distance. She stared at the stormy sky with horror on her face.

"No," she gasped and fumbled with her car keys. "Not now."

She bolted from the porch and hurried for her car. Sage jumped into the car, started it, and turned for the driveway. She hit the gas a little too hard and the car burned out on the dirt road. Sage drove across the ranch toward the long driveway as thunder rumbled loudly and lightning flashed. Sage jerked in time with the lightning. Her eye then caught the symbol on the braided leather bracelet she wore. There was a brilliant flash, and Sage was transported back to that night.

As Sage ran for the back road in the dark, she saw headlights from a jeep. She had to stop that vehicle. She heard movement behind her, but she couldn't look back. Sage ran out into the road in front of the swiftly moving jeep and raised her hands in the air despite the pain it caused her. The vehicle slammed on its brakes and skidded loudly across the wet road. The jeep came to a sudden stop only inches before hitting her. Sage clutched the front of the vehicle and hurried for the passenger side as the driver's side door opened. She panted while waving to the driver.

"We have to go," she gasped, feeling her legs becoming almost too heavy to move.

Sage returned to reality with a loud crack of thunder. She saw a horse and rider in the driveway in front of her. Sage screamed, spun the wheel to avoid the horse, and attempted to slam on the brakes. The horse squealed and reared up as the lightning flashed. The car flew off the side of the road and struck a tree with a loud bang, bouncing Sage's head off the steering wheel. She tried to focus, but everything became dark.

Sage stood in the pouring rain, soaked and exhausted. Her once white shirt was now stained pink from her blood being washed away from her shoulder wound. She gasped to catch her breath and stared down the barrel of a large .357 Magnum revolver. Despite the nearly deafening sound of the pouring rain, Sage could hear the revolver's hammer as it rotated back. She could see a man's finger squeezing the trigger. She lifted her eyes and cast them upon the man holding the gun. She could hear herself screaming something at him, but the words were inaudible. She stared at the man's face beneath the wet black cowboy hat as the trigger suppressed. Jackson's eyes were cold as he fired the weapon.

Sage suddenly gasped and jerked awake as blood-streaked her temple near her eyebrow. She was still behind the wheel of the car with its airbag deflated. Jackson crouched within the open doorway and placed his handkerchief on her bleeding temple while staring at her with concern.

"Are you okay?" he just about gasped.

Sage stared at Jackson, uncertain what was real and what wasn't. "What happened?"

"You nearly ran me down in the driveway," Jackson replied. "You veered and hit a tree." He checked her head wound. "You got a nasty bump on your head. We should get you back to the house and take a look at it."

Sage stared at Jackson as the images from her flashback now came flooding back. As the thunder cracked, she twitched. Despite her urge to curl into a ball, she didn't take her eyes off Jackson. She couldn't get the image of him aiming a gun at her and pulling the trigger out of her mind. He lied! He lied about having seen her before! It was him! He attacked her that night! Jackson took her hand in his and helped her from the car. Her legs were incredibly weak, and she nearly collapsed. Jackson caught her and, without hesitation, swept her off her feet and into his arms.

"It's okay, Sage," he assured her while clinging to her. "You're going to be fine."

He carried her to the waiting horse and let her feet touch the ground. The rain poured down, drenching them and the horse.

"Let's get you on the horse, and I'll take you back to the house," he insisted with compassion. Jackson met her gaze despite the pouring rain and touched her face. "Hey, can you hear me?"

Sage stared at him, but all she could see was his face from the past as he aimed his weapon at her and pulled the trigger. He indicated the horse and placed her hand on the saddle horn above her.

"Come on," he announced. "Let's get your foot in the stirrup."

Sage couldn't take her eyes off Jackson. She couldn't unsee what she'd seen in her flashback. She couldn't stop seeing Jackson shooting her. When she didn't respond to his request, he placed his hand on her face.

"Sage, I need you to stay with me here," he announced. "We need to get you back to the house. Can you get on the horse, or do you need me to carry you?"

Sage's head was pounding almost as bad as it was spinning. Despite her condition, she was thinking clearly. She needed to get away from Jackson, and there was only one way she could do that. She gripped the saddle horn and struggled to get her foot in the stirrup. Jackson helped place her foot in the stirrup and then heaved her up into the saddle with his hands on her backside. She nearly fell off the other side but did her best to maintain her balance. Jackson rounded the front of the horse and helped her secure her right foot in the opposite stirrup. Once he had her foot secure and was out of her path, Sage kicked the horse and sent it into a gallop past the wrecked car and away from the ranch.

"Sage!"

As the horse ran along the dirt driveway, Sage did her best to keep her seat and stay on the horse. With the pouring rain and her blurred vision, she almost couldn't tell where she was going, but the horse seemed to know. She had to stay awake or risk the horse turning around and heading back to the ranch. Falling off was also not an option. Jackson would almost certainly be heading back to the ranch to retrieve a car and come after her. She slowed the horse near the end of the long driveway and found a path in the woods. She veered the horse into the woods and took it slow on the trail. She stopped the horse when she thought she was far enough away yet close to the back road. Sage removed her cellphone and pressed the button for her sister. Her vision seemed to worsen, and there was a loud ringing in her ears. She feared passing out or simply falling off.

"Hello?" came Toby's familiar voice.

"Toby," Sage gasped into the phone and felt her heart pounding with hope. "I'm in trouble. I need you to come and get me."

"Where are you?" Toby asked with concern. "Hold on. I'm coming for you."

"I'm about two hundred yards from the Morgan Ranch driveway," Sage told her sister. "I'm hiding about twenty yards in the woods. I'll come out when I see you."

"I'm on my way, Sage," Toby assured. "I'm getting in my car now. What's going on? Is someone after you? Did Jackson hurt you?"

"It's a long story, Toby," Sage replied. "Whatever happens, don't let Jackson take me back to his ranch."

"You're scaring me, Sage."

"Just hurry, okay?"

§

Jackson's newer truck reached the end of the driveway and stopped. Lance's saddled horse, without its rider, trotted down the driveway past the pickup truck and headed back to the ranch.

"Christ," Jackson cried out and jumped from the truck. "Sage!" He ran along the driveway and looked in the nearby woods. "Sage!"

Jackson stopped at the end of the driveway and looked down the road. He saw Sage getting into Toby's car. The car burned out on the wet road and sped away. Jackson stood in the pouring rain staring after the car as it disappeared.

CHAPTER 22

Now in dry clothes, Sage sat at the kitchen table within her sister's apartment above the bookstore. Toby applied surgical strips to the cut on Sage's temple and watched as she dried her phone.

"Are you going to tell me what's going on?" Toby finally demanded. "Why was Jackson Morgan chasing you? Did he hurt you?"

"I don't know what happened," Sage replied.

Toby appeared alarmed. "Your amnesia?" she practically gasped. "Did he hit you on the head?"

"No, I wrecked my car leaving his ranch," Sage informed her sister.

"So you do remember what happened today?"

"I need to show you something, Toby," Sage announced. "I can't explain it. You have to see it for yourself."

Sage plugged her cellphone into Toby's laptop computer and pulled up her photo files. Toby pulled a chair up alongside Sage's chair and waited while watching the screen. The first picture on the screen was Jackson sitting naked on his horse, wearing only his cowboy hat. Sage gasped and swiftly moved to the next picture. Toby stared at Sage with near horror.

"You didn't see that," Sage muttered, then pulled up the next picture of Jackson's whiteboard.

"What is that?" Toby practically gasped.

"It's a track board," Sage informed her.

"Like on the detective shows?"

"Exactly," Sage replied.

"What's he tracking?"

"Murders," Sage announced, then found the picture of her and the journal pages. "I found this."

Toby stared at the picture on the screen and immediately tensed. "That's us," she gasped.

"Yeah," Sage replied and shivered. "Taken two months ago when I first arrived in town. I found it in this old journal in the basement."

Toby squinted at the screen. "What language is that?"

"I don't know," Sage insisted, "but the entry was probably the day he took that photo of us."

"So Jackson Morgan was stalking you?" Toby asked, then shot a concerned glare at her sister. "Do you think he's dangerous?"

Sage groaned and ran her fingers through her damp hair. "I don't know," she replied and sighed.

"This is really starting to freak me out," Toby remarked.

"Oh, it gets creepier," Sage insisted, then pulled up the picture of the newspaper article. "I didn't get to read the entire article, but this came from the newspaper here in Great Bend." Sage looked at her sister and raised her brows. "According to this article, you and Mom were killed here in Great Bend. It's weird because Mom died in Colfax, and, obviously, you're still alive."

Toby seemed unusually tense as she stared at the article. "I'm sure there's some explanation for that," she insisted, unable to take her eyes off the article.

Sage gave her a strange look. "You're not freaking out nearly as much as I expected," she remarked. "What possible explanation could there be?"

"I, well, I don't know," Toby replied and remained transfixed on the photo of the article. Finally, she snapped out of her thoughts and glanced at Sage. "What happened with Jackson? Why was he chasing you? Did he catch you looking at this stuff?"

"No, but I wanted to get out of there before he came back," Sage insisted. "That's when I wrecked the car. He was only trying to get me to go back to the ranch. He didn't actually *do* anything, but I wasn't about to sit around and wait for him to actually do something."

"He must have done something," Toby muttered, then ran her fingers through her hair and seemed unusually tense while staring at the laptop.

Sage stared at her sister and her strange reaction. "What's wrong?" she asked.

"Nothing," Toby announced and just about jumped from her seat.

"There's more," Sage remarked.

Toby released her breath and eyed Sage while sinking back into her chair. "What else?" she practically gasped.

Sage showed her the pendant bracelet. "Jackson was wearing this," she remarked. "From the moment I saw it, I've been having flashbacks of that night." She nervously fidgeted. "Right before I wrecked the car, I had a flashback of the night Mom was killed and I was attacked."

"What did you see?" Toby practically gasped with a somewhat hopeful look.

"I saw Jackson," Sage insisted. "He aimed a very large gun at me, and then he pulled the trigger."

Toby's eyes widened in horror as she stared at Sage. "He what?"

"It was Jackson," Sage informed her. "I don't know how, but it was him. I saw him clear as day." She held her breath. "He must have recognized me from that night. That's the only explanation for my picture in his secret lair."

Sage and Toby stared at each other for a long moment in silence. Sage's cellphone rang, startling both. She glanced at her cellphone and saw Jackson's name on the caller ID. Both women tensed.

"Think you should answer it?" Toby whispered almost as if he'd be able to hear her.

"No," Sage replied. "We need to go to the police, but I don't know what to tell them."

"You can't exactly go to the police," Toby insisted, then hesitated. "I mean, he's in good with them."

"Then we need to call the state police," Sage replied.

They heard the doorbell to the shop downstairs ring within the apartment. Toby appeared alarmed. She nervously stood and headed for the main door. Sage stood a little too quickly and nearly fell back down. She held her head a moment, again stood, and followed her sister. Toby got halfway down the stairs to the shop before turning around and meeting Sage at the top of the stairs. She ushered her back into the apartment.

"It's Jackson," Toby gasped. "He's outside the front door."

Once Sage and Toby entered the apartment, Toby locked and bolted the door.

"We have to call someone," Sage insisted.

Toby paced the living room and appeared deep in thought. "Give me a minute, okay?"

Sage waited impatiently. Her cellphone again rang almost in time with the downstairs doorbell. Her cellphone no sooner stopped ringing when the shop phone rang.

"Son-of-a-bitch," Toby cried out, then approached the laptop. She hit the print button and waited for the page to print.

Sage joined her sister by the printer. Toby held the paper to her chest a moment and shut her eyes. She released a breath and looked at Sage.

"Sage," Toby announced with distress in her voice. "You'd better sit down."

Sage stared at her sister for a long moment, then slowly sank into the chair. "What is it?"

Toby met her gaze and trembled while holding the paper to her chest. "I don't know how to tell you this without completely freaking you out," she announced.

"Tell me what?" Sage asked with concern. "You're scaring me."

"Do you remember when you showed up at my doorstep two months ago?"

"Of course," Sage replied. "It was after Mom was killed. I had just been released from the hospital and needed a place to recover."

Toby trembled slightly. "Sage," she announced, almost unable to get the words out. "Mom was murdered twenty years ago."

She stared at Toby, baffled by her words. "What are you talking about?" she gasped, then shook her head. "It was two months ago."

"Sage," Toby just about whispered while cringing. "When I say *Mom* was killed twenty years ago, I mean *my* mother. Toby Remington."

Sage couldn't take her eyes off Toby. "What? We have the same mother," she insisted. "And *you* are Toby Remington."

"No," Toby replied with a soft groan. "I'm named after my mother, who was also Toby Remington. My father ran off before I was born, so I was given my mother's surname. Grace Remington, your mother, was my grandmother."

Sage's head was pounding again, and she suddenly felt lightheaded. "You're cracking up, Toby."

"At first, I thought so too," Toby nervously informed her. "Imagine my surprise when my Aunt Sage showed up at my door two months ago. You were missing for *twenty years.*" Toby now trembled. "You showed up the same age as when you disappeared." She reluctantly handed her the article that she had printed from the screenshot. "Look at the date on the article."

Sage hesitated, then accepted the printed article and looked at the date. Horror swept over her. Toby was telling the truth. The article was from twenty years ago!

"No, this can't be," Sage gasped, unable to take her eyes off the paper.

Toby slowly sank into the chair facing Sage. "I don't know what happened to you," she insisted. "At first, I thought you were a ghost, but you're obviously not."

Sage lifted her gaze and looked at Toby. "I don't understand--"

"I don't either," Toby assured her. "I'll tell you everything I know." She drew a deep, shaken breath. "Twenty years ago, Grandma was coming to visit us. We lived in a house on that back road near the apple orchard. I was six at the time. The night my mother and Grandma were murdered, I was staying overnight at a friend's house. My first sleepover." She shuddered slightly and rubbed her chilled arms. "After the murders, the authorities were trying to track you down to take me in. Apparently, one of your college friends from Colfax said you decided last minute to go with your mother to visit your sister in Great Bend. I guess it was supposed to be a surprise. They never found your body, so it was never reported that you were even there that night."

Sage couldn't tear her eyes away from Toby.

"I don't know what happened, Sage," Toby insisted. "I don't know where you were for the last twenty years, and I have no idea why you hadn't aged a day. When you showed up with no memory and assumed I was your sister, I didn't know what to do. They'd lock us both in the loony bin if I told anyone. I certainly wasn't going to tell you the truth. I didn't understand it myself. It was just easier to let you and everyone else think you were my sister. I figured I'd worry about it if and when you got your memory back. Until then, I was just happy to have my aunt back. Having you as a sister worked for me."

"All this time," Sage whispered to the woman she thought was her sister. "You were only six?" She shook her head. "I'm so sorry, Toby. What you must have gone through--" She then eyed her niece. "Who took care of you?"

"Mom's boyfriend wanted to take me in, but the courts said 'no'," Toby remarked, then offered a tiny smile. "It wasn't so bad. My best friend's parents took me in. I was young; I bounced back. My childhood isn't important." Her look turned more serious. "What's happening, Sage? None of this makes any sense."

Sage placed her hand on her head and gently rubbed her temple. "I started seeing flashes of that night when I first saw Jackson's pendant. That's why I initially pursued him," she announced, then shook her head. "Jackson was lying when he said we'd never met before. We met the day he tried to kill me."

"If he remembered you from twenty years ago," Toby announced, "then I can only imagine he must have thought he'd seen a ghost just as I had."

Sage groaned and shut her eyes. "The tracking board," she muttered and looked back at Toby. "He had all this stuff about ghosts. I can't believe I walked right into that. He just strung me along." She sank into thought and shook her head. "Why didn't I age? Why did I suddenly start having flashbacks when I saw the bracelet?"

"Because it was your bracelet," Toby informed her. "I remember you having it when I was a kid. You're wearing it in several pictures."

"Mine?" she asked with surprise. "How did Jackson end up with it?"

"If he tried to kill you, maybe it fell off," Toby suggested. "I guess he kept it."

Sage glanced at the bracelet. "There has to be something significant about the bracelet," she announced. "It has to mean something."

"The design is similar to some hex spells often associated with voodoo and witchcraft," Toby replied. "I've seen similar symbols in my research."

Sage snorted a laugh. "Yeah, like the bracelet has some sort of magical powers. Be real."

"Why not?" Toby asked. "Can you come up with a better explanation?"

The store phone rang again in sync with the doorbell, sounding like some creepy horror movie.

Sage jumped, then groaned. "We need to do something about him," she muttered. "Before he breaks in and kills us both."

"He can try to break in," Toby remarked, "but he's not getting in. As a child whose entire family was murdered in their home, all my doors are reinforced steel with floor and ceiling bolts. Paranoia at its finest." Toby turned her chair to her laptop. "Let me do a little research on that symbol and see what I come up with."

Sage's cellphone rang again, and she glanced at the caller ID. "He just doesn't give up."

"Answer it," Toby announced with a shrug. "Tell him I'm waiting inside the door with a shotgun, and you called the state police."

"Do you really think it's a good idea for me to talk to a potential serial killer?" Sage asked with concern.

"Sage," Toby remarked while glaring at her aunt. "You've been sharing a bed with the guy for a week now. Talking to him is the least of your worries."

"Yeah, I realize that," Sage remarked with some annoyance. "I mean, if I talk to him, won't that just piss him off?"

"Maybe," Toby replied, then shrugged. "But I do have a shotgun."

Sage held her breath, stood, and pressed the button on her cellphone. She placed the phone to her ear and paced the living room.

"Jackson," she announced softly.

"Sage," Jackson gasped from the other end. "Thank God you're okay. What happened? Why did you run away from me?"

"You know why," she announced without emotion. "I found your armory and your psycho board."

There was a strange moment of silence. "Sage, I can explain all of that," he insisted from the other end. "Let me in. We'll talk about it."

"I'm not letting you in," Sage remarked and managed a tiny laugh. "Do you think I'm crazy?"

"Considering the company you keep, yeah, I think you're a little crazy," Jackson replied over the phone. "I can explain those boards. I watched one too many crime dramas. At least come downstairs and let me see that you're okay."

Sage fell silent a moment while considering the request. "Okay, I'll come downstairs, but I'm not opening the door," she announced.

Toby gave Sage a sharp look. "Are you insane?"

Sage disconnected the call and looked at Toby. "I'm going to talk to him through the glass," she insisted. "You said it's shatterproof, right?"

"Yeah, but not if he drives his truck through it," Toby huffed.

"I'll be fine," she replied somewhat insecurely. "Where's that shotgun?"

CHAPTER 23

Sage entered the bookstore on the first floor and approached the front door. Jackson paced before the door with his cellphone in his hand and looked almost like a caged panther. He turned toward the door when he saw her and stepped closer to it. Sage held the shotgun cradled in her arms. Jackson immediately noticed the shotgun and shook his head in disapproval.

"Come on, Sage," he announced through the glass. "Is that really necessary? I'm not a serial killer."

Sage approached the door and stared at him through the glass. Her look was hard and cold. "I know everything, Jackson," she informed him.

He gave her a puzzled look and cocked his head. "What do you mean?" Jackson stared into her eyes and appeared sympathetic. "Please, Sage. Open the door. Let's just talk about this."

"We can talk through the door."

Jackson appeared defeated. He placed his cellphone in his jacket pocket and moved closer to the glass. "That board doesn't mean anything," he insisted. "This is all a big misunderstanding. Don't make me beg. I will, if I have to, but it's not a good look on me."

"I know what you did."

He gave her a strange look and shook his head. "I don't know what you're talking about."

Sage drew a deep breath and leaned the shotgun against the doorframe. Jackson watched through the glass as Sage held up her left wrist, revealing the bracelet. "This," she announced firmly. "It was mine."

Jackson's expression suddenly dropped to something resembling horror, although he was still attempting to put it together.

"Right before I wrecked the car, I had a flashback," she informed him. "I saw you with a .357 Magnum aimed at my face, and you pulled the trigger."

He suddenly turned pale and seemed unable to look away. "No," he announced and shook his head. "That's not possible."

"I saw it," she snarled. "It was you. We were in a field in the middle of a thunderstorm. I was bleeding from my shoulder. You were there. You shot me."

Jackson continued to shake his head, the horror clearly in his eyes. "That wasn't you," he insisted. "That was twenty years ago."

"I know what happened," she insisted in anger. "I was there."

Jackson remained stranded in his own thoughts as if desperately attempting to piece it together. He lifted his eyes and met her gaze.

"Please, Sage," he announced. "Let me in. I don't know what's happening, but we need to talk about this."

"If I let you in, it'll be to shoot you," she informed him. "I'm calling the state police. It's over."

Sage snatched the shotgun and walked away from the door. She hurried into the stairway and headed to the apartment above the shop. Sage entered the apartment and locked the door behind her. Toby briefly glanced at Sage, then looked back at her laptop.

"This is some weird shit," Toby informed her.

"Did you find something?" she asked and hurried to her niece.

There was a crude drawing of the pendant on the computer screen. "According to this, it's a spell symbol," Toby informed her. "Witchcraft."

"I'm not a witch," Sage informed her.

"I'm not suggesting that you are," Toby replied. "That would be ridiculous, but the pendant itself may have been enough. In those last moments before Jackson shot you, your adrenaline was probably skyrocketing. You feared dying and projected yourself out of the situation. Sort of like when you have a bad dream and magically transport yourself somewhere else."

"This isn't a dream."

"I know," Toby replied, "but it works on the same principle. There's a time travel spell. Best I can come up with, something you thought at that moment somehow triggered it, and it shot you twenty years into the future."

"If it shot me into the future, wouldn't that mean it could also take me back?"

"Yes, hypothetically," Toby replied, then eyed her. "But back to what? The moment Jackson pulls the trigger? There's nothing to go back to."

"There's you," Sage insisted with hope in her eyes. "I could go back for you."

"Why risk it?" Toby asked. "I'm right here. You're here. We're both alive and safe. There's no reason for you to go back."

There was a long moment of silence.

Sage suddenly felt her heart race. "What if I could go back before Jackson killed our family?" she asked and lunged into the chair facing Toby. "What if I could prevent them from being killed?"

Toby stared at Sage and appeared unable to speak. "My mother would be alive," she whispered.

"We'd have our family back."

Toby returned to reality. "The only way we'd be able to do that is if there's a way to choose the time and date," she informed her.

"It's worth looking into," Sage replied. "I can make this right. If I could come to 'here and now', there's no reason to think I couldn't go back to 'then and there'."

§

Later that evening, Sage slept peacefully on the sofa while Toby continued to work on her laptop. Toby gently nudged Sage awake. She looked at Toby with some disorientation.

"What? What is it?"

Toby grinned. "I found it."

It was already dark outside when Sage and Toby ventured downstairs into the bookstore. There was no sign of Jackson outside beyond the glass door or windows. Perhaps he gave up and went back home. Maybe he feared her calling the state police. Sage cradled the shotgun and looked around.

"I don't understand why we couldn't do this upstairs," Sage remarked.

"Twenty years ago, someone else lived in that upstairs apartment," Toby informed her. "You're going to show up where you left. We can alter the day and time, but I couldn't find any way to alter the location."

Toby handed Sage a piece of paper.

Sage studied the phrase. "I don't understand how I did this in the first place," she remarked. "I don't even know what language this is."

"Stop worrying about how you got here," Toby insisted. "Concentrate on going back. You don't even have to say the words aloud. You just need to say them in your head and concentrate on the date and time. The time I provided will be right after the shop opens on Thursday morning. The murders happen late Tuesday night almost a week later." Toby hesitated and looked around. "Hopefully, there won't be anyone in the shop to see you when you appear."

Sage tensed and took several deep breaths.

"You have your cellphone?" Toby asked.

Sage nodded and patted her jacket pocket. "And a pocket full of cash dated twenty years ago." She then cocked her head in question. "You are aware that I won't have cellphone service on this particular phone twenty years in the past, right?"

Toby gave her a condescending look. "I realize that," she huffed. "You were never to our house in Great Bend, so I put the old house address in your phone as well as directions to get there."

Sage nodded, now understanding.

"It's a bit of a walk from here, but at least it'll be daylight," Toby said, then took the shotgun from Sage and took a step back. "It's all you, Sage. I know you can do it. Good luck."

Sage smiled at Toby, then eyed the paper. She shut her eyes and concentrated on the words and the date and time. There was a clunk within the shop. Sage opened her eyes and saw Jackson approaching.

"Sage," he announced.

Toby cried out in panic and raised the shotgun. Sage gasped at what she was witnessing, but no sound came out. Suddenly, there was a blinding light. When Sage opened her eyes, she was standing alone in the shop, now filled with sunlight. Toby and Jackson were gone! As she looked around, Sage realized she was in the middle of the old general store. She stood near the cashier's counter at the front of the empty store and again looked around. An older man entered from the back and paused when he saw her.

"Oh, I'm sorry," he announced pleasantly. "I didn't hear you come in."

Sage again looked around the general store, almost disbelieving what she was seeing. "Uh, do you have the morning paper?"

The man smiled and indicated the counter behind her. Sage turned, saw the stack of papers, and picked one up. She stared at the date on the paper. It was the Thursday before her mother and sister were killed twenty years ago! Sage breathed a sigh of relief and then smiled at the shop owner.

"I'll just take the paper," she announced and pulled some change from her pocket.

CHAPTER 24

S age walked along the back road from town and took it all in. Although she'd only been living in Great Bend for two months, she was familiar with many roads, but everything looked completely different in the past. There were fewer homes and more farmland. Walking, it took nearly an hour to reach Toby's house. As she passed the apple orchard, a chill ran down her spine. Sage stopped and stared at the orchard filled with well-groomed trees. She saw a brief flash from the stormy night, and she now remembered running through the apple orchard. The flash ended as quickly as it had started. She saw a police cruiser pull up alongside her as if perfectly timed. Sage eyed the police car somewhat suspiciously and immediately recognized the much younger sheriff. Now only in his mid-thirties, Sheriff Baxter looked almost exactly the same except a little less round. The sheriff leaned across the center console and offered a mildly creepy smile that sent a chill down Sage's spine.

"Morning, sweetheart," Sheriff Baxter announced a little too pleasantly. "Are you lost?"

"No," Sage replied while attempting a false cheerfulness. "Just taking a walk."

"Can I give you a ride somewhere?" he pressed.

Sage maintained her smile, although she was immediately suspicious of the lazy sheriff's much younger alter ego. "No, thank you," she again replied. "Just getting some fresh air."

"You aren't from around here," Baxter remarked and now seemed somewhat stern.

"No, I'm visiting my sister," she informed him.

"Who's your sister?" he pressed.

Now, the man was starting to make her uncomfortable. "Toby Remington," she reluctantly responded, then pointed to the apple orchard. "She's probably wondering where I am so long. I need to get back."

"I can take you there," Sheriff Baxter again insisted as his creepy smile returned.

"Thanks, but I prefer to walk," Sage informed him and continued walking.

The sheriff's police cruiser backed up until it was once again alongside her. "You're not being very polite," he announced somewhat curtly. "Maybe you should show me some ID."

"I don't have it on me," she informed him, although that was a lie. Unfortunately, her ID had an expiration date of twenty-some years in the future.

"I think you should come with me," Sheriff Baxter announced commandingly. "Take you to the office and get this straightened out."

"There's nothing to straighten out," Sage informed him, now becoming flustered. She removed her cell phone and pushed a button, even though her current cell phone didn't have service in this time period, and pretended to wait for an answer. "I'll just call Jackson Morgan and ask him to come out here and confirm my identity."

Although Jackson didn't even know who she was, and he and his brothers didn't have the clout that they'd have in the future, it would carry more weight than threatening to have her sister come out.

"I'll let you off with a warning this time," Sheriff Baxter announced, appearing displeased, then drove away, burning out on the road.

Sage lowered the phone and shook her head. Let her off with a warning? For what? Taking a walk? She hadn't been expecting that. Older Sheriff Baxter was too lazy to cruise the back roads for damsels in distress. She didn't realize that younger Sheriff Baxter was some sort of roaming pervert. Sage picked up the pace in case he thought about returning. By the time she reached her sister's house, she had finally relaxed after her odd run-in with the sheriff. The two-story house was on the other side of the orchard and not far from a new development. The house was only a few years old with plenty of landscaping and flowers. Sage walked up to the house, drew a deep breath, and knocked on the door. Only a moment passed when the door opened, revealing a six-year-old girl. Little Tobias Remington had long medium brown hair with plenty of waves, and her emerald green eyes sparkled like large jewels. Memories of this little girl suddenly came flooding back, and Sage couldn't help but stare at her niece.

Little Tobias's expression turned to glee. "Aunt Sage!"

Tobias practically jumped into her arms. Sage held the little girl and just about broke down into tears. There was no mistaking that this was the same girl she'd been living with for the last two months thinking she was her sister. As soon as Sage released the little girl, Tobias ran into the house.

"Mommy, Mommy, it's Aunt Sage!"

"Aunt Sage?" a familiar female voice was heard from within the house.

Sage's sister, Toby, approached the door and stared at Sage with surprise. Sage immediately recognized the woman in a flood of memories. Her twenty-six-year-old sister, Toby Remington, was a beautiful young woman with dark eyes and dark shoulder-length hair. She stood about five-foot-six with enough generous curves to gain plenty of attention. All of Sage's earlier memories had been with her adult niece's face, possibly some sort of mind hocus-pocus to keep alive the lie she had to tell herself. Now, all her memories were returning with her actual sister's face. Sage couldn't believe she'd forgotten her own sister like that. It didn't seem possible. Toby cried out excitedly, overjoyed to see her sister, and hugged Sage while laughing.

"You should have told me you were coming," Toby announced happily. "I would have done some baking."

Sage smiled and was almost down to tears seeing her actual sister. "I wanted to surprise you."

"You know Mom's coming on Tuesday, right?" Toby remarked, now curious. "You could have driven together from Colfax."

"I know," Sage replied as she smiled brightly while secretly wiping her tears of joy, "but I wanted to spend some alone time with my sister."

Toby eyed Sage somewhat suspiciously but maintained her smile. "Paul will be home a little later, so we have the entire afternoon to ourselves before he gets here," Toby happily informed her.

Paul? Some memories of him also returned. Paul was her sister's boyfriend. Toby had been dating him for a couple of years, but he wasn't Tobias's father. Sage had met him a couple of times when Toby came to Colfax to visit.

"Did you want some tea?" Toby asked cheerfully, knowing her younger sister all too well.

"Absolutely."

§

Sage and Toby sat in the living room with their tea while young Tobias was upstairs playing in her room. The house had a living room and dining room combination, which was small and cozy. Unlike Tobias's apartment above the bookshop in the future, Toby's home had contemporary furniture, which included a sofa, loveseat, and several overstuffed chairs. A large bay window allowed plenty of sunlight to enter and brighten the room. Toby kept her house just about spotless, which was another thing her daughter didn't inherit from her. Once Sage was sure her six-year-old niece was out of earshot, she unloaded on her sister. Toby sat in complete silence, listening to every crazy thing that Sage had to say, from the future murders to her time travel and memory loss. Once she had finished telling her sister every frightening and unimaginable detail, Toby sat in silence, staring at her as if she were crazy. Sage tensed while waiting for her older sister to offer some comment or even call her crazy.

"Well," Toby announced and leaned back on the sofa, "that's a fascinating story you've told."

Sage frowned while groaning. "I knew you wouldn't believe me," she muttered with a defeated groan as she propped her cheek on her fist.

"Of course, I believe you," Toby replied with little hesitation and even managed a tiny laugh while shaking her head. "If anyone could pull off a stunt like time displacement, it would be you." She then grinned. "I can't wait to see Mom's face when we tell her."

Sage stared at her sister with some surprise. "Wait, what?" she practically gasped.

"You must have received one hell of a bump to your head," Toby announced, then leaned forward and gently touched the cut on her temple.

Sage realized she retained the injury she sustained twenty years in the future. It must have been the same type of situation when she was injured and traveled to the future for the first time. That's how she ended up in the hospital's intensive care unit with her shoulder injury.

"You were always better at spell casting than I was," Toby informed her sister. "I think Tobias is going to be gifted like you. Only six years old, and she sketches these amazing life-like pictures. It's incredible."

"So you're saying I'm actually a witch?"

"We all are," Toby replied, then shook her head with a strange look on her face. "I'm not sure how that got erased from your memory, but you have been through a lot."

"I can't believe this," Sage remarked and shook her head. "I've been so lost these last two months living twenty years in the future."

"You actually lived with Tobias in the future?" Toby asked, still astonished by it.

"Yeah, she let me think she was you," Sage replied, then managed a tiny, humorous laugh. "She's an amazing woman. Well, she will be."

"Well, the goal is for the rest of us to live long enough to find out," Toby remarked while sinking into thought. "By the time Mom arrives on Tuesday, we'll have this all figured out."

"I don't think Mom should come," Sage insisted, feeling her anxiety spiking. "In fact, I think you and Tobias need to take a long vacation."

"Oh, no," Toby announced in a stern tone. "We're going to tackle this thing head-on. Now that we know the score, we can prevent it. You said you know who the killer is, right?"

"Jackson Morgan," Sage informed her.

"Jackson Morgan?" Toby just about gasped. "The reclusive cattle rancher? Are you sure?"

"Oh, I'm sure," Sage replied and shuttered. She couldn't bring herself to tell Toby about her relationship with the man prior to her findings. "I have large chunks of my memory still missing, but I saw him shoot me." She then removed her cellphone from her pocket. Despite that she didn't have any cellular service, she was still able to pull up her photos file and showed her sister the pictures she'd taken. "I found this in his basement. It's a tracking board of murders committed over the course of decades."

"And you definitely saw him shoot you?"

"Oh, it was definitely him," Sage insisted as her eyes widened. "That image is burned into my mind. He also had my pendant bracelet." Sage then sifted through the pictures and found the one of the journal. "He kept a journal. In it, I found a photo he'd taken of me shortly after I showed up in town. He denied having met me before, yet he had a picture of me in his journal. He also had this board with ghost hauntings. It must have freaked him out when he saw me twenty years later, alive and looking the same as the day he shot me."

Toby stared at the photo a moment, and her expression suddenly dropped. "Is that Tobias?" she practically gasped.

Sage smiled warmly and nodded. "Yeah, that's your daughter in twenty years."

Toby placed her hand to her mouth and held back her tears. "She's so beautiful." She immediately composed herself while returning the cellphone to Sage and attempted to push her emotions aside. "Well, Jackson doesn't launch his murder spree for another few days, so that gives us time to check him out. I want to be one hundred percent certain it's him before we take action."

"I can't believe I let him manipulate me like that," Sage muttered and shook her head. "I can't believe I fell for his charm."

Toby gave her sister a strange look. "Now you're really making no sense," she remarked and cocked her head. "Jackson Morgan? Charming?"

"Trust me; he's charming when he needs to be," Sage insisted.

"I think we should call your two college friends, Lindsey and Courtney, in on this," Toby informed her. "They're outsiders to Great Bend, so your Morgan boys won't suspect them of anything. The three of you can hang out at the tavern and keep an eye on them."

Sage tensed and frowned while looking at her sister. "I'm in no particular hurry to face Jackson Morgan again," she remarked.

"You don't have to worry," Toby informed her. "He has no idea what happens twenty years from now. He has no memory of you, and he doesn't try to kill you for another few days."

"Okay, I'll call Lindsey and Courtney," Sage reluctantly replied.

Toby's look then turned stern and commanding. "Just in case your memory is a little fuzzy," she announced. "Paul doesn't know anything about our family secrets."

Sage snorted a laugh. "Well, that makes two of us then," she replied.

"I'm serious," Toby scoffed. "I haven't told him, so you can't mention anything about all this. He's a great guy, and I don't want to scare him away."

"You two don't live together, do you?" Sage asked, somehow not remembering that detail.

"No, not exactly," Toby replied. "He splits his time between here and his apartment in Colfax, but he can work remotely, if he gets that promotion. If that happens, we've discussed him moving in with us permanently."

"Is that why he wasn't here?" Sage asked, then hesitated and reconsidered her question. "Is that why he isn't here during the attack?"

"Actually, he's going away on a business trip in a couple of days," Toby informed her. "When I told him Mom was coming for a visit, he asked if he should try and get out of it, but I told him no." She suddenly stared at Sage with horror in her eyes. "He can't be here. He can't know anything about what you've seen."

"Relax," Sage announced with a groan. "I'm not going to say anything. Just let him continue on his original path. We don't need him here."

§

After putting in a call to her college friends, there was nothing left for Sage and Toby to do until they arrived tomorrow afternoon. Thankfully, her friends would stop off at her apartment and pack some things for her, including her driver's license, credit card, and working cellphone. Once little Tobias joined them, they played board games and pretended nothing bad ever happened. Toby started dinner shortly before Paul was supposed to come home. Although Sage didn't remember much about Paul, she instantly recognized him when she saw him. She had mixed feelings about her sister's boyfriend if she remembered correctly. Paul was an undeniably handsome and rather charming man. He stood a little over six-foot-tall with an athletic build and an ego to match. His light brown hair was kept short and neatly styled. While Sage and little Tobias set the dinner table, Paul opened a bottle of wine. He eyed Sage several times before finally commenting.

"What did you do to your head?" Paul asked and indicated the small contusion on her temple that was practically hidden by her hair hanging close to her brow.

Sage subconsciously touched her temple and grimaced slightly with pain. "Oh, that," she replied. "I hit a deer on my way here."

Tobias looked at her Aunt Sage and gasped in horror. "You didn't kill the deer, did you?"

Paul grimaced and looked away, not wanting to touch that one.

"Of course not," Sage replied, which wasn't a lie because there hadn't actually been a deer.

"Is that why you don't have your car?" Paul asked.

"Uh, yeah," Sage replied and doubled down on her lie. "I got a ride here with the tow truck guy."

"Well, if you're staying a while," Paul announced, "you can always drive back to Colfax with your mother. I'm actually surprised you didn't just come with her."

"Toby and I needed a little extra sister time," Sage informed him. "But I'll ride home with her."

Paul poured three glasses of wine and then poked inside the dinner pots while Toby cooked. She swatted his hand.

"Too many cooks in the kitchen," Toby announced. "Tobias will help me. You two enjoy your wine in the living room."

Paul handed Sage her glass of wine and grinned. "We have some catching up to do," he announced cheerfully. "You can tell me all about the city and all the men beating down your door."

Sage groaned. Somehow, she felt as if she'd had this conversation with Paul before. Sage sat on the sofa while Paul took the plush chair not far from her.

"Well, the city is crowded and dirty," she informed him while sipping her wine. "And the man I'm seeing is probably a psychopath."

Paul casually nodded and leaned back in the chair. "Sounds like you're living the dream," he replied with a chuckle before manspreading in the chair.

Sage took one look at Paul, where he sat spread out, and shut her eyes. She sank into the sofa and muttered, "Like mother like daughter."

CHAPTER 25

Lindsey and Courtney, Sage's two college friends, arrived in town just before dinner the following evening. Lindsey was an attractive twenty-two-year-old woman with long, straight dark hair and dark eyes. She was a petite girl not much taller than five-foot-four, and she looked much younger than her age suggested. Courtney was a beautiful young woman with a tall, slender body. She stood almost five-foot-seven with long sandy blonde hair and hazel eyes. She came across as flirty and bubbly, but she was more intelligent than most people gave her credit. Sage and Toby got the two women up to speed without mentioning time surfing and witchcraft. The adventurous young women enjoyed flirting with danger and were up to the challenge. Both were eager to get to work, so they opted to have dinner with Sage at the tavern that evening. Since it was Friday night, going to the tavern early was a good idea.

Before they left for the tavern, Sage took a moment to transfer her photo file from her future cellphone to her present-day cellphone. She needed a working cellphone, but she didn't want to sacrifice her photo files from the future. Call her sentimental. Despite that Sage borrowed her sister's car, Courtney also wanted to drive her car. Courtney almost always drove her own car in case she found an after-party, but Sage knew her friend would have difficulty finding any local place open after the tavern closed. When they arrived at the tavern, Sage thought it looked pretty much the same as it had but twenty years newer and with a fresh coat of paint. The three women found a table not far from the Morgan boys' usual table, which would give them a better view. Time wasn't on their side, with the murderous attack on Sage's family happening in about four days. Naturally, Sage didn't mention her knowledge of future events with her friends either. While waiting for the Morgan boys to show that evening, Sage remained rigid in her seat. Even though Jackson wouldn't have any memory of her from the future, Sage couldn't deny that she was anxious about seeing him again.

As Sage looked around the tavern, she thought it was strange how different some things were but not others. She recognized Dusty, the bartender and owner, who was almost unrecognizable twenty years younger. He looked so young in his thirties with a moderately trim build and seemed physically fit. The bigger surprise was a much younger Kennedy waiting tables. She appeared genuinely happy and full of life. Kennedy may have been a vision of beauty at forty-five, but twenty-five-year-old Kennedy was a bombshell. Her straight, dirty blonde hair was longer, hanging partway down her back, and she looked so young and full of hope. When Kennedy approached their table to take their order, Sage couldn't stop staring at the young woman.

"Good evening," Kennedy announced cheerfully. "What can I get for you, fine ladies?"

Sage couldn't get over how different the waitress looked and acted. Twenty years later, she seemed so broken and defeated. What changed? Sage then saw Kennedy's brand new diamond engagement ring with a brilliant sparkle. That's when it dawned on her. Kennedy went through that messy divorce, and it must have broken her spirit.

"I'll have an iced tea," Sage replied.

Courtney and Lindsey looked at Sage with the same dumbfounded look.

"Iced tea?" Courtney gasped with surprise. "We're in a bar, Sage. It's Friday night."

"I think it's best if I stay clear-headed," Sage insisted.

Both her friends groaned and ordered mixed drinks. Within the next hour, they had dinner that was quite possibly prepared by the same line cook as in the future. Sage couldn't get over how the food tasted exactly the same. When she looked at the Morgan boys' table, another group of men and women was sitting there. Sage guessed some things were bound to be different twenty years earlier, but it seemed almost foreign to her. When the clock struck eight, and there was still no sign of the four brothers, Sage was starting to think they weren't going to show. They usually showed up for dinner, but not this particular Friday. Maybe they had a different routine twenty years in the past.

"I think your Morgan boys are a no-show," Lindsey remarked and seemed almost disappointed.

"Want to play a little pool?" Courtney suggested and indicated the empty back room. "Both tables are open."

Sage felt some pressure now. If the boys didn't show up at the tavern, it would make poking around that much harder, and she only had a short time to get ahead of the upcoming attack. Sage reluctantly joined her two friends in the pool parlor. She wasn't used to the back room being empty this time of night, especially on a Friday. Twenty years in the future, Dean, Lance, and Creed dominated the back room. It was practically their domain. Now, even though they would be much younger, they weren't even at the tavern. It seemed strange. Sage and Courtney had just about finished their first game when Creed, Dean, and Lance appeared in the back room without their usual rowdy reign of terror and claimed the second pool table.

Sage just about did a double-take when she saw the three brothers. She had almost forgotten they would be in their twenties. Baby brother Lance, being only twenty-three, looked nearly the same but so much younger. His clean-shaven baby face now made him look almost like a teenager. Dean was only twenty-five, and he was even more handsome than his older counterpart. He was borderline muscular with a devilish smile that could quite possibly charm any woman. Although still serious, Creed, being only twenty-seven, looked so much younger. Even in his youth, he remained clean-shaven with neatly trimmed hair. Sage found herself staring at the three younger Morgan boys in stunned disbelief. Courtney and Lindsey sent silent messages to Sage indicating the three men. Sage nodded.

"Oh, my God," Courtney gasped softly to Sage, barely able to control her grin. "They are so hot!"

"Focus," Sage quietly threatened.

Although the three men enjoyed their game and joked around, they weren't nearly as rowdy as they would be twenty years in the future. Sage couldn't stop staring at the three men and how different they looked and how they acted. It didn't seem possible. Sage sat out the next game to keep an eye on the three men. Lindsey and Courtney just started their second game when Dean moved in a little closer to observe their play. He smiled almost charmingly at both women.

"Haven't seen you ladies around," Dean announced cheerfully.

"We're visiting with some friends," Courtney informed him while returning the smile. "I'm Courtney, that's Lindsey, and that's Sage."

"It's a pleasure to meet you ladies," Dean announced, sounding almost respectful. "I'm Dean, and these are my brothers, Creed and Lance."

All six exchanged pleasantries. Sage was blown away by their politeness. It seemed almost impossible that they would transform into the brothers she'd come to know.

"Would it be okay if we bought the next round of drinks?" Dean then asked.

"We'd like that," Courtney replied while maintaining her grin.

Sage felt panic sweep through her. While Lindsey was making her next shot, Sage pulled Courtney aside to speak privately to her.

"What are you doing?" Sage asked with some concern. "We're supposed to be observing."

"We are," Courtney insisted and patted her shoulder. "The best way to observe the enemy is to get close to them."

"I'm uncomfortable with this, Courtney," Sage remarked and fidgeted. "I told you they can't be trusted. That's why we're keeping an eye on them."

"Sage," Courtney announced firmly while staring into her eyes. "They're young, horny men. We have the greatest weapon against them God ever created."

"What weapon?"

"Lust," Courtney remarked while grinning. "You wanted to spy on them and see what they're up to? Getting close to them is the easiest way to do it."

"Easiest way to get us all killed," Sage informed her. "This is a bad idea."

Courtney frowned and shook her head. "I know this is outside your comfort zone on many levels, Sage," she announced, "but this is the best way. Do you want to know what they're up to or not?"

Sage could feel her tension rising. Forcing her sister's family out of town seemed to be the path of least resistance now. This was just playing with fire. What if Jackson's brothers were all in on it together? Now she involved her friends, who were regarding life-and-death as a game. Unfortunately, she couldn't be completely honest with them either.

"Fine," Sage groaned while shifting uncomfortably, "but no one is going home with any of them tonight. Those are my terms."

"Sage, you know us better than that," Courtney insisted and added a flirty smile. "I know what I'm doing, okay? Just play along." She cast a sly look at the three men at the next pool table over. "We'll even let you have first pick which one you want if it makes you feel better."

"I don't want any of them," Sage snapped.

"You know what I mean," Courtney announced, then groaned. "Just some light flirting. You can do it; I know you can. Which one do you want?"

Sage felt the entire situation already spiraling out of control. She tensed and glanced at the three men at the next pool table. They seemed to be having their own quiet meeting, possibly having the same discussion but without all the cloak-and-dagger.

"The older, serious one," Sage informed her friend, indicating Creed.

"Really?" Courtney asked with some surprise. "I thought for sure you'd go for the gorgeous one."

"Trust me," Sage informed her friend. "Creed isn't nearly as gullible as his two younger brothers. He's not going to fall for that sort of flirting."

"I thought you'd never met these guys before," Courtney remarked.

"I haven't," Sage easily lied, although it was actually true. They hadn't met yet in this particular timeline, but that didn't alter the fact that she knew the Morgan boys from her visit to the future. "My sister fed me enough information on them that I have a pretty good idea of what to expect."

"It'll be fine," Courtney insisted.

A gorgeous woman in her mid-twenties entered the pool parlor and cozied up to Dean, commanding his attention. All three women immediately noticed the sexy, slender woman with a more than generous bosom casting her sights and hands onto Dean. Courtney silently seethed at the prospect of this woman stealing her would-be date. The woman Sage had never met or seen before had straight, jet-black shoulder-length hair and amazing ice blue eyes that commanded attention.

"Hey, Dean," the temptress cooed through ruby red lips while placing her hand on Dean's shoulder.

Dean glared at the woman and took a step away from her. "Hey, Leigh," he replied, showing a complete lack of interest in her.

Leigh seductively leaned against the pool table while giving him what was clearly a come-hither look. "Mind if I hang out with you for a while?"

Dean casually moved Leigh away from the table so he could make his shot. "Whatever you're peddling, Leigh, I'm not buying," he scoffed without even looking at her while he lined up his next shot. "Go sell it to someone else."

Leigh sneered at Dean and immediately turned defensive. "One day, you're going to come crawling back to me," she huffed.

"Doubtful," Dean muttered in a cold tone. "I'm not into psycho chicks."

Leigh gave him the middle finger and then left the pool parlor. Lance and Creed groaned and shook their heads.

"Certainly one of your less classy ex-girlfriends," Creed remarked while Dean made his shot.

Dean sank the corner ball and straightened. "At least I have ex-girlfriends," he announced to his brother. "The woman you're looking for doesn't exist."

"I'm selective," Creed informed him.

"Hey, I'm selective," Dean remarked defensively. "I'll never date a woman taller than me, and I've held fast to that rule."

"You're six feet tall," Creed scoffed while glaring at his brother. "This is Great Bend, not Beverly Hills. There are no women taller than you around here."

Dean offered a playful smile at his brother. "See," he announced. "Selective."

CHAPTER 26

As the evening progressed, Lindsey and Courtney inserted themselves into pool games with the Morgan boys, now switching things up. Unlike in the future, there were no wagers on games. The three seemed almost too gentlemanly. It actually made Sage uncomfortable. While Courtney played pool with Dean, Lindsey played a game with Lance, leaving Sage and Creed to play the winners. Sage's friend and the younger Morgan boys seemed to be hitting it off. Sage had a tougher time connecting with Creed, but it was possible she wasn't trying nearly as hard as her friends were trying with the younger boys. Despite that he was twenty years younger, Creed seemed almost as serious as she had remembered from the future. He was rigid around Sage, possibly even disinterested or distracted, at the very least.

Sage attempted to hold up her end of the deal with Courtney and Lindsey and made an effort to entertain Creed. Both leaned against the back wall and watched the others play pool.

"Something tells me this isn't how you wanted to spend your evening," Sage remarked to Creed, attempting to get past the awkwardness.

Creed glanced at her and tensed slightly. "My brothers are easily distracted by attractive women," he replied with little interest. "Just another typical Friday night."

"I get it," Sage remarked while nodding. "After a long week, you just want to blow off some steam and have a little fun with the boys, right?"

"Something like that," Creed replied with little emotion. "I'm sorry you were dragged into this. Me? I'm used to it. I'm often the third wheel." He then glanced at her. "I guess your friends do this to you a lot too, huh?"

"Well, like you, I'm used to it," Sage teased while turning. She leaned her shoulder against the wall and faced Creed. "So, what do you and your brothers do for a living?"

"We work the family cattle ranch," Creed replied, then shrugged. "I guess you could say we're professional cowboys." A tiny, humorous smile crossed his face. "It's not exactly an attractive lifestyle to many women. Dean and Lance are young enough to make the best of it, but it's tough for either of them to hold onto a girlfriend for very long. You probably saw his ex-girlfriend, Leigh, in here earlier." He drew a deep breath. "Unfortunately, that's pretty typical."

"I guess it's hard work--being a professional cowboy," Sage remarked.

"Well, kind of. Our older brother is a bit of a slave driver," Creed informed her.

Sage's heart skipped a beat at the thought of Jackson. She silently cursed herself. She knew what the man was, and she couldn't let her feelings for him cloud her judgment and her mission. Saving her mother and sister was all that really mattered to her.

"He did practically raise us, so I suppose I can't really complain," Creed remarked.

"So you work for your brother?"

"No, not really," he replied. "The ranch belongs to the four of us, but Jackson has, well, always been in charge ever since our father died."

Creed's eyes strayed beyond the pool area to the barroom. Sage followed his gaze to Kennedy waiting tables. Sage looked back at Creed and wondered if he had actually been watching the attractive waitress. He frowned and now avoided staring at the woman. Sage was momentarily stunned at the new revelation. Creed liked Kennedy!

"She's very pretty," Sage remarked.

Creed fidgeted and ran his fingers through his hair. "She and her boyfriend just got engaged. They're getting married next spring."

"You like her," Sage remarked.

Creed tensed and avoided looking at Sage. "Well, like I said, she's engaged."

"Everyone knows that marriage isn't going to work," Sage announced, practically waving him off. "I wouldn't doubt she even knows it."

"I thought you weren't from around here," Creed remarked while eyeing her somewhat suspiciously.

"My sister hears a lot of gossip," Sage informed him, then flashed a smile. "She likes repeating a lot of gossip too."

Creed didn't question her source further. "It doesn't matter," he replied while frowning. "Even if she decided not to marry the guy, I'm not her type. Kennedy is looking for the successful businessman type, not a cattle wrangler with twenty-five percent interest in the family ranch."

"Do you think she's that shallow?" Sage suddenly asked with surprise.

Creed looked at her and appeared almost offended. "Of course not," he protested, then resumed his usual demeanor. "It's just, well, she can do better."

Sage again watched Creed's gaze stray to the waitress. He had it bad for the young woman. It seemed odd that, even after Kennedy's divorce in the future, Creed never made a play for her. Or had he, and she shot him down? Sage was starting to think she needed to mind her own business. For all she knew, Creed could be a psychopath like Jackson. If all four were in on the killings together, she certainly didn't need to be playing matchmaker. It would possibly get the poor woman killed. Sage focused her attention on her college friends, who were actively flirting with Dean and Lance. Lance was rather shy with Lindsey, but Dean was taking Courtney's flirting in stride. It seemed almost strange seeing both men filled with hope and lust in their youth. What changed?

Sage smiled at Creed and played the role she had been assigned. "So what's this other brother of yours like?" she finally asked.

It was a fair question. Toby didn't really seem to know much about the Morgan boys. Their infamous rise to power didn't happen until many years later. Most in town didn't really seem to think about the brothers one way or another right now. Twenty years later, they were practically running the town.

"He's my brother, and I love him," Creed informed her, then drew a deep breath, "but he pretty much has a stick up his ass. When he turned into our mother after she died, he wasn't so bad, but when he turned into our father--" Creed shook his head. "I'd love to say his bark is worse than his bite, but they're both pretty severe."

Sage couldn't believe what she was hearing. In the future, Creed seemed to idolize Jackson.

"He sounds like fun," Sage retorted while grinning. She tensed before putting on a false smile. "Is he here?"

"No, Jackson doesn't come to the tavern with us very often," Creed replied, then rolled his eyes. "He doesn't drink much, and he's not exactly a people person."

Jackson didn't drink much? Sage found that quite surprising.

§

Later that evening, Sage was starting to worry about her friends. Perhaps they were just really good actresses, but they seemed to be having a little too much fun with Dean and Lance and ramped up their flirting. They were both hanging on the guys, and there was a lot of unnecessary touching. The younger Morgan boys were definitely enjoying the attention. The behavior of all four made both Creed and Sage a little uncomfortable, although Creed was possibly used to it with his brothers. Creed checked his watch, then cast a look at his two brothers, indicating the time. Neither man was happy with what Creed was signaling.

"Your brothers don't look too happy," Sage remarked, wondering what was happening.

Creed shrugged and finished his beer. "It's ten o'clock," he informed her. "It's time to go home."

Sage raised a curious brow at the comment. "You have a ten o'clock curfew?"

"Jackson runs a tight ship," Creed reminded her. "It's a ranch. We have an early morning tomorrow, and we're short a few hands. We don't have a curfew on Saturday nights since we have off on Sundays."

"I see," Sage replied, then smiled warmly at the man. "I had a nice time, Creed."

"Yeah, me too," he replied and smiled a little more naturally. "It was a pleasure meeting you, Sage."

Dean approached Creed with his arm over Courtney's shoulder. They looked a little too chummy. Although Sage was sure Courtney wasn't drunk, she seemed unusually giddy.

"I'll ride home with Courtney," Dean informed his brother.

Creed didn't appear pleased. "You're not bringing her home, Dean," he announced in a stern tone. "You know how Jackson gets about unannounced overnight visitors on a work night. You'll have to go to her place."

"She's staying at Sage's sister's house," Dean protested to his brother. "She's sharing a room with Lindsey. We can't go back there."

"Dean--"

"You let me worry about Jackson," Dean insisted.

Sage watched the unfolding events in silent horror. Before they could leave the pool area together, Sage approached her friend.

"Courtney," Sage announced with a stern look. "Could I talk to you a minute?"

Courtney managed a tiny smile, released Dean, and joined Sage on the opposite end of the pool area where they could speak privately. Lindsey was too busy saying 'goodnight' to Lance, now making out in the back corner, and didn't seem to notice anything else. Sage spun to face her friend and gave her a disapproving glare.

"What the hell--?" Sage demanded. "What happened to sticking to the plan?"

"Change of plans," Courtney insisted, then smiled reassuringly. "Dean is an absolute stud." She placed her hand on Sage's shoulder. "Don't worry about me. I'll give him an amazing night, he'll pass out, and I can do a little snooping. I'll check out that room in the basement you mentioned while everyone is asleep and be back in bed before he wakes for round two. It's foolproof."

"I did mention one of them could be a serial killer, right?" Sage snapped. "It's bad enough you're putting yourself in that house, but going alone? Are you insane?"

"It'll be fine, Sage," Courtney reassured her. "You and Lindsey go back to your sister's place. I have my car. I'll call you in the morning."

Sage knew she wasn't going to win an argument with Courtney, and she was now wishing she hadn't included her college friends. She didn't remember them being quite so gullible back in college. Sage felt completely helpless as she watched Courtney leave with Dean.

CHAPTER 27

The following morning, Sage clutched her cellphone while pacing Toby's kitchen. Lindsey entered the kitchen looking weary but cheerful.

"Morning," Lindsey announced and headed for the filled coffeepot.

"Courtney didn't call," Sage informed her friend as her anxiety increased.

Lindsey poured a cup of coffee for herself and then eyed Sage. "It's kind of early, don't you think?" she remarked with little concern. "It's only eight in the morning. She's probably still asleep in her stud's arms."

"Her *stud* had an early morning," Sage reminded her.

"Maybe he invited her to stay for breakfast," Lindsey remarked.

"You're taking this too lightly."

"The guy may be a rancher, but he's still a guy," Lindsey reminded her. "You don't think he'd tell his brother to go fuck himself if it meant morning sex?"

"Maybe," Sage replied while frowning, "but I'm not counting on it."

"Relax, Sage," Lindsey insisted and seemed almost humored at her friend's concerns. "You're worrying over nothing. She'll be here before ten, I promise."

§

Wh
hen ten o'clock rolled around, Sage paced the living room while Lindsey pressed redial on her cellphone. She'd no sooner disconnect before pressing the button again. Toby sat on the arm of one of the chairs and nervously wrung her hands together.

"You should never have let her go home with him," Toby muttered to her sister under her breath.

"I was opposed to it," Sage snapped back.

"It keeps going straight to voicemail," Lindsey informed them, then nervously ran her fingers through her hair. "What are we going to do?"

"Drive out there," Sage announced and turned to Toby. "Can I use your car?"

"Maybe we should call the sheriff," Toby suggested.

"That creepy pervert? And tell him what?" Sage asked while raising a curious brow. "Our friend went home with a guy last night, and we haven't heard from her this morning? He's going to laugh in our faces and tell us we're overreacting. Besides, the Morgan boys have some clout in this town. The sheriff doesn't even know Courtney."

"Maybe you should wait for Paul," Toby announced. "Let him go out there with you."

"That won't be until dinnertime," Sage protested. "If something happened to Courtney, we need to go out there now."

"Then I'm going with you," Toby insisted.

"And take Tobias?" Sage remarked, then shook her head. "No, Lindsey and I will go out there. We'll see if her car is at the ranch and take it from there."

"I don't like this idea," Toby informed her.

"It's the best I've got," Sage assured her and held her hand out.

Toby reluctantly handed her the keys to her car. "One hour," she announced. "If you're not back in an hour, I'm calling the sheriff and telling him my car was stolen, and it was last seen driving down Morgan's driveway."

"I can agree to that," Sage replied, then nodded for Lindsey to join her.

Both women hurried from the house.

§

Sage and Lindsey stared out the windshield as they pulled up to the Morgans' plantation-style house. The property was in a lot better shape than it was twenty years in the future. Surprisingly, there was even some landscaping around the porch. Both women held their breath as they drove up to the house.

"I don't see her car," Lindsey just about gasped and quickly looked around. "If her car isn't here, why isn't she answering her phone?"

"Good question," Sage muttered and threw the vehicle into park. She turned off the car and faced Lindsey. "Wait in the car with the doors locked and your finger on 9-1-1."

"I don't think you should go in there alone," Lindsey protested.

"I'm not going in there alone," she insisted. "You're my backup. Anything happens, you call the sheriff."

Sage got out of the car, leaving the keys in the ignition, and locked the door before shutting it. She took a moment to look around for signs of life. Everything seemed quiet, although that wasn't surprising. She was sure the guys were out in the pastures tending to the herd. Sage cautiously headed to the porch and walked up the steps. Despite her little trip to the future, which technically hadn't happened, she could still remember every detail. When she thought about Jackson, her heart ached. She knew he was a monster, but she couldn't stop thinking about him and how he made her feel each time he'd made love to her. Sage paused before the door, drew a deep, nervous breath, and knocked, although she wasn't expecting anyone to answer. She waited a moment, then placed her hand on the doorknob and gently turned it.

It wasn't locked. She actually hadn't expected it to be. Sage quietly pushed open the door. The car horn tooted as if by accident, startling her. Sage spun around and came face-to-face with a much younger Jackson Morgan. Thirty-year-old Jackson appeared to have a bit more muscle mass to back him up, and he actually seemed a little taller. His shoulders definitely appeared broader. Despite not having any gray in his hair, he already had some gray starting in his beard. He was still incredibly handsome, but the look in his eyes was anything but friendly. Her relationship with his older alter ego aside, this younger version of Jackson was both frightening and intimidating. Sage jumped and stared at the stern look on his face.

"Can I help you?" Jackson just about snarled, possibly not appreciating that Sage had opened the door to his house uninvited.

Somehow his voice even sounded deeper and more intimidating than before. Jackson stood unusually close, towering over her, and had no problem crowding her near the house. Considering the early hour, he was unusually dirty with a strong odor of horse and sweat wafting from his stained clothes. Sage couldn't take her eyes off him, and she knew she must have looked like a deer in headlights with the way she stared. She couldn't help herself. Her heart was pounding with fear at the imposing man and the hardened look on his face. She'd seen the same face behind the gun aimed at her just before he pulled the trigger.

"I, uh," she stammered a moment, then quickly pulled herself together and straightened proudly. "I'm looking for my friend. She left the tavern last night with Dean Morgan. I'm told he lives here."

Jackson's look didn't soften. "Well, you missed her by about four hours," he announced with no compassion. "No sleepovers on a school night."

Sage didn't see any resemblance to the man in the future who had made passionate love to her so many times. When she saw what looked like bloodstains on his hands and shirt, Sage felt a cold shiver run down her spine. She needed to pull herself together for Courtney's sake.

"She didn't return home."

"Don't care," Jackson countered sharply.

Sage was slightly surprised by the hostility, especially when all she could think about was her sexual escapades with his older counterpart. Who the hell was this man? He was cold and cruel.

"Maybe Dean cares," she snapped back, refusing to be intimidated by him. "I'd like to speak to Dean."

"Dean's working," he countered, remaining curt and impatient.

Sage dug deep and refused to let Jackson intimidate her despite every fiber of her body screaming for her to run. She stared into his eyes and showed no emotion.

"Maybe you'd better start caring. My friend is missing, and your brother was the last person to see her," Sage scoffed as her eyes narrowed. "So you can either let me talk to Dean, or I'm coming back with the sheriff."

Jackson suddenly cocked his head and offered an unsettling smirk. "Are you threatening me on my own goddamned property?"

He was going to shoot her; she just knew it.

Sage buried her fears, folded her arms across her chest, and shook her head. "No," she casually replied. "If I intended to threaten you, I'd tell the sheriff I heard a woman's screams coming from your basement."

Although his expression didn't change any, Jackson maintained his stare and raised his brows. "I doubt you'd get that worthless excuse of a lawman off his fat ass, let alone get him to drive out here," he remarked while showing little emotion. "But, if you did somehow manage it, I suppose having to explain my pleasure room would be a bit of an inconvenience."

Sage felt her entire body stiffen at the sexual innuendo, particularly when he showed no emotion. She attempted to control her rising hostility since it wasn't doing her any good and get him off the defensive. Sage drew a deep breath, held it a moment, and tried to relax.

"I think we got off on the wrong foot, Mr. Morgan," she remarked less confrontationally. "Think we could try again?"

"I wasn't even in the mood to have this conversation the first time around," Jackson informed her, then seemed to dial his aggression down a notch as well, although his look didn't soften any. "Dean is riding fences in the north pasture. He turned his radio off so he wouldn't have to talk to me, which means it's highly unlikely he'll show his face before dinnertime tonight." Jackson cocked his head and raised his brows. "You want to know about your little friend? She rolled up to the ranch last night around quarter after ten with Dean riding shotgun. My half-lit and excessively horny brother politely told me what I could do with myself before scooting the young lady upstairs to his room, where they prayed loudly to God while presumably jumping up and down on the bed."

Sage internally squirmed and had to look anywhere but in Jackson's cold, emotionless eyes. It's possible he would have enjoyed it if she had. She finally felt compelled to look back at him and his mocking gaze.

"Forty minutes and two orgasms later, your friend fell asleep with my brother." He folded his arms across his chest while maintaining eye contact, enjoying making her squirm. "Fast-forward six and a half hours later, the two of them prayed for another thirty minutes at dawn. I'm guessing they were praying doggie style by the sound of the headboard being driven against the wall dividing our two rooms. No orgasm for the lady, but Dean had a big finish." Jackson's eyes pierced through hers as he cocked his head. "Back to my original, *shortened* version of the story. At six this morning, she walked down the stairs looking a little saddle sore but satisfied, got into her car, and drove away. She was heading north--down the driveway." Jackson's sly, devious grin once again returned. "Anything else you'd like to know, darling?"

Sage didn't take her eyes off him. "Just one," she remarked, revealing little emotion. "Are you always this big of a prick? Or am I just special?"

Jackson grinned and chuckled lowly. "You *definitely* don't want me answering that," he remarked. "I'm liable to say something crude and offensive."

"Well, too late for that," she scoffed while avoiding looking at him. She then shook her head as she walked past him. "I don't know what I ever saw in you."

Jackson turned and watched her head down the porch steps with a bewildered look on his face. "What did you say?" he demanded.

"Nothing," she muttered and headed for the car.

Jackson frowned, folded his arms across his chest, and leaned against the support beam while watching her. The passenger side door on the car opened, and an excitable Lindsey leaped out with her cellphone to her ear.

"Damn it, Courtney," Lindsey cried out. "Where the hell are you?"

Sage hurried for the car and stared at her friend on the cellphone.

Lindsey looked up and met Sage's gaze. "You're at Toby's house?" she suddenly gasped. "Why didn't you call?" There was a pause. Lindsey groaned and looked back at Sage while frowning. "Her cellphone battery died, and she didn't have a charger."

"Where was she for over four hours?" Sage demanded, then waved her off. "Never mind. I'll yell at her when we get there."

"I think you owe me an apology, darling," Jackson called after her while his grin mocked her.

Sage shot a hateful look at Jackson. She wanted to wipe that smug smile off his face. "Fuck you," she scoffed.

Jackson chuckled, humored by her lack of refinement. "Wrong brother, darling," he called back, then winked at her. "But you're welcome to try and change my mind."

Sage jumped into the car and slammed the door. "I'm going to kill Courtney."

CHAPTER 28

Sage paced the kitchen while Courtney sipped her coffee and showed no signs of remorse for what she'd put her friends through.

"Four hours," Sage huffed at her friend. "We thought you were dead!"

"It was six in the morning," Courtney announced in her defense, then casually shrugged. "I didn't see the point in waking the whole house."

"Where were you for four hours so early in the morning?" Lindsey then started in.

"I ran back to my apartment in Colfax," Courtney replied, taking the interrogation in stride. "I needed a few things. Since I assumed the rest of you were all sleeping, I thought it'd be a good time to run and get some things I'd forgotten." She eyed both her friends. "I'm fine. Nothing weird happened at the Morgan ranch. I spent the night with Dean, and when he got up, I left."

"Yeah, we heard all about your night with Dean in graphic detail," Sage scoffed. "Thanks to Jackson Morgan."

"Jackson," Courtney huffed while rolling her eyes. "Now there's a real prick."

"Why didn't you just hang around and snoop," Lindsey remarked, now feeling a little agitated by what they'd been put through as well. "That was the plan, right? All four of them would have been gone."

Courtney frowned and stared at her coffee mug. "Unfortunately, Dean suggested I leave early to avoid Jackson's wrath. There was no way that prick brother of his was going to leave me alone in the house while they were gone."

"Dean wasn't being melodramatic either," Sage reported while shifting uncomfortably. "Jackson's a miserable prick. He probably would have thrown you out."

"Well, the good news to come out of all of this," Courtney announced and turned almost cheerful. "Dean wants us to meet them at the tavern tonight. Sunday is their day off, so we'll be able to spend the night."

"What do you mean by 'we'?" Sage asked suspiciously.

"Just how it sounds," Courtney replied almost casually. "We spend the night and search that room while they're sleeping."

"Who is 'we'?" Sage just about demanded, not believing what she was hearing.

"You, me, and Lindsey."

Lindsey and Sage squirmed at the comment.

"That didn't exactly work out for you last night," Sage reminded her. "I don't know how you think involving me and Lindsey is going to change that any."

"I couldn't search the house last night because Dean was making up for lost time," Courtney informed her. "Considering what little sleep he got last night, he's going to crash tonight." She then eyed Sage and Lindsey. "You can't honestly say you want me to go back there alone again, can you?"

Sage knew she couldn't go through another morning like this morning, but there had to be another way.

"I want to have a look in Jackson's basement," Sage insisted and shook her head. "But I'm not willing to jump into bed with one of Jackson's brothers in order to do that."

Courtney groaned, then looked at Lindsey. "How about it, Linds? You got my back on this?"

Lindsey shifted uncomfortably. "I like Lance," she remarked, "but I don't know if I'm ready to jump into bed with him just to satisfy Sage's suspicions about this basement murder board."

"Bunch of prudes," Courtney muttered and groaned. "Fine. I'll do it myself." She eyed her friends. "But the two of you are going out tonight. Lance and Creed will be expecting you two."

"I'll agree to that," Lindsey replied.

Sage nodded. "We'll go out together tonight," she replied, then sighed. "Maybe I'll come up with some sort of plan. If they have Sunday off, maybe we can get them to invite us over for the afternoon."

§

Later that afternoon, Sage and Toby entered the general store and greeted the owner on their way through to the back of the shop. They entered the personal care aisle and explored feminine care products. Sage paused by the condoms, glanced at the assortment, and shook her head.

"I can't believe Courtney talked me into buying condoms for her," Sage muttered.

"Seems to me that her date should be purchasing them," Toby remarked while shaking her head. "Times certainly have changed, that's for sure." She then looked around the store and seemed lost in her thoughts. "Tobias actually buys this place when she's older?"

Sage looked around and couldn't help but smile. "It's a beautiful vintage bookstore," she replied and sighed. "I don't know if that'll happen once we prevent--" Sage hesitated and eyed her sister. "You know."

"You still have no memory of the attack?" Toby asked, sounding somewhat defeated.

Sage shook her head. "No, none," she replied, disgusted with herself. "And Tobias wasn't there that night, thank God, so she could only tell me what the newspaper reported about the incident."

Toby shivered, then focused on the items on the shelf before her. "I don't want to think about it," she remarked, then glanced at Sage, who plucked a box of condoms from the rack. "You're sure we can change those events by leaving town, though, right?"

"Of course," Sage replied and attempted to sound more optimistic. "By Monday, no matter what I discover or don't discover, you guys are on an extended vacation, Mom stays at home in Colfax, and we avoid the entire mess."

"What about you?" Toby asked.

"My friends and I are getting out of Dodge long before D-Day," Sage insisted.

Toby sank into thought, then eyed her sister. "If this truly is the work of a serial killer," she remarked. "Wouldn't he just find another target?"

Sage tensed and glanced at her sister. "That's why I'm trying to stop it," she insisted. "In saving ourselves, it's possible someone else will become the victim."

"I wish we could confide in the sheriff," Toby muttered.

"He'd never believe us," Sage remarked. "I wouldn't even believe us."

"The sheriff is lazy and incompetent," Toby scoffed and shook her head. "The deputies are completely clueless. I just wish there was some way we could put the town on alert. We know the 'who, when, and where'. You'd think we'd be able to stop it."

"Still working on it," Sage reported, then attempted to lighten the mood as she held up two boxes of condoms with a cheap grin on her face. "What do you think? Glow in the dark or ribbed for her pleasure?"

Toby laughed a moment, then suddenly tensed, fidgeted, and gently cleared her throat while looking away. Sage glanced behind her and saw Jackson towering over her while eyeing both boxes of condoms in her hands. He tapped the box of ribbed condoms and then continued past without a word. Toby sheepishly glanced at Sage, who was now three different shades of red.

"That was embarrassing," Toby muttered while looking away.

Sage shook her head in disgust. "I'm never speaking to Courtney again after this is over," she muttered.

As they headed up to the register, Sage was still suffering the effects of her earlier embarrassment. Her cheeks felt hot, and she was certain her face was still red. She placed the box of ribbed condoms on the counter along with a few other items. When the owner totaled the items, Sage handed him her credit card. She was lucky that her friends had stopped off at her apartment in Colfax and retrieved her personal items before driving out to meet her. The older man eyed the credit card and gave her a strange look.

"We can't take credit card," he informed her. "Machine's been broken for days."

Sage groaned and looked at Toby. As luck would have it, Jackson was now standing behind them at the counter and seemed to be in his usual foul mood. Toby searched her pocket and groaned.

"I left my wallet in the car," Toby announced. "I'll be right back."

Sage felt her heart sink as her sister hurried from the shop, leaving her alone and embarrassed alongside Jackson Morgan. Sage briefly met Jackson's somewhat mocking gaze. He then turned to the older shopkeeper.

"Put it on my account," Jackson informed the owner.

Sage was about to protest when the older man nodded and proceeded to put the order on Jackson's tab.

"That's not necessary," Sage insisted with a slight hiss in her tone, wanting to get as far away from Jackson as possible. "My sister is coming right back with the money."

"I'll get it from Creed," Jackson muttered with little concern. "He should be buying his own damned protection anyway." He frowned and shook his head with disappointment. "So much for him being the responsible one."

Sage suddenly felt horror sweep over her. He thought she was buying condoms for her date with Creed! She couldn't let him think that.

"They're for Courtney," Sage insisted, turning defensive. "Certainly not for me."

"Huh?" he casually remarked without looking at her. "Poor Creed."

"I wouldn't worry about poor Creed," Sage announced while avoiding looking at Jackson. Instead, she watched the shop owner place her items in a bag. "He and I are fifth wheels tonight, and we're both okay with that."

"Not into dumpster diving like your sorority sisters?" he teased, although his tone remained dry.

Sage shot a look at him and saw the smirk on his face. As she stared at Jackson, it pained her to think about what she once had with his older alter ego. She had difficulty seeing the man with whom she had shared so many intimate moments in their week-long affair. How was it possible he was that big of a prick in his younger years? Maybe older Jackson was just playing her for sexual gratification. Perhaps this side of him was his true personality. She was furious and hurt that he could be so cruel toward her and treat her this way. Sage needed to remind herself that this younger version of Jackson didn't even know her. Even so, wouldn't he feel some sort of attraction toward her? Unfortunately, even knowing what he was, she still missed older Jackson and desperately wished she could be back in his arms. Maybe it was a blessing that younger Jackson was swiftly erasing any feelings she'd once had for his older counterpart.

"I feel sorry for you," she announced, then snatched her bag and just about stormed from the store.

Sage practically collided with her sister, who had been on her way back into the store with her wallet. Sage took a moment to collect herself and wiped the stray tears from her eyes. Toby stared at Sage for a moment with surprise and concern.

"Are you okay?" Toby just about gasped. "What happened?" She immediately turned angry. "Did Jackson say something to upset you?"

When she heard the bell ding above the store door, Sage pulled it together and hurried to Toby's car while angrily wiping the tears from her cheek. She didn't want Jackson to see her crying.

"Just get me out of here," she scoffed.

CHAPTER 29

S age, Lindsey, and Courtney entered the tavern a little before six o'clock that night. They were supposed to meet Dean, Lance, and Creed for dinner and spend the evening together. The three women helped Kennedy push two tables together for their party, who hadn't yet arrived, then ordered drinks while they waited. Two men at the bar were checking them out. Sage recognized them as Jackson's poker-playing buddies in the future, Fat Matt and Slim. Of course, they were much younger now. Fat Matt wasn't as heavy in his twenties as he was in his forties, although his hair was still unkempt and his sideburns were still long. Surprisingly, Slim looked almost exactly the same in his twenties as he did in his forties. Sage wasn't sure if her friends noticed the two men, but she avoided looking at them and hoped they wouldn't find an excuse to come over.

Obviously, the three women were expecting friends with the larger table, but that didn't seem to matter to the two men, who now approached them. Being they were Jackson's poker-playing buddies in the future, it also meant they were in tight with the tavern owner, Dusty.

"Mind if we join you?" Fat Matt asked, then sat down without waiting for permission.

"We're expecting some friends," Lindsey politely informed him.

Fat Matt grinned and nodded while completely ignoring everything she said. "We'll just keep you company until they arrive," he announced, then focused his attention on Sage. "I'm Fat Matt. What's your name, little lady?"

"Sage," she replied but kept her tone with the man somewhat cool.

"How about we buy you ladies a drink?" his counterpart, Slim, suggested.

"We're waiting for friends," Sage again reminded him. "We already have drinks, and we already have company for the evening."

"Plans can change," Fat Matt replied while grinning slyly and reaching out to place his hand on Sage's leg.

Sage angrily swatted his hand. "Back off," she snarled.

"Oh, you're feisty," Fat Matt announced with a laugh. "I like them feisty." He then reached for her face.

Fat Matt's hand was caught and bent backward. He cried out in agony, then looked up. Jackson stood over him without releasing his hand. The look in his eyes was cold and emotionless.

"Touch her again, Matt, and you'll be picking up your teeth off the floor," Jackson snarled at him as he swiftly released his wrist.

Fat Matt stared at Jackson with some surprise. "Jackson," he announced, then managed a tiny, nervous grin. "Are these ladies with you?"

"Yeah, they're with me," Jackson scoffed, lacking emotion. "New rule. You don't touch *any* of the ladies in this bar unless they give you permission. Now get your ass out of my seat."

Fat Matt leaped from the chair, and both men scurried across the barroom. Jackson didn't bother looking at Sage or her friends; instead, he seemed to case the bar. As his three brothers approached, Jackson headed for the bar without a word and found a vacant seat. His three younger brothers had puzzled looks on their faces.

"What was that about?" Dean asked as he approached Courtney and affectionately placed his arm around her.

"Protective big brother?" Courtney questioned but seemed as perplexed as the others.

Sage's eyes strayed to Jackson at the bar as the three brothers joined them at the table. Creed sat beside Sage and gave her a strange look. She snapped out of her thoughts and looked at Creed.

"Jackson decided to tag along, huh?" Sage remarked, seeming a little more than curious.

"He's in one of his moods," Creed informed her.

"I'm sure I can guess why," Sage muttered as she shifted uncomfortably, recounting her run-in with Jackson at the ranch and again at the general store.

"One of his moods?" Dean suddenly laughed while taking his seat alongside Courtney. "That's a good one," he announced as he eyed his brother, then glanced at Sage and raised his brows. "Jackson's going to get plastered tonight and probably pick a fight. If we're lucky, it'll be with someone other than the three of us."

"He had a rough day," Creed reminded his brother, seeming almost sympathetic. "Cut the guy some slack." He eyed Sage. "And it didn't have anything to do with you stopping by the ranch this morning, I promise."

Dean rolled his eyes and snorted a laugh. "Cut him some slack?" he scoffed and became offended. "Maybe he should cut me some slack. He's the one busting my balls and insulting my lady friend."

"Something happen?" Sage asked Creed while ignoring Dean's rant.

"His favorite mare lost her foal this morning--again," Creed informed her. "I know it sounds trivial, but it's kind of a big deal to Jackson."

Sage's mind immediately reeled at the news. She remembered fifty-year-old Jackson telling her about that particular incident and how he wrecked his truck leaving the tavern that night. She now wondered if the horse losing her foal happened prior to her arrival at the ranch as well. It might explain why he was there at that time of the morning, the stains on his clothes, and why he seemed so angry with her.

"He invested too much money in that damned mare," Dean scoffed while frowning. "God only knows how much he paid for her. He should just breed his stud to one of the other mares and be done with it."

Creed managed a tiny smile at Sage while avoiding looking at Dean. "Big deal to Jackson," he remarked, then gave a nod to his younger brother. "Trivial to Dean. His current horse, Raven, is getting up in years. Jackson keeps breeding him to his prized mare, and she keeps losing the foal."

"Maybe we should ask him to join us for dinner," Sage suggested and was met with a round of groans.

"He's already in a foul mood," Dean informed her. "Once you add alcohol, he's going to be twice as bad."

"I have to agree with Dean," Creed remarked with a defeated sigh. "It's best just to leave Jackson alone."

Sage sank into thought while staring at Jackson sitting at the bar, downing a glass of whiskey. He was going to drink himself into a stupor. Was his rage and hostility all because of the mare losing her foal? Or was he just angry at the world? The difference between his younger self and his older self was staggering. What was she missing?

CHAPTER 30

Shortly after they finished dinner, Sage noticed Creed secretly watching Kennedy while she waited tables. Her boyfriend seemed to be hounding her with some ongoing argument they were having. Despite that Kennedy was working, her boyfriend didn't seem to care that he was upsetting her. The dispute eventually led to him storming out and Kennedy stepping out back. Sage saw Creed watching the entire event unfold with all the concern of a man in love. Sage placed her hand on his arm and leaned closer to him to speak privately.

"Comfort her," Sage insisted while staring into his eyes. "She needs a shoulder to cry on."

"I wouldn't know what to say," he replied timidly.

"You don't say anything," Sage informed him. "You let her talk. Lend a sympathetic ear and a strong shoulder."

"Are you sure--?"

"Go."

Creed excused himself and headed across the tavern toward the bathrooms and the back exit of the building. Sage held her breath a moment, hoping she did the right thing. She didn't want to think she was sending Creed to slaughter, but the poor waitress had no future with the man she later marries. Sage certainly couldn't make the situation any worse for Kennedy.

Speaking of making things worse, Sage noticed Dean's ex-girlfriend, Leigh, hanging out at the bar, watching their table. She didn't seem happy when she saw Dean and Courtney looking cozy together. It was going to be one of those nights. Dean and Courtney finally found their way to the jukebox, under Leigh's watchful eye, and made several song selections. Half the patrons gathered on the dancefloor to "Boot Scoot Boogie" when one of the more popular country line dance songs played. Courtney and Dean were joined on the dancefloor by Lance and Lindsey.

Unfortunately, Leigh inserted herself into the line dance as well. At least she was far enough away from Dean and Courtney that it didn't seem like it would turn into an issue. Sage didn't feel like joining them and was once again off in her own thoughts. She fiddled with her pendant bracelet, allowing her thoughts to stray to older Jackson in the future. Every time she looked at younger Jackson drinking at the bar, it made her miss older Jackson that much more. The music and commotion within the tavern suddenly fell unusually silent. Sage didn't hear a sound, which was almost alarming. She looked up and saw everyone frozen in time. Sage sprang up from her chair with a gasp and looked around. Nothing moved!

Sage nervously walked around the bar, glancing at the motionless people frozen in moments of happiness. Frozen mid-step, her friends and the Morgan boys remained on the dancefloor with the others. Smoke from cigarettes was frozen in the air, and a falling bottle was frozen halfway to the floor. Sage slowly walked around the tavern and stared at the motionless scene with confusion. She'd never witnessed something like this before. At least, she was pretty sure she'd never seen this before. Since she was still able to move, it was obvious she had somehow caused time to stop. She cast a quick look at her bracelet. She'd done something: a thought, a spell. Something caused the world to stop abruptly. She wasn't sure how she did it, which meant she didn't know how to undo it.

"Well," she huffed and threw her arms in the air. "This is fantastic. Now what?"

Sage looked around the crowded room a moment longer, then stared at Jackson sitting at the bar with his whiskey glass in his hand and a lost look on his frozen face. She had been thinking about him just before time froze. Sage approached Jackson and studied his handsome profile for a long moment. Sadness swept over her. She placed her hand on his beard and gently nuzzled her face against him.

"I'm sorry I left," Sage whispered as her eyes swelled with tears, "but I had to save my family." She sniffed softly. "Why did you do it, Jackson?"

She lifted her head and stared at his profile only inches from her face. Sage warmly kissed him on the cheek and again nuzzled his face with hers. A strange revelation suddenly hit her. She straightened and looked around. How had she stopped time? If she could figure out how she did it, she could use that power to solve the riddle of Jackson's crime board. Sage crossed the bar and returned to her seat. She then looked at her pendant bracelet and tried to remember what she had been thinking just before time froze. She shut her eyes, drew a deep breath, and concentrated. The loud music all of a sudden blared, nearly startling her. Sage jerked and looked around. The room was once again alive with activity. She took several deep breaths while attempting to sort it out.

Sage once again looked at her bracelet and concentrated. Instead of stopping time, she saw a flashback of a stormy night. *Sage ran through the apple orchard near Toby's house while rain drenched her. She could feel the intense pain in her shoulder, and her feet were bruised and sore. She heard something behind her and gasped.* Sage jolted back to reality. Well, that wasn't what she had been attempting to achieve, but it was enough to quicken her pulse. A crash from the bar got half the barroom's attention. Sage looked at the bar and saw Jackson punch a man in the face. The man was thrown backward and into another man. Jackson was now on his feet and seemed somewhat unsteady. He was obviously drunk, but that didn't seem to hamper his ability to fight. Sage groaned and shook her head. She couldn't even have a civil conversation with him while he was sober and mildly rational; there was certainly no talking to him while he was drunk.

"That's it, Jackson," Dusty snarled at his friend. "You're cut off the rest of the night."

Jackson sneered at his friend, then looked across the tavern and saw Sage staring at him. It was too late for her to look away. He'd already caught her looking at him. Jackson approached her table while putting on his best, sober appearance. He was almost convincing.

"Where's Creed?" Jackson demanded, then looked around. "Why did he leave you here alone?"

"He's taking care of some business," Sage replied and indicated the bathroom area. She didn't feel the need to elaborate.

"Kind of rude for him to leave you alone so long," Jackson muttered, sounding annoyed as he collapsed into the vacant chair alongside hers and helped himself to Creed's glass of scotch. Jackson took a large swallow from the glass and immediately made a face. "How can he drink this shit?" He then set the empty glass down and casually looked around while sneering. "How could he leave you alone like this? Now every man in the bar is sizing you up for his next conquest."

Sage glanced around the bar but didn't see any sign of anyone in the room 'sizing' her up. "Yeah, I'm beating them off with a stick," she muttered.

"Don't you worry," Jackson announced in a serious tone as he placed his arm around her shoulder. "I'll keep an eye on you until Creed comes back."

While consciously aware of his arm over her shoulder, Sage looked at him moderately puzzled. Who was going to keep an eye on him? Out of everyone in the bar, he was the only one who didn't seem to like her. Jackson's arm over her shoulder made her mildly uncomfortable, but it was best not to say anything that would upset him in his current condition. Despite the strong smell of whiskey on his breath, Sage detected a more pleasant, light scent of aftershave. It was the same musky aftershave he wore that first afternoon when they had lunch at the ranch.

"Where is he so long?" Jackson finally demanded while again looking around while flawlessly moving his chair closer to hers without releasing her.

"I told you before, Creed isn't interested in me," Sage remarked to the imposing man, who had now made himself comfortable while practically holding her to his side.

"Why not?" Jackson asked while eyeing her with a puzzled look. His face was now close to hers, making her slightly uncomfortable. "I mean, if women of your caliber are going to dumpster dive, the least he can do is take advantage of the situation." He snorted a laugh, amused with himself. "God knows the guy needs to get laid."

"I wish you'd stop referring to it as 'dumpster diving'," Sage scoffed.

Jackson gazed into her eyes close to his with a serious look. "We're cattle ranchers, darling," he informed her matter-of-factly. "Blue-collar all the way. Hell, we're probably what people like *you* would call rednecks." He snorted a laugh. "The four of us barely made it through high school, while you and your little college friends--" He shook his head and smirked. "It doesn't take a college degree to know there's something wrong with this picture."

"Is that why you don't like me?" she asked, now putting it together. "You think I look down on you?"

"I never said I didn't like you," Jackson replied with little emotion. He then shifted in his chair, removed his arm from her shoulder, and turned to face her while gazing into her eyes. "I just don't understand your kind. Women." He moaned dramatically, then leaned forward and placed his hands on her legs without taking his eyes off hers. "You smell good, dress nice, travel in your little herds, giggling at God knows what.

Our father told us always to be a gentleman and treat women with respect."

Sage was consciously aware of his hands caressing her legs almost sensually, but she was positive he wasn't aware of his own actions.

"And we did that," he insisted, sounding almost angry. "But every time he brought a new woman home, she always ended up leaving us. No matter how respectful we were. No matter how hard we tried." He turned somewhat angry. "He'd tell us ranch life wasn't for everyone, but I never really understood that until I got older." He now looked into her eyes. "Ranch life isn't for *women*. Every time my brothers try to have relationships, it always ends in heartache for them." His hands continued to caress her legs firmly. "It's bad enough when they seek out local women, but high maintenance city girls--?" He shook his head. "You know someone's getting hurt."

Sage placed her hands on his to keep them from traveling too far up her thighs. "I don't think Dean and Lance are interested in any kind of relationship with Lindsey and Courtney. I'm pretty sure it's just casual sex. I doubt anyone's getting hurt."

"I guess I used to feel that way when I was their age," Jackson remarked, then sighed. "Casual sex gets old fast. In a few years, you'll understand."

Sage caressed his hands on her legs and offered a tiny, knowing smile. "I'm, uh, not really the casual sex kind of girl," she informed him.

Jackson grinned and appeared slightly humored by the comment. "Require a bit of commitment, eh?" he remarked while offering a sly wink.

"I prefer an emotional connection with a guy, if that's what you mean," she informed him. "You don't get that in a bar."

Jackson stared at her a moment as if attempting to sort out the string of words. "So poor Creed really isn't getting any tonight, huh?"

"I told you we're just fifth wheels," she reminded him. "But you were too busy insulting me to listen."

Jackson frowned and seemed to turn serious. "I'm really sorry about this afternoon in the general store," he remarked with genuine sincerity. "I shouldn't have been so rude, and I certainly didn't mean to make you cry." He hesitated while staring into her eyes. "Just because I was in a bad mood, that isn't any excuse for my behavior."

Sage stared into his eyes while feeling a dull pang deep inside her body. He was apologizing to her because he had made her cry. How could this be the man that tries to kill her in a few days? Jackson drew a tense breath and avoided looking at her a moment, although it didn't stop his hands from caressing her legs.

"You should give Creed a chance," he gently remarked, then met her gaze. "If anyone can provide you with an 'emotional connection', it'd be him. He's not so bad."

"Nothing against Creed," she remarked and avoided looking into his eyes, "but he's not the man for me. There aren't any sparks between us."

"Are you one of those 'love at first sight' kind of girls?" he asked with a playful smile and snorted a laugh. "If you are, you're going to be lonely for a very long time."

"No, I don't believe in that sort of thing," she remarked, then hesitated and drifted off a moment. Remembering the first time she'd seen older Jackson sent her heart aflutter. It was possible she was instantly attracted to him. She looked at younger Jackson, meeting his gaze, and realized she saw the same thing. She wanted to caress his beard but resisted. Sage tensed a moment and gently cleared her throat. "I've only ever been in love once, but it was *complicated*."

"I respect that," Jackson announced, surprising her.

"You do?"

"Yeah, of course," he replied, then straightened, removing his hands from her legs. "Everyone seems to think sex is a purely physical act, but there are a lot of psychological and emotional elements to it. Even among animals." Jackson again leaned forward and eagerly returned his hands to her legs. He now grinned almost playfully. "I've bred my horse, Raven, to probably a dozen mares on the ranch, but Karma is his favorite. He pays attention to her even when she's not in season." Jackson grinned and winked. "You know, just a bunch of little things. Like showing off in front of her to get her attention. Strutting his stuff."

"He sounds like an amazing horse."

Jackson's smile increased, possibly pleased with her interest in his horse. "He's the best horse *ever*," he informed her. "If there's one thing a cowboy can count on, it's his relationship with his horse. True partners for life. A good horse doesn't betray you."

Sage stared into his eyes that seemed to sparkle when he talked about his horse. At least that was one thing he had in common with his older counterpart. His love for his horse. Sage was happy to see him finally smiling.

"Maybe you could introduce me to Raven and Karma sometime," Sage announced.

Jackson's smile suddenly increased at the suggestion. "I'd love to." He then removed his truck keys from his pocket and held them up. "Want to go now? I was just about to leave anyway."

"I hope you don't think you're driving in your condition," she announced in a stern tone, remembering that he said he put his truck in a ditch on this particular night in the past.

He maintained his smile and handed her the keys. She accepted the keys. Accident averted. That was easy enough.

"Okay," she announced while hiding her smile. "Let me tell the guys we're going to your ranch."

CHAPTER 31

Sage leaned against the fence while Jackson stood just inside the well-lit paddock and played with his large blue roan stallion. The older horse, Raven I, looked very similar to Raven II twenty years in the future. Karma, the mare that stole Raven's heart, was in the next fence over. She was a 15.1 hand, pure black mare with a thin white strip down her face and four white socks. Karma was built solid and thick, looking every bit as impressive as the stallion.

"Raven's getting up in years," Jackson informed her. "I'll need to retire him soon. I was hoping he and Karma would have a colt, but Karma can't seem to carry a foal." He frowned and sank into his own thoughts. "She lost another foal this morning."

"I'm sorry, Jackson," she replied timidly. "That must have been difficult for you."

He nodded but didn't comment, obviously hurting. A tiny smile then crossed his face. "We'll try again in August," he informed her. "Raven doesn't mind trying." Jackson stroked the horse's large head and patted his neck. "Isn't that right, boy?" He then kissed the horse on the nose while the horse played with his shirt.

Sage smiled, enjoying the tender moment Jackson shared with his horse. He still had a heart somewhere in that semi-cold exterior. She just didn't see how he could be a cold-hearted killer.

"I'm sure he doesn't mind doing his part," Sage announced with a smile, knowing that Raven and Karma would successfully produce his new cowpony partner next spring, but she couldn't very easily tell him that. Just like she couldn't comment about that deer they nearly hit on the way to the ranch. She could see how Jackson had initially put his truck in the ditch. Had Jackson been driving, it would have been a spectacular crash.

Jackson smiled at her and laughed. "No, he doesn't mind at all," he replied.

He affectionately patted the horse and then climbed the fence with little difficulty, despite how drunk he must have been. He jumped down on her side and immediately placed his arm over her shoulder, partially leaning on her.

"How about a drink and a tour of the house?" he suggested.

Despite that she'd already seen the house twenty years from now in the future, she eagerly accepted. "I'd love to," she replied.

Sage's main purpose for returning to the ranch with Jackson was to have another crack at the armory since she now had the ability to freeze time on her side. She couldn't deny that she also wanted to spare him that accident that ruined his truck and gave him a nasty concussion. Her feelings for him would be her undoing.

§

Sage sipped her strong drink while Jackson took her on a tour of the house. To her surprise, the house was nearly spotless. Everything within the house was clean, polished, and put in its proper place. Thirty-year-old Jackson was a far better housekeeper than fifty-year-old Jackson, except when he was trying to impress a much younger woman. Did Jackson just give up later in life? Or did something happen? His older and younger self was very similar in many ways, being they were the same man, but somehow they were also very different. Not including their first meeting, he wasn't nearly as rough around the edges as his older counterpart. Perhaps life hadn't beaten him down yet.

"And your family owned this ranch for generations?" she asked as they roamed the hallway, although she already knew the answer.

When they stopped in the study, he approached the portable bar and refilled both their drinks for the third time. She was already starting to feel tipsy as it was. Despite being drunk, Jackson was in an oddly good mood. Keeping him inebriated seemed to be in her best interest.

"Since the 1800s," he replied proudly. "My family built the first home on the property, and between my father, grandfather, and great-grandfather, they handcrafted most of the furniture." He chuckled while sipping his whiskey. "That shit will outlast me."

Sage encouraged him to drink more, despite that she was forced to join him. He was in a good mood, and she intended to keep him that way.

"So how about showing me the wine cellar," she announced.

He gave her a slightly surprised look. "You know about the wine cellar?"

"I heard your father had quite the collection," Sage replied, not letting him know that she'd actually heard that from him twenty years in the future.

"It's kind of creepy down there," he remarked while making a face, seeming reluctant to take her downstairs. "Are you sure?"

"It's not haunted, is it?" she teased.

"Haunted," he announced, then laughed. "You don't actually believe in that shit, do you?"

Sage was a bit surprised by his comment, especially considering he had articles about hauntings on the armory wall in the future.

"Don't you?' she asked.

"Hardly," he replied and topped off their drinks for the basement tour. "Just so you know, it was my father's wine collection. I don't really know a lot about wine."

"Neither do I," she replied, now feeling the full effects of the alcohol, then giggled. "It's okay if you want to make shit up. I'll believe you."

Jackson grinned and chuckled. "You're cute when you cuss," he remarked.

As they headed into the basement, Sage could feel her anticipation rising. She was starting to wish she hadn't drunk as much as she did. If she could manage it, she'd attempt to stop time as she did in the tavern and take a look inside the connecting room. When they entered the wine cellar, she couldn't help but marvel at how it looked almost exactly the same. It was still coated in a layer of dust, and not a single bottle had been disturbed in twenty years.

"Wow," she announced and looked around. "This is quite the collection. I didn't know you meant an actual wine cellar. It must have taken your father years to put this sort of collection together."

"A lot of the wine came from friends who traveled abroad," Jackson informed her. "My father didn't really travel much. I suppose none of us really has."

Sage glanced at the side door and felt her heart pounding. Despite feeling slightly dizzy from drinking too much, she managed a smile and indicated the door.

"What's in there?"

"Nothing you'd be interested in," Jackson announced a little too quickly.

"Is it as cool as this room?" she asked.

Jackson seemed to tense and managed a smile. "I don't want you to get the wrong impression," he replied.

"Now I want to know even more," she remarked and indicated the door while grinning. "What's behind door number two?"

Jackson groaned and approached the door. Once he unlocked it, he looked back at her and appeared serious. "Don't freak out, okay?"

Sage nodded despite her pounding heart. Jackson opened the door, turned on the light, and indicated for her to enter. She entered the room and looked around at the familiar armory, although it seemed to be missing some of the weapons she'd remembered seeing.

"Now, this isn't something you see every day," she remarked and allowed her eyes to stray to the back wall. The board was missing, and the wall was empty.

"I'm not a terrorist," he insisted, then managed a slightly drunken smile. "I'm a collector."

"That's an impressive collection," she replied and looked at the weapons.

"It doesn't frighten you?" he asked while following her across the room.

She looked back at him and raised a brow. "No," she replied while cocking her head. "I understand the concept of collecting. If you say you're not building your own army, I believe you."

Jackson hid his smile and laughed. "I've never shown my gun collection to any woman before," he remarked. "Most of them seem squeamish just talking about guns. Not that I haven't found a thousand ways to repel women before even talking about my gun collection."

"Well, I come from a cool family," she replied while glancing at the different weapons. Her eyes then fell upon the .357 Magnum revolver.

Sage's heart pounded while staring at the familiar weapon. She saw a flashback of the gun aimed at her and Jackson squeezing the trigger while rain drenched them. She returned to reality and shuttered slightly.

"I have a shooting range out back," he informed her. "Sometime, when we're both sober, I'll take you out for target practice."

Sage glanced at him and smiled. "I'd like that."

Jackson managed a tiny laugh. "You actually would, wouldn't you?"

Sage returned the smile and then glanced at her bracelet. For a brief moment, she concentrated on it. When she looked up, Jackson was frozen in time with a tiny smile on his face. Sage waved her hand in front of him and sighed with relief. She hurried across the room for the desk, now realizing the full effects of her drunken condition. She caught onto the desk for support and opened each of the drawers. Besides gun cleaning supplies, she didn't find any of the information on the whiteboard. It hadn't happened yet. She wondered what that meant. Something suddenly didn't add up. Did she really see Jackson in that flashback? Or had she created his face as she had with Toby? Maybe she was mistaken about him. She really wanted to believe that. Sage finally gave up trying to figure it out and returned to Jackson. She glanced at her bracelet, and time resumed.

"Booze and weapons don't mix," he informed her, finishing his conversation prior to the time freeze, completely unaware that it had even happened. He then indicated the door. "We should probably go."

§

It was just before sunrise, and the bedroom was moderately dark but rapidly getting lighter. Not too surprising, Sage had one erotic dream after another that night. She dreamt she was once again back in Jackson's arms as he made love to her. She couldn't believe how real it felt. Sage was nestled against Jackson's chest as he held her in his arms while his warm lips kissed her forehead.

"Sage," he whispered against her forehead between kisses. "Are you awake?"

She groaned softly against his chest and nuzzled him as his hand firmly caressed her naked body.

"Hmm," she cooed while smiling. "Just start without me." She rubbed her leg against his hip and rolled partially onto her back. "I'll catch up with you in a minute."

As Jackson maneuvered himself on top of her, Sage groaned at the sensation and lightly clung to him while drifting in and out of sleep. She woke just long enough to caress his chest, then slipped back out again. His hot kisses ravaging her neck again woke her while he gently grinded against her. She loved when he woke her that way. There was always a flurry of erotic dreams interrupting reality. She sighed contentedly to the pleasure he brought her and now clung to his hips with her legs. It was time to wake up and enjoy her early morning delight. Jackson warmly kissed her face, then ravished her lips with his. As his breathing became heavier, the movement of his body against hers increased in intensity. Sage smiled and finally opened her eyes, looking at him. She just about gasped when she saw thirty-year-old Jackson on top of her.

"God, you're amazing," he whispered and again kissed her lips.

Sage sharply tensed, startled by Jackson's younger alter ego enjoying their moment. When she tensed, it seemingly enhanced his pleasure. Sage couldn't take her eyes off younger Jackson, not sure how she even ended up in bed with him. As his hands firmly caressed her body, he groaned with pleasure. Sage tightened her arms around his neck, buried her face into his shoulder, and shut her eyes while clinging to him with her entire body. Jackson groaned sharply and then relaxed on top of her while firmly holding her in his arms.

"Oh, Sage," he gasped softly near her ear. "That was the best night of my life."

She then realized it was possible that she hadn't been dreaming at all and that she had been with younger Jackson several times throughout the night. She couldn't even remember how they got into his bed, but she was grateful it had happened. She missed him so much and needed to be with him.

"You're pretty damned amazing, Jackson."

He groaned softly and kissed her warmly on the lips. She eagerly returned the kiss while clinging to him.

CHAPTER 32

W ithin Sage's dream. *A crack of thunder woke her from her sleep, and her eyes popped open to the familiar sound. She recognized the guest bedroom in her sister's house and saw the open bedroom window. The night seemed almost peaceful except for the nearly deafening sound of crickets. Had she actually heard thunder? Sage, wearing an oversized t-shirt as her nightgown, leaped from the bed with mild disorientation. Without hesitation, she hurried from the guest bedroom. Her heart was already racing, although she wasn't sure why. Sage rushed down the stairs just in time to hear a crash coming from the kitchen. She was about to run for the kitchen when she saw her mother lying face down, butchered on the living room floor. Her throat had been slashed, and a large amount of blood was already pooling around her. Sage gasped in horror, but her mind immediately reeled at her next thought.*

"Toby," she gasped.

Sage remembered the crash she'd heard and ran for the nearby kitchen, bolting through the archway. Toby lie on the floor, blood pouring from her throat and swiftly collecting into a pool of blood on the tile floor. Sage then heard something behind her and turned just in time to see a decorative dagger thrusting downward for her throat. Sage thrust her hand outward, barely connecting with the masked attacker. The killer was thrown across the kitchen but not before the knife plunged into her shoulder. Sage cried out as blood seeped from the deep wound. Before she could react, she was alerted to another sound from nearby. She barely had time to turn when a second masked killer lunged for her. In no condition to fight, Sage clung to her bleeding shoulder and ran for the kitchen door.

Sage ran across the dark orchard and saw the approaching headlights from a jeep on the road ahead. As she ran into the road, the jeep slammed on its brakes and skidded, coming to a sudden stop. Sage hurried for the passenger side while frantically waving to the driver.

"We have to go," she gasped.

She no sooner heaved herself into the passenger side when the jeep sped off down the road. Sage turned to the driver, once again clutching her bleeding shoulder, and stared at the concerned look on Jackson's face as he glanced at her several times while driving.

"We need to go for help," she cried out while gasping in pain.

§

Sage woke from her dream with a loud, horrified gasp and immediately clutched her shoulder. She gasped several times as she stared at the dimly lit bookstore from where she kneeled on the floor. Twenty-six-year-old Tobias kneeled alongside her while gently rubbing her shoulder.

"Hey, are you okay?" Tobias asked with concern.

Sage stared at her *adult* niece, recognizing her, and immediately became alarmed. "Toby?" she gasped. "What am I doing back here?"

"I'm pretty sure you passed out," Tobias informed her, then tensed slightly. "Not exactly the outcome we'd been hoping for."

Sage followed Tobias's eyes to fifty-year-old Jackson as he angrily slammed the shotgun down on the counter and glared at Tobias while speaking to Sage.

"Care to explain why your sister just tried to shoot me?" Jackson demanded.

"You broke into my shop," Tobias launched back at him. "That's called breaking and entering!"

Sage slowly moved to her feet. She was somewhat unsteady now, and, although she couldn't be sure, she felt as if she were stiff and sore from her extended night of drunken sex with younger Jackson. As strange as it sounded, she almost felt hungover. Was that even possible? Tobias took a step toward her, but Jackson forced her back and just about lunged for Sage. Sage saw his aggressive approach and reached for her bracelet. Jackson snatched the bracelet from her wrist, startling her. He clutched it in his hand with rarely seen anger and stared into Sage's eyes.

"I don't know what's going on around here, but I'm going to be the one asking questions this time," Jackson informed her in anger. "Right before you collapsed, I saw a light. Whatever happened--wherever you went, I'm not giving you a chance to do it again."

While his attention was focused on Sage and his back turned to Tobias, she inched her way closer to the shotgun on the counter. Without looking back, Jackson held up his finger behind him.

"Don't even think about it," Jackson snarled at Tobias without taking his eyes off Sage. He once again focused his attention on Sage. "You and I need to talk."

Sage stared at Jackson with concern while feeling confused and hungover. "I'm so confused right now."

"I don't care," he snapped back with little concern. "You can stay confused a little while longer. At least then we'll be on equal ground."

Sage stared into his eyes a long moment and nodded. "Fine, we'll talk."

"I saw you get zapped into a light," Jackson informed her. "Tonight was the second time I'd witnessed that. That was you that night twenty years ago, wasn't it? But how is that possible?"

"As far as I can tell, it's some sort of spell," Sage informed him and then sneered in increasing anger. "I did it the night you tried to kill me."

He was obviously drowning in confusion. "What are you talking about?" Jackson asked with surprise. "I never tried to kill you."

"I saw it, Jackson," she insisted. "I have enough of my memory back to piece together what happened that night. After you murdered my family and attacked me, I managed to get away. It was you in the jeep. I thought I was flagging down help, but it was you returning to finish the job. I have a big blank spot from the time I got into your jeep, but I know how it ended. I saw you shoot me with a .357 Magnum revolver. The same one in your armory."

"I didn't kill anyone, Sage," he insisted somewhat docilely. "And I certainly didn't shoot you. I just--I need to understand how you're here. That happened twenty years ago, yet you haven't aged a day. I'll admit; when I first saw you in town two months ago, I thought you resembled that woman, but I don't understand how it's possible."

"I was injured," she informed him. "I was dying. When you pulled that trigger, I removed myself from the path of the bullet."

"Removed?"

"A time spell," she informed him. "I traveled twenty years into the future. That's how I got here. For you, it's been twenty years. For me, it was a split second."

Jackson continued to stare at her as if he saw a ghost. "I didn't shoot you, Sage," he whispered while shaking his head.

"Everything that happened from the time you got in my jeep until the time I pulled the trigger makes all the difference."

"What happened?"

"The man who attacked you crashed my jeep," Jackson informed her. "He pulled you from the wreckage and dragged you into the field. You came too, but he already had you. I pulled my weapon, and he used you as a shield. He had some sort of decorative dagger to your throat. I didn't want to take the shot, but you kept screaming, 'take the shot'." Jackson held his breath. "I took the shot, and I *didn't* miss. Even though I knew I didn't hit you, there was this brilliant flash of light. He went down, and you were gone. I mean gone. Vanished. Honestly, I thought I was crazy. I searched for you, thinking you had to be close by and that my mind was just playing tricks on me." He hesitated, then shook his head. "Then, when I returned to the place where'd I shot the killer, he was gone too. I never reported it to the state police or our sheriff even though I knew I killed the man."

"That explains why they never mentioned finding the killer," Sage remarked and again met his gaze.

"I didn't even tell my own brothers what I'd seen that night, but it fucked me up pretty badly," he admitted.

"I saw your whiteboard, Jackson," she whispered and shook her head. "How can I trust you? Every person who's ever died a bloody death is on that board. My own family included."

"Your family wasn't the first to die, Sage," he announced without taking his eyes off her. "There were others." He hesitated. "My mother was one of the victims. My father saw the pattern and waited for him to return. That's how he died as well." Jackson tensed. "The night your family was killed, my brothers and I were ready for him. We were hunting him, but we didn't know where to look."

Sage stared at him for a long moment in silence. "I believe you."

Jackson shut his eyes and appeared relieved, then glanced at the bracelet he held in his hand. "This time spell," he announced. "How does it work? Can we use it to stop this guy?"

"As far as I can tell, I can travel back to a day and time of my choosing, but the location was supposed to be wherever I'm currently standing," she informed him. "Something isn't right with the whole spell. I'm still trying to figure it out."

Jackson held his breath, then sighed. "He's coming back any day now," he informed her. "He operates on five-year intervals, striking during the full strawberry moon. There have been reports of dogs barking all over town."

The comment caught her attention. "Is that why Sheriff Baxter stopped by and asked if we saw anything?" she asked. "What do dogs barking have to do with any of this?"

"Well, that's just another part of the puzzle," Jackson informed her. "That and stray cats going missing."

"Really?" she asked with surprise. "That is strange."

"Yes, it is," he replied with a sigh. "Unfortunately, I've missed the last three times. My brothers and I have been killing ourselves trying to calculate where he's going to strike next. We don't have a definitive 'when', let alone any idea of 'where'. We know his preferred victims, but that could be anyone anywhere in a fifty-mile radius."

"We already know when and where," Sage informed him.

Jackson stared at her a moment and squinted. "Did I just miss something?"

"If I can fine-tune time travel, I can show up at the exact time and location he strikes in the past," Sage informed him.

"So you want to kill him *in the past?*" Jackson asked, then raised his brows. "Is this a solo act, or can anyone hitch along? Because I think I should go with you."

"I don't need you to hitch along," Sage informed him. "I just need to knock on your door twenty years ago."

"Thirty-year-old me?" Jackson asked while cringing. "He's kind of a prick."

Sage managed a tiny smile and shrugged. "Turns out, he just needed to get laid."

Jackson eyed her almost suspiciously. His eyes then widened. "Wait a minute," he suddenly demanded. "Do you mean you--?"

She grimaced and shrugged. "It just, well, kind of happened."

"I realize we never formally discussed being exclusive," he remarked. "But you stepped out on me kind of fast."

"Are you actually accusing me of cheating on you *with you?*" Sage demanded.

"I guess not," he remarked, then raised a brow. "I am questioning your screening process a little, though. I excelled at repelling women in my thirties."

"Wait a minute," Tobias blurted out, interrupting them and reminding them she was there. She eyed Sage and raised a brow. "If *you* slept with *him* in the past, why doesn't *he* remember it?"

"She does have a point," Jackson remarked while eyeing Sage. "Apart from the night you were attacked, I don't even remember running into you twenty years ago, let alone spending the night together. If I can't remember something like that, how do we think killing him in the past is actually going to work?"

"Maybe it has something to do with me coming back at the exact moment I left," Sage suggested. "Maybe my presence counteracts anything I changed in the past."

"Like the future following your original destiny," Tobias suggested.

"Something like that," Sage replied, then glanced at Jackson. "Any thoughts?"

Jackson seemed to be deep in thought before nodding. "Yeah, I have a thought or two," he replied while glaring demandingly at Sage. "You'd have sex with thirty-year-old me despite what kind of bastard he is? What the hell is wrong with you?"

"You're not helping, Jackson," Sage remarked and looked at Tobias. "Think you can find any answers in one of these old books?"

"It's worth a shot," Tobias announced with a defeated sigh. "It'll probably take all night, and even then, I'm not promising anything. This is uncharted territory."

CHAPTER 33

It was after one o'clock in the morning. Tobias had fallen asleep on an open book at the desk, unable to stay awake any longer while Sage and Jackson sat on the floor surrounded by old books stacked around them. Both were exhausted and frustrated.

"This is like looking for a needle in a haystack," Jackson huffed and tossed another book aside. "If I read one more supernatural lore, I'm going to puke."

"As much as we want to find answers," Sage insisted. "We're not going to accomplish anything if we don't get some sleep. I think I read that last page ten times already, and it still doesn't make any sense."

"Trust me," he muttered. "Most of what we've been reading is beyond comprehension even if we weren't tired. Reading dead languages is more Lance's thing." He then considered the comment. "We should sic him on it tomorrow."

"If you think it'll help," she announced with a defeated sigh. Sage studied Jackson for a long moment as he stretched his aching legs across the floor where he sat. "Can I ask you a personal question?"

He eyed her, cocked his head, and immediately grinned. "Of course," Jackson replied. "I love personal questions. Ask away."

"What happened?" she asked almost timidly.

"What do you mean?"

Sage drew a deep breath and held it a moment. "Your bad reputation," she replied somewhat delicately. "Thirty-year-old you has a bit of an edge, but he's not--"

"A bully?" Jackson asked with a humored grin.

Sage looked away, slightly embarrassed. "I'm sorry I called you that."

"No, you're right," he insisted, catching her attention. "I am a bully. My brothers and I are everything you think we are, but it's not something I'm proud of."

"Well, what happened?"

He leaned back against the bookcase and sighed. "We have weak and corrupt law enforcement in this town, as you're well aware," Jackson informed her. "It never really affected us on the ranch, so we minded our own business. Then, one Friday night at the tavern about nineteen years ago, this attractive girl came in. Not local. I believe she had car trouble and wandered in looking to borrow someone's cellphone. Dean moved in on her like a heat-seeking missile." Jackson flashed a tiny smile, but it immediately faded. "I think he really liked her, even if he wouldn't admit it. He offered to drive her back to her car and take a look at it. I was in one of my usual foul moods, got a little mouthy with Dean, and I guess it scared her." He held his breath a moment. "She refused Dean's offer to help and accepted an offer from some other guys." Jackson was silent a moment as the expression left his face. "As they drove away, they tried to force themselves on her."

Sage stared at him with horror on her face.

"Thankfully, she was able to fight them off and got away before they got out of the tavern parking lot," Jackson remarked. "She ran back inside." He sneered while staring blankly across the room. "The idiots actually followed her into the tavern; claimed she was lying about what they'd done." Jackson finally looked at Sage. "What happened to that girl was on me. It was my fault she didn't let Dean take her back to her car. It was my fault, and I owned it." He cocked his head while staring into her eyes. "My brothers and I roughed up the two men and held them until the sheriff arrived."

Sage couldn't take her eyes off him.

"When Sheriff Baxter showed up, he threatened to arrest us for assault and battery," Jackson remarked.

"What about the two men who attacked the girl?" Sage practically gasped.

"He let them off with a warning," Jackson replied matter-of-factly.

She stared at him with a surprised look and immediately asked the follow-up question. "What about the girl?"

Jackson's eyes narrowed. "Sheriff Baxter told her she should have known better than to get into a car with strange men," he replied, causing Sage to gasp in horror. Jackson nodded, then smirked. "Yeah, he actually said that. Of course, Sheriff Baxter had roaming hands back in the day too."

Sage had wished he'd shared that information with her prior to her time jump. Her run-in with the sheriff on that deserted back road was cringe worthy.

"Kennedy took the girl to her car and stayed with her until a tow truck arrived," Jackson informed her. "Physically, she was unharmed, but, emotionally, she was a wreck." He released a sigh. "Dean was completely pissed at everyone, including me, and I don't blame him. I was upset with myself as well." Jackson shrugged. "After the guys left the tavern, my brothers and I followed them home, and we beat them within an inch of their lives. Although they didn't tell anyone what had happened, Sheriff Baxter took it upon himself to question us. When he came out to the ranch to confront us, we educated him on how things would be from there on out."

Sage knew what he was going to say next after hearing part of the story from Toby.

Jackson offered a tiny, unsettling smile. "Sheriff Baxter saw it our way, and we've been keeping the town safe for the last nineteen years," he informed her. "No one fears Sheriff Baxter, but they fear us." He studied her a moment. "Looking back, I know there was probably a better way of handling Sheriff Baxter, but I opted for the harshest possible way."

Sage stared at him in silence.

"Do you hate me?" he finally asked.

"No, I don't hate you," she finally replied. "I understand you a lot better, though." Sage released a sigh and shifted uncomfortably. "Is the back door secure? Can we let Toby sleep down here?"

"Yeah, I fixed it," he replied with a moderately humored smirk. "No one's breaking in. Although, no one's exactly breaking out either. I nailed it shut."

"Maybe we should try and get a little sleep then," Sage suggested.

Jackson grinned somewhat slyly. "I thought you'd never ask," he teased.

Sage groaned while hiding her smile and shook her head. "Nothing wrong with your sex drive," she remarked and wearily moved to her feet, feeling stiff from sitting on the floor for too long.

Jackson extended his hand to her, and she helped pull him to his feet. "Sorry," he reported while grinning somewhat deviously. "I'm still making up for my insanely long dry spell. It's nice having someone else to play with. I get tired of playing with myself."

Sage cast a look at him, then shook her head and headed upstairs to the apartment. "I'm not sure which of you is worse," she remarked.

"The real question is," he remarked, following her with renewed enthusiasm. "Which of us is *better*?"

Sage cast a disapproving look back at him as they entered the apartment. "I'm not even dignifying that with an answer," she insisted while heading to her bedroom with Jackson only a step behind.

"Oh, we all know the answer to that one," he replied. "Older and more experienced always wins."

She looked back at him. "Solo acts don't count toward experience," Sage reminded him.

"Ouch, that hurt," Jackson remarked, then chuckled deviously.

CHAPTER 34

Sage nuzzled Jackson's chest while he gathered her in his arms. She felt at peace while listening to his heart pounding from their aggressive lovemaking. She'd accuse him of trying to prove he was better than his younger self, but she knew his aggressive sexual drive was just who he was.

"Are all cowboys this great in bed?" she asked while clinging to him.

She knew she shouldn't have given him the opening when he chuckled almost deviously.

"Hours of our asses slapping saddles prepares a cowboy for slapping--"

"Please don't finish that sentence," she practically begged. "I still haven't recovered from that whole you wanting to put your brand on my ass thing."

Jackson chuckled, amused at the thought. "And I still say it would add a whole other level to doggie style."

"Do all cowboys like to mark their territory?" she asked while grinning.

"I don't know," he replied. "I never had an actual girlfriend before. Certainly, no woman I wanted to brand, that's for sure. I kind of want something that says, without a doubt, this ass belongs to Jackson Morgan."

"I'm thinking I should be offended by you treating my ass like a piece of property," she informed him.

"And yet I have zero problem with you carving your initials on my dipstick," he announced cheerfully. "If I thought you'd say yes, I'd marry you tomorrow."

Sage suddenly tensed.

Jackson immediately fidgeted. "Well, I really shot myself in the foot with that one," he remarked. "Is it too late to pull my boot out of my ass and walk it back?"

Sage relaxed and again nuzzled his chest. "I know you're too old for me," she informed him. "But I really don't care. I won't let that keep me away from you."

"Do you mean that?" he asked somewhat timidly.

"Very much," she insisted while caressing his chest. "I just don't know what's going to happen tomorrow. If we can stop the killer and save my mother and sister, I need to do whatever it takes."

"And that means going back to your right time," he replied gently.

She sighed while clinging to him. "Yes, I have to stay there," Sage replied. "It's where I belong."

Jackson reestablished his hold on her and seemed to fear letting go. "Do you think, maybe, this will be us in twenty years? What I mean is, do you think there's a chance when you go back that you'll decide to, well, you know, stay with me? Younger me. That maybe this future will one day be our reality?"

Sage lifted her head and met his gaze. "You know, Jackson," she remarked. "I've only ever been in love twice in my life. Both times it's been with you."

Jackson attempted to hide his smile but couldn't. "So you'll give the prick a chance?"

Sage lightly caressed his face. "When I'm with him, I see you in there," she assured him. "I promise; I'll do my part. The rest is up to him."

Jackson drew a deep breath while reestablishing his hold on her. "I remember just about every detail of that night when I nearly hit you on the back road near the apple orchard," he remarked almost timidly. "I remember seeing you standing in front of my jeep, soaking wet, blood covering your shirt--" He hesitated a moment, then groaned. "Your beautiful, perky breasts visible through that wet t-shirt."

She lifted her head and glared at him. "Stop embellishing," Sage scoffed.

Jackson grinned and chuckled. "Oh, I'm not embellishing," he announced. "I'd never been in love before, but I took one look at you, and it was love at first sight. When you got in my jeep, I was already thinking of the stories I'd tell our grandkids about how we first met. How I rescued you that night." He shuddered slightly and clung to her almost insecurely. "Then, when you just vanished--" He drew a deep, shaken breath. "That broke me in ways I can't begin to describe. I didn't know what happened to that beautiful, injured girl, and I blamed myself. That's why I kept your bracelet when I found it. I was a different man after that."

Sage stared at him as he held her and realized she might have had more to do with Jackson's downfall than she initially thought. How much had that incident changed him? How much for the worse?

"I rarely went to the tavern in those days," he informed her. "If memory serves correct, the night you got together with younger me would have been shortly after Karma lost her foal. I was all kinds of crazy miserable that week."

"Yeah, that just happened yesterday," she remarked, then hesitated. "Well, you know what I mean."

He drew a deep breath and sighed. "If I knew at that time that she'd deliver a healthy foal the following spring, I probably wouldn't have taken it that hard." Jackson groaned and shook his head. "I let Creed talk me into going out that night to the tavern. What a mistake that was. I got completely wasted, got into a fight, and Dusty cut me off. I was so pissed off, I drove home drunk and put my truck into a ditch." He again shook his head. "Less than a week later was when I ran into you, almost literally. My life just kind of went downhill from there."

"In my alternate reality, you got into a fight, the bartender cut you off, and I drove you home," she informed him, then offered a tiny smile. "I didn't let you drive home and kept you from wrecking your truck."

Jackson shook his head in stunned disbelief. "And yet I still remember wrecking my truck," he informed her. "You'd think I'd remember these things if you actually altered what happened in the past."

"You heard what Toby said," she reminded him.

Jackson appeared deep in thought, then gave her a strange look. "Wait a minute," he announced. "You drove me home that night? Is that when--?"

"Yes," she replied with a soft groan. "I already told you that."

Jackson cast a glare at her. "Seriously?" he just about demanded. "You jumped right into bed with him, well, with me?"

"Well, in my defense, when we went to the ranch, he got me drunk," she informed him. "I must have been pretty drunk because I actually thought it was you. This you. Older you."

"I'm noticing a pattern with you," he remarked, then chuckled. "Tequila makes you all kinds of stupid horny." There was a pause as his mood shifted. "I'm serious, though, Sage. I want to spend the rest of my life feeling the way I feel right now with you. And as much as I'd love to have that here and now, I want it even more for me twenty years ago. I want the chance to grow old with you."

Sage lifted her head, met his gaze, and kissed him warmly on the lips. "I'd like that too."

"Will you promise me something?" Jackson asked almost timidly.

"Depends, I suppose," she remarked while hiding her tiny smile.

"Make me a better man," he replied. "I could have done the right things sooner with a gentle but firm nudge. I didn't want to be a bully. All the drinking. All the fighting." He held his breath a moment. "I want to be a better man for you."

Sage affectionately caressed his face and nodded. "I'll do my best to make us both happy."

§

Sage woke to warm sunlight on her face. She stretched and clung to Jackson, nuzzling his bare chest as he held her securely in his arms. She caressed his chest and shoulder, feeling contented and relaxed. He affectionately kissed the top of her head.

"Good morning," he whispered with his lips against her head.

Sage continued to nuzzle his chest and firmly caressed his body. "Good morning."

Jackson groaned softly then, without warning, tackled her to the bed, rolling on top of her. She giggled, pleased with his enthusiasm, before opening her eyes and meeting his gaze. Sage was just about shocked when she saw thirty-year-old Jackson grinning back at her. He gently caressed her face.

"I think I'm calling in sick today," he remarked.

Sage immediately hid her shock and surprise, but she had no idea how she got back to the past. And how did she get from Toby's bookstore to Jackson's bedroom at the ranch? Oddly enough, she seemed to have returned to the exact time and place she had initially left as well. Jackson affectionately kissed her neck and worked his way down her chest. Sage's heart was now racing while almost unaware of Jackson's sexual advances. There were too many unanswered questions. What caused her to jump into the future in the first place? And in her sleep, no less! What brought her back? Again, in her sleep. If she couldn't control her time surfing, and it could happen in her sleep, she could be riding some torturous time loop forever. Jackson's lips made their way back up her body to her mouth, and he kissed her warmly before pulling back and meeting her gaze with a strange look.

"Is everything okay?" he asked, sounding concerned. "Drunken night and morning regret?"

Sage snapped out of her own thoughts and stared into Jackson's concerned eyes. If she remembered correctly, which was doubtful at this point, she and younger Jackson had copulated several times throughout the night. If she actually thought about it, she'd probably had more romps in the last forty-eight hours than she had in the last year. She smiled warmly and placed her hand on his bearded face.

"No, not at all," she replied, then eagerly kissed him on the lips. Sage moved her leg out from under him, straddling him with one leg, and gently rubbed her ankle against his bare hip. "I enjoyed every intense minute of it."

Jackson nuzzled her face with his while hiding his proud yet devious grin. "Is that a fact?" he announced boldly and chuckled. "Then I should probably knock you up before you come to your senses."

He resumed kissing her neck with some aggression, causing her to squirm in ecstasy. She managed a tiny giggle, but it quickly turned to a moan of pleasure.

CHAPTER 35

Once she had showered and dressed, Sage sat on the window seat within Jackson's bedroom and smiled while watching him pull on his cowboy boots. He saw the way she looked at him and couldn't help but grin. Jackson stood and immediately slid onto the window seat with her, stalking her before kissing her warmly on the lips.

"I can't even begin to understand what happened over the last twenty-four hours," he remarked, unable to wipe the grin from his face. "I mean, no disrespect, but who the hell are you?" He let out a tiny chuckle. "You show up at my door yesterday morning prepared to rip out my throat, and the following morning I wake up with you in my bed." Jackson shook his head while appearing almost amused. "I mean, my head is spinning, and it's not from a night of heavy drinking." He continued to stare at her with a strange fascination. "I don't have much experience picking up women in bars, but I know last night was not typical."

Sage smiled and cocked her head. "Can I assume that's a good thing?"

Jackson let out a throaty chuckle and affectionately caressed her leg. "Absolutely," he replied. "I won't lie. You pretty much blew my mind. The third time I rolled over on you, I was sure you would chase me away, but you just kept welcoming me back. By the fourth time, I was like, 'fuck it', and just went for it."

Sage considered the comment and nodded. "That would explain the explicit dream I had."

"Sorry," he remarked with some embarrassment.

"No, it's okay," she replied and smiled. "I enjoyed it."

Jackson shook his head and marveled at her response. "That's what I mean," he announced. "You made it so easy. Almost *familiar*."

His 'familiar' comment blindsided her a little. She'd been with his older alter ego many times in the last week that she knew what to expect and how to please him.

"If I promise to keep it in my pants, will you consider sticking around today?" he asked, fidgeting. "I could take you out riding or let you take out some frustration at the shooting range. Whatever you like."

Sage stared at him and the permanent smile on his face. She touched his face, kissed him on the lips, and smiled. "I'd love to," she replied and warmly kissed him several times on the chin and cheek while working her way down to his neck. "Keeping it in your pants is *not* a requirement."

Jackson suddenly groaned, sought her mouth, and aggressively kissed her. He broke off the kiss but kept his mouth close to hers while clinging to her.

"I'll admit; I have a lot of pent-up sexual frustration that needs to be worked off," he gently informed her.

"Maybe we could take that ride to some nice, secluded spot and see what we can arrange," she announced while grinning somewhat deviously.

Jackson groaned and allowed his hand to travel her body firmly. "I'd love nothing more."

She kissed him quickly, then pulled away and turned serious. "But we have some time to kill before that little adventure," Sage announced. "And I'm starving."

"In that case," he announced and stood while extending his hand to her. "Are you ready for an awkward breakfast with your friends and my brothers?"

Sage smiled, accepted his hand, and stood. "As ready as I'll ever be," she replied.

§

Jackson and Sage were the first to arrive in the kitchen that morning. Sage watched as Jackson pulled together a large Sunday brunch for his brothers. He made a large batch of scrambled eggs with onion, ham, peppers, mushrooms, and hot sauce. There was also a plateful of bacon and a large stack of pancakes. He knew he was cooking for Sage's two friends as well, being confident his brothers had brought their dates home. Sage eyed the feast and shook her head, marveling how easy he made it look.

"Do you ring the dinner bell?" she teased. "How do you get them up?"

Jackson set the last of the pancakes on the table and looked at his watch. It was ten in the morning. Within seconds, they heard footfalls on the back stairs.

Jackson glanced at Sage and smiled almost knowingly. "Sunday morning brunch is a Morgan family tradition," he informed her. "Everyone shows up, and they're always on time."

Sage wasn't surprised that both her friends had hooked up with Dean and Lance, but they were possibly surprised to see her with Jackson. Creed entered the kitchen last, which Jackson found unusual.

"You're usually the first one down here," Jackson announced to his brother. "It's a good thing Sage was here to help."

Creed appeared slightly embarrassed and unkempt, whereas the rest of his brothers were showered and ready for their day off.

"Don't make a big deal out of it," Creed announced in a gruff tone.

Before Jackson could question the comment, Kennedy appeared on the stairs looking equally bedraggled. Jackson stared at the woman with shock and dismay. Creed threatened his brothers with his glare. Jackson hid his smile and glanced at Sage. Sage wondered what her part had been in getting those two together. Jackson pulled out the chair to his right for Sage and then took his seat at the head of the table. Once everyone was seated, they said grace before diving into the mammoth breakfast. Jackson had a difficult time hiding his pleased grin. It was possibly a first for them. All four Morgan boys got laid on the same night.

"Seeing as today is our day off," Dean announced cheerfully while placing his arm over the back of Courtney's chair in an intimate gesture. "I think the ladies should stay and make a day out of it."

"I agree," Courtney announced while clinging to Dean seated alongside her.

It had originally been Sage's plan, but now she wasn't so sure she should involve her two friends. She accomplished what she set out to do. She'd seen Jackson's basement room, had a long discussion with older Jackson, and she knew he couldn't possibly be the killer.

"I'd love to stay, but I can't," Kennedy informed Creed, then smiled. "You can call me later."

"I'd like that," Creed replied while hiding his boyish grin.

"The three of us could return home this morning and come back later," Courtney announced and eyed both her friends. "It'll be fun."

Dean grinned and raised his brows deviously. "Skinny-dipping in the pond."

"I think I'm just going to hang out," Sage informed her friends. "Jackson's going to take me horseback riding after breakfast."

"Oh, okay," Courtney replied while grinning slyly at her friend. "Then we'll see you when we return later this afternoon."

CHAPTER 36

That afternoon was sunny and warm. Two saddled horses, Raven and Karma, grazed in the lush field while their bridles hung from the saddle horns. Underneath a nearby tree, Sage, wearing just her tank top and underwear, clung to a bare-chested Jackson, where they relaxed on a blanket. Jackson groaned and then sighed while gripping her tighter in his arms.

"For an angel, you have quite a devilish streak," he informed her and kissed her head.

"Well, I'm far from an angel," she insisted.

"Yeah," he agreed. "You're more of a goddess." He sighed deeply and glanced around the massive field in the middle of nowhere. "This ranch really needs a cowgirl." He looked at her with a devious smile. "If you keep blowing my mind like this, I'll never let you leave."

"Well, prepare to have your mind blown a little more," Sage informed him while tensing. "Because there are some things I need to tell you that will *completely* blow you away."

He groaned almost lustfully. "I'm looking forward to it," Jackson announced.

Sage pulled away from him just far enough to kiss him warmly on the lips, then met his gaze while giving him a slightly sympathetic look. She almost hated to spoil his perfect day, but she needed to have an uncomfortable conversation with him. Sage smiled and affectionately caressed his chest.

"Storytime," she announced as she pulled away from him while sitting up.

Jackson attempted to keep her on the blanket with him while maintaining his devious grin. "Can't we have storytime and cuddle?"

"This is more of a discussion than a story," she replied. "It requires pants and maybe even boots."

Jackson groaned and reluctantly sat up. "I'm already not liking it," he remarked, then slipped into his shirt while Sage finished dressing.

Once they had both dressed, Sage turned on the blanket to face him. She pulled her knees to her chest, relaxed her chin to her knees, and stared into his eyes. Jackson immediately tensed at the way she looked at him.

"Now you're making me uncomfortable," he remarked and frowned. "Are you married?"

"That might be an easier conversation," she announced, then summoned all her courage. "We need to talk about the murders that happen every five years."

Jackson's expression suddenly dropped. "What are you talking about?" he asked as his entire body involuntarily stiffened.

"Every five years, a serial killer emerges and goes on a killing spree," Sage informed him. "I know you've been trying to stop this killer, and I know it's personal for you. In two days, it becomes personal to me."

Jackson seemed unable to move or take his eyes off her. She could tell he was attempting to sort out what she'd just told him.

"How do you know about that?" he asked while struggling to remain calm, but she could see an explosion building up beyond his eyes. "And how does it become personal to you in two days?"

"We should probably skip that part for now. You wouldn't believe me if I told you," she informed him. "I can help you stop this, but you have to trust me."

Although he didn't seem reactive, Sage knew he was possibly processing everything that had happened from the moment they'd met.

"Trust is a two-way street, Sage," he informed her slightly gruffly, making her somewhat uncomfortable. "If I'm going to trust you, then you need to trust me. You need to tell me how you know all this."

Sage drew a deep breath, held it a moment, and then confessed everything. "In two days, the killer comes after my family," she informed him. "They all die. He tries to kill me too, but I manage to escape."

Jackson gave her a bewildered look, obviously not believing her. "In two days?" he remarked skeptically.

"The night I'm attacked, I run into you, and you save me," she informed him somewhat delicately. "Only the man you kill isn't in on it alone."

Jackson stared at her for a long moment, possibly considering everything she said. "There's something seriously fucked up in your head," he finally replied. "You're talking as if you can see the future."

"I can't *see* the future," she announced, then hesitated and shifted uncomfortably, "but I've been *to* the future." He already thought she was crazy; she may as well go for the trifecta. "My near-death experience shot me twenty years into the future with no memory of what actually happened." Sage hesitated while staring into his eyes, knowing by the way he looked at her that he didn't believe her. "Bits and pieces of what I saw led me to believe you were the killer, but we worked that out after a nice long chat."

"We?" Jackson asked while cocking his head. "Who's we?"

Sage held her breath. "You, twenty years in the future," she gently replied.

Jackson stared at her and seemed unable to move. "You talked to *me* twenty years in the future?" he asked, then raised a cocky brow. "I'm guessing that must have been an interesting conversation."

She knew he'd never believe her, but she had to sell it. "Believe it or not, you're very open-minded in the future," she informed him. "You have this whole NCIS crime board, serial killer tracker thing going on in the armory."

He couldn't take his eyes off of her. "Now, you're starting to scare me," he remarked while tensing. "I keep that in the attic, but I was thinking about moving it into the gun vault because it's cooler down there."

She should have been surprised to hear that, but she wasn't. "I know this is a lot to take in, Jackson," she announced delicately while keeping him from reacting poorly, "but I really need you to believe me."

As Jackson stared at her for a long moment, it was difficult to tell what was going through his head.

"Let's say, for argument's sake, I do believe you," he announced while studying her. "I'm compelled to ask--?"

Sage held her breath, not sure what to expect. "What do you want to know?"

"How the hell did you get fifty-year-old me to believe any of this bullshit?" he asked while raising an arrogant brow.

Sage tensed slightly but maintained eye contact. "A twenty-two-year-old woman paying attention to a fifty-year-old man," she remarked. "You figure it out."

Jackson snorted a laugh. "In other words, I wanted to get in your pants. Yeah, that sounds about right." He appeared amused. "I'm guessing that didn't work out for him, huh?"

Sage shifted uncomfortably and avoided looking at him. Despite both incidents being him, she still felt oddly uncomfortable discussing it.

Jackson's smile faded to surprise. "No," he just about gasped, then suddenly grinned and laughed. "You can't seriously tell me that you jumped into bed with a fifty-year-old, geriatric version of me." He shook his head. "You're obviously some psycho chick with serious mental issues." Jackson hesitated a moment before chuckling. "Fortunately for you, I'm willing to work around that."

"I'm not crazy," she snarled, then realized her response sort of made her sound unstable. "You know that comment you made this morning about how easy I made it. Almost familiar?" Sage shifted uncomfortably. "It was easy and familiar because I'm your girlfriend twenty years in the future."

"Hmm? Well," he announced and smiled humored. "Lucky me."

Sage drew a deep breath and ran her fingers through her hair a moment. Her eyes shifted back to meet his, and she just about lunged for her discarded phone.

"I think I can prove I'm not crazy."

"Hey, it's okay, Sage," he announced while grinning. "I already said I'm okay with you being crazy."

Sage slid alongside him and held her cellphone in front of him. He saw the picture of his older self, wearing nothing but his cowboy hat, sitting naked on Raven. Jackson stared at the picture as he took the phone from her.

"Did you photoshop this?" he asked with a hard-to-read expression on his face. He then smiled and laughed. "You're good."

"Start scrolling," Sage announced while groaning, knowing what he was going to find.

Jackson browsed through more pictures of his older self from their drunken afternoon in the horse pasture twenty years from now. With each picture, his expression changed. When the video of Sage having sex doggie style began to play, she gasped and attempted to grab the phone from him. He kept the phone from her and moved to his knees while grinning.

"Oh, look at you," he teased, now humored as the sex video played. "Aren't you the naughty one?"

His smile slowly faded as he continued to watch the video. Sage could only hear her moans of pleasure from the phone, but something else seemed to catch his attention, and his expression dropped. Sage moved onto her knees and looked at the screen that had horses in the background. He paused the video.

"That looks like Raven," he informed her, then pointed at the screen. "But there's *two* of him."

"That's Raven I and Raven II," she informed him. "Raven I is in the far pasture. You told me he's a very old man. I think you said he's thirty-five. Raven II is nineteen, and Raven III is just a month old."

Although he didn't look at her, he stared at the two horses in the background. "Raven III?" he practically whispered, choking on his words. "I have a Raven III?"

"Yeah," she replied and smiled warmly. "You told me you're a 'sentimental old prick'."

Although it was unclear if he believed anything she was telling him, Jackson chuckled at the comment.

"You said you usually put Raven II out in the pasture with the mares on Sundays for Woodstock, but this was taken on Monday," she informed him, then considered the comment. "I guess we wanted to be a part of Woodstock."

Jackson suddenly eyed her with a strange look and indicated the video. "You mean that's *me* filming *us*?"

Sage drew a deep, tense breath. "Give it another couple of seconds," she reluctantly replied.

Jackson pressed play and returned his attention to the raw, X-rated footage. The cellphone camera image turned, revealing a drunken, fifty-year-old Jackson grinning deviously before continuing to film their sexual act. Jackson's expression turned to something resembling shock as he watched the remaining footage.

"That's me," he just about gasped in astonishment. "It's actually me but a lot older."

"I tried to tell you," Sage informed him and again reached for the cellphone.

He again prevented her from taking it and continued watching the raw footage. When it ended, he looked at her with a strange expression.

"So you're actually my girlfriend when I'm fifty?" he asked with some surprise.

"Yeah, pretty much," she replied and finally took the phone from him.

Jackson fell onto his backside and remained stranded in his thoughts, scratching his beard and attempting to come to terms with what she told him. He finally looked at her as she sat in front of him. Jackson suddenly appeared puzzled and tensed.

"So your original timeline is here, but the attack that happens in two days sends you twenty years into the future," he announced.

"Yes," Sage replied, feeling a new round of questions coming her way.

"As bizarre as that is," he remarked. "How the hell did you get back here from there?"

Sage tensed and held her breath. "That's where it gets a little complicated," she remarked.

"It was already complicated."

"My niece in the future helped me find a way to bring myself back," Sage informed him and cringed. "But then it happened again without my knowledge or consent. Twice, actually."

"When?"

She tensed slightly. "After we made love," she informed him.

He cocked his head and gave her a strange look. "Which time?"

Sage appeared slightly embarrassed, being reminded how many times she'd had intercourse with him last night. "Prior to dawn," she informed him. "It just, sort of, happened in my sleep. I was shot back to the exact place and time I originally left in the future."

"And then you were returned to my time," he announced while eyeing her. "How long were you in the future, and what were you doing when you were thrust back to this day and time?"

Sage shifted and was unable to look him in the eyes. "I was there five or six hours," she replied and fidgeted. "I was thrust back after, well, after I was *with* older you."

Jackson stared at her with some surprise while trying to understand. "And you popped back in my bed as if you had never left?"

"I think so," she replied, then shifted. "I was back with you for, well, the last round."

Jackson gently cleared his throat and rubbed his eyes. He finally looked at her. "So we had sex, you passed out, and then you returned to the future where you proceeded to service older me." He raised his brows while gesturing. "After which, you popped back into my bed for another round with me."

Sage felt her cheeks become hot and red. "It would seem that way."

"Jesus, you've had a full dance card," he remarked.

She sneered at him. "That's not funny."

He grinned slyly. "It is a little."

"Anyway," she announced with a groan. "Tobias was trying to find out why my interaction with you, here and now, didn't seem to affect you in the future. It doesn't do any good to have a 'do-over' if it doesn't change the future."

Jackson was now curious. "So you're saying fifty-year-old me had no memory that he'd met you in the past or, more importantly, that you'd slept with him when he was thirty?"

"Yes, exactly," she replied. "But I'm also a little worried about non-consensual time surfing. The whole time travel thing seemed like a bit of a fluke to begin with. Consciously doing it was a stretch. Subconsciously can't be good. If I can't control it, I could be jumping back and forth randomly for the rest of my life."

Jackson studied her a long moment, then seemed unusually serious. "I need to ask you something, Sage, and I need you to be completely honest with me."

"Yeah, sure." She raised a brow. "As long as it doesn't have to do with anything sexual with your older counterpart."

"I'll get that information out of you another time," he announced, then returned to his serious demeanor. "Just a quick, yes or no question." He stared into her eyes. "Are you a witch?"

Sage stared at him with some surprise by the question. With the time travel information, it didn't seem as if 'witch' would have been the first best guess. She didn't know how he even came up with that question.

"Yes," she replied somewhat insecurely, reluctant to share that information. There was no telling how he'd handle it.

Jackson stared at her a moment after hearing the response and seemed unusually rigid. His reaction was hard to read. "Well, that certainly explains a lot."

Sage was now uncomfortable by the way he reacted. She barely remembered her lineage, but she was sure she didn't readily share that information with most people. She attempted to relax but found it difficult.

"Why do you ask?"

"Because that's what all the victims have in common," Jackson informed her.

"All the victims were witches?" Sage asked, then vigorously shook her head. "That doesn't make any sense. How would the killer know?" A strange thought then swept over her. "If that were true, why wouldn't fifty-year-old Jackson have told me that? He knew my mother and sister were killed and that I was attacked. Wouldn't he have known I was a witch? Why wouldn't he say anything?"

Jackson shifted uncomfortably and drew a tense breath. "Probably because he didn't want you asking the follow-up question, fearing he'd lose you."

Sage stared at Jackson a moment and suddenly put it together. "Your mother was one of the victims."

"Yes, my mother was a witch," Jackson informed her, then frowned. "And my father died five years later trying to stop the killer."

Sage stared at him a long moment and fidgeted slightly. "Then that makes you at least part witch."

Jackson nodded.

"Is that how you knew who the potential victims would be?" Sage asked.

"Yeah, well, with some help," he informed her. "Creed is amazing with lineage and has half the town dated back to the beginning of their ancestry. Each of us has our own unique talents."

"What's your talent?" she asked, a little concerned by what she might learn.

"Numbers, patterns, putting together random pieces," he informed her.

"Which would explain why you play poker," she remarked with a tiny laugh.

"I don't play poker," he informed her somewhat sternly. "That'd be cheating."

"You don't seem to care later on in life," she reported while raising her brows. "That's how fifty-year-old you spends almost every Friday night."

"Well, that's just wrong."

"What about Dean and Lance?" Sage asked.

"Dean can spot a liar a mile away," Jackson replied. "He can hear their heartbeat. I mean, *literally* hear their heart. When a person lies, their heart rate increases."

"Sounds pretty useful," Sage remarked.

"Except those who lie professionally can do it without their heart rate increasing," he informed her.

"And Lance?"

"Lance can read and understand every language known to man," he replied. "What about your family?"

It felt weird talking about her family history since it was something they never did. "My mother can communicate with spirits," she replied. "But she chooses to ignore them. Long story."

"And your sister?"

"She's a chemist," Sage replied. "She knows exactly what to mix with what to create something. Anything from an amazing chili recipe to bombs."

Jackson hesitated and raised his brows. "Your sister and I need to get together," he teased while grinning, then winked at her. "Swap recipes."

"Not on your life," Sage replied with a tiny smile.

"What about your niece?"

"She's only six," Sage informed him. "She mostly colors and sketches."

"Sometimes the gifts come before puberty," he informed her.

"Well, she owns an antique bookstore in the future," Sage replied. "She has a real passion for reading."

"Spells and hexes?"

"Not funny."

"Wasn't trying to be," he replied. "Your family lineage seems to be pretty strong. I need to sic Creed on you. Find out where you come from."

"Didn't he already check into my sister?" she asked, now curious. "She's lived here a few years. You said he knows the family history of everyone in town."

"Almost everyone," Jackson corrected. "He needs to know mothers and fathers in order to begin. He's never gotten a clear line on your father."

"My mother never talked about our real father," Sage insisted, then frowned at the thought. "I don't know if the man is alive or dead. I've never even seen a picture of him."

"But your sister is a few years older than you, so he must have hung around long enough for you to be conceived," Jackson insisted.

"My sister doesn't remember him, and my mother doesn't talk about him," Sage informed him. "She never even mentioned his name. I used to think it was too painful for her to talk about, but now I believe he wasn't a very good man, and she just wants to forget about him."

"Which tells me he was at least part witch," Jackson remarked.

"Not necessarily."

"Sage, your family is a lot stronger than mine," he informed her. "You can time surf."

"I have a charm for that," she replied.

"That piece of junk you wear?" he insisted, then shook his head. "That's not even antique. That bracelet has nothing to do with your abilities."

"I'm pretty sure it does."

"There's no known spell or object that can do something like that," he informed her. "That's something you carry inside you. That's why it happened without you consciously willing it. You willed it in your subconscious."

"For what purpose?"

"I suppose you needed something from the future," he replied, then shrugged. "Initially, you needed to escape to avoid death. You transported yourself out of this reality and into the future in that split second, but you got stuck when you lost your memory."

"And when I hopped back to the future?" she asked. "Why would I do that?"

"Unfinished business," Jackson suggested. "You thought I was a killer. You couldn't find the answers here, so you went to my older alter ego."

"Why would you say that?"

"Did the Jackson of the future help you?"

Sage hesitated while staring at him. "Yes, he did."

"When you got what you needed, you came back."

"I didn't get what I needed," she insisted defensively. "Tobias was going to find information for me, but I came back before she could find it."

"You don't need information from her," he replied confidently. "Because the answers to your questions are already inside you."

"You're infuriating; you know that?"

He shrugged and smirked. "It's a gift."

CHAPTER 37

Jackson and Sage returned from their horseback ride an hour before Sage's friends would be returning that afternoon. Jackson entered the kitchen in a bit of a hurry, with Sage only a few steps behind him. He found all three of his brothers planning the BBQ for that afternoon.

"Family meeting," Jackson gruffly announced. "Study. Now."

Jackson turned and escorted Sage from the kitchen. All three brothers exchanged looks.

"Well," Dean announced with a defeated sigh. "I guess that ride wasn't nearly as romantic as he had hoped."

The three brothers followed Jackson and Sage into the study. His brothers suspiciously eyed the young woman that had joined them.

"If it's a family meeting, why's she here?" Dean was the first to ask.

"It involves Sage," Jackson informed them with little emotion.

"Are we going to be uncles?" Dean asked while grinning, then winked at Sage.

Sage groaned and rolled her eyes.

Jackson gave Dean a commanding look. "Put your ass in a chair," he scoffed.

Dean frowned and flopped into a nearby chair. After his brothers each took a seat, they gave him their full attention. Jackson leaned against his desk, drew a deep breath, and indicated Sage.

"Sage is a witch," Jackson announced.

All three looked at Sage with surprise.

Creed nearly jumped out of his chair and practically lunged for her. "Who's your father?" he asked while whipping a notebook from his pocket. "Birthdate, if you know it."

"She doesn't know who her father is," Jackson informed Creed, who immediately frowned. "Guys, Sage survived an attack by our serial killer."

All three were stunned while staring at her.

"--in two days from now," Jackson informed them.

He received strange looks from his brothers.

"She can time surf?" Creed just about gasped while studying Sage. "No way."

Sage was stunned at how easily Creed put that together. Why did everyone else in the world know more about these things than she did?

"Her family makes ours look like sideshow freaks in a circus," Jackson remarked.

"I need to know who her father is," Creed announced, now ready to jump from his seat.

"Well, you'll have to ask her mother," Jackson remarked, then raised an arrogant brow, "but I wouldn't count on her being very helpful. She's kept it a secret from both of her daughters."

"Oh, I'll find out," Creed announced in all seriousness. "If Sage can time surf, the possibilities are endless."

"I was thinking the same thing," Jackson insisted.

Sage eyed both men with some surprise. "What are you talking about?"

Creed remained moderately excited. "You don't *just* time surf," he insisted. "If you can time surf, you have endless other abilities."

"I assure you, I don't."

"Some witches go their entire lives without knowing the power they possess," Creed remarked, then shook his head while grinning. "You could be a nuke waiting to explode."

"I don't want to explode," Sage gasped in horror.

"Metaphorically," Creed insisted.

"Maybe literally," Dean teased and winked at her. "You never really know."

"If you can time surf, that means you can manipulate time," Creed informed her. "You can go to the future; jump into the past; freeze time."

Sage suddenly tensed. Dean was the first to pick up on her mood, possibly hearing her heart beating faster.

"You can freeze time?" Dean asked with surprise, then pointed at Sage while looking at his brothers. "She can freeze time!"

"I only did it twice," she informed them. "Trust me; time jumping should be the main focus."

"Imagine," Creed announced while staring at her. "The ability to simply disappear before our very eyes. It's definitely a big deal."

"I did some reading on that once," Lance insisted, now jumping into the conversation. "It's possible to manipulate others during a time stop."

"Doubtful," Sage informed him. "No one could see me. I tried to make them see me."

"I'll read up on it," Lance replied.

"This isn't helping," Sage announced with increasing frustration. "We need to come up with some sort of plan to stop them from killing my family in two days."

"Sounds like we already tried and failed," Dean boldly announced.

"Maybe we need to be concentrating on Sage's memory loss," Jackson informed his brothers. "She was attacked. She obviously saw who attacked her. If we could jump-start her memory, maybe she could just tell us who it was."

"It might be more complicated than that," Lance insisted and eyed his brothers. "We're obviously dealing with a killer who has supernatural abilities much like our own. I think our killer or killers might be shifters."

"Now you're talking out of your ass," Dean scoffed while rolling his eyes. "No one's seen a live shifter in over a hundred years."

"Shifters used to hunt witches to absorb their power," Lance insisted. "Like a fountain of youth. A witch or two would easily sustain a shifter for five years, explaining the pattern."

"It's possible," Jackson announced in agreement. "The killings have been happening for over one hundred years. So unless someone is taking over the family business, it makes sense."

"And it always happens during the full moon in June," Lance added.

"The strawberry moon," Creed added while looking at his brothers. "June has been known to be breeding season for shifters. It could also explain the vanishing cats and why dogs all over town go crazy the week leading up to that particular full moon."

"Why do cats vanish?" Sage felt the need to ask, now curious.

"They eat them," Dean casually informed her.

Sage stared at him with a horrified look. Dean raised his brows and nodded.

Creed swatted his brother's shoulder while giving him a disapproving look, then focused his attention on Sage. "The cats go into hiding," he informed her. "Animals are very perceptive."

"Shifters would make sense," Lance then remarked. "All the murders happened during a strawberry moon. It's possible they need to feast on that particular day."

"And the next strawberry moon is right around the time Sage said she and her family are attacked," Jackson replied.

"Okay," Sage announced while eyeing the guys. "Pretend I'm stupid. What's a shifter?"

"A mostly human creature," Creed informed her, sounding almost clinical. "It has the ability to take on human form as well as animal or insect."

"So it could be one of us right now?" she asked with surprise.

Dean laughed at the question and immediately received glares from Jackson and Lance.

"No," Creed replied without passing judgment on her lack of shifter knowledge. "Although they can take on multiple human forms, male or female, they can't replicate, say, you or me."

Dean groaned and rubbed his eyes. "Jesus, I can't believe we're actually having a serious discussion on shifters," he moaned dramatically, then eyed his brothers. "The whole idea is ridiculous."

"You've always been so closed-minded," Lance scoffed at his brother.

"Okay, this isn't getting us anywhere," Jackson announced with a sigh. "Sage saw something the night she was attacked. We need to see if we can get that part of her memory to return."

"I'll do some research," Lance replied. "Maybe I can find a spell or something that will help."

Jackson nodded. "That's a start," he announced.

"We need to find out who Sage's father is," Creed again insisted. "Her mother needs to tell us. She has just as much at stake in this as the rest of us. In two days, they come after her and her family."

"I've asked about my father in the past," Sage informed him. "She shuts down that conversation. My mother is, at times, difficult."

"I'm difficult too," Creed replied without emotion. "I'll talk to her."

Sage snorted a laugh. "Good luck."

"We should include your sister," Jackson informed Sage. "Being a chemist, we could use her talent. If it is a shifter, between her and Lance, they may be able to come up with something to unmask them."

Dean groaned and threw his head back against the chair. "Again, with the shifter theory."

"I'm sorry if you don't share our ideas, Dean," Jackson scoffed at his brother. "If we are dealing with a shifter, the killers could be anyone already in our circle."

"That's a scary thought," Sage remarked.

"And there's no 'one size fits all' in that scenario either," Creed announced.

"What do you mean?" Sage asked.

"Well, if our shifter is over one hundred years old, it could be someone we've known forever," Creed informed her. "Someone already in our lives. Someone we trust."

"Even multiple people," Dean remarked while straightening. "If you want to explore that possibility, you can't ignore the fact that a shifter can change appearance." He shrugged, almost mocking them. "He could be the sheriff during the day and, let's say, your new girlfriend, Kennedy, at night."

Creed sneered at his brother, who enjoyed his torment. "And he could also be your girlfriend."

Sage became alarmed at the comment and eyed the guys. "Is he being serious?" she suddenly asked. "Could one of my college friends actually be a shifter?"

"Possibly, but doubtful," Lance replied and cocked his head. "Logically speaking--"

"There's nothing logical about speculating a shifter," Dean muttered.

"Logically speaking--" Lance announced a little louder while glaring at his brother. "It would be someone in town. All the killings happen in this area. A predator always remains close to his food source."

"That's pleasant," Dean muttered.

"Well, we can all vouch for one another," Jackson announced, then looked at Sage. "Memory loss aside, can you vouch for your sister?"

Sage considered it a moment and nodded. "Yes, of course."

"Why did you hesitate?" Creed asked with a slightly curious look.

Sage fidgeted, now uncomfortable. "With my memory loss and the time jump, my mind has played tricks on me," she gently replied. "I lived with my grown-up niece in the future, thinking she was my sister. All my memories of my sister were with my niece's face. Then, when I reunited with my actual sister, they all returned to her face."

She was met with several concerned looks. Sage tensed while eyeing the four. "Is that bad?"

"The night you were attacked, future me said he shot the killer when he tried to finish the job," Jackson remarked while eyeing her.

"Yes," Sage replied and again eyed the four men.

"If it had been a shifter stealing power--" Creed began, then stopped when Jackson stiffened.

Sage was now alarmed. "What?" she just about gasped. "What are you not telling me?"

"Memory loss with no head injury," Jackson replied while remaining tense. "If it was a shifter, he could have gotten inside your mind. The shifter may have caused your memory loss."

"Are you saying my mind may have been corrupted?" Sage practically gasped. "Or are you suggesting I may be the shifter?"

"No, definitely not that," Jackson insisted, turning defensive. "Your sister, niece, and college friends all recognized you."

"Then what are you suggesting?" Sage asked.

"Nothing you think you saw or did really happened," Creed gently replied. "Or maybe twisted truths."

"I *was* to the future," Sage insisted and looked at Jackson. "I did meet you in the future. You saw the pictures and the video."

"It's true," Jackson informed his brothers. "She had some documented proof on her camera."

"A video?" Creed asked and now appeared curious. "Can I see that?"

"No," Sage and Jackson announced a little too quickly in unison, surprising the three brothers.

Dean's eyes suddenly lit up, and his grin increased. "A porno?" he eagerly cried out.

Sage felt her cheeks redden at Dean's educated guess while Jackson fidgeted.

Dean suddenly laughed while pointing at his brother. "Your heart rate is up. It was a porno," he cried out enthusiastically. "You dog!"

Sage shifted uncomfortably and eyed Jackson. "Can you make him stop?"

"Don't worry about him," Jackson casually replied while glaring at Dean. "I'll tie him down and castrate him in his sleep."

Dean squirmed in his chair and seemed to mind his manners.

"So we can all agree I was actually to the future?" Sage asked, looking for some reassurance that she wasn't crazy or imagining things.

"The pictures and video confirm your story," Jackson replied.

Dean again grinned and snickered.

Jackson pointed a warning finger at his brother without looking at him. "Last warning, Dean."

Sage breathed a sigh of relief at Jackson's confirmation. For a moment, she actually questioned what she had gone through. It hurt her head, thinking it may not have been real but just her imagination.

"But that doesn't mean you remember *everything* correctly," Creed informed her.

Sage felt annoyed by the entire conversation.

"You people are making my head hurt," Dean announced in frustration, sharing Sage's sentiment, and then stood. "Keep your crazy shifter talk to yourselves. Courtney's coming back for a picnic this afternoon, and I have things to do."

CHAPTER 38

Courtney and Lindsey returned later that afternoon and planned on spending the rest of the day at the ranch with their favorite Morgan boys. Once they learned the pressure was off regarding their covert mission, everyone was able to relax and enjoy themselves. Creed was the only one not partnered up that afternoon, which was possibly a good thing. He was still brooding from his not-so-pleasant phone conversation with Sage's mother in Colfax. Obviously, he was unwilling to give up certain details regarding his questions about Sage's father. It possibly wouldn't have mattered anyway. Sage's mother tore into Creed, leaving him a little angry and emotionally battered. Sage found it hard to believe her mother went off on Creed like that. Certainly, he exaggerated. Growing up, her mother rarely had a bad temper.

Closer to dinnertime, Jackson prepared baked potatoes for the grill since they would need about an hour to cook. The corn on the cob and the steaks would be prepared closer to dinnertime. Sage watched her friends enjoying their afternoon with Lance and Dean. All four seemed to be having a good time. She finally joined Jackson near the grill.

"You've been quiet most of the afternoon," Sage remarked while studying him. "Everything okay?"

"I have a lot on my mind," he replied, then glanced at his brothers laughing with Sage's friends. "This morning, the world was good. Better than it had been in a long time, but this afternoon--"

"I know," Sage replied with a sigh. "I kind of killed the mood."

"It wasn't your fault," he announced. "You had to warn us. It was coming whether you spoke up or not. There's just so much preparation needed, and I can't get Dean to take the threat seriously." Jackson frowned and shook his head. "He sometimes thinks he's invincible."

"He'll figure it out," Sage remarked. "You raised him right."

Jackson gave her a strange look, then smiled. "I keep forgetting you have inside information about my family and conversations with me from a different time." He chuckled at the thought. "Makes me wonder what sort of secret things I told you about me. Things that I might find a bit embarrassing. My deepest darkest regrets."

"I think your biggest regret was that none of you had any children," she informed him. "You worried about the Morgan legacy ending."

Jackson eyed her and appeared somewhat surprised. "None of my brothers got married or had kids?" he asked, stunned by the admission.

Sage slowly shook her head. "You blamed yourself for giving up on women," she replied.

"Lead by example," he muttered, then managed a tiny laugh. "My twenties were pretty discouraging. I can't imagine my relationship with women got much better in my thirties."

Sage fidgeted and looked away.

Jackson snorted a laugh and shook his head. "Figures," he scoffed. "I probably isolated myself on the ranch, turned bitter, and started drinking myself into an early grave."

Sage eyed him with some surprise. "How did--?"

Jackson cast a look at her and managed a tiny laugh. "That's what my father did after his last failed attempt at a relationship." He sighed with defeat. "After he died, I turned into him." He eyed her. "How much of an asshole did I become?"

"I'll admit; fifty-year-old Jackson has his flaws," Sage informed him, then hesitated. "Remember when I told you I was only in love once, but it was complicated?"

Jackson stared at her a moment, then groaned softly. "Fifty-year-old me?"

"Yeah, fifty-year-old you," she replied.

Jackson pulled Sage into his arms and held her in a warm embrace as he nuzzled the top of her head. "I'm looking forward to falling in love with you, Sage," he whispered into her hair before kissing the top of her head. "You're making it very easy."

She sighed and pulled away, attempting to hide the tears in her eyes, then offered a tiny, tense smile. "I'm afraid I'm going to screw up," she confessed to him. "My emotions are all over the place. I'm so terrified that I'm going to time surf back to the future again that I can't even relax."

"I wish I could say something to help," Jackson replied with compassion. "Unfortunately, if your prediction is true, future events are already set in motion. The killers are out there preparing their attack on you and your family, and we can only sit and wait for them to come. We know where and when they're going to strike, but we could be proactive if we knew who they were."

"I wish I brought more to the party," Sage remarked while rubbing her chilled shoulders. "If I could control 'time freeze', maybe I could actually be useful."

"You're plenty useful," Jackson informed her. "Someone needs to guard your sister and niece in the gun vault."

Sage shot a look at him. "Seriously?" she just about demanded. "You're benching me?"

"Well, according to you," Jackson remarked. "My brothers and I live, whereas you barely make it out with your life. It's probably best if you weren't in the danger zone."

"Once we move my sister and niece to your ranch, we alter what happens," Sage informed him. "We don't know what the new outcome will be."

"Are you really going to argue with me on this?" Jackson demanded.

"I may still have gaps in my memory, but I remember finding my sister and mother butchered," Sage informed him. "I intend to do everything in my power to erase that memory and stop that future."

"Lance is confident you can control time freeze," Jackson insisted while resuming his job at the grill. "Maybe you need to work on that. You can practice before dinner. Apparently, I won't know if you do anyway." He set his glass of iced tea on the counter to the right of the grill. "Move my glass to the other side." He then offered a playful grin. "Call it my entertainment while I grill."

Sage eyed the grin on his face. "Great, now I'm doing parlor tricks."

"Humor me," he replied.

Sage sat on the bench near the grill and stared at her bracelet.

"That thing has no power, remember?" he insisted.

"I don't care," she informed him. "I need something to focus on. Now be quiet."

Jackson chuckled. "Jesus, you're cute when you're feisty," he remarked. "Like an angry little Chihuahua."

Sage glared at him. "Just remember, you're at my mercy when I freeze time," she reminded him. "Don't piss me off, or you'll be wearing your iced tea."

Jackson maintained his humor and then suddenly became silent. Sage recognized the deathly silence and looked around. Everyone was frozen in place. Sage looked up to the sky and saw a bird that had been flying overhead was now motionless as well. She couldn't deny it was pretty cool. Sage stood and looked around a moment. She picked up Jackson's glass and looked at the contents. They, too, were frozen. She turned the glass upside down and marveled at the liquid that stayed in place. She moved the glass to the opposite side of the grill, then studied Jackson and the sly grin frozen on his face. She hesitated only a moment before smiling and gently caressing his beard. She moved closer to him, warmly kissed his cheek, and pulled back just far enough to gaze into his eyes that remained fixated on the grill. She moved into his line of sight and again caressed his face.

"It's so quiet and peaceful in here," she whispered to him. "I wish I could share it with you."

Sage considered it only a moment, then warmly kissed him. Jackson returned the kiss. Sage jumped with surprise as his arms circled her waist, pulling her against him. She broke off the kiss and met his gaze.

"Sneaky little witch," he joked with a chuckle.

Sage continued to stare at him with a strange mix of fear and surprise.

Jackson appeared humored by her reaction. "What's that look about?"

"I pulled you in," she gasped.

He seemed bewildered at first, then looked at the frozen flames on the grill. Jackson released her and turned around. He stared at the frozen world around them.

"Holy shit," Jackson just about exclaimed as he took a few steps across the patio. When he was convinced of what he was actually seeing, he looked back at Sage and grinned. "How did you do that?"

She shook her head. "I don't know," Sage replied. "I just said I wished I could share this with you, and you slipped into this reality with me."

Jackson laughed enthusiastically. "Absolutely wild," he cried out and continued looking around. He then looked back at her. "Can you wake Creed? He's got to see this."

"I don't know," Sage replied and walked over to Creed, where he sat away from his other brothers and their lady friends. Sage crouched down in front of Creed and attempted to look in his eyes. "Creed?" There was no response. "Creed, I want to share this with you."

Nothing happened.

Sage groaned and looked back at Jackson. "I don't know how I did it with you," she insisted. Something then occurred to her. She leaned closer to Creed and kissed him quickly on the lips.

"Hey!" Jackson cried out, scolding her.

Creed looked down at her with some surprise. "Did you just kiss me?"

Sage sprang upright and laughed. "Can you believe that?" she announced excitedly.

"Figures," Jackson scoffed.

Creed looked around, and his expression immediately dropped. "What the--?" He sprang to his feet and checked out the patio and the bird frozen in the sky before returning his gaze to Sage and Jackson. "She pulled me in."

"Yeah, with an unauthorized lip lock," Jackson huffed his annoyance as he folded his arms across his chest.

"Oh, so you did kiss me," Creed remarked before sinking into thought. "I seriously doubt that's what did it. There has to be more to it than that."

"I should hope so," Jackson muttered. "The last thing I want is my girlfriend kissing my brothers."

"Girlfriend?" Sage asked while eyeing him.

"Hey, if fifty-year-old me was your boyfriend, that means I am too," he insisted.

Creed walked around the patio while marveling at the frozen scenery and people surrounding them. "This is incredible," he remarked. "If we can perfect whatever this spell is, we can use it to our advantage. We wouldn't even have to fight the killers. We could actually take them down without bloodshed."

"Yeah, well," Jackson casually announced. "That's not happening. I see them; I kill them. End of story."

"How long can you keep time frozen?" Creed asked.

Sage shrugged. "I'm not sure," she replied. "It's not exactly an effort. I'm guessing I can keep it like this for a while."

"Well, this is certainly going to add a whole new level of kink to our sex life," Jackson informed her.

Creed and Sage cast disapproving looks at him.

Jackson snorted a laugh. "Oh, come on," he announced boldly to Sage. "All women wish men could last a little longer. This is the perfect solution."

Creed groaned and shook his head. Sage had to hide her smile.

Jackson caught her look and chuckled. "I saw that," he teased, then winked at her. "You naughty girl."

Creed picked up his drink and turned it upside down. He chuckled his amusement at the frozen contents, then looked back at Sage.

"How do you unfreeze time?" Creed finally asked.

"I just will it," she replied while looking around.

Time resumed mid-conversation for the others. All four looked at Jackson and Sage, somewhat startled.

"How the hell did you get over here so fast?" Lance asked.

"You really need to be more observant," Jackson scoffed, leaving his brothers in the dark about what had happened.

CHAPTER 39

The dinner cookout was enjoyed by all, despite the looming threat of what would happen in the next couple of days. Somehow, Dean and Lance were able to put their problems out of their minds while entertaining Sage's friends. Possibly a gift of being young and feeling invincible. Jackson and Creed seemed to be in better spirits after their new discovery regarding Sage's time freeze ability. Sage remained cautiously optimistic, but her mother and sister's lives were on the line if they failed. They had no sooner finished eating when a woman in her late forties appeared around the side of the house, receiving looks from everyone. Sage was somewhat shocked seeing her mother at the Morgan ranch.

Grace Remington was a beautiful middle-aged woman with long, straight dirty brown hair. The years had been kind to her, making her seem almost younger than her actual age. She stood almost five-foot-seven with a generous amount of cleavage. Just by looking at her, anyone could see she was a confident, strong woman. Grace immediately received looks from all four Morgan boys, who had no idea who she was.

"Who's that?" Dean asked.

"My mother," Sage replied as she stared at her mother with disbelief while standing.

Grace sneered and just about stormed across the backyard, pausing only a few feet away from the gathering. Sage took a step closer to her mother, who immediately held her finger up, stopping her. Sage stopped on command and watched as her mother glared at the four men.

"Which one of you bastards is Creed?" Grace demanded with a growl in her tone.

Creed took a step toward her. "I spoke with you, Mrs. Remington," he announced without backing down.

Sage's mother locked eyes with Creed, and her glare turned even colder. "Who the hell do you think you are?" she snarled at him.

"Mom," Sage announced in an attempt to smooth things over.

Her mother glared at her. "What are you doing hanging around with men like this?" she demanded.

Toby and young Tobias hurried around the side of the house and quickly approached.

"You're not going to help matters, Mom," Toby informed her mother.

"I don't know what's going on around here," Grace announced in anger while eyeing the four brothers, "but I don't appreciate receiving phone calls from strange men interrogating me about my past."

"No one was interrogating--" Creed insisted but was immediately silenced.

"I've heard enough from you," Grace snapped at him, then glared at Sage. "Let's go, Sage. I don't want you hanging around with these men."

"Okay," Jackson bellowed loudly, standing his ground. "That's enough. I won't have you insulting my brothers and me on my own goddamned property."

"Jackson," Sage lightly scolded.

He didn't even look at her. "I don't care if she's your mother," Jackson announced without taking his eyes off the irate woman. "Someone's got to be the adult in the room."

Grace's eyes lit up at the comment. "You're saying I'm acting like a child?" she just about cried out.

"We've obviously gotten off to a bad start," Creed announced, attempting to smooth things over.

"You should have thought about that before you brought up Sage's father," Grace snarled at Creed.

"I'm sorry if you're offended, Mrs. Remington," Creed blurted out. "But there are bigger issues at stake here than whatever emotions and insecurities you're feeling."

"That's it; that right there," Grace fired back. "It's that attitude."

"Your mother is a completely unreasonable woman," Jackson informed Sage.

Grace sneered at Jackson. "Unreasonable," she scoffed in anger. "I know *what* you are, Mr. Morgan. I'm not being the least bit unreasonable. I don't want you anywhere near my daughter. I don't need someone like *you* corrupting her."

Jackson snorted a laugh. "Too late for that," he scoffed while smirking.

Sage gasped in horror at Jackson's words, purposely fanning the flames.

"Sage," Grace launched in anger and pointed behind her. "Let's go. Now!"

"Everyone stop!" Sage shouted.

There was absolute silence. Sage looked around and saw everyone frozen around her. She was slightly surprised that she had stopped time without even thinking about it. She took several deep breaths, attempting to calm herself before thinking of her next step. Finally, she approached her mother and placed her hand on her shoulder.

"We need to talk," Sage announced.

Her mother moved and was about to speak when she suddenly looked around. "What the hell--?" She looked back at Sage. "Did you do this?"

"Yes," Sage replied, then drew a deep tense breath. "I need you to put your defenses on the back burner because this is serious."

"Serious?" Grace scoffed and seemed mildly humored. "That man Creed rattling on about foreshadowing the future? Is that what I'm supposed to take seriously?"

"It's all true, Mom," she insisted.

"How do you know?" Grace demanded, then sneered at Jackson, who was frozen a few feet from her. "You can't trust *his* kind."

"What do you mean *his* kind?" Sage asked while shaking her head. "You don't even know Jackson and his brothers. They're witches like us."

Grace snorted a laugh as her eyes widened, and she vigorously shook her head. "Oh, no," she announced. "They're nothing like us. They're warlocks. They come from evil stock."

Sage stared at her mother with some surprise. "Why would you say that?"

"Because it's true," Grace informed her.

Sage eyed her mother for a long moment, then slowly shook her head. "You don't know them," she remarked and appeared curious. "Or do you?"

Grace sneered at Jackson, who was frozen with that smug smile on his face. "Oh, I know their family lineage," she remarked, then met Sage's gaze. "Not them personally, but I'd met their father."

"You knew their father?" Sage asked with surprise, then immediately tensed. "Please don't tell me we share the same father."

Grace suddenly shot a look at Sage and appeared almost horrified. "Heaven's no!" she launched, then shook her head. "You didn't actually have relations with that swamp dweller, did you?"

Sage held her breath a moment, then attempted to relax. "Jackson's not a bad man," she insisted. "And he's certainly not a swamp dweller."

"Your sister will need to develop a particularly strong bath salt for you to soak in," her mother remarked. "Probably take hours to detox his evil from your skin."

"Okay, that's enough," Sage growled at her mother while folding her arms across her chest. "I'm extremely fond of Jackson, and there's nothing that you can say or do that'll stop me from seeing him."

"Careful," Grace remarked and raised a brow. "I may accept that as a challenge."

"Okay, enough," Sage scolded her mother, surprising her. "I know the subject of my father is a sore one for you, but we need that information. Our future; our lives may depend upon it."

"Again with the future?" Grace demanded. "What have those filthy warlocks indoctrinated into your mind?"

"They didn't do anything to me," Sage insisted. "In fact, I'm pretty sure it was the other way around."

Grace studied her a moment and cocked her head. "What's that supposed to mean?"

"I time surfed twenty years into the future," Sage informed her mother.

Grace's expression suddenly dropped. "What?"

"I was stuck twenty years in the future after some psycho killer attacked me--two days from now," Sage informed her astonished mother. "He attacks me after he kills you and Toby."

CHAPTER 40

While Dean and Lance entertained Courtney and Lindsey on the back patio, Sage and her family joined Jackson and Creed in the study. Tobias was given a pair of noise-canceling headphones and watched a movie on Jackson's computer at his desk. The little girl seemed oblivious to the conversation being had by the adults. Grace had finally cooled off despite giving Jackson and Creed dirty looks.

"Thank you for helping us, Mrs. Remington," Creed announced while studying her where she sat on the sofa between Sage and Toby.

"I'm doing this for my daughters," Grace informed him with a slight hiss in her tone. She seemed unusually uncomfortable while fiddling with her glass of brandy. "I don't like talking about their father. It was never my intention that they know anything about him."

"If it's that important to you," Creed insisted with some compassion, "you and I could discuss it in private."

"No," Sage and Toby launched in unison.

Jackson remained comfortably leaning against the front of his desk and eyed Grace. "Seems as if your daughters want to know," he announced.

Grace glared at Jackson with daggers in her eyes. "It's none of your business."

"Kind of is," Jackson muttered.

"Don't start," Sage announced while shooting glares at both. "Let's just get this over with so we can figure out our next move."

"Fine," Grace scoffed and sat back on the sofa, folding her arms across her chest. She glared at Creed and remained uncomfortable. "Their father was Wolfram."

Sage and Toby cast looks at each other past their mother as if waiting for the rest of the name or some explanation. Were they supposed to know him? Grace locked eyes with Creed, who stared at her with a strange look of horror on his face. Jackson immediately straightened and seemed tense.

"Wolfram?" Creed asked while starting to fidget, now uncomfortable as well.

Sage and Toby were slightly surprised by both men's reactions to the name drop.

"Yes, Wolfram," Grace scoffed and now appeared uncomfortable herself.

Sage and Toby shot looks across the room.

"Who's Wolfram?" Toby was the first to ask.

"And why is everyone suddenly so uncomfortable?" Sage asked the logical follow-up question.

"Wolfram was a powerful warlock," Creed replied and seemed unable to relax now. "Had a seriously bad, uh, reputation."

Jackson again leaned against the desk and thoughtfully scratched his beard. "It was rumored he sired about, oh, five hundred or so children over the last two centuries." Jackson then raised his brows while eyeing Grace. "With five hundred *different* women."

Grace sneered at Jackson. "I'm going to kill that man," she scoffed.

"Just stating facts, *Ms.* Remington," Jackson informed her. "And maybe a polite suggestion about checking the skeletons in your own closet before looking for them in mine."

"That's it! He's dead!" Grace shouted and just about jumped up from the sofa to reach Jackson.

Although Grace didn't take her eyes off Jackson, Sage and Toby caught her arms and pulled her back down.

"Hey," Jackson announced with a humored smirk on his face. "I can't help it if I was born a filthy warlock, but you were the one who was fuck--"

"Jackson," Sage cried out in anger. "That's not helping!"

"I don't understand," Toby now announced, almost horror-stricken, and turned on the sofa to face her mother. "Who was this infamous warlock? And why is he our father?"

"We have five hundred brothers and sisters?" Sage demanded with the follow-up question.

Jackson again rested against the edge of his desk, folded his arms across his chest, and stared at Grace. Creed seemed less arrogant but was just as curious to hear the answer.

Grace was now squirming in her seat while eyeing both her daughters and then the two men before them. "I don't feel comfortable discussing this in front of *them*," she informed Sage and Toby. She then focused her venomous wrath on Creed. "You have your name. Do whatever it is you need to do with that information. The rest is none of your business."

Grace sprang up from the sofa and stormed out of the study, slamming the door behind her. Toby groaned and hurried after their mother. Sage remained silently seated and stared at the floor for a long moment. She finally lifted her eyes and glanced at Jackson and Creed.

"If this guy is my father, what does it mean?" Sage asked either man who'd respond.

"Well," Jackson announced with a deep sigh while straightening. "It *definitely* means your family is more fucked up than mine."

"I'm being serious, Jackson," Sage launched back. "Who is this warlock? Is it bad?"

"Wolfram was a powerful warlock," Creed informed Sage.

"Was?" she asked. "So he's dead then?"

"Unknown," Creed replied almost dryly. "No one has seen him in the last couple of decades."

"Do I really have that many brothers and sisters?" she pressed.

"According to legend, yes," Creed replied. "No one really knows for sure." He then shook his head. "It's strange, though."

"Yeah, you can say that again," Sage muttered while gently massaging her temple.

"I meant, strange that he impregnated your mother twice," Creed remarked. "Wolfram was--" He hesitated. "How do I say this politely?"

"A 'once and done' kind of guy," Jackson replied. "He put himself out to stud. Saw himself as the perfect breeding stock. Like me breeding Raven."

Creed cast a look at Jackson.

Jackson caught his brother's look and groaned. "Yeah, I'll be quiet now," he muttered.

"No, that was actually pretty accurate," Creed remarked, then looked back at Sage. "He sought out women who were, shall we say, worthy to bear his offspring. The fact that he returned to your mother is quite strange. Jackson is correct. According to my research, he only ever copulated once with any one witch."

Sage eyed Creed almost suspiciously. "How could he possibly impregnate that many women on the first try?" she finally asked.

Creed shifted uncomfortably, then cast a quick glance at Jackson before looking back at Sage. "Wolfram was a powerful warlock and notoriously evil," he replied somewhat delicately and again looked back at Jackson, hoping for some sort of rescue.

"He was shooting with loaded dice," Jackson bluntly informed her.

Sage eyed Jackson with some confusion, then suddenly realized what he was saying. "He knew exactly when the women were fertile?"

"Close," Creed replied while remaining uncomfortable. "It was rumored he used his powers to ensure each woman became pregnant on the first try."

Sage stared at Creed with something resembling shock. "How is that possible?" she gasped.

"It's an old warlock trick," Creed gently explained while shifting. "Centuries ago, warlocks would often use it to ensure the survival of their lineage."

Sage sat still and silent a moment as his words sank in. Jackson's words from early that morning came back to haunt her. *"Then I should probably knock you up before you come to your senses."* Sage looked at Jackson with something resembling horror.

"Is that why my mother freaked out about us?" Sage gasped.

"I'm sure she's had her fair share of morning regret," Jackson informed Sage. "It would only be natural for her to think the worst."

Sage continued to stare at him. "You joked around about 'knocking me up'," she reminded him as her mind reeled. Sage slowly stood without taking her eyes off him. "Was it just a joke?"

Jackson appeared surprised at the question and stood somewhat defensively. "I didn't impregnate you, Sage," he insisted. "I wouldn't *intentionally* do that."

"But you know the spell?" Sage practically demanded.

There was an unusual hesitation from both men, shocking Sage. She glared at Jackson and his brother.

"You both know the spell?" she cried out.

"It's a puberty thing," Jackson insisted, waving it off. "All warlock boys *know* the spell, but we also know it's against our code of honor to use it."

"That's the interesting thing about warlocks," Sage scoffed defensively. "They don't exactly have a code of honor."

"I resent that," Creed was the first to launch back, now offended. "Our father instilled the warlock code of honor upon us. He raised us right."

Sage looked from Creed to Jackson with surprise. "Your father was a warlock?" she asked, then raised a cocky brow. "You said your mother was a witch."

Jackson fidgeted while Creed shot a surprised look at his brother.

"You didn't tell her about our father?" Creed asked.

"If I had told you, you'd freak out, just like your mother had," Jackson insisted, then held his breath a moment. "Yes, our mother was a witch, and our father was a warlock."

She couldn't believe what she was hearing and then quickly turned angry. "If I'm pregnant, you'll have a lot of explaining to do," Sage snarled.

"If you're pregnant, I'm not the only possible candidate," Jackson responded defensively.

The comment took a moment to register. "Jackson in the future?" Sage demanded, then shook her head in anger. "He wouldn't do that."

"Wouldn't he?" Jackson asked while cocking his head. "He's a lot older and probably more desperate than I am to carry on the family name." He then raised an arrogant brow. "You also said he didn't tell you that our mother was a witch. Sounds like he has more motive than I do."

"Now you're just making excuses," Sage snarled in anger.

Jackson drew a deep breath and held it, attempting to keep the conversation from spiraling into an argument. "I wasn't shooting with loaded dice, Sage," he gently replied. "I wouldn't do that to you--or myself for that matter."

"What's that supposed to mean?" Sage asked, not convinced but now curious.

"It's very easy to terminate a pregnancy in today's day and age," he informed her. "I couldn't live with myself knowing I caused that."

"Well, you'll understand if I don't take your word on that," Sage insisted. "I'll be taking a test first thing tomorrow morning. I'm also going to suggest it to Lindsey, Courtney, and Kennedy as well."

Creed frowned and glared at Jackson. "Now I'm being dragged into this?" he snarled at his brother.

"Oh, as if this is my fault?" Jackson snapped back. "I'm not the one who knocked up five hundred women. Blame that guy."

"Can we just stop talking about this?" Sage blurted out, then groaned. "The whole conversation is making me sick to my stomach."

Creed again glared at his brother, then stood. "Excuse me," he announced. "I'm just going to run out to the pharmacy and end this right now."

Both watched Creed leave the study.

"I wonder how long it'll take him to remember that the pharmacy is closed on Sundays," Jackson remarked.

"Aunt Sage," Tobias announced, reminding them that she was still there.

Sage and Jackson looked back at the little girl behind the desk, now holding her headphones.

"Are you going to be a mommy?" Tobias asked.

Sage managed a tiny, tense smile and approached her niece. "No, Tobias," she replied. "I don't know what you heard, but we were just joking around." She cast a look at Jackson. "My *new friend* has a warped sense of humor."

"Well, at least we're still friends," Jackson muttered.

"For now," Sage scoffed.

CHAPTER 41

Despite what happened in the study between Sage's family and Jackson and Creed, Sage's friends remained oblivious to everything. If Lance had been interested, he quickly forgot while in Lindsey's company. Dean was more interested in Courtney than any 'family business'. Sage finally joined her mother and Toby on the patio with little Tobias in tow. Grace saw them and practically jumped up from her seat.

"We should go," their mother announced. "We never should have come here in the first place."

"Come on, Mom," Sage moaned and frowned at her mother's poor attitude. "This is important."

"Yes, and we can handle it ourselves," Grace insisted. "We don't need those men hanging around. We already know everything we need to know to remain safe. The three of us can handle this."

"I understand your reluctance," Sage replied, then shifted uncomfortably. "But we're stronger together."

Grace groaned and rolled her eyes. "Dear Lord," she announced. "He's gotten into your head."

"He and his brothers have already dealt with this on several occasions," Sage reminded her mother. "I know you don't want to hear it, but we're safer with them."

"With them?" her mother gasped with horror on her face. "You mean you want us to stay here?" She shook her head. "You can't let that man get into your head, Sage. You don't know what he's capable of doing."

"Believe me," Sage announced with a defeated sigh. "I got quite the education, but we're still safer here and in greater numbers."

"What about Paul?" Toby asked.

"They don't want Paul," Sage reminded her. "Besides, he wasn't around for the final act. He'll be fine. He just needs to continue on his current path."

"What about your friends?" Toby then questioned.

"They were planning on going home tonight," Sage remarked. "Besides, they're not targets."

"Maybe we should all just go to my house in Colfax," Grace insisted. "That would be the better solution."

"We don't know that we'll be safe there," Sage reminded her mother. "If this has been pre-planned, it may just follow us there."

"What's following us?" Tobias asked, now curious.

"Nothing, sweetie," Toby replied to her daughter's question. "Why don't you ask Lindsey to take you to the barn and show you the horses?"

"Okay," she replied, then hurried across the back patio, interrupting Lindsey and Lance, who were practically cuddling around the fire pit.

"I don't want Tobias anywhere near this," Toby insisted firmly. "We need to get her out of here."

"We all need to get out of here," Grace replied. "We'll take a nice, long road trip."

"Creed mentioned the possibility of shifters," Sage informed her mother and sister.

Both stared at her a moment with some surprise and possible concern.

"Shifters?" Toby just about gasped. "Are they even real?"

"Of course they're real," Grace replied, then shook her head. "But no one has seen one in over one hundred years. The chances this involves a shifter is slim to none."

"Over the past week, I've seen and done things I would never have imagined," Sage informed her mother and sister. "I'm not ruling anything out at this point. You could tell me aliens are behind it, and I'm keeping an open mind." She glared at both women. "In two days, I'm attacked along with my mother and sister. I intend to do everything in my power to stop that from happening." She then glared at her mother. "I don't care how much you hate warlocks. Those four men are our best hope for getting through this and stopping it from ever happening again. Just put your personal issues aside for the rest of our sakes."

Grace brooded a moment and finally looked at Sage. "I can make an effort," she replied. "But I want full disclosure from them. I want to know what they bring to the party, and I don't mean weapons. I want to know what 'talent' they have. What they can do."

"And when this is all over," Toby announced, then looked at their mother. "I want to know what happened with our father."

Grace had to look away. She didn't seem pleased by the demand. "We'll have a rational discussion."

§

Despite being unpopular, Sage and Jackson had to get Courtney and Lindsey away from the ranch. Getting her friends to leave wasn't difficult, but not going with them was a bit of an issue. Dean and Lance weren't very happy with their brother for suggesting they send their 'company' away, but it was a school night for the brothers. Eventually, Lindsey and Courtney left for the tavern with the false claim that Sage would join them a little later before they returned home to Colfax.

Sage used a fight with Jackson that needed to be sorted out first as an excuse. It wasn't exactly a lie. This time, they held their meeting in the living room so Tobias could watch a movie in one area while they were free to talk just out of earshot. Grace was still in a foul mood, but she reluctantly agreed to play nice with Jackson and his brothers for her daughters' sake.

"Can we at least agree that we'll hole up here in two nights?" Jackson asked somewhat gruffly, already having his fill of Sage's mother.

"Under extreme duress, yes," Grace remarked with her arms folded across her chest and her crossed leg swinging aggressively enough to convey her annoyance.

"I can get my hands on some security cameras," Lance informed them. "I can mount them around the house. Anyone coming at us will be seen a mile away."

"And then we'll blast them full of holes," Dean remarked, clearly irritated with the entire topic. "It's not rocket science. We know when they're going to hit. If they even find us out here."

"If they're actually shifters--" Creed began.

"They're not shifters," Dean scoffed while glaring at his brother. "Do you know how ridiculous you sound?"

"I don't care," Creed snapped back. "We need to be ready in the event that they are."

"Okay," Toby announced while shifting her attention to Creed. "Let's suppose they are shifters. They can live one hundred years or more, right?"

"Yes," Creed replied.

"And if they choose their targets in advance, they're probably someone we already know," Toby continued, then looked around the room. "Anyone in town, for that matter."

"Yes and no," Creed informed her. "According to Sage, Jackson kills one of them two days from now, but there was a second one. So we're dealing with at least two. In order to fit into that particular shifter box, it would have to be someone with few people to vouch for them."

"That makes no sense," Grace scoffed.

"It actually does," Toby informed her mother. "The three of us are related and grew up together. We're not shifters. Jackson and his brothers grew up together, so they're not shifters." She then shrugged. "Courtney and Lindsey--? We don't know much about them. They could be shifters."

"They're not," Dean remarked.

"Yeah, I don't think so either," Sage announced. "I mean, I went to college with them."

"But if you don't know their family, you can't be sure," Creed reminded her. "Just because the murders take place here, that doesn't mean you and your mother weren't being watched in Colfax. We don't know if Grace or Toby was the killer's initial target."

"Or both," Lance added and received looks. He then shrugged. "We know there are two of them. One could have been keeping an eye on Sage, sticking close to her while the other was here in town, watching Toby."

"Then the killers could be almost anyone," Grace scoffed, somewhat outraged. "If there are two of them, they can vouch for each other."

"True," Creed replied.

"Maybe Sage's trip to the future can shed some light on our killer," Jackson remarked, then eyed Sage. "Is there anyone conspicuously missing in the future that you've seen around town? If I kill one of them in two nights, they wouldn't be around in the future."

"I don't know the people in this town as well as the rest of you," she reminded him. "I know a few more in the future, but only by a couple of months."

"Such as--?" Lance pressed.

"Well, Jackson's poker buddies," Sage replied.

"I don't play poker," Jackson again reminded her.

"You do in the future," she reminded him. "The bartender, Fat Matt, and Slim play poker with you on Friday nights."

"Some pretty scummy company I keep in the future," Jackson muttered.

"Well--" Grace was about to add when Sage shot her a look, silencing her.

"Uh, there's Kennedy," Sage remarked. "In the future, she divorces her husband."

"Who didn't see that coming?" Toby muttered.

"Focus," Creed remarked, not wanting to trash talk Kennedy.

"There's the sheriff and his deputy," Sage continued. "A whole bunch of people I've seen but don't really know all that well."

"Anyone different in the future?" Creed pressed.

"Lots of different people," Sage insisted. "My friends Shelly and Henry. They're sister and brother. They only lived in town about a year. Uh, Toby's boyfriend."

"Paul?" Toby asked with surprise.

"Uh, no," Sage replied, then fidgeted. "Your daughter Toby when she's in her twenties."

"That creeps me out," Toby muttered. "My little girl dating."

"Well, she's not so little in the future," Sage responded, then frowned. "Although her boyfriend is cringe-worthy."

Toby rolled her eyes. "Don't tell me," she announced. "I don't want to know."

"She grew up differently than she would have with you in her life," Sage reminded her. "Things will be different, I promise."

"Who are these friends of yours in the future?" Creed asked.

"Just friends," Sage replied with a shrug. "She's nice. He's a bit of a prick. He's always getting into fights with the Morgan boys." Sage hesitated and looked at the four Morgan boys, who were now staring at her. "You know, the four of you in the future."

"That's interesting," Creed announced while considering it. "This guy, Henry, is friends with you, but he's also in our circle?"

"Yes, but Shelly is his sister," Sage reminded him. "They vouch for each other, remember?"

"Maybe, but what if the one Jackson shot that night didn't actually die?" Creed asked while eyeing her. "Jackson of the future said he couldn't find the body."

"Enough with the shifters already," Dean moaned and sat forward. "Can we just discuss the plan where we shoot them in the head?"

"Look," Grace announced and finally sat forward, putting Sage and Toby on edge. "I agreed to play nice with you boys. Now, I want full disclosure. What do you boys bring to the table?"

"A secluded ranch and an arsenal of weapons," Jackson informed her, then returned the cocky look. "What do you bring?"

"Let me rephrase that for the less developed warlocks in the room," Grace announced while squinting at Jackson. "What sort of powers do the four of you have?"

"Powers?" Jackson asked, then shook his head. "We don't have any powers that would be useful in battle." He hesitated and eyed her. "Do you?"

"Considering my daughters' pedigrees--" Grace announced, then raised her brows.

"Did I miss something?" Dean asked while casting looks around the room.

Creed and Jackson hesitated a moment before exchanging looks. They finally looked back at Grace.

"You say that as if you hand-picked their father," Jackson remarked.

Grace's smile faded at the comment. "That's ridiculous."

Sage and Toby glanced at their mother, who now seemed tense and fidgeted.

"Did you?" Toby asked.

Grace's expression turned into a frown. "Wolfram sought out witches based on their bloodlines," she remarked. "I don't see why I shouldn't expect the same of the man who father's my children."

"Wolfram?" Lance asked as his expression dropped. He then looked at Sage and Toby. "Your father is Wolfram?"

"Don't look so surprised," Sage scoffed with disgust. "Five hundred children. Eventually, you'd have to run into one of them."

Dean groaned and rubbed his eyes. "This day just keeps getting weirder," he muttered.

"You knew it was him," Creed announced with some surprise. "You knew it was Wolfram and that he'd impregnate you."

Grace frowned and avoided looking at him. "I wanted children," she insisted. "I wanted *exceptional* children."

"Okay," Jackson replied with a sigh. "So back to my original question. What sort of powers do you have?"

Grace again glared at Jackson. "I'm starting to hate you all over again," she scoffed. "I have a few tricks up my sleeve." She then eyed Sage. "Stay out of that man's bed."

"Don't worry," Jackson scoffed. "You already killed any chances Sage and I have for a relationship with your warlock bashing. Maybe she'll grow old and miserable with her mother."

Grace looked as if she would leap from her chair for Jackson. Sage and Toby placed a hand on her to keep her from reacting. "Better than hooking up with some filthy warlock," she scoffed. "You'll just knock her up and abandon her."

"Oh, you're not actually brooding over Wolfram, are you?" Jackson remarked, then smirked. "You don't knowingly jump into bed with someone like that and expect a commitment. That would be plain stupid."

"Maybe I was young and naïve," Grace scoffed while glaring at Jackson. "But my daughters won't make those same mistakes."

"Well, in one regard, she already did," Jackson snapped back. "But, hey, why would you want her to be happy? Right? If you're lucky, she'll never find a suitable partner, and then she won't leave you like the other one did."

Toby now shifted uncomfortably.

"Ironically, Toby never moved back to Colfax when things didn't work out with Tobias's father," Jackson remarked, then eyed Grace. "I wonder why that is?"

"Okay," Sage snarled, interrupting the two. "That's enough from both of you." She then looked at Creed. "This isn't getting us anywhere. Maybe we should come up with two separate plans, compare notes, and combine forces later."

"Great idea," Dean announced and jumped from his seat. "I'm heading to the tavern to meet Courtney."

"It's a school night," Jackson reminded him in a stern tone. "You have an early morning."

"Hey," Dean announced boldly. "Just because you ruined your love life before it started, don't try to sabotage mine." He straightened proudly. "I'm going out."

As Dean left the room, Lance glanced at his oldest brother. Jackson rolled his eyes and nodded, releasing Lance from his invisible hold. Lance jumped up from his chair and hurried after Dean.

"We should get going," Toby announced and glanced at her watch. "It's past Tobias's bedtime."

Grace was quick to leap from the middle seat on the sofa. "Thank God," she cried out. "Let's go home."

As Toby headed across the room to get Tobias, Grace turned toward Sage. "I'll drive home with you," she announced matter-of-factly. "That way, we can speak privately without Tobias listening in."

"I'll be along later," Sage informed her mother, surprising her. She then indicated Jackson. "Jackson and I have some things we need to discuss."

Grace stared at Sage a moment and appeared almost concerned. "You are coming home, though, right?"

"Eventually," Sage replied with little emotion. "You don't need to wait up."

Her mother didn't seem happy about the lack of an answer but reluctantly left. Creed walked them to the door, giving Sage and Jackson some privacy. Jackson had a difficult time looking her in the eyes.

"I'm sorry for being a prick to your mother," he remarked and shook his head. "I have a difficult time letting people talk down to me."

"Actually, I understand," Sage replied, surprising him.

"Really?"

"She wasn't exactly nice to you either," Sage reminded him. "I certainly didn't expect you to take her abuse. If the situation had been reversed, I know I wouldn't have handled it well either."

Jackson now stared into her eyes and sighed. "I know there's a lot of negative opinions of warlocks, particularly in the witch community, but we're not all bad," he remarked. "I'm not trying to trap you or turn you into the human version of Karma. I enjoy being with you. You're the first woman, witch or not, that I've connected with in a long time." He then considered the comment. "Maybe ever. I just don't want that thrown away because your mother hates warlocks."

Sage placed her hand on his face and gently caressed his beard. "I'm not going to let my mother ruin anything," she informed him. "Of course, I'm going to religiously pee on a stick once a week just to keep you honest."

Jackson smiled with relief. "I'll buy you a whole case of them, if it'll make you happy," he insisted, then took a step closer to her while placing his arms around her waist. "I know it's a school night, but I'd love for you to sleep over."

"Maybe tomorrow night," she replied while caressing his chest.

Jackson offered a tiny, disappointed smile. "I'll take whatever you're offering," he replied.

Sage glanced at her watch, met his gaze, and smiled. "I should probably leave," she remarked, then shrugged. "--in an hour or so."

He seemed intrigued and raised his brows. "Oh?" Jackson asked, then chuckled. "Did you want to watch a movie?" His grin increased. "Or mess around?"

Sage grinned, pulled away while taking his hand, and led him from the living room.

CHAPTER 42

Jackson groaned while gathering Sage in his arms and pulled her against his bare chest, where they collapsed on his bed together. His room was dimly lit, allowing for a romantic glow. Jackson attempted to look at Sage while she clung to him, nuzzling his chest.

"I'll admit," he announced with a tiny laugh. "I was afraid you weren't going to let me touch you ever again."

"Fortunately for you, you're the only Jackson in this timeline," Sage remarked, then flashed a smirk before shutting her eyes. "You're also a little too good in the sack."

Jackson chuckled lowly and kissed the top of her head. "Whatever reason you choose to keep me around, I'll take it," he replied cheerfully. "You were out of my league *before* I found out you were a witch."

"That makes me more attractive, huh?"

"Having Wolfram as your daddy, not so much," he replied, then chuckled. "But most warlocks would kill to be in a relationship with a witch." He shrugged. "Witches, on the other hand, not a big fan of warlocks. Even us half breeds."

"Yeah, I get that," Sage replied before sighing dramatically. "My mother's probably already working on a spell that'll make you impotent."

"Keep talking about your mother, and she won't need a spell," he remarked.

Sage smacked his chest and then lightly laughed. "You're horrible."

"Yeah, but you knew that going in," he insisted and again kissed the top of her head. "Stay."

"I can't," she replied.

"Actually, you can," he remarked and reestablished his hold on her. "I refuse to let go."

Sage nuzzled his chest and sighed softly. "A few more minutes." The words barely left her lips before she drifted off to sleep.

§

Sage woke in Jackson's bed and immediately realized she was alone. She slowly sat up while clutching the sheet to her naked body and looked around the dimly lit room. She could see the beginning of sunrise through the part in the bedroom curtains. She'd spent the entire night! She looked at the bedside clock and saw it was five in the morning. Sage groaned and reached for her discarded clothes. Curse Jackson for letting her sleep all night. He was probably already outside feeding the horses. Once she was dressed, she headed down the hall for the back stairs. Despite the early hour and a Monday, no less, Sage expected more activity this time of the morning, but there wasn't any activity from any of the brothers' bedrooms. The brothers would be having breakfast by six, so they could be out with the cattle by seven.

It seemed strange that she didn't hear anyone rustling around, and when she entered the kitchen, she discovered it was still dark. Sage headed through the kitchen, down the hall, and for the front door. Jackson had to be in the barn, still feeding the horses. Since his brothers went out last night, against Jackson's wishes, it was possible they got in late and wanted a few more minutes to sleep. As Sage stepped onto the porch, she looked out to the barn with an interior light on. Her eyes then strayed to a man sprawled out, face down on the ground, halfway from the barn to the house. Sage gasped in alarm and bolted from the porch. As she got closer, she saw it was Dean. She prayed he had been drunk and just passed out. Sage dropped alongside him and touched his shoulder.

"Dean?" she gasped.

To her horror, Dean was cold to the touch. Sage removed her hand and gasped, her heart now racing at the discovery. It had to be a mistake. To be certain, she felt his neck for a pulse and immediately felt something wet and sticky against her fingers. When she pulled her hand back, she saw blood on her fingertips. Sage wanted to shout for help, but she felt compelled to roll him over instead. With some effort, she rolled Dean's cold body onto his back. When she saw the jagged knife gash across his throat, the horrifying images of her dead mother and sister flashed through her mind. There was no mistaking the manner of Dean's death. Horror filled her. She wanted to scream, but she resisted. It was possible she was also in danger. Her thoughts then raced in the brief seconds she remained kneeling on the ground alongside Jackson's dead brother. If he was that cold, he'd been dead for hours. Possibly all night.

Jackson would have seen his dead brother on his way to the barn. Her heart suddenly sank. Why was the ranch so quiet? The revelation frightened her. Sage sprang to her feet and looked around. Nothing moved. She ran to the barn, slowing before the open door. She hesitated a moment and cautiously peered inside in case it was a trap. Lance was partially sprawled across a displaced bale of hay toward the middle of the barn. His eyes were open, and dried blood soaked the front of his shirt from a large gash across his throat. Sage held back her horrified scream. Her heart was now pounding as her fears spiked. She saw the shotgun near his outstretched hand. Sage took a deep breath and darted across the aisle closer to him to retrieve his weapon. She looked in each stall as she hurried past, but she didn't see anyone.

Sage picked up the pump-action shotgun and pumped it. It made a distinctive, loud clatter that would terrify even the hardest of men. As she cautiously crossed the barn for the main entrance, she glanced inside the tack room. Several saddles were thrown across the room while others were missing. Someone saddled horses! Jackson and Creed? Where were they? She had to find them. As she left the barn, she looked around at the rapidly brightening countryside surrounding the farm. She then saw something mildly frightening down the driveway. Her eyes widened in horror, and she took off down the driveway toward a wrecked car just before the tree line. As she got closer, her fears were confirmed. It was Toby's car! Sage nervously slowed as she neared the badly demolished vehicle.

The driver's side door was open, and a woman was on the ground not far from the open door. Sage continued closer, unable to take her eyes off the motionless woman. She felt her body tremble as she was now able to identify her sister. The entire front of Toby's shirt was covered in blood from a deep slit across her throat. Sage fought her tears, then quickly pulled herself together and scanned the surrounding woods. In her emotional state, the killer could have been standing alongside her, and she wouldn't have noticed him. She just about broke down when she saw someone in the vehicle's passenger seat. Sage took several deep breaths, burying her emotions deep inside, and then rounded the car while raising the shotgun. She scanned the area with a little more conviction as she approached the passenger side. Sage swiftly opened the door and looked at the dead man slumped in the passenger seat.

Before she even got a good look at him, he fell from the car and onto the ground. Sage stared at Paul, who had been stabbed in the chest and shoulder. He, too, was dead. Why had Toby and Paul come to the Morgan ranch last night? Had they come looking for her? Was this her fault? Tobias! Sage looked in the back seat. Thankfully, it was empty. She must have left Tobias at home with their mother. Sage knew she had to find Jackson and Creed. They had to be alive. Someone saddled some horses. Certainly, they'd gotten away. But why didn't they wake her? If the killer didn't know she was there, maybe they were leading the killer away from the house to keep her safe.

CHAPTER 43

Sage hurried back to the house while keeping the shotgun raised and ready to fire. Nothing seemed to move. It was now light enough that she could see the entire ranch except for a few shadowy areas. She scanned the area while approaching the house with caution. Sage then caught a glimpse of a saddled horse grazing not far from the fence line. She approached the horse and recognized it as Dean's horse. Sage's head was now spinning. She didn't know if she should phone the sheriff, search the house, or check the nearby pastures for Jackson and Creed. It was getting harder and harder to keep it together, especially after finding her sister dead. The killers struck two days early! Why? How could she let this happen? How had she slept through the attack?

When the horse lifted its head, she felt compelled to touch its nose. Sage could feel her entire body trembling. She was going to lose it, but she needed to hold it together. She needed to find Jackson and Creed. Sage looked past the horse to the path alongside the fenced pasture. In the distance, she saw

Raven saddled and grazing near the tree line. It was Jackson's horse! Sage slung the shotgun over her shoulder and jumped onto Dean's horse without hesitation. She was barely in the seat when she kicked it, racing in the direction of Jackson's beloved horse. As she got closer, she could see Raven had his head hanging down close to the grass, but he wasn't grazing. She then saw the second saddled horse flat on the ground.

Sage dismounted Dean's horse so fast that she nearly fell to the grass. She hurried for the two horses and saw Raven was standing over Karma. The mare was dead. Sage slowly approached Raven, feeling the horse's anguish. Raven barely lifted his head as she approached and looked at her. His mouth hung open with blood dripping from his tongue that was hanging out. The horse's breathing was heavy and labored. She then saw the jagged gash across Raven's throat with both fresh and dried blood. He was dying a slow, painful death. Sage felt her eyes swelling with tears as she comforted the dying horse. She swiftly removed the bridle, tossed it aside, and rubbed Raven's forehead gently. She drew a deep breath before hastily removing the saddle, wanting to make the horse as comfortable as possible.

She no sooner tossed the saddle to the ground when the horse groaned and sank to his front knees. His hind end swiftly followed, and he fell to his side with a loud groan. Raven took two deep breaths and then became motionless while his eyes remained open. The image of the dead horse with his eyes open and blood covering his mouth would haunt her forever. She felt compelled to stare at the dead horse a moment longer. Under what circumstance would Jackson leave Raven to suffer? He would never have taken off without putting the suffering animal down. Sage felt almost weak now. She needed to find Jackson and Creed. They had to be somewhere. Had they been riding the horses? Or had the horses gotten this far without riders? She was about to mount Dean's horse when she caught a glimpse of someone sitting beside a tree in the woods. She raised the shotgun and stared a moment.

"Jackson?" she finally called out. "Creed?"

There was no answer, but there also wasn't any movement from the person she'd seen either. Sage kept the shotgun raised and quickly but cautiously approached the woods. As she got closer, horror swept over her. Creed sat on the ground with his back against the tree. His throat was covered in dried blood with a large amount of blood down the front of his shirt. Sage felt panic sweep through her as she fought her tears. She saw the second body close to his as she walked closer to him. Sage stared at her dead mother with a slit across her throat and her eyes wide open. Sage could barely control the tears when something suddenly dawned on her, and her heart nearly stopped. If her mother, sister, and Paul were at the ranch, where was Tobias?

Sage felt a sudden surge of energy sweep over her. Tobias wasn't at home by herself! She had to be here! Two horses, two bodies. Sage hurried back for Dean's saddled horse and sprang onto its back. She raced the horse along the fence line, past the barn, and back to the house. She pulled the horse into a sliding stop not far from the porch steps and leaped off before the horse had even fully stopped. This time she did fall to the ground. Sage picked herself up and ran onto the porch. She pulled the shotgun from over her shoulder and held it in her trembling arms as she entered the house. It was too much ground to cover, and she needed to find her niece now!

"Toby!" she screamed as loud as she could, then listened a moment. "Toby!"

Sage ran toward the kitchen while looking around. That's when she saw the droplets of blood near the open basement door. Sage lurched for the open doorway, turned on the stairwell lights, and aimed the shotgun down the steps. There were more droplets of blood leading into the basement.

"Toby!" she again screamed and listened.

Sage thought she heard something, although she could have been mistaken. She didn't hesitate and rapidly headed down the steps while keeping the shotgun aimed. Once she reached the bottom of the steps, she looked around. The blood led into the wine cellar.

"Toby!"

"Aunt Sage," Tobias called back, sounding muffled and far away.

Sage ran for the closed wine cellar door and attempted to open it, but it didn't budge. "Toby, are you in there?" she cried out.

"I'm in here!" Toby cried back, although it sounded as if she were in the armory and not the wine cellar.

"I'm coming, Toby," she called out through the door. "Don't be scared! Get down on the floor and stay away from the door!"

Sage raised the shotgun, aimed it at the wine cellar lock, and pulled the trigger. With the shotgun blast, the lock was obliterated. She kicked in the door and looked across the wine cellar. There was more blood leading to the armory.

"Toby?"

"I'm in here, Aunt Sage!" Toby cried out in a frightened voice. "Is it safe?"

Sage shut her eyes and held her breath. "Yeah, it's safe," she replied.

The armory door was unlocked and opened, revealing Tobias with blood covering the entire front of her shirt. Sage hurried for her niece.

"Are you okay?" Sage gasped and quickly looked over her. "Where are you hurt?"

"I'm okay," Tobias softly replied, then backed away from the door.

Sage could feel her heart pounding so hard that she thought it would rip through her chest. She stepped inside the armory and saw Jackson propped against the wall alongside the door with a shotgun across his lap. There was a cut on his throat. It wasn't enough to kill him immediately, but with the amount of blood on his shirt, he didn't make it much beyond securing Tobias in the armory. Sage sank to her knees, dropped the shotgun, and placed her hand on Jackson's face. She sobbed softly over the dead man. She only allowed herself to break down for a minute or two. She needed to think about Tobias and keep her safe. Sage aggressively wiped the tears from her face and turned toward her niece while opening her arms.

"It's okay," Sage whispered to her.

Tobias leaped into Sage's arms and clung to her on the floor not far from Jackson's dead body. Tobias sobbed along with Sage.

"Where were you, Aunt Sage?" she softly cried.

"I'm sorry I didn't come home," Sage whispered close to her ear. "I fell asleep. I'm so sorry."

Tobias sniffed while pulling away, wiped her eyes, and met her aunt's gaze. "Fell asleep?" she asked, bewildered. "For two days?"

Sage stared at Tobias for a moment with some confusion. "Two days?"

"You were gone for two days," Tobias insisted while sniffing. "Uncle Jackson came to the house yesterday looking for you. Creed said we had to come here when we couldn't find you. He said a bad man was coming, and we needed to hide from him."

"Do you remember the picnic we had here?" Sage asked Tobias while studying her.

She nodded.

"When was that?"

"Two days ago," Tobias insisted. "When you didn't come home."

Sage heard the words and felt her heart pounding. She'd time jumped again in her sleep! This time, she went two days into the future. But why? Sage placed her hands on Tobias's shoulders and stared into her eyes.

"I can fix this, Toby," she whispered to the little girl. "I know I can fix it."

"I know," Tobias replied, then threw her arms around her neck and hugged her.

Sage held Tobias tightly in her arms while shutting her eyes. She drew a deep breath and held it.

§

Sage shot up in Jackson's bed with a loud gasp. Jackson jerked awake and sprang from the bed, just about stumbling into his gun vault. Thunder cracked loudly outside, and lightning lit the room. Jackson groaned and raked his fingers through his hair.

"It's just a thunderstorm," Jackson gently informed her and flopped back onto the bed. He attempted to pull her into his arms. "It's okay."

Sage clung to him and trembled, although it wasn't from the thunderstorm. She held onto him so tight that he had to loosen her grip.

"It happened again," Sage whispered into his chest.

"What happened again?" he asked, then hesitated and attempted to look at her. "You time surfed?"

"We're not safe here," she announced in a trembling voice. "He finds us here. Everyone dies."

"Are you sure?" Jackson asked with surprise.

"Yeah, I'm sure," she replied, then finally pulled away from him and attempted to collect herself. She looked at the bedside clock. It was three o'clock. "I have to go home."

"You can't leave now," Jackson insisted. "Not in your condition and in the middle of a thunderstorm."

Sage climbed out of bed and began dressing despite her trembling hands. "I have to go home," she insisted. "I need to be with my mother and sister."

"Sage," Jackson groaned while shaking his head. "You're not going to do anyone any good going home now. It's late. They're sleeping. There's no reason to wake them with more bad news."

Sage just about jumped onto the bed and threw her arms around his neck, burying her face into his chest. "Everyone dies," she whispered. "I feel so helpless."

Jackson held her in his arms in a warm embrace. "I don't care what you saw in your future excursion," he insisted. "We're going to stop this. I won't let him kill you or your family."

"He kills you too," she whispered, then pulled away and met his gaze while touching his face. "I love you, Jackson. I don't want to see you die."

He stared into her eyes and kissed her warmly but quickly. "I'm not going to die," Jackson insisted, then caressed her arm. "I'll go with you to your sister's house."

"Are you sure?"

Jackson smiled gently and nodded. "Yeah, I'm not leaving you alone."

CHAPTER 44

Sage entered her sister's house a little after three o'clock in the morning with Jackson only a step behind her. Sage was somewhat surprised to find her mother sitting at the kitchen table with a cup of tea. Grace saw Sage, then eyed Jackson and groaned.

"Really?" Grace scoffed. "You brought him here? It's too early, and I haven't slept yet."

"Good morning to you too," Jackson growled lowly at Grace.

"What are you doing up?" Sage asked her mother with some surprise.

They heard thundering footfalls on the stairs. Little Tobias appeared in the kitchen.

"Aunt Sage," she cried out and threw her arms around her hips, clinging to her.

Sage held her niece a moment, although remaining puzzled. "What are you doing up?" she asked Tobias.

Toby entered the kitchen and appeared relieved. "Thank God you're home," her sister remarked.

"What? Why?" Sage asked and eyed her sister. "Did something happen?"

Tobias remained clinging to Sage. "I had a bad dream," she announced.

"There's a lot of that going around," Jackson remarked and leaned against the archway.

Sage pulled away from Tobias and met her gaze. "Me too," she informed her niece.

Tobias stared up at Sage with a concerned look. "You can fix it, though, right?"

Sage stared at Tobias and almost felt her heart stop. "What did you say?" she gasped.

"In my dream," Tobias announced. "You said you could fix it."

Jackson straightened and eyed Sage with a strange look. "Does that mean something?" he asked.

Tobias looked at Jackson and seemed relieved. "Uncle Jackson," she cried out and ran to him, hugging him around his leg since he was so much taller than she was.

Jackson was surprised by the warm reception from the little girl he barely knew but gave her a tiny hug. "I'm surprised you remember my name," he remarked to the little girl.

She clung to him as if she'd never let go. "You were there when I was scared," Tobias insisted without releasing him. "You kept me safe in that gun room."

Sage shot a look at Jackson, who remained confused. She then looked back at the little girl who refused to release the man she barely knew.

"The gun room?" Sage asked her niece with some surprise.

"It was her nightmare," Toby informed her sister. "She said we all died. *Uncle* Jackson came back for her in some gun room in the basement and kept her safe."

"Except you died," Tobias added without releasing Jackson. "I was so sad."

Jackson exchanged looks with Sage. "Didn't I die in the armory in your dream as well?" he asked with some concern.

"This isn't a coincidence," Sage whispered, hoping her niece wouldn't hear.

Grace, Toby, and Jackson stared at Sage, attempting to understand the comment.

"You two shared the same nightmare?" Grace finally asked, unable to look away.

"It wasn't a nightmare," Sage whispered to her mother, not wanting Tobias to hear it. "I time surfed two days into the future."

"Is that why Tobias said you weren't at the ranch for two days?" Toby asked softly while eyeing her sister.

"She saw," Sage whispered back. "Somehow, Tobias saw the future."

"We need Creed," Jackson muttered to them while still ensnared by the little girl clinging to him. "This is not a coincidence."

§

It was close to four o'clock in the morning by the time Creed arrived at Toby's house. Despite the hour, he was shower fresh and full of energy.

"What's happening?" Creed asked and looked at those within the living room.

Tobias jumped up from where she was sitting on the floor, drawing in her sketchbook, and ran for Creed. She hugged him the same as she had Jackson. Creed was almost as surprised as Jackson had been.

"I'm glad you're alive," Tobias announced, unwilling to release him.

"Of course I'm alive," Creed remarked while uncertainly patting her shoulder. "Why wouldn't I be?"

"Because you died with Grandma while escaping on the horses," Tobias informed him.

Creed eyed the others. "Is this why you called me?" he asked.

Grace stood and gently pried Tobias from around Creed's leg. "Come on, honey," she announced while rousing her best smile. "Let's put a movie on in your bedroom."

Once Tobias and Grace left the room, Creed eyed the others. "What's going on?" Creed demanded.

"I time surfed earlier tonight," Sage informed him while running trembling fingers through her hair. "Two days into the future. We were all at your ranch, and everyone was dead." She then held her breath. "Tobias supposedly had a nightmare, but it was exactly what I saw in the future."

"How is it possible?" Jackson asked his brother.

Creed sank into thought while attempting to process the information. He then looked at Toby. "Is there coffee? This is going to take a while."

CHAPTER 45

Creed returned to the living room an hour later while flipping through his small notebook. He shook his head with a moderately stunned look on his face.

"The little girl's dream was exactly the same as Sage's recall from her time jump," Creed announced and eyed all four. "She has some sort of power, but I don't know if she time surfed with Sage or if it's a premonition."

"Are you saying it's possible that she was actually there?" Toby just about demanded. "That she actually lived through that horror?"

"No matter what happened, the memory is fading fast," Creed insisted. "By morning, she may not even remember any of it."

"I don't understand," Sage remarked. "Twenty years in the future, Tobias didn't have any sort of power. She had a love for old books, but that was about it."

"Powers sometimes fade as we get older," Toby informed her sister.

"What are you talking about?" Grace just about demanded while eyeing her daughter. "They don't fade. If anything, they get stronger."

"I can attest that they sometimes fade," Toby insisted while eyeing her mother. "I used to have more powers when I was younger; then, they weakened considerably a few years after Tobias was born."

"That's not normal," Grace informed her daughter matter-of-factly.

"I may not know a lot about a witch's powers," Creed informed them. "But I've never heard about them decreasing with age."

Grace cocked her head and indicated Creed. "See," she announced. "The derpy warlock agrees with me."

Creed glared at Grace and squinted, taking offense by the comment. "I'm far from derpy," he scoffed, then looked back at Toby. "Exhaustion can affect a witch's powers, but they would typically improve after a day or two of rest."

"Well, I'm the mother of a six-year-old," Toby informed him. "So I never get any rest."

"That shouldn't matter," Creed insisted before looking at Grace. "How strong are your powers?"

"Better than average," Grace replied with some arrogance.

Creed then looked at Sage. "And yours?"

"Whatever powers I have seem to be locked by my memory loss," she replied.

"Before she started time surfing," Grace remarked to Creed, "she had pretty strong powers."

"Being they're both daughters of Wolfram, their powers should be stronger than their mothers," Creed insisted as he eyed Grace. "I can perform a simple test on each of you that will gauge your powers, if you'll allow."

Grace held her breath a moment, then frowned. "I despise the thought of a warlock testing me for anything," she remarked and sighed. "But, I suppose it's important." She then shrugged. "And, according to Tobias, you did try to save me in her dream." Grace eyed Creed with some disapproval. "What sort of test?"

"I just need you to hold my hands and look into my eyes for about thirty seconds," Creed replied.

Grace groaned and shifted on the sofa. "Sounds like an eternity," she muttered, then sighed. "Okay. Let's get this over with."

Creed moved onto the sofa across from Grace, faced her, and held out his hands. She frowned and reluctantly placed her hands in his.

"You'll provide the baseline for your daughters," Creed informed her. "It'll tell me how strong they should be."

"Yes, just get on with it," Grace muttered while remaining uncomfortable holding his hands.

There was a tense silence as Creed held Grace's hands and stared into her eyes. Once he released her hands, Grace moved further away from him.

"Good strong baseline," Creed informed her. "You didn't embellish your powers either."

"Told you so," Grace muttered somewhat proudly.

Toby sat on the other end of the sofa and faced Creed. He turned to face her and took her hands in his. They gazed into each other's eyes for more than a minute, catching everyone's attention. Creed appeared almost puzzled.

"What's wrong?" Grace was the first to ask, breaking Creed's concentration.

Creed remained staring at Toby while releasing her hands. "I'm getting next to nothing," he remarked, then shook his head. "I find the results difficult to believe."

"I told you so," Toby remarked and shrugged. "I'm always tired."

Sage nudged her sister from the sofa and took her spot. Grace seemed more confused than Creed. Sage placed her hands into Creed's hands and met his gaze. Creed almost immediately tensed but didn't take his eyes off hers. Thirty seconds later, he released her hands and looked away.

"What?" Sage asked. "Nothing?"

"On the contrary," Creed informed her and shook his head. "It's like a storm building. Increasing in intensity with each passing second."

"What does that mean?" Jackson just about demanded. "Does it have something to do with her time surfing? Is it harming her?"

"I don't think so," Creed replied but remained perplexed. "It's as if her powers are building rapidly. Her current baseline is possibly quadrupled that of her mother."

Grace smiled proudly. "That's my girl," she announced, then turned concerned. "So, what's wrong with Toby?"

Creed shook his head and glanced at Toby. "I don't know," he replied. "Maybe it's some factor I'm not considering."

"Yeah, I'm a mother," Toby again insisted.

Creed then glanced at his brother.

Jackson eyed Creed. "What?" he demanded. "You're not holding my hands and gazing into my eyes."

"I want to test a theory," Creed insisted.

Sage jumped up and practically pulled Jackson to the sofa. "Sit down, you big baby," she announced. "Hold your brother's hands."

Jackson groaned and reluctantly sat facing his brother. He took his hands, met his gaze, and frowned. "Make it quick, you pervert."

"Shut your yap, and I will," Creed muttered.

They sat on the sofa for nearly a minute before Jackson became uncomfortable and started fidgeting. Creed finally released his brother's hands and shook his head.

"What?" Jackson demanded.

"Your baseline is higher than Ms. Remington's," Creed informed him, surprising Jackson and horrifying Grace.

"Impossible!" Grace shouted.

"Considering he had no powers ten years ago," Creed remarked. "Yes, it does seem impossible."

"What would change that?" Jackson just about demanded, now eyeing his hands as if waiting for some secret power to materialize.

After a moment of uncomfortable silence, Creed, Jackson, Grace, and Toby all looked at Sage.

Sage eyed all four and cocked her head. "What's everyone looking at?" she just about demanded.

"Are you actually suggesting I'm tapping into Sage's powers?" Jackson asked.

"I'm suggesting her levels are so high that she's passing them onto you," Creed announced. "Like an overflow reservoir. Being a warlock, you're the perfect sponge, absorbing her excess powers."

"I don't understand," Sage remarked with some confusion while fidgeting.

Creed glanced at Sage and raised his brows. "You and Jackson have been going at it like bunnies the last two days, and I think it's causing a nuclear reaction, increasing both your powers."

"So Sage is making me a more powerful warlock?" Jackson asked with some surprise.

"Oh my God," Grace gasped, filled with horror and catching everyone's attention. "When I was with Wolfram, I felt spikes in my powers. I just assumed it had to do with the pregnancy."

"That's an interesting theory," Jackson remarked and now appeared curious. "What if Wolfram wasn't just impregnating women to bolster his ego? What if, with each witch, he became a more powerful warlock?"

"He'd be drunk on power," Creed replied, then cocked his head.

"Well," Grace announced with a sigh. "That certainly sounds like Wolfram." She then shrugged. "And it actually makes a lot of sense. By the time I was pregnant with Sage, I was certainly more powerful."

"Your two encounters with him wouldn't really have that much effect," Creed informed her.

Grace eyed him and raised a condescending brow. "Who said it was only twice?"

"Wolfram never hung around with any woman for longer than that," Creed reminded her.

"And yet I have two daughters by him," Grace remarked almost casually.

"You were with him longer than conception?" Toby was first to ask.

"He visited me many times," Grace informed her daughter. "He wasn't the only one capable of casting spells."

Jackson grinned slyly while chuckling. "Well, how about that?"

Grace sneered at Jackson. "Watch it, warlock."

"Maybe you should watch it," Jackson replied, maintaining his sense of humor, then suggestively raised his brows. "Remember, I'm going nuclear."

"Well, you're never touching my daughter again," Grace informed him.

"Not your call, Mom," Sage muttered to her mother, surprising her.

"Argue about it later," Toby scoffed, then looked back at Creed. "Will you do that little test on Tobias?"

"I'd like to," he replied.

CHAPTER 46

A few minutes later, Tobias eagerly sat on the living room floor across from Creed. She seemed giddy at the game they were playing.

"Remember the rules," Creed informed her while using a slightly childish tone to make it seem like a game. "You have to stare into my eyes as long as you can without looking away. First one to look away loses."

"I'm ready," Tobias announced enthusiastically and placed her little hands in Creed's much bigger ones.

Toby, Grace, and Sage sat on the sofa and stared at Creed with Tobias on the floor. All three were just about holding their breath as Tobias stared into Creed's eyes. Within the first few seconds, Creed started twitching. His expression dropped while keeping his gaze on the little girl's emerald green eyes. At the end of the thirty seconds, he gasped and looked away. Tobias cried out excitedly and pulled her hands from his.

"I win!" she cried out, then laughed. "I get ice cream for breakfast!"

Creed managed a tiny smile and laughed. "You certainly do," he replied.

Tobias jumped up from the floor and ran into the kitchen. Grace, Sage, and Toby stared at Creed, who remained sitting on the floor.

"Well?" Toby asked.

Creed looked at the three women and his brother. "Her powers are off the charts," he replied and shook his head. "You're sure her father wasn't a witch or warlock?"

Toby shook her head. "He barely qualified as a man," she scoffed. "He took off before she was even born."

"Like Wolfram did with his baby mamas?" Jackson remarked, catching the women's attention.

"Wouldn't I know if he was a warlock?" Toby demanded.

"Not necessarily," Grace muttered.

Horror crossed Toby's face as she eyed all four. "You don't think her father is Wolfram?"

"No," Grace gasped in horror. "No, he'd know his own children, and I met Tobias's deadbeat father when you first hooked up with him. He *definitely* wasn't Wolfram."

"Would you have known if he was a warlock?" Toby asked, now curious.

"You knew about Jackson and his brothers," Sage remarked to her mother.

"That was different," Grace informed them. "I did my research when I first suspected there were warlocks in Great Bend."

"So Tobias's father could have been a warlock without our knowledge?" Toby asked.

"Did you feel an increase in your powers those few months you were with him?" Grace asked.

"Well, yeah, I guess," Toby replied. "But I was stupid crazy about him." She then frowned. "Right up until he abandoned me."

"While Tobias eats her ice cream," Creed announced, "I think I should see what I can learn from her regarding her dreams." He then eyed Toby. "Will you help me gain her trust?"

"She seems to like you," Toby remarked, "but I would like to be there when you talk to her. She'll be more receptive if we talk to her while she watches one of her favorite movies in her room."

Creed nodded and left the room with Toby.

§

It was now close to five o'clock in the morning and nearing sunrise. While waiting for Creed to conduct his Q&A with young Tobias, Sage and Jackson spent an uncomfortable hour or more with Sage's mother in the living room. Grace cast evil looks at Sage and Jackson, where they sat cozily together on the sofa. Jackson might have been twice as affectionate, knowing Sage's mother was watching their every move. When he kissed the back of Sage's hand while speaking softly to her, Grace groaned loudly.

"Get a room," Grace announced, clearly annoyed.

Jackson cast a look at Sage. "Which room are you staying in?" he teased.

Sage lightly smacked his leg. "Behave."

"Your mother started it," he insisted.

"You need to take the high road, Jackson," Sage insisted. "Be the grown-up."

Grace gasped at the comment while Jackson snickered. He again kissed her hand.

"Anything you say, darling."

Someone was heard on the stairs. Creed appeared at the bottom of the steps and entered the living room. All three looked at him with great interest. Creed seemed slightly anxious.

"Well?" Grace asked, ready to leap from her chair.

"After having an in-depth conversation with the young lady, I've come to a somewhat disturbing conclusion," Creed announced, putting everyone on edge.

Toby entered the living room as well and appeared equally disturbed while rubbing her chilled arms.

"Tobias is able to see into the future," Creed informed them. "It's possible she shares a strange bond with her Aunt Sage. One she isn't even aware of. When little Tobias sees future events, mostly in her dreams, she connects with her Aunt Sage. I think Tobias might be partially responsible for Sage's time jumps."

Sage and Grace were equally horrified. "What?" both cried out.

"How is that possible?" Jackson asked his brother.

"She has a connection with her Aunt," Creed again insisted. "When something bad happens, she connects with Sage, who must make things better on some spiritual level." He then looked at Sage. "Without knowing it, the two of you are communicating the whole time. She knew everything that happened when you visited the future."

Sage suddenly tensed. "Everything?" she gasped, then glanced at Jackson.

"That little girl's going to be fucked up," Jackson muttered while squirming in his seat. "More of an education than she'd intended."

"I don't think she witnessed anything like that," Creed insisted and brushed the comment aside. "She didn't mention anything, well, X-rated, but she did refer to Jackson as Uncle Jackson on many occasions." He then looked at Sage. "That little girl is in your head. There's no telling what the two of you discuss in an alternate dimension. When the killer seriously injured you, it's possible Tobias knew you were in trouble and helped you 'escape'. It's difficult to tell what was her and what was you."

"So you think we may be connecting on a subconscious level?" Sage asked. "Maybe in our sleep?"

"It's possible," Creed replied, then looked at his brother. "We need Lance and Dean over here. The girl has tablets full of drawings that might mean something."

"I'll call them and tell them to come over after they feed the horses," Jackson replied, then removed his cellphone and crossed the room to make his call.

"Even if what you say is accurate," Sage remarked to Creed. "How is it possible? When I was twenty years in the future, Tobias had no powers. There's no way she could have lost them like that, and she certainly wasn't hiding anything from me."

"You're positive?" Creed asked.

"Yes, absolutely," Sage insisted. "She wasn't even aware that she was a witch. Future Tobias was six years old when she lost her family. If she had any clue that she was a witch, she would have shared that with me when we were attempting to figure out time travel."

"With as strong as she is," Creed informed them. "I don't see how she could simply lose her powers. Even if she wasn't aware that she was a witch, she'd eventually figure it out."

CHAPTER 47

Dean and Lance showed up around six o'clock that morning as Toby and Grace made a big breakfast to feed the large group now at the house. Surprisingly, everyone enjoyed a pleasant breakfast together. Despite everything Sage's little niece had been through that night, Tobias was now her usual self and didn't seem to remember how upset she was just a few hours earlier. After breakfast, Dean and Lance encouraged Tobias to show them her artwork, which she was happy to do. After that, Sage and Creed decided to join them in Tobias's bedroom. Tobias's room was pretty much like any little girl's bedroom with frilly pink bedding, a collection of toys and dolls, and tiny furniture. Dean sat on a little chair at the little table with Tobias.

While the little girl drew pictures, Dean colored in a coloring book. To anyone else, it would seem as if Dean found a way to connect with the six-year-old girl, but in reality, he was just embracing his inner child. While Sage and Creed sat on the frilly bed, Lance sat on the chest at the foot end of the bed and leafed through Tobias's sketches.

"She's an amazing artist," Lance informed them. "She even dates all her artwork. That's next level."

"Is this really going to help?" Sage asked, somewhat uncomfortable with their situation.

"She's a little girl seeing adult things," Lance informed her. "She's going to process those things differently so her mind can understand it. Her drawings are the perfect outlet."

"Let me know if you see anything about me and Jackson that might scar her for life," Sage muttered.

"She won't process that sort of thing in a way she can't understand," Lance insisted.

"What do you mean?" Sage asked. "She saw death. She knew what that was."

"Because she's seen death before," Lance informed her. "Maybe something she saw in a movie once. But where you may have seen a bloody and graphic death, Tobias would have seen it as a princess in a dreamless sleep. You know, holding daisies or something." He cocked his head while studying Sage. "If she witnessed you and Jackson having adult relations, she may have seen cupid shooting an arrow."

Dean eyed what Tobias was sketching and then showed her his coloring book. "Trade you," he announced.

Tobias smiled and handed him her sketch pad. Dean gave her his coloring book and then approached his brothers and Sage.

"Hey," Dean announced. "Check this out." He handed Lance the sketchpad and indicated the drawing. "She's been drawing our ranch."

Lance flipped through several pictures and nodded. "Yes, she has," he replied, then handed the book to Sage. "Could this be from last night's jump?"

Tobias's sketches were amazingly realistic for a six-year-old. There were people, horses, and scenery that looked very accurate. Dean pointed to the one picture with the barn in the background.

"That's me," Dean announced. "She drew me sleeping in the driveway."

Sure enough, the lifelike sketch was of Dean in a sleeping bag on his stomach, cuddling a pillow.

"Why am I sleeping in the driveway?" Dean asked.

"That's what she drew," Lance informed his brother. "That's how she's choosing to remember it."

"That's where you were killed," Sage muttered just loud enough for the other three to hear, so she wouldn't upset Tobias.

Dean's expression suddenly dropped. "You're saying I died in the middle of the driveway?" he asked loud enough for Tobias to hear, but she wasn't paying attention.

"Keep your voice down," Creed shushed him.

They flipped to the next picture, which was Lance sleeping in the barn. He was positioned exactly as Sage remembered him, but Tobias had him sleeping on the bale of hay with a horse standing nearby. It was enough to unnerve Sage. She could still see the graphic image fresh in her mind. The next sketch was of Toby and Paul with Toby's car near the tree line. Instead of a wrecked car, the car had a flat tire, and the couple seemed to be arguing about it. The next one was of two saddled horses grazing in the field. The detail of Raven and Karma was almost stunning. Creed and Grace were having a picnic lunch by the woods not far from the horses. The last one was the toughest for Sage to look at. It was Tobias and Jackson in the armory. Tobias was sitting on his lap while he read a book to her. Sage was now curious and looked at her niece coloring in the coloring book.

"Tobias," Sage asked.

Her niece didn't even look up. "Yes, Aunt Sage?"

"In these drawings," Sage announced while holding up the sketchpad. "Where am I?"

"You're inside the book," Tobias informed Sage.

"Inside the book?" Sage asked with some surprise. "What am I doing inside the book?"

"Fixing everything," Tobias informed her almost matter-of-factly.

"Do you know how I fix everything?" Sage asked and received looks from all three men.

"Really?" Dean remarked somewhat skeptically to Sage.

"I don't know," Tobias replied without looking at her aunt. "I think Uncle Jackson helps."

"Uncle Jackson," Dean muttered while chuckling. "That's too funny."

Tobias eyed Dean with some surprise. "What's funny about that, Uncle Dean?"

Dean eyed Tobias before looking at Lance and Creed. "Hear that?" he announced and grinned. "I'm Uncle Dean." He then looked back at Tobias. "And that's Uncle Lance and Uncle Creed, right?"

Tobias looked from Dean to Lance and Creed. "Just Uncle Lance," she replied.

"Why are we your uncles?" Lance asked the little girl.

"More importantly," Creed remarked, seeming concerned. "Why am I *not* your uncle?"

Tobias looked at Creed and seemed almost surprised. "Because you're my daddy."

All eyes were suddenly on Creed, who appeared stunned at the comment.

"I'm your daddy?" Creed asked Tobias with some surprise.

"In one story, you are," Tobias informed him. "You don't remember?"

"Tobias," Sage announced somewhat delicately. "You're seeing future events. Some of those things haven't happened yet."

"I know," Tobias casually replied, then appeared curious while staring at Sage. "Don't you see the future too? I saw you there."

Lance and Creed exchanged concerned looks.

"She's under too much stress," Lance whispered to his brothers and Sage. "I think she's losing touch with her current reality."

"Her mother isn't going to like that," Creed muttered.

"What do we do?" Sage asked with concern.

"There's nothing we can do," Lance replied just loud enough for them to hear. "Her powers are all over the place.

It's possible she doesn't even know what reality she's living in right now."

"Will she be okay?" Sage asked Lance with concern for her niece.

"I think once we're past the traumatic event causing her premonitions, she'll return to normal," Lance replied while frowning, then looked at Sage. "Until then, if she has any more premonitions, you could be thrown just about anywhere and anytime."

"Great," Sage muttered and shivered. "Last night was almost more than I could handle."

"I know a lot is being asked of you," Creed announced to Sage, "but is there anything from your last jump that might help us."

Sage drew a deep breath and flipped through each of Tobias's sketches to jog her memory. She studied each one, remembering in great detail the horror, despite Tobias's happy pictures. Jackson appeared in the bedroom doorway and eyed his brothers with a stern look.

"Heads up," Jackson announced gruffly. "The boyfriend is coming home soon. We may need to bug out, so Toby doesn't have to explain anything to him."

"I thought he wasn't going to be home until after--" Creed hesitated and eyed Tobias, who wasn't paying attention. "You know, *after.*"

"I guess he's heading back out tonight," Jackson replied. "Toby didn't elaborate."

"He has some conference on the West Coast," Sage informed them. "That's why he was absent during--" She hesitated and shrugged. "*You know.*"

"Well, let's start wrapping things up," Jackson informed them. "I want to be out of here before he shows up this morning."

As Jackson left the bedroom, Sage sank into thought. She then flipped through the sketches and paused on the one of her sister and Paul standing by the car with the flat tire. Sage thought about what she saw. She remembered her sister's death vividly. Her throat was slit. She revisited Paul's death. Two puncture wounds. One to his chest and then a fatal one to his neck. Was Paul not killed in the same manner because he wasn't a witch or warlock? Sage continued to stare at the sketch that depicted Toby and Paul arguing over the flat tire. Sage sprang to her feet, grabbed Creed's hand, and practically pulled him from Tobias's room. He was a bit surprised by the force she used to move him. She stopped him just outside Tobias's bedroom and spun to face him.

"You said being with Jackson is increasing my powers at a significant rate," Sage remarked, then cocked her head. "Jackson's powers have also significantly increased."

"Yes," Creed replied while studying her. "It's a sort of chemical reaction of your powers combining. Why?"

"You said Tobias's powers are off the chart, yet I know she had no powers in the future," Sage announced. "And Toby's powers are significantly weakened. If Jackson and I are able to increase each other's powers, what would it take to drain Toby and Tobias's powers?"

"It could be almost anything," Creed replied and eyed her almost suspiciously. "What are you getting at?"

"Paul wasn't home during the attack. He never died," Sage informed him. "And he's leaving for that convention tonight, which is what keeps him safe."

"Yes, that's what Toby said," Creed agreed.

"When I found everyone dead at the ranch, he died in the car with Toby," Sage informed him.

"You think he comes back?" Creed asked.

"Maybe he never leaves," Sage suggested. "Everyone had their throats slashed, but Paul was stabbed in the chest and then stabbed in the throat."

"What are you suggesting?"

"What if Paul is one of the killers?" Sage asked with concern. "What if he tried to kill Toby in the car, but she got in one or two shots before he got her?" She cocked her head.

"Could Paul be the reason Toby lost her powers? Could he somehow be draining her?"

Creed stared at Sage for a long moment while considering the question. His eyes suddenly widened. "Paul is a shifter," he gasped, then thundered down the stairs.

Sage ran down the steps after him.

CHAPTER 48

T oby stared at Creed and Sage from where she sat on the sofa with a stunned look.

"Paul?" Toby gasped. "A shifter?" She shook her head defensively. "No, that's not possible."

"Your powers are drained," Creed insisted. "Your daughter and sister see Paul dead at the ranch in two days, but he's leaving tonight."

"Maybe I ask him to stay," Toby replied.

Grace stared at her daughter on the sofa alongside her. "Would you ask him to stay?" her mother asked somewhat skeptically.

Toby sank into thought a moment, then shook her head. "No, I wouldn't do that," she replied.

"Can a shifter drain powers from a witch over time like that?" Jackson asked his brother.

"They can drain powers while they're dying," Creed insisted, "but I hadn't considered it while they are alive. Considering you and Sage are increasing power between the two of you, I think it's possible for a shifter to drain power in the same manner."

Grace studied Toby for a moment with a sympathetic look. "When did you first notice your powers had decreased?" she asked.

Toby was silent a moment, then fidgeted. "A year or two ago," she replied almost timidly.

"After you started dating Paul?" Grace asked.

She fidgeted and then nodded. "But if he could steal my powers, wouldn't he have drained Tobias as well?"

"No, because he's not in an intimate relationship with her," Creed informed her. "He wouldn't be able to do it without some sort of connection. It'd be like ripping an organ from her body. That's why they slash the throats of their victims to drain their powers."

"Even if it is Paul," Grace announced while looking at the guys, "that still doesn't explain why Tobias loses her powers in the future. Paul *has* to be stealing her powers too."

Sage considered the comment a moment. Something then hit her, and she practically jumped. "Tobias has a boyfriend in the future," she gasped. "He man spreads."

"Man spreads?" Jackson asked, not understanding. "What does that even mean?"

Grace mimicked how Paul would sit, spreading her legs. "Yeah, manspreading," she announced. "Sitting wide open."

"I don't get it," Creed remarked, just as confused as Jackson. "What does that have to do with--?"

Toby shot a look at her sister with horror in her eyes. "Paul does that!"

"Now I know who Leo reminded me of," Sage announced. "He reminded me of Paul!"

Creed and Jackson came to the same conclusion.

"It has to be Paul. Paul is a shifter," Creed announced in stunned disbelief. "Twenty years later, he takes on the form of a different man and dates Tobias."

"Where he slowly drains her powers the same way he did her mother," Jackson replied.

Toby's look turned from horror to anger. "You mean Paul dates my daughter in the future?" she gasped, then sneered. "He kills her family and then becomes her boyfriend twenty years later so he can drain her as well?"

"I'll kill him," Grace snarled in anger.

"Get in line," Toby scoffed.

"If Paul is actually Leo, Tobias's boyfriend in the future," Sage remarked while eyeing Creed. "Then that means Leo knew who I was. He knew I wasn't actually Tobias's sister but her aunt."

"Yes, he would have known who you were," Creed replied, then cocked his head. "I'm guessing he was almost as surprised to see you as your niece had been."

"All things considered, you'd think he would have killed me the first chance he got," Sage remarked.

Creed eyed her, then shook his head. "No, he wouldn't have any reason to do that," he informed her. "You wouldn't have recognized him even if you had your memory. He looked nothing like Paul from your past. He just needed to sit back and wait for the right moment, killing you when he killed Tobias." Creed raised his brows. "It actually worked to his benefit." He looked at the three women. "We need to be sure that Paul is actually a shifter and our man. We need to approach with caution, test him, and then take him down."

"He's going to be here soon," Toby reminded them and just about jumped from her seat. "We need to come up with a plan real fast."

§

Around nine o'clock that morning, Paul opened the front door and entered the living room. He glanced at Grace and Toby, who were sitting on the sofa while having a cup of tea, and smiled at them.

"Good morning, ladies," Paul announced pleasantly, then looked around. "Where's Tobias?"

"She went to her friend's house this morning," Grace replied with a false smile. There was no denying the venomous look in Grace's eyes.

"Did you want some coffee?" Toby asked while just about leaping to her feet. She seemed to have a difficult time looking her boyfriend in the eyes.

"I'd love some," Paul replied cheerfully. "I'll be leaving for my business trip after dinner this evening so I can get there before dark."

"I'll be sure to send a thermos of coffee with you after dinner," Toby replied, then headed into the kitchen.

Paul watched her with a strange look. He then glanced back at Grace. "Is everything okay?" he asked. "Toby seems upset."

Grace retained her 'if looks could kill' smile and waved Toby off. "She's just worried about her sister," she replied. "She spent the night at the Morgan ranch with her new, ill-mannered boyfriend."

"Is that who she's been seeing?" Paul asked with surprise and flopped into his favorite chair. He shook his head while making a disgusted face. "I honestly thought she was smarter than that."

"Well, you know how conniving and sleazy some men can be," Grace replied with a sigh while keeping her eyes locked on Paul. "They come across as charming when they're actually more like a cancer that needs to be cut away."

Paul cringed slightly and managed a tiny laugh. "Wow, you really don't like Jackson Morgan."

"Jackson?" Grace remarked while suddenly raising a curious brow. "What makes you think she'd get involved with that one?"

Paul appeared surprised by the question and seemed to backpedal his earlier response. "Oh, I guess I assumed--" he began, then changed direction. "Her college friends were hooking up with Dean and Lance. I just assumed she got together with Jackson."

"Her date was with Creed Saturday night, not Jackson," Grace reported without taking her eyes off Paul.

Paul managed a smile and nodded. "Yes, that's right," he replied. "I remember now."

Toby returned to the living room with Paul's cup of coffee. While handing it to him, she offered a pleasant smile. "How long will you be on your business trip?" she asked.

"I'll be home by Friday," he replied and sipped his coffee.

"Then it'll just be us girls," Grace announced and cast a look at her daughter while smiling slyly. "We're going to need a lot more wine."

"Did you want some more tea, Mom?" Toby asked with little emotion.

"I can get it myself," Grace replied.

"I'm already up," Toby insisted, then took their cups and returned to the kitchen.

"Isn't she sweet?" Grace remarked while eyeing Paul and adding a slightly psychotic smile. "How's that coffee?"

"It's wonderful," Paul replied and took another sip.

"I brewed that pot myself," Grace announced while grinning, then raised a devious brow. "Would you like a scone to go with that?"

Paul hesitated and eyed the cup of coffee. He stared at the contents for a long moment as his expression changed. "Huh?" he remarked without looking up.

Grace maintained her grin and cocked her head. "What is it, Paul?"

"Was there alcohol in this?" he asked, still unable to look away from the mug.

"Of course not," Grace replied almost sweetly as Toby returned to the living room without their tea. "Just an old *family* recipe."

"Family recipe?" Paul asked and seemed almost sedate.

Sage, Jackson, and Creed appeared on the stairs and entered the living room past Toby, who remained just inside the doorway and watched. Sage and Jackson stood near the main entrance while Creed crossed the room. He paused before Paul's chair and sat on the coffee table facing him.

"Paul," Creed announced, barely catching the man's attention. "Paul."

Paul lifted his eyes and stared at Creed. "You," he gasped, although barely getting the words out. "What are you doing here?"

"I wanted to ask you a few questions," Creed casually replied, then pointed back at Grace. "Do you know who that woman is?"

Paul looked at Grace, who remained comfortably seated and showed no reaction. "Toby's mother," he replied.

"Yes, that's Toby's mother," Creed replied, then raised his brows. "What do you think Toby put in your coffee?"

Paul looked back at the cup of coffee still in his hand. His expression changed slightly, although he still remained sedate. "Witch's spell."

Toby exchanged looks with Sage and shook her head. "I never told him *what* I was," she whispered.

"Is Toby a witch?" Creed asked.

"Yes," Paul replied.

"Are you a shifter?" Creed then asked.

Paul met Creed's gaze with something resembling mild surprise. He suddenly dropped the coffee cup and gripped the arms of the chair. A strange snarl came from his throat. Creed casually stood while keeping his eyes on Paul.

"I'm going to kill him," Grace growled while sneering as she jumped from her chair.

Creed held his hand up to Grace, silencing her without taking his eyes off Paul. "Who else is in your pride?" he demanded.

Paul continued to snarl and dug his fingernails into the armchair. He met Creed's gaze with a mostly psychotic look but didn't respond.

"*Who* is in your pride?" Creed shouted, now turning angry. "Tell me!"

"He's shifting," Jackson announced and took a step closer.

As Creed took a step back, Paul lunged for him, changing mid-air into a grizzly bear and breaking the spell from the tainted coffee. He knocked Creed to the floor and lunged for his throat. Grace screamed and cast her hand out in front of her, a beam of blue light shooting from her fingertips. The magical force held back the bear, keeping his teeth from sinking into Creed. Grace braced her legs while attempting to hold the bear back with her powers. The weight of the large bear was stronger than she was. Jackson lunged for the bear with a shotgun in his hand. He rammed the butt of the shotgun into the bear's head several times. Grace cried out in anger while attempting to keep her hold on the bear's head. By the third strike with the shotgun stock, the bear was thrown off Creed.

The bear immediately shifted direction and lunged for Grace, who had now lost her magical hold over the beast. The shotgun fired, striking the bear in the side. The bear was thrown off course and collided with the chair instead of Grace. Grace leaped away from the bear, drained of her powers after the strain. The bear spun and lunged for Jackson. Jackson pumped the shotgun and fired again, striking the bear in the shoulder. The bear roared and was momentarily stopped by the buckshot tearing into its body. Jackson again pumped the shotgun as the bear again lunged for him. As he raised the barrel, aiming for its head, the bear vanished. Something flew past Jackson's face. He immediately lowered the shotgun, swatted at the bug, and looked around.

"Where did he go?" Jackson shouted.

"He turned into an insect," Sage cried out.

Everyone looked around, but there was no sign of him or any insect.

Grace looked at the floor and suddenly pointed. "There!" she shouted, indicating a spider.

Jackson sprang forward and stomped on the spider. There was a moment of silence as everyone stared at Jackson's booted foot. He lifted his foot off the crushed spider.

"No," Toby gasped, then pointed across the room.

Everyone looked toward the fireplace and saw a mouse run into a small hole in the hardwood floor. No one moved. They had no way of telling if Paul had been the crushed spider or the mouse.

"He got away," Toby whispered.

"We don't know that," Sage remarked.

"No," Toby moaned while rubbing her chilled shoulders. "That was him, I know it. He got away."

CHAPTER 49

Toby paced the living room while Creed and Jackson discussed what had happened with Paul. Grace and Sage brought coffee for the men and spiked tea for Toby to help calm her nerves.

Grace impatiently eyed the two men and offered her usual condescending look. "Are the two of you any closer to solving the world's problems?" she just about demanded. "If not, I'd like my granddaughter returned from those two savage brothers of yours."

"You're not helping, Mom," Toby muttered while continuing to pace.

Creed and Jackson now included the women in their conversation.

"Despite that Sage was my date Saturday night, Paul somehow knew she got together with Jackson," Creed remarked, indicating his brother. "How?"

"No one told him," Toby insisted while looking at Creed. "As far as he knew, Sage went out with you."

"That means whoever the other shifter is, he or she had to be at the tavern that night," Creed insisted.

"Someone who saw Sage leave with me," Jackson announced.

"The shifter you later kill," Sage informed Jackson. "So it had to be someone who was at the tavern, but someone who was missing from my visit to the future."

"So, who was missing?" Toby asked.

"We should make a list of everyone at the tavern," Creed insisted. "Between Sage and my brothers, we should have a decent account of everyone there."

"There's no reason to bring Tobias back here," Jackson remarked and eyed the women. "We're safer at the ranch. Less chance of anyone sneaking up on us, and we have an armory filled with weapons."

"According to Tobias's premonition, it's not all that safe," Toby reminded him.

"It has to be safer than here," Sage admitted, then groaned in frustration. "Let's just get some things together and wait it out at Jackson's ranch. We'll work on the list there."

"We're cutting it kind of close," Grace remarked. "According to the premonitions, all of us die sometime tomorrow night."

"But we already have the identity of one shifter," Creed insisted. "A very important one at that. Paul was the inside man. Maybe that's what will save us."

§

By the time Sage, her mother, and sister arrived at the ranch with Jackson and Creed, they found Tobias and Dean sprawled out on the living room floor with coloring books in front of them. With the way Dean was talking to the little girl, it almost seemed as if he had regressed into his own childhood. It was endearing and possibly somewhat embarrassing for the adult man. Jackson shook his head as the two hung out on the floor and compared their coloring activities.

"Who would have thought Dean would make a great babysitter?" Jackson remarked.

"Well," Lance announced. "He is the closest thing we've got to a child around here."

"I didn't think he even liked kids," Creed muttered.

"In his defense," Jackson remarked. "He's never really been around any."

"Can we ride the horses?" Tobias asked her new friend, who was stretched out on the floor alongside her, where they colored.

"Sure," Dean replied while taking his coloring almost too seriously.

"Not today," Jackson announced, interrupting their 'play time'.

Both looked up at Jackson and pouted. "Oh--"

"Why not?" Dean asked. "We were supposed to be out in the pasture hours ago."

"The ranch hands can take care of the cattle today," Jackson informed his brother. "We have other things to worry about at the moment, and straying away from the house isn't a good idea."

"Uncle Jackson is no fun," Dean informed Tobias.

"No, he isn't," the little girl agreed.

Dean and Tobias laughed at Jackson's expense.

Toby sat on the floor near where her daughter colored and gently stroked her hair. "Tobias," she announced in a gentle tone. "Something bad happened this morning."

Tobias looked up at her with some concern.

"Paul is no longer part of our family," Toby informed her daughter. "If you see him, you're not to talk to him. In fact, if you see him, I want you to run away from him and get one of us immediately."

Tobias stared at her mother for only a moment, then resumed coloring. "He's a bad man," she responded with little emotion. "He tried to hurt you, Grandma, and Aunt Sage."

Everyone stared at the little girl, who seemed unaffected while coloring beside Dean. Dean looked from Tobias to his brothers.

"How did you know that?" Toby asked her daughter.

She shrugged with little interest. "I saw him in the living room trying to hurt you," Tobias replied.

"When did you see that?" Toby asked, now somewhat startled.

"Earlier," the little girl replied almost casually. "Before you came here."

Toby looked back at the others. "She saw it as it happened?"

Creed stared at the child with astonishment, then removed his notebook. "It's possible but very surprising," he remarked and scanned through his notebook.

Toby again stroked her daughter's hair. "What else did you see?"

"He turned into a mouse and slipped into a hole," Tobias replied.

There were several soft groans around the room, realizing that he did escape.

"Honey," Toby quietly announced. "What else have you seen? We need you to tell us everything."

Tobias stopped coloring but didn't look up. "Everything?" she asked.

"Yes," Toby replied.

"Some of it is bad," Tobias gently reported.

"We need to know," Toby informed her. "It's important that we know."

Tobias resumed coloring. "I don't want to talk about it," she replied.

Dean sat up and picked up her sketchbook. "What if you told us some stories?" he asked while skimming through the sketches. "That would be fun, right?"

Tobias sat up and faced Dean, now grinning. "Okay," she replied. "What kind of stories?"

Dean showed her the picture of himself asleep in a sleeping bag in the driveway. "This picture of me," he announced.

"Why am I sleeping in the driveway? Is it nighttime? Aren't you worried I'll get run over by Uncle Jackson's big truck?"

"It's nighttime," Tobias informed him. "No one is driving anymore. It's dark."

"Why am I sleeping in the driveway?" Dean pressed and cocked his head. "Why not in the barn with Lance? Or in my bedroom?"

Tobias studied the drawing a moment and seemed to consider the questions. "Lance was supposed to be saddling horses, but he fell asleep. You were with your girlfriend in the driveway when you fell asleep."

"My girlfriend?" Dean asked with some surprise.

"Courtney?" Sage asked, now interested.

"No, not Courtney," Tobias insisted while briefly glancing at Sage. "Courtney and Lindsey went home to the city."

"So, who is my girlfriend?" Dean asked somewhat suspiciously.

"The pretty one."

Dean glanced at his brothers and groaned. "That certainly narrows it down."

"Yeah, to about a hundred different women," Lance muttered.

Dean glared at his brother. "Hey, I can't help it if I'm so damned loveable."

Toby studied her daughter and appeared curious. "Tobias, is Dean's girlfriend in any of the drawings?"

"No," Tobias replied, then looked at Dean and appeared enthusiastic. "Would you like me to draw her?"

"Yes, I would," Dean replied while rousing his best smile.

As Tobias worked on her sketchpad, Dean cast looks at the others around the room. They all shared the same concern. Tobias knew who killed Dean, even if she did remember the incident differently. Her young, innocent mind was blocking out the unpleasant parts. Dean stared over her shoulder while she sketched.

Tobias stopped sketching and looked at him. "I don't like being watched while I draw," she informed him.

Dean straightened and held his hands in the air. "Sorry," he replied. "How about I get you some ice cream?"

Grace and Toby glared at Dean, but he ignored the looks he received.

"It's a little early for ice cream," Toby informed him.

"I'd like some ice cream," Tobias reported.

Dean sprang to his feet. "Two scoops coming up," he announced, then hurried from the living room.

By the time Dean returned with Tobias's ice cream, she had finished the sketch. Dean handed her the bowl of ice cream as she handed him the sketch pad. Dean looked at the drawing, and his expression immediately dropped. He turned the pad toward the others. It was his ex-girlfriend, Leigh.

"Son-of-a-bitch," Dean groaned.

"Mommy," Tobias announced while eating ice cream. "Uncle Dean said a bad word."

"I'll make sure he puts a quarter in the swear jar," Toby replied while remaining focused on the woman in the drawing. "So that's her?"

"That's our other shifter," Jackson muttered.

"She was also at the tavern that night," Creed remarked while eyeing the others. "She probably would have seen Sage leave with Jackson, explaining how Paul knew they were together."

"I'm glad everyone is taking this so lightly," Dean scoffed somewhat defensively. "I was banging a shifter!"

"Mommy," Tobias asked while briefly looking up. "What's banging?"

Toby glared at Dean while answering her daughter. "It's when you speak without thinking first," she scoffed.

"There's a good chance Paul went straight to her," Jackson insisted and eyed his brothers. "We need to pay Leigh a little visit."

"She'll be at the tavern tonight," Dean informed them. "She's there most evenings."

"It could be Leigh," Sage remarked. "I don't remember seeing her in the future."

"Dean and Lance are with me," Jackson announced, then eyed Creed. "We'll head to the tavern after dinner. Creed, you stay here and keep an eye on our houseguests."

"Maybe I should go along," Sage announced.

"Sage--" Grace scolded, then gave her daughter a mildly threatening look.

Jackson ignored Grace's threatening stare and eyed Sage with a curious look. "Are you any good with a rifle or handgun?" he asked.

"I have a working knowledge of firearms," Sage replied somewhat casually. "You point and shoot."

"So, basically, no," Jackson casually remarked. He shook his head. "Sorry, you're staying behind." He indicated Creed. "Creed can take you out back for some target practice this evening. Get you ready for tomorrow night."

Sage frowned, but there wasn't much she could say. Even her own mother was better equipped for the upcoming battle than she was.

CHAPTER 50

Jackson leaned on the wooden fence not far from the barn and stared into the pasture where Raven grazed alongside Karma. Sage approached him and leaned on the fence as well, mimicking his posture, and watched the horses in silence. Several minutes passed without either saying a word. Sage finally spoke.

"You're worried about them, aren't you?" she asked somewhat timidly.

"No, of course not," Jackson softly replied without looking at her.

"I know you would never breed Karma so soon after she lost her foal," Sage remarked.

"She's not in heat," he reported, lacking emotion. "They're okay out there together." Jackson maintained his gaze at the grazing horses. "If anything happens to them, at least they'll be together."

"Jackson," she announced sympathetically while studying him. "I know how you feel about your horses. You don't have to pretend."

He shifted uncomfortably, then cast a quick look at her. "Sounds kind of trivial, huh?" he muttered, then drew a deep breath. "Our lives are on the line, and I'm concerned about a couple of horses."

Sage turned toward him, clung to his arm, and rested her head against his shoulder. "No, it's not trivial," she remarked while nuzzling his shoulder. "They're not just a couple of horses."

Sage couldn't get the image of Raven slowly dying while standing over Karma out of her mind. It was painful to relive, and she hoped none of that future premonition would come true. The fate of his beloved horses was the one part of her time jump she couldn't share with him. She knew it would tear him apart.

"They're part of you," Sage remarked. "Part of your family."

Jackson gently maneuvered her into his arms and held her affectionately against him, then warmly kissed the top of her head.

"Thanks for not seeing me as weak," he whispered into her hair.

Sage nuzzled his chest while clinging to him. "Love doesn't make you weak," she gently informed him. "It makes you stronger."

"Do you remember at the tavern when I poked fun at the whole notion of love at first sight?" he spoke into the top of her head.

"Vaguely," she replied.

Jackson pulled back just far enough to meet her gaze without releasing her. "When you showed up at the house that morning looking for your friend, despite my foul mood, I knew I'd met my Karma." He offered a tiny smile. "I also knew Creed saw you first, which meant you were off-limits." Jackson withheld his chuckle. "I guess that kind of made me a little less tolerable."

Sage smiled and affectionately caressed his beard. "Yeah, you were a bit of a prick."

Jackson managed a tiny laugh, then placed his hand on her face and stared into her eyes. "I've never been in love before," he informed her. "I never thought it would happen." His grin increased. "How lucky am I that I got to fall in love with you twice."

Sage held back her laugh and then moved onto her tippy toes to kiss him. Jackson leaned down, meeting her halfway, and kissed her warmly. As their kiss turned more passionate, they heard horses and riders approaching. Jackson broke off the kiss and looked across the driveway. Sage immediately recognized Jackson's two ranch hands, Marv and Gus, although each was now twenty years younger. Despite their younger age, they seemed to retain their playful personalities. Both men grinned as they stopped their horses.

"Well, now we know why he took off today," Marv remarked and chuckled.

Gus grinned slyly while eyeing Sage. "Can you blame him?" he added.

Jackson smirked at the two men while releasing Sage. "Yeah, okay," he scoffed. "Get it out of your system. Why are you here?"

"Just checking on you and the kids," Marv insisted but retained his grin. "It's not like the four of you to all call in sick at the same time." He then indicated Sage. "Of course, now we know why."

"Having a bit of a family situation," Jackson informed his ranch hands. "We won't be out tomorrow either, but on the bright side, you can clock out early tomorrow."

Gus and Marv appeared surprised, then grinned.

"Well, that's a first," Gus announced.

"Don't get too used to it," Jackson replied while maintaining his gruffness. He had to keep up appearances so his men wouldn't ask too many questions and somehow get involved. "I'll check in with you tomorrow morning before you head out. We have things to discuss."

Gus and Marv both nodded.

"Catch you tomorrow morning," Marv replied.

Then, both men tipped their hats to Sage with a polite 'ma'am' and rode away. Sage snorted a laugh, catching Jackson's attention.

"What?" he asked, now curious.

"They don't change much in twenty years," she informed him.

Jackson raised a brow while eyeing her. "You mean those two are still working for me twenty years from now?"

"Well, yeah."

He shook his head. "I can't believe I didn't kill either of them," Jackson remarked.

§

Shortly after dinner, Jackson, Lance, and Dean left the ranch for the tavern in search of Leigh. Once they were gone, Creed took Sage to the outdoor shooting range beyond the patio to give her a crash course in firearms. Her mother joined them while Toby and Tobias remained on the porch, drawing at the picnic table. Grace watched Creed's weapons instruction with some interest. Sage practiced shooting for nearly an hour, and she was finally able to hit the target more than she missed it. Grace seemed lost in thought once they removed their protective eye and ear gear.

"With all your powers," Grace remarked to her daughter, "I can't believe you can't cast spells or even throw a good power ball. Have you even tried?"

"I'd love nothing more than to lob a fireball at Paul or Leigh for that matter," Sage informed her mother. "But if I possessed that sort of power, I would have used it the night you and Toby were killed."

"But you still have memory loss from that night?" Grace asked.

"Yes," Sage replied.

"So, how do you know you didn't use witchcraft prior to your travel spell?"

"I don't," Sage insisted. "But, if I had, I'm sure I'd be able to use it now."

"It's not uncommon for witches to develop the sort of power you possess after age thirty," Creed reminded Grace. "What age did you learn?"

Grace considered the question, then frowned. "I suppose you're right," she replied with a defeated sigh. "It was long after thirty for me. Years after I had the girls."

Creed collected the weapons, and they headed back to the patio. "Just out of curiosity," he remarked. "How do you summon your power?"

They paused before the picnic table where Toby and Tobias waited. Tobias happily sketched, but Toby was now interested in the question presented to her mother.

Grace placed both hands before her lower abdomen. "I reach deep down inside," she informed him. "Imagine a flame burning deep inside." She rotated her hands in the form of a ball. "You press it together. Then, there's this warm sensation rising up through your body." She lifted her hands while seemingly rolling a ball. As she moved her hands upward, the blue fireball magically appeared. "When your fingertips feel like they're on fire--" She cast the ball across the yard and struck the distant shooting target, evaporating it. "You throw it." A sly grin crossed her face.

Toby and Sage attempted to do what their mother had just done. Grace watched both women straining to produce the flaming blue ball.

"Not like you're constipated," Grace informed her daughters with a groan. "Nice and easy. Like you're caressing a kitten. Happy thoughts are the best way to start. Later, anger gets you there quicker, but you really want to learn to control it first."

Toby and Sage made another attempt to recreate a fireball like their mother's. Tobias was heard giggling. When they looked back at the little girl, she used a blue colored pencil to draw a ball of flame in one of her sketches. Tobias looked up and smiled proudly.

"I did it first," Tobias announced. "I win."

"And a very lovely fireball it is, honey," Grace announced while brushing the hair from Tobias's face.

§

Jackson's truck pulled into the tavern parking lot and stopped alongside many other pickup trucks. Although the tavern wasn't packed, plenty of vehicles were already outside, given the early hour. Jackson put the truck into park, and all three glanced around. Dean, who was sitting in the passenger seat, pointed across the parking lot.

"There's her car," Dean announced. "I knew she'd be here tonight."

Lance moved between the two front seats, poking his head between his two brothers. "So, what's the plan exactly?" he asked.

"She's been trying to get back together with me for a while," Dean replied, then casually shrugged. "I'll just lure her out with the promise of reconciling."

"That should work," Lance replied. "I mean, her goal was to get close to our family to take us out, and you were the obvious choice."

Dean looked back at his brother between the seats. "That's not why she wanted to go out with me," he remarked, somewhat offended.

"She's a shifter, Dean," Lance reminded him matter-of-factly. "She was never interested in you. She and her partner, Paul, killed our parents. She just wanted to get close enough to take out the rest of us."

"First, you tell me I was boning a shifter," Dean scoffed, turning defensive. "And now you're telling me she was just using me?"

Jackson groaned and rubbed his eyes. "I don't give a fuck if she was head over heels in love with you, Dean," he announced, interrupting his brothers. "The fact remains that she killed our parents, and she wants us dead. No amount of charm is going to change her primary goal." He glared at his brother. "Got it?"

Dean frowned, possibly believing his brothers were right. "Fine," he scoffed. "I'll lay on the charm, get her to leave the tavern with me, and go back to her place."

"We have to assume Paul told her what happened at Toby's house," Lance reminded them. "If he filled her in, she'll be suspicious of Dean's motive."

"Paul doesn't know we suspect Leigh of anything," Jackson reminded him. "Of course, that doesn't mean she won't plan some sort of ambush anyway."

"I appreciate you guys using me as bait," Dean muttered. "So brotherly of you."

"Hey," Jackson announced with little emotion. "It's the price you pay for being so Goddamned loveable."

Dean's eyes narrowed as he glared at his brother. "I hate you."

"Yeah, tell it to your therapist," Jackson muttered and motioned him from the car.

"This feels familiar," Lance muttered. "Why am I suddenly having flashbacks of high school?" He then collapsed back in his seat and rubbed his eyes.

"Probably because this was how we spent every Monday morning when I'd drop you kids off at school," Jackson remarked.

Dean gave Jackson the middle finger, then jumped out of the truck and headed into the tavern.

Jackson nodded. "Yep, exactly like that," he remarked with disgust.

§

Jackson and Lance only waited an hour within the truck before Dean appeared from the tavern with his arm around Leigh's shoulder. He was grinning, and she was giggling. Lance, who was now in the passenger seat, cast a look at his oldest brother behind the wheel.

"You realize we're basing this assumption off a little girl's say-so, right?" Lance reminded him.

Jackson started the truck while watching Dean and Leigh head for her sports car. "Actually," he remarked without taking his eyes off the couple in the parking lot. "I'm putting my faith in Creed and Sage. Creed says that little girl has powers beyond anything he's ever seen, and Sage saw the same thing. We have to act."

As the sports car pulled out of the parking lot, Jackson shifted his truck into gear and followed them from a distance. It was only a few miles to Leigh's house in a small development on the edge of town. She owned a quaint little, two-bedroom home with a small yard and plenty of flowers as landscaping. Jackson parked his truck, shut it off, and both men removed their seatbelts while watching Dean and Leigh get out of the sports car.

"It is strange that Leigh can afford this house all on her own," Lance remarked while eyeing the cute, smaller home. "I'm pretty sure a bank teller in her twenties doesn't make enough to afford a place like this."

"She's only been in town a few years," Jackson added. "No family that anyone's met. Fits the profile perfectly. Besides, I doubt she's living here alone."

"What do you mean?" Lance asked with surprise as he eyed his brother.

"I wouldn't doubt she and Paul live here together," Jackson replied and briefly eyed his brother. "You know, when he goes to that job in the city that probably doesn't exist."

They watched as Dean and Leigh paused before the front door while she found her house key. If Dean was nervous, he didn't look it.

"I'm heading around back," Jackson announced to Lance. "As soon as they go inside, you head for the front door just like we discussed."

CHAPTER 51

Dean entered the dimly lit house and scanned the area as Leigh shut and locked the front door. Just because there wasn't any sign of Paul, that didn't mean he wasn't there. Dean turned toward Leigh while rousing his finest smile at the beautiful woman. Leigh wore her best come-hither look and took two steps toward him.

"Considering everything that's happened between us since we were last together," Dean announced in a serious tone while stopping her approach by holding his hand up. "I think we should, you know, clear the air first."

Leigh maintained her smile and laughed softly while waving him off. "You said things; I said things," she replied. "That's in the past."

She again took a step toward him, preparing to cozy up to him, when he once more stopped her.

"Maybe so," Dean announced, attempting to avoid her advances. "But I'd like to think I've grown since our break-up, and I think some things need to be said."

Leigh stared at him with surprise as her look turned serious. "I'm offering you sex, and you want to talk first?" she remarked slightly gruffly.

Dean tensed and refrained from fidgeting.

Leigh suddenly smiled and laughed. "I guess you have grown," she announced and indicated the sofa. "Okay. Let's talk then."

Dean glanced at the sofa and seemed to hesitate before approaching it. There was a knock on the door, stopping him in his tracks.

Leigh appeared bewildered and glanced back. "Who the hell is that at this hour?" she demanded, then turned for the door.

Dean took two quick steps toward the nearby archway and peered into the kitchen. Jackson crossed the kitchen from the back door while eyeing his brother. Leigh looked out the peephole and groaned.

"It's your brother, Lance," Leigh scoffed before glaring at Dean. "Did he follow you?"

Dean gave her an innocent look and shrugged. "He's probably upset that I ditched him and went to the tavern without him," he remarked.

Leigh groaned, then unlocked and opened the door, revealing Lance. "What do you want, Lance?" she demanded. "Dean and I are sort of in the middle of something."

"I need to talk to him," Lance informed her. "It'll just take a minute."

Leigh frowned and walked away from Lance. As Dean walked past her toward the door, Leigh heard it close. She spun and saw Lance was now inside the house.

"What's going on?" Leigh demanded.

"Cut the shit," Jackson announced from the kitchen archway.

Leigh spun back around and saw Jackson staring at her. She seemed to tense, then eyed the three men on either side of her.

"What are you doing in my house?" she demanded, turning angry and pointing to the door. "All of you! Get out!"

"We know who and what you are," Jackson informed her with little emotion. "Paul ratted you out."

Leigh stared at him with some surprise, but there was a tiny flicker of arrogance. "I don't know what you're talking about," she insisted, again turning angry. "I want you out of my house."

"I saw the bloody rags in your kitchen garbage can," Jackson informed her. "We know Paul was here after I wounded him."

Paul suddenly appeared behind Jackson and plunged a dagger for his throat. Jackson must have been aware of his presence and immediately caught his wrist with the dagger before catapulting him over his shoulder and onto the floor. The moment Paul hit the floor, he changed into a large, gray fur-covered werewolf and slashed at Jackson's legs with his razor-sharp claws. Jackson leaped from his path and pulled his .357 Magnum from an interior pocket in his jacket. Before he had a chance to aim the weapon, the creature vanished. Leigh cried out in anger while transforming into an equally frightening werewolf creature and attempted to slash Dean and Lance with her claws.

Jackson aimed his weapon at her, looking for a clear shot so he wouldn't accidentally shoot one of his brothers. She took one step in the right direction, and Lance moved just enough to take him out of the line of fire. Jackson pulled the trigger, and the revolver fired. The werewolf Leigh turned for Lance at the same time, and the bullet grazed her side. She cried out and vanished. Lance and Dean looked around for any sign of her. Dean feverishly swatted at a fly while Lance attempted to stomp on a mouse scurrying across the floor. Jackson took a step closer and aimed his revolver at the mouse. He fired the weapon and splintered the wooden floor directly behind the mouse just as it disappeared into the wall. Jackson cursed under his breath while Dean and Lance continued to look around.

"They're gone," Jackson insisted.

His brothers looked at him with some doubt. "How do you know?" Dean then asked.

"Too many neighbors," Jackson informed him while indicating the revolver. "There's a good chance someone called the police already. We can't stick around."

§

When Sage and Grace saw Jackson's truck pull up to the house, they ran onto the porch. Creed and Toby were only a few steps behind them and waited for the three brothers to get out of the truck. All three frowned at those near the front steps and shook their heads.

"Was it her?" Toby asked.

"Yeah, she's the other shifter," Jackson replied as he hurried onto the porch and greeted Sage.

"She got away," Lance muttered as they joined the others.

Jackson placed his arms around Sage and pulled her against him, holding her in a tight embrace.

"And Paul?" Toby asked.

"He was there too," Dean remarked while shaking his head. "Jackson must have gotten a piece of him at your place, but his injuries weren't serious enough to slow him down."

"Shifters are made of pretty tough stock," Creed reminded them. "Even when in human form. They can also change into creatures with thicker hides to absorb impact."

"Like when Paul changed into the bear," Grace replied.

"Exactly," Creed responded. "They can transform into smaller creatures, like insects, to escape, but that also makes them more vulnerable."

"So if they change into a fly, we can squash them?" Dean asked.

"Probably a little tougher than an ordinary fly, but yes," Creed replied.

Dean and Lance looked around the porch, making Toby and Grace slightly insecure and forcing them to look around as well.

"They could be almost anywhere," Lance muttered.

"I probably shouldn't leave Tobias alone in the living room," Toby announced, then hurried back inside.

CHAPTER 52

Despite all evidence that supported the attack not happening until the following night, during the strawberry moon, Jackson didn't want to take any chances after their confrontation with Leigh and Paul. He and his brothers would take turns standing guard inside the house. Even though there was plenty of room at the farmhouse, Grace, Toby, and Tobias shared a bedroom. Her mother would have preferred if Sage stayed with them as well, but she'd already made up her mind that she'd stay with Jackson in his room. Dean and Lance were on first watch, which meant Jackson would turn in early to get some sleep before his shift. As Sage entered Jackson's bedroom, only a step behind him, he locked the door and offered a mildly pleased smile as he turned to face her.

"I'll be honest," he announced. "I had my doubts that you'd be joining me tonight."

Sage affectionately ran her hands along his chest and then placed her arms around his neck while meeting his gaze. "I'm terrified about what will happen tomorrow," she insisted while tensing against him. "If this is really it, I don't want any regrets."

His arms tightened around her waist as he held her close to him. "I'm glad you decided to stay with me tonight," Jackson gently replied. "It was hard enough fighting this evil knowing my brother's lives were at stake, but the thought of anything happening to you is a thousand times worse." He frowned and looked down. "I wish you weren't involved."

"Well, we have no choice in the matter," she reminded him. "If we try to outrun them, there's a good chance they'd just follow us. But, despite my little peek into what happens tomorrow, I'm still convinced all of us sticking together is for the best."

"Yeah, me too," Jackson replied, then met her gaze and tensed. "Are you worried Tobias might have you time surfing half the night?"

"I hope not," Sage announced and released a soft sigh. "But it's possible."

Jackson warmly kissed her forehead and met her gaze. "If you travel into the future," he announced, affectionately caressing her face as his look turned stern. "Tell the old man to keep his hands off you."

Sage managed a tiny laugh and clung to him. "I can't believe you're jealous of your older alter ego."

"He's perverted and creepy," Jackson remarked with some annoyance. "Christ, he's old enough to be your father. You'd think he'd know better."

She offered a playful grin. "Maybe you should wear me out, so I don't have any energy for him," Sage teased.

Jackson chuckled warmly and lowered his mouth to hers. "Challenge accepted."

He warmly kissed her on the lips while holding her against him. The moment she returned the kiss, his kiss turned more aggressive.

§

Sage's dreams were all over the place that night. It was hard to distinguish whether they were dreams or time jumps. Whatever they were, she wasn't in one spot long enough to really figure it out. A loud crack of thunder woke her from her restless sleep. Sage opened her eyes and looked around the familiar, dimly lit bedroom. Although she recognized the room, it wasn't Jackson's bedroom. She was somewhat surprised to discover she'd been sleeping on the carpeted floor. A familiar lullaby was playing and caught her attention. Sage slowly stood while looking around the dimly lit room and saw a toddler's bed. She approached the small bed and peered at the sleeping three-year-old girl beneath the blanket. Sage stared at the little girl for a long moment, deep in thought. She again looked around the room with a strange realization. She was in her childhood bedroom! Sage looked back at the little girl and realized it was her older sister, Toby.

Her mother's bedroom door softly creaked, alerting her that her mother was still awake. Sage looked back at the partially open door to the dimly lit hallway. She cautiously approached the door, pulled it open, and peered into the corridor. She stepped into the hallway when nothing moved and headed for the stairs. As quickly and quietly as possible, she hurried down the steps. She didn't know what she was doing before her own existence in the past, but she knew she needed to get back to her current situation. As she reached the bottom of the stairs and turned toward the front door, Sage was suddenly grabbed from behind with a hand over her mouth and a dagger to her throat. She released a muffled gasp and immediately tensed.

"I should kill you where you stand," a man whispered close to her ear. "Fortunately for you, I don't like killing women, so I'm willing to listen while you beg for your life." The man kept his mouth close to her ear and held her against him with the knife snug against her throat. "Who are you?"

He removed his hand from her mouth but didn't ease up with the knife to her throat.

"My name is Sage Remington," she just about gasped. "This is my mother's house."

The man tensed against her. "Who's your mother?" he demanded.

"Grace," Sage replied. "Grace Remington."

Sage could feel the man's apprehension, although he still made no attempt to release her.

"Grace Remington's daughter is three years old," he informed her with a snarl in his tone. "Want to try again?"

"It's difficult to explain," Sage remarked, then hesitated. "I'm her *other* daughter."

"She only has one daughter," he informed her. "My daughter, Tobias."

Sage felt her entire body suddenly stiffen. "Wolfram," she gasped with something resembling horror. She could feel his entire body stiffen against her.

"How do you know who I am?" he demanded while just about grazing her throat with the knife. She could hear the concern in his voice. "Who are you?"

Sage held her breath a moment. "If Toby is three," she remarked, "that would make me your daughter in about nine months."

There was a moment's hesitation. The man removed the knife from her throat, spun her around, and just about slammed her against the nearby wall. He hit the light switch not far from her head, and the kitchen brightened. Although Wolfram was just a tick under six-foot-one, he seemed more imposing than his stature. Built moderately athletic, he had broad shoulders and carried himself with more than enough confidence. His thick hair was dark with a few wisps of gray. He had a short, neatly trimmed beard that was mostly gray, giving him a silver fox sort of appeal. Sage and Wolfram stared at each other with strange looks on their faces.

"How?" he just about demanded while lowering the knife, possibly believing her.

"Your granddaughter, Toby's little girl," Sage gently replied. "She has premonitions. Apparently, we somehow link up when she sleeps, and I time surf on her whims."

Wolfram stared at her. It was unclear if he believed anything she was saying. He suddenly grinned. "You can time surf?" His smile faded just as quickly. "Why should I believe you?"

Sage raised a cocky brow while studying him. "Did you just knock up my mother?"

He stared at her for a long, silent moment. "Okay," Wolfram replied and replaced his knife. "I believe you." His smile again returned with added arrogance. "I have a daughter who can time surf." He shook his head. "I'm damned proud of you." Wolfram then cocked his head while studying her. "What else can you do?"

"What else?" she asked, then shook her head. "Nothing."

"Nothing?" he just about demanded. "That's not possible. If you're linking up with my granddaughter and time surfing, you must have unlimited power. My granddaughter can't be more than six or eight. She can only link up with someone extremely powerful at that young age, and my children are bred to be powerful."

"Yeah, let's not open up that particular can of worms, okay?" she muttered.

"I guess you've done your homework on me, huh?" he remarked.

"Yeah," she replied with little enthusiasm.

"I'm sorry if you don't approve," he replied and casually leaned against the nearby wall. "But I'm not going to turn down any true blood witch that wants my offspring. I'm fulfilling my destiny, and it's made a lot of witches very happy." He then casually shrugged and grinned. "And I haven't exactly been suffering either."

Sage stared at him with bewilderment. "Wait," she remarked and cocked her head. "They ask you to impregnate them?"

Wolfram raised a cocky brow. "Of course," he remarked, then snorted an almost humored laugh. "How else would it happen?"

She shifted uncomfortably. "From everything I heard, you did it without their knowledge."

His arrogance quickly diminished. "Did Grace tell you that?" he suddenly demanded, turning angry. "Is that what she tells you about me when you're older?"

"Actually, she never mentioned you," Sage informed him matter-of-factly. "I had to drag it out of her that you were my father. I guess there was a rumor that you got witches pregnant without their consent."

"Well, that's absolutely not true," he insisted, then pointed to the stairs. "Visiting Grace more than once is not something I normally do, so she'd better not spread lies about me either." He then hesitated and appeared curious. "Why did my granddaughter send you here?"

"I don't know that she's aware of where she's sending me when I jump," Sage informed him.

"If she has premonitions, she'd sent you here for a reason," he insisted. "She must have seen something traumatic."

"Well, that's an understatement," Sage muttered, then met his gaze. "Tomorrow night, my time, two shifters kill my mother and my sister. Tobias saw it happen and shared it with me via a time jump."

Wolfram straightened without taking his eyes off her. "Shifters?" he asked with surprise. "Two shifters kill Grace and Toby?"

"As well as my new friends," she informed him.

"If she's at the helm, she's sending you on these journeys for a reason," he insisted. "Obviously, she saw something, and she wants you to see it too."

"Yeah, that's what Jackson said too," Sage replied, then shook her head. "She's launched me twenty years into the future and now twenty-three years into the past."

"You met someone in the future, I assume," he replied.

"Yes, the man who saved me the first time I was attacked, twenty years after that night," she informed him. "He helped me get some of my memory back."

"You had memory loss?" Wolfram asked, now interested.

"Yeah, I kind of still do."

He motioned her to him. She uncertainly took a step closer. Wolfram reached out and touched her temple. Sage suddenly gasped as a flash of memories from her missing two weeks flooded back to her.

Sage sat in the passenger seat in her mother's car as her mother drove from Colfax to Great Bent.

Grace looked at Sage and smiled happily. "I'm glad you're coming along to visit," she remarked to her daughter. "I know you don't care for Paul, so what made you change your mind last minute like that?"

"I had this really freaked-out nightmare," Sage replied while fidgeting in her seat. "Tobias was distraught in the dream." She then smiled and shrugged. "I guess I was just feeling guilty about never visiting Toby's house in Great Bend."

Flash forward to that night. Sage rushed down the stairs just in time to hear a crash coming from the kitchen. She was about to run for the kitchen when she saw her mother butchered on the living room floor. Sage gasped in horror, but her mind immediately reeled.

"Toby," she gasped.

Sage ran for the kitchen and bolted through the opening. Toby lie on the floor with blood pouring from her throat and collecting in a pool around her. Sage turned just in time to see a decorative dagger plunge downward for her throat. She thrust her hand outward, sending a blue ball of power into the masked attacker. It was her first-ever power ball, and she didn't even know how she did it. The killer was thrown across the kitchen but not before the knife tore into her shoulder. Sage cried out as blood seeped from the fairly deep wound. Despite her pain, she was alerted to another sound from alongside her. A second masked killer lunged for her. Sage clung to her bleeding shoulder and bolted for the kitchen door. As she ran from the house, she looked behind her and saw what appeared to be a werewolf chasing her, but it was dark, and she must have been mistaken.

The flashback jumped forward to the dark road past the apple orchard. As the jeep sped off down the road, Sage turned to the driver while clutching her bleeding shoulder.

"We need to go for help," she insisted.

As he drove down the back road, Jackson eyed her and then her bleeding shoulder. He grabbed a towel from the center console.

"Put pressure on that wound," he instructed while handing her the towel. "Who's chasing you?"

Sage applied pressure to her wound and cringed from the agonizing pain. "You wouldn't believe me if I told you."

A gray blur suddenly ran into the jeep's front fender, rocking the vehicle and tossing it across the road. Jackson slammed on the brakes, causing the jeep to skid along the wet road. A tree suddenly appeared in the headlights directly in front of them. Sage cried out as the jeep slammed into the tree. The flashback jumped again. Sage slowly regained consciousness while the rain drenched her. She saw a woman with dark, wet hair dragging her along the ground behind her. As Sage began to struggle against the hand clutching her ankle, the woman stopped and spun to face her. Sage watched in horror as the woman she recognized as Leigh transformed into a much larger man. He grabbed her by the arms and pulled her to her feet. She then saw the decorative dagger in his hand as he placed it to her throat.

"Let her go!" Jackson cried out through the pouring rain.

The man spun Sage around and held her against him from behind with the dagger to her throat. Sage saw Jackson holding the Magnum revolver aimed at her abductor.

"Drop the gun, or she dies!" the man shouted in anger.

Jackson gripped the gun in his wet hand and appeared to assess the situation.

"Take the shot!" Sage cried out, knowing her fate if he didn't. "Take the shot!"

Despite the nearly deafening sound of the pouring rain, Sage could hear the hammer of the revolver as it rotated back. She watched as Jackson's finger squeezed the trigger. She stared at the cold yet somehow concerned look on Jackson's face beneath the wet black cowboy hat as the trigger suppressed. Sage drew a deep breath and held it as she heard the bang of the gun firing. When she opened her eyes, she saw the bright lights above her in the hospital's emergency room.

Sage was lost in her own memories for a moment before finally looking at Wolfram with some surprise.

"How did you do that?"

"I'm a warlock, remember?" he teased while grinning. "It's why I'm so popular with the ladies." He shrugged. "Not that I'd ever time surfed, but I know it can scramble your brain a little." He then considered her situation. "My granddaughter must have sent you here to this place and time to meet me. She must have thought I could help."

"Can you?"

"I can't time surf to the future with you if that's what you're asking," he informed her. "Even if I could manage it, everything I did will be undone when I return to my correct timeline."

"I traveled back and forth unexpectedly, with Tobias's help, I assume," she informed him. "Jackson of the future didn't remember my interactions with him in the past, and I thought he should have."

"Because you were erased for those twenty years that you jumped," he informed her. "You're going to follow your original timeline. You can go back for a do-over, but you can't skip. Going back just resets everything."

"What about the 'you' of my timeline?" she asked. "Would older you be able to help us?"

"I'm sure I would," he insisted, then managed a tiny smile. "But considering you found me here and now, I'm guessing I cease to exist beyond tonight."

"What do you mean?" she asked with some surprise. "You think you're dead?"

Wolfram casually shrugged. "Why did your niece send you back twenty-three years to find me? Why not a month or a week?" He sighed, although he didn't seem too upset. "The only logical explanation is I cease to exist much beyond tonight."

"You don't seem unwell," she informed him. "How could you die?"

"I can die just like anyone else," he informed her. "Who knows? Maybe a shifter gets me too."

"Maybe you time surf to the future and decide to stay there," she remarked.

"Not one of my tricks," he replied with a tiny, humorous smile.

"I don't want to think that you die," Sage informed him, then shifted uncomfortably. "For what it's worth, you're still my father. I honestly never thought I'd meet you."

"That's one of the conditions. I don't get to know any of my kids," he informed her.

"Why don't you want to know your kids?" she asked. "Seems kind of sad."

He snorted a laugh. "I never said it was one of my conditions," Wolfram replied. "Witches only want me around for one thing, and I'm good at that one thing. So your mother requesting encores is actually a first for me." He shrugged. "Probably the most time I'd ever spent with one of my baby mamas. Most of them don't even want to talk."

"That's kind of sad," she reported.

"It is what it is," he replied with a sigh. "I didn't mind so much the first one hundred years. These last fifty have been exhausting." Wolfram studied her a moment and managed a tiny smile. "I wish I could get to know you and your sister a little better. Seeing little Tobias upstairs in her room is a rare treat for me. I never get to see my children, much less interact with them. This is a first for me."

Sage smiled warmly, then shrugged. "That time travel spell might be worth looking into," she informed him, then gave a general nod across the house. "I should find my way back to my timeline." Sage hesitated. "It was nice meeting you--Dad."

Wolfram leaned against the nearby wall and watched her with a tiny smile on his face. "Yeah, it was nice meeting you too, Sage."

CHAPTER 53

Sage woke in Jackson's mostly dark bedroom and stared at the part in the curtains as pre-dawn replaced the darkness. It would still be another hour before sunrise. She heard Jackson enter the bedroom after his perimeter watch. She listened as he undressed, then felt him crawl into bed. Jackson immediately spooned against Sage from behind, nuzzled her shoulder with his face, and clung to her. She caressed his hand over her abdomen.

"I didn't mean to wake you," he whispered close to her ear and then warmly kissed her.

"I was already awake," she informed him.

Her time jumping to the distant past and meeting her father was a little more real than she would have liked, making her sad. She didn't know the man, but she suddenly missed him.

"Did you get any sleep?" he asked softly.

"Some," she replied. "I time surfed last night."

"Oh?"

"Into the past," she replied, then held her breath. "I met my father."

"Wolfram?" Jackson asked with a slightly concerned tone in his voice as he tensed against her.

"I think he died shortly after I was conceived," Sage remarked while continuing to stare at the part in the curtains.

"How--?"

"Long story." She caressed his arm across her abdomen. "Hold me."

Jackson tightened his arm around her and clung to her while lightly kissing her shoulder. "I'll never let go."

§

Breakfast that morning was unusually somber. No one was in the mood to talk, and most just picked at their food. Little Tobias didn't seem to mind since it gave her a chance to sketch while she ate. Since Jackson and Sage cooked breakfast, Creed, Grace, and Toby cleaned up. Lance, Dean, and Jackson then went outside to discuss the day with the ranch hands. When they returned to the house an hour later and joined their guests in the living room, all three brother's moods were equally foul.

"The ranch hands are leaving early today," Jackson informed Creed. "They'll be gone by early afternoon."

"I think it was a mistake," Dean remarked while glaring at his brother.

"We can't have them here," Creed insisted. "We don't need more collateral damage."

"Not the ranch hands," Dean launched in anger. "The horses." He looked at Creed while indicating his oldest brother. "Jackson had the ranch hands take every last one of them out to the back forty."

"I'm sorry," Jackson scoffed, clearly annoyed. "I don't want any of the horses caught in the crossfire."

"What if we need them to escape?" Dean demanded.

"If we need them to escape, we've already lost," Jackson insisted. "Sage saw that future."

"You're just worried about your damned Bonnie and Clyde," Dean scoffed.

"Raven and Karma," Jackson snarled while glaring at his brother. "And, yes, I'm worried about them."

"I know this may sound like simplicity at its finest," Grace remarked while eyeing the guys. "But if these shifters can only siphon our powers every five years during a strawberry moon, wouldn't it be smart if we just locked ourselves in the gun vault." She looked around, then glanced at Sage. "You said Tobias survived in the vault. We just need to stay there until morning, right?"

"We don't know that she was actually safe because she was in the vault," Creed reminded her. "It seems pretty obvious they were saving her for some future attack."

"Draining our power during the strawberry moon is their ultimate goal," Lance remarked, "but leaving us alive is no longer an option for them. We already know who they are, and they know we'll hunt them. If we don't kill them, they'll almost certainly kill us. Strawberry moon or not."

Dean flopped onto the floor near Tobias and leaned on his elbow while watching her. "Tobias," he announced, catching her attention.

"Yes, Uncle Dean?"

He indicated for her to stare into his eyes. "Any words of wisdom for your old uncle?"

Tobias stared into his eyes with a strange look. "If you add chocolate to milk, it doesn't make chocolate milk."

Dean stared at her, somewhat baffled, then groaned. "Not what I meant, but good to know," he announced. "You got any pictures you want to share with us. You know, to help us get through the day. I really don't want to fall asleep in the driveway."

"Ask Grandpa," Tobias replied while she continued sketching.

"Grandpa?" Dean asked with surprise. "He's been gone a long time. A very long time."

"Aunt Sage talked to him last night," Tobias casually remarked.

Sage received strange looks from everyone except Jackson and Tobias.

"You were talking to Grandpa?" Grace remarked lowly while glaring at her daughter. "Does she mean her grandfather or your grandfather?"

Sage shifted uncomfortably. "I had an unexpected time jump last night," she informed her mother and the others staring at her. "I may have bumped into Wolfram."

Grace sneered. "Seriously?" she demanded. "How did that happen?"

"I don't know," Sage replied defensively. "How did any of my time jumps happen? I showed up at our old house and ran into him."

"Our old house?" Toby asked with a look of surprise. "When was he at our old house?"

"Shortly after, well, after I was conceived," Sage replied while fidgeting.

Grace's eyes widened as she stared at her daughter. "You ran into Wolfram after we--?" She suddenly groaned and shook her head. "I think I'm going to be ill."

"You and me both," Sage announced.

"Grandpa Wolfram died," Tobias remarked while resuming sketching.

Grace looked at her granddaughter on the floor. "He died?" she asked with some surprise. "When?"

Tobias shrugged without looking up. "Not long after Aunt Sage spoke to him," she replied. "A day, I think."

"What would possibly have killed him?" Grace asked while everyone exchanged looks. Obviously, they were all thinking the same thing.

"He was pretty powerful," Creed remarked. "And he wasn't actually all that old for his kind."

"He seemed to think he could die just as easily as anyone else," Sage informed Creed.

"Well, not *just* as easily," Creed informed her. "But a guy like that doesn't unexpectedly get hit by a car, die in a crash, or drown in a lake. He's a little more bulletproof than that."

"What if a shifter got him?" Lance then asked and immediately received several looks. "What if he had been one of the victims?"

"Then I'd feel bad for all the bad things I'd said about him," Grace muttered.

"Why would that change?" Toby asked her mother.

Sage stared at her mother for a moment as if attempting to read her thoughts and body language. Her eyes suddenly widened. "Oh, my God!" Sage exclaimed. "You wanted him to father another child!"

Grace shifted uncomfortably and avoided looking at Sage. "Not the time," she muttered.

"I'm really starting to question your relationship with him," Sage remarked.

"Fine," Grace scoffed while avoiding looking at anyone. "I had a weak spot for the guy. I was captivated by his strength." She hesitated, then grinned almost slyly. "And he was amazing in bed."

Toby and Sage cried out and had to look away. "No one wants to hear that," Toby announced.

"Well, he certainly had enough practice," Creed remarked in all seriousness and immediately received several looks.

CHAPTER 54

A̲s the afternoon passed, everyone became a little more tense and anxious about the upcoming battle. It would almost certainly happen after sunset, but they needed to remain alert for an earlier attack. Although Paul and Leigh knew they'd been called out, the shifter duo didn't know their victims had insider knowledge of the 'when'. Even though they had information on the sneak attack, Sage was still burdened with the reality of the time jump where everyone died. In that reality, they also had prior knowledge of the attack, and the shifters still managed to wipe them out. It wasn't doing much for Sage's confidence. Jackson stood on the porch an hour or two before sunset and stared out at the ranch in silence. Sage joined him on the porch and clung to his arm.

"Are you okay?" she asked gently.

"This is the first time I've stood here without seeing the horses," Jackson replied, then held his breath. "It feels like the end of the world."

"Aren't you supposed to be optimistic?" she asked, feeling uneasy.

"Seven to two," he remarked while patting her hand on his arm. "Those odds sound pretty good, but shifters are tough bastards to kill. They change into something small to escape and then sneak up on you. It was easier when I thought the killer was human." He glanced at her. "If we had known then what we know now and coordinated our attack, the shifter that killed my father may have gotten all of us."

"And maybe you would have gotten the shifter," she reminded him.

"I know you don't want to hear this," Jackson announced while staring at her. "But maybe you and your family should lock yourselves in the vault until morning. In your premonition, you said Tobias survived in there. So maybe all four of you will survive as well."

"You heard what Lance said," Sage reminded him. "They're coming for us no matter what. You need us. We already know the four of you aren't enough."

"That was before we knew who they were," Jackson reminded her. "For all you know, we were ambushed between Paul and Leigh because we didn't know they were the killers. This time, we know."

"We need to watch one another's backs," Sage insisted. "They aren't going to simply drive up to the ranch in a frontal assault. They can change into any living creature. They could be birds sitting in a tree watching the house for all we know. They could be a mouse already inside the house walls. We just don't know. I don't think any of us is safe. Hiding isn't the answer."

"I understand your reservations," he replied, then sighed. "At the very least, Tobias needs to go into the vault, which needs to happen soon."

"She can't go alone," Sage remarked. "Toby will have to stay with her."

"Agreed," he replied, then held her in a warm embrace before kissing the top of her head. "Let's go."

They entered the house and found Grace, Toby, and Tobias in the living room, where they'd been most of the day. Grace was now on edge, preparing to defend the fort, while Toby seemed somewhat emotional, worrying about her daughter and the rest of her family.

"It's time," Jackson informed them, then indicated the little girl sketching on the floor. "You need to take her downstairs and lock yourselves in."

Toby looked at Jackson and appeared concerned. "I don't want to leave her in there alone, but I don't think I can simply hide with her."

"It's not hiding," Grace insisted somewhat sternly. "It's called the last line of defense. You need to be there to protect her."

Tobias now seemed interested in the conversation. "I don't want to go into the vault," she remarked, then looked at Sage. "If you're scared, Aunt Sage, maybe you should talk to Grandpa again. He made you feel safe."

"No," Sage replied a little too quickly, then fidgeted. "I need to stay here, Tobias. I can't risk leaving again." She crouched on the floor alongside her niece. "I need to stay here. I can't go on any more time jumps."

"Is that what you want?" Tobias asked while looking concerned.

"Yes, that's what I want."

§

Creed and Dean went downstairs with Toby and Tobias. They entered the gun vault, which now had a mattress, blankets, pillows, food, and water.

"You'll be safe in here," Creed informed them.

Dean held his arms open to the little girl. "We'll be back for you in the morning," he announced.

Tobias jumped into Dean's arms and hugged him. "Be careful, Uncle Dean."

Dean smiled and hugged her. "I will," he replied, then released her and returned to the wine cellar.

"Did you need anything else?" Creed then asked Toby and her daughter.

Toby nervously rubbed her chilled arms and frowned. "How will we know what's going on up there?"

"You won't," Creed informed her. "There's no reception in here, so we can't contact you. You'll just have to wait until we come to the door." He indicated the clock on the wall. "By sunrise tomorrow, you can unlock the vault and leave if we're not back. You'll be safe after sunrise." Creed managed a smile at both the mother and daughter. "Stay safe."

Toby stared at the doorway after Creed left. She pushed the vault door closed and was about to secure it when Tobias stopped her.

"Mommy, I'll be okay by myself," Tobias insisted while clinging to her thick sketch pad. "You should look after Daddy. He needs you."

Toby stared at her daughter and remained tense. "Creed isn't your father," she reminded Tobias.

"He is in one story," Tobias insisted while staring back at her mother. "But he doesn't survive in any of them without you to protect him."

Toby couldn't look away from her daughter. "If I leave you here, do you survive?" she asked with concern. "I don't want to leave you all alone."

The little girl considered the question. "You don't have to worry about me," she replied. "I always survive, and I'm never alone. Keep Daddy safe."

Toby hugged her daughter while fighting her tears. "I'll be back for you, I promise."

CHAPTER 55

Toby received strange looks from the others as she walked through the house. Her mother hurried after her with a concerned expression on her face.

"I thought you were staying in the vault with Tobias," Grace remarked. "Is something wrong?"

"No," Toby replied and glanced at her mother without stopping. "Tobias told me to leave."

"She what?" Grace practically gasped as they approached Sage and Jackson, who joined in on the strange looks.

"She told me I needed to look after Creed," Toby remarked, then eyed Jackson. "Where is Creed? He left the vault a few minutes before I did. He couldn't have gotten far."

"He's on the front porch," Jackson informed her, then cocked his head as she continued past. "She must be having some sort of premonition. What else did she say?"

Toby paused and turned to face Jackson. She fidgeted and rubbed her chilled shoulders. "She told me that the only way Creed survives is with me there to protect him."

"In the scenario she showed me, you died in your car with Paul," Sage informed her. "Creed died with Mom."

"It's possible she's having premonitions of every possible outcome," Jackson remarked, then frowned. "You should go with Creed. Stick with him."

He removed a revolver from the back of his pants and handed it to her. Toby uncertainly accepted it and placed it down the back of her pants.

Grace groaned and shook her head. "I don't like this," she scoffed.

"I don't like it either," Jackson informed Grace. "But if Toby staying with Creed ensures the two of them possibly live, it's better than all of us dying."

"When we discovered Paul and Leigh were the shifters, we changed the outcome of Tobias's last premonition," Sage reminded her mother. "I'm guessing in that timeline; Paul got the slip on Toby because she trusted him. Maybe the rest of that future changed as well."

"I don't know," Toby announced with a sigh. "I just know that I need to stick with Creed. If Tobias says I should, I'm doing it."

Toby headed outside and onto the front porch, where Creed kept watch while sitting on the porch railing. He gave her the same quizzical look she'd received from the others.

"I thought you were staying with Tobias in the vault?" Creed asked.

"Tobias said I needed to stay with you," Toby informed him and joined him on the railing.

Creed drew a deep breath and stood while reaching behind him. "You should have a weapon."

"Jackson gave me one," Toby informed him

He returned to his spot on the porch railing. "That's one amazing little girl you have there," Creed remarked. "Her father must have been at least part witch."

"If he was, he didn't tell me," Toby muttered. "Of course, his plan was to abandon us from the beginning, so who knows." She then snorted a laugh. "I really know how to pick them, huh?"

"Taking up with Paul wasn't your fault," Creed insisted. "Shifters can be relentlessly charming. Once he was in your life, he was able to cloud your judgment."

"And suck my powers from me," Toby muttered, then frowned. "Like he does with Tobias in the future." She shook her head. "I can't believe Tobias ended up with Paul in the future like that. Charming the daughter of the woman he killed twenty years earlier. Makes me sick."

"Hopefully, that all changes tonight," Creed reminded her. "If at least one of us survives this, she won't be conned by him in the future."

"I want Paul dead so he never has the opportunity to touch my daughter," Toby scoffed while running trembling fingers through her hair.

Creed glanced at Toby's profile, fidgeted, and then looked away just as quickly. "Did, uh, Tobias say why you should stay with me?" he asked. "Some sort of premonition about our fate?"

It was Toby's turn to shift uncomfortably. She again raked her fingers through her hair, held her breath, and then met Creed's gaze. They stared into each other's eyes for a long, silent moment. Toby was forced to look away.

"She, uh," Toby tensed and again looked at Creed. "She called you 'Daddy'."

Creed and Toby gazed into each other's eyes for a long, silent moment. Creed appeared uncomfortable and looked away.

"She said something similar yesterday," he timidly remarked and again met Toby's gaze. Creed then offered a tiny, embarrassed smile. "I suppose I've heard stranger things the last twenty-four hours."

Toby laughed softly and looked down while hiding her smile. "Yes, I suppose so," she replied.

Creed maintained his smile and gazed across the farm at the empty pastures. "I'd be kind of interested to hear that story though," he remarked, then cast a quick, sideways glance at Toby.

Toby caught his warm gaze and quickly looked away while possibly blushing. "Yeah, me too."

Creed studied her profile a moment longer and appeared lost in his thoughts. He looked away but couldn't stop smiling. Toby shyly glanced at his profile and studied the handsome, quiet man for a moment. She drew a deep breath and proudly raised her head as she gazed out across the farm.

"It's not far-fetched," Toby remarked, then shrugged while smirking. "Not far-fetched at all."

After hearing the comment, Creed cast a surprised sideways glance at her profile and was momentarily at a loss for words. As Toby turned her head and met his gaze, Creed appeared embarrassed and hid his smile.

"No," he replied while looking away, unable to control his grin. "Not far-fetched at all."

They heard a car driving down the driveway. Both looked while straightening, hearing the car long before seeing it. Jackson stepped onto the porch with Grace and Sage only a second behind him.

"Who's that?" Grace asked as the car finally came into view.

Creed suddenly groaned. "It's Kennedy," he muttered, then looked at Jackson. "I've been avoiding her since Sunday morning. I didn't want to involve her."

"Well, she has bad timing," Jackson remarked and nodded to the car as it approached. "Get rid of her."

"Why would Kennedy get involved?" Toby asked with some surprise and seemed to put it together. "I thought she was engaged."

"Are we sure she's not Paul or Leigh?" Grace then asked. "You said shifters can take on more than one form."

"No, she's not Paul or Leigh," Creed insisted, now seeming flustered. "She's been waitressing at the tavern for a few years now, and she's been in the company of both Paul and Leigh many times. Paul was with her fiancé at the tavern when she'd first met him."

"Get rid of her," Jackson again insisted. "And make it fast. Two minutes or I chase her off."

"I have it under control," Creed informed his brother before stepping off the porch as the car stopped.

Kennedy got out of the car, eyed those on the porch, and then looked back at Creed. "Looks like you're having a party," she scoffed, clearly irritated. "Is this why you haven't been returning my calls?"

"I can explain everything," Creed informed her while tensing. "Just not right now. We're sort of in the middle of a family crisis."

"Oh?"

Creed looked back at the porch and saw Jackson cradling his shotgun while impatiently glaring at them. He then looked back at Kennedy and shifted uncomfortably.

"Jackson's in a really foul mood about it," Creed informed her. "I'll call you tomorrow, I promise."

"I broke off my engagement with my fiancé for you, Creed," Kennedy reminded him. "I thought you actually liked me. Now, it kind of feels as if you were taking advantage of my situation."

"It wasn't like that at all," Creed attempted to explain, becoming flustered. "I just need to straighten this out. I promise. I just need tonight."

Kennedy stared into his eyes a long moment before nodding. "Fine," she replied. "You can call me tomorrow afternoon, but if I don't hear from you by then, I don't want to see you ever again."

"I promise," he replied and smiled with relief. "Tomorrow afternoon."

Kennedy managed a tiny smile and opened her arms to hug him. As Creed moved in to hug her, Toby was suddenly standing alongside him and yanked him back, surprising him.

"Paul introduced her fiancé to her," Toby announced while glaring at Kennedy.

Creed was moderately confused, then turned stern while glaring at Toby. "We were already over this," he informed Toby.

"That's how I know you," Kennedy scoffed and glared at Toby while indicating Creed. "I guess we know why you broke up with Paul, huh?"

Creed looked at Kennedy with surprise and possible horror. "How did you know she broke up with Paul?" he just about gasped.

Kennedy sneered and suddenly slashed at him with a carefully hidden knife that neither had seen. Creed attempted to block the knife, but it slashed him across the lower arm. Toby went for the gun tucked in the back of her pants while Jackson raised the shotgun from his position on the porch. Kennedy cried out and lunged with the knife for Toby, tackling her to the ground. As Jackson moved toward the porch steps to assist, the screen door was thrown open to reveal Paul behind Sage and Grace. Both women screamed with surprise and bolted from his path. Jackson spun to their screams with his shotgun aimed. Paul plowed through both women, knocking them to the porch floor, as he leaped onto Jackson. Jackson was thrown backward, down the porch steps, and onto the ground with Paul on top of him. The shotgun flew from his hands upon impact. Paul raised a dagger above his head, attempting to plunge it into Jackson, while sharp teeth were revealed in his almost beastly mouth.

Jackson held back the hand with the dagger and grabbed Paul by the throat in an attempt to keep his teeth away from his face. There was a crash from inside the house, followed by gunfire. Grace and Sage jumped to their feet. While Sage ran down the porch steps, Grace produced a blue ball of fire and threw it across the yard, striking Kennedy on the back. Kennedy wailed and snarled from the hard hit. It was enough to send her rolling off Toby. She immediately changed into a bird and flew away. Sage leaped for the discarded shotgun as Jackson fought to keep Paul from tearing his throat out. She didn't have a clean shot at the man on top of Jackson. Sage cried out in anger, flipped the shotgun in her hands, and struck Paul along the side of his face with the stock. Paul rolled off

Jackson from the intense pain, dropping his dagger. He, too, turned into a bird and flew away. Sage flipped the shotgun, aimed it at the bird, and fired. The bird dipped slightly but flew away.

There was another crash from inside the house, followed by silence. Toby helped Creed to his feet. Sage grabbed the discarded dagger, and all four hurried to the porch. Dean and Lance ran from the house and looked around.

"Leigh got away," Dean gasped while breathing heavily. "Turned into a mouse. There's no telling where she got to."

"Back inside," Jackson ordered, forcing them into the house. "Kennedy's a shifter as well."

"Kennedy?" Lance gasped. "Creed's Kennedy?"

"So now there's three of them?" Dean demanded, then frowned. "That's just great."

CHAPTER 56

The sunset that evening was spectacular, but no one was outside to watch it. Tobias remained safely tucked away in the gun vault while the seven adults stayed together in the living room. Sticking together was the best way to ward off any surprise attacks. Creed continued to blame himself for being charmed by Kennedy and not seeing through her façade while Toby bandaged the injury to his forearm. Despite shifters being notorious charmers, Kennedy hadn't pursued Creed. He made the first move. Sage couldn't help but blame herself for his anguish and near-fatal attraction. She was the one who encouraged him to follow his heart and pursue the woman, which put him in her crosshairs.

Dean shifted uncomfortably in his chair and eyed those within the room. "We're going to need a lot of coffee if we're going to sit around like this all night," he finally insisted.

"We need to be cautious," Creed reminded his brother. "It's possible all three of them are inside this house waiting for us to break rank."

"No one goes anywhere alone," Jackson announced in a stern tone.

"Well, that kind of sucks," Toby remarked while squirming in her seat. "Because I have to go to the bathroom."

"Me too," Sage muttered.

"Then I suggest you partner up," Jackson informed them. "Even the bathroom isn't safe. They could be hiding in any of the walls."

Grace groaned and stood. "I'll go to the hall bathroom with my daughters," she announced. "After that, we can go to the kitchen and make some coffee."

Jackson eyed his brothers as if silently relaying some sort of message.

Creed sighed and stood. "I'll go with them," he remarked. "All three won't fit in the hall bathroom. I'll wait in the hallway with the other."

"Take your weapons," Jackson insisted.

The three women and Creed were only gone a couple of minutes when they heard the sounds of a panicked horse outside. Jackson, Lance, and Dean exchanged looks, then ran for the window and looked outside. All of the horses were supposed to be in the far pasture. As the men looked toward the barn, they saw Raven and Karma run across the driveway and into the barn with two wolves chasing after them.

"Son-of-a-bitch!" Jackson cried out.

"It's a trap," Lance shouted at his brother.

"I know," Jackson lashed back. "But I'm not going to let them kill my horses!"

As Jackson ran from the house, Lance and Dean exchanged looks, then groaned and ran after him. Sage stood in the hallway outside the bathroom with Creed and saw all three men run from the house. As Toby and Grace emerged from the bathroom, Sage looked back at them.

"Stay here," she shouted while removing the gun from the back of her pants. "I'm going to help them."

Grace and Toby looked at Creed with concern as Sage ran for the front door.

"What's happening?" Grace asked.

Creed frowned and shook his head. "Jackson's Achilles heel," he replied with defeat. "Leigh was around long enough to know how Jackson feels about his horse." He looked at both women. "We should stick together."

"I'm all for that," Grace scoffed and rolled up her sleeves while heading toward the door. "Let's get this party started."

§

Jackson ran into the barn and immediately slowed when he saw Raven and Karma near the back of the aisle, crowding each other and looking spooked. Both wolves were gone. Jackson raised his shotgun and scanned the interior for any sign of the two shifters. Lance and Dean entered and immediately stopped, also looking around with their weapons raised. The horses stomping around within the aisle was the only sound any of them heard. Sage paused within the open barn doorway and looked around, but she didn't see or hear anything. She drew a deep breath and briefly shut her eyes. When she opened her eyes, all three men and the two horses were frozen within the aisle. Sage walked along the aisle and squeezed Dean's arm. He suddenly looked around.

"What the--?"

Sage continued past him and squeezed Lance's arm. The youngest brother looked around with some surprise as well. Sage continued to look around as she approached Jackson and touched his arm. When he moved, Dean and Lance looked around the barn with astonishment as time stood still.

"How long can you hold it?" Jackson asked while walking through the barn toward the frozen horses.

"I don't know," she replied as she continued to search the barn. "They could be anywhere."

Lance and Dean hurried to catch up to them and also searched the area.

"If they turned into a fly, mosquito, or ant, we'll never find them," Dean muttered.

Jackson cautiously approached his frozen horses and gently placed his hand on Raven. He flicked a fly from the horse's shoulder and then checked each over for injuries.

"One thing's for sure," Jackson announced. "When time resumes, those bastards are going to wonder how we disappeared from one spot and ended up in another."

"Good," Dean scoffed while continuing to scan the barn. "Let's blow their minds. Might disorient them just enough."

Jackson looked back at Sage and indicated his horses. "Can you unfreeze them?" he asked. "Get them out of the danger zone?"

"I can try," Sage remarked and approached the horses. She then eyed Jackson. "You may want to stand aside. If I unfreeze them, they will be extremely spooked at our sudden appearance."

All three men moved to the side of the aisle. Sage moved between the two horses, not wanting to be in front of them when they were brought out. She placed her hands on each horse near their shoulders. Both horses suddenly bolted with loud snorts, lunging away from Sage. They seemed equally spooked to see the three men now within the barn. Both horses galloped through the aisle and out the main door. Dean and Lance joined Sage and Jackson in the area where the horses once stood. All four scanned the back of the barn for any signs of the shifters. Jackson saw a spider frozen on the wall. He slammed the side of his fist against it, crushing it, then flicked the dead carcass from his hand.

"Is that the big plan, Jackson?" Dean demanded while glaring at his brother. "Are we going to squash every insect in the barn?"

"If we have to," Jackson scoffed in response without looking back at his brother.

Lance snorted a tense laugh. "Might be a good time to set off an insect fogger," he remarked.

"Won't work," Sage informed him. "The mist would be frozen until I restart time."

Jackson glanced at his shotgun. "So buckshot won't work either," he remarked.

"No," she replied. "Just like the iced tea in the glass. It'll stay in place until time restarts."

All four looked around the general area where the horses had originally gathered, assuming the wolves changed into something else around that point. They couldn't find any visible creatures, although they could have easily turned into something hard to see with the naked eye.

"Well, we don't want to be standing here when time restarts," Lance insisted. "We want the element of surprise, not hand it to them."

"Then we should use that to our advantage," Jackson announced and eyed his brothers. "If we assume they're somewhere in this general area and anticipating us coming through the main door, we should be somewhere behind them." He looked around and indicated the loft ladder. "Up in the loft." Jackson then looked across the barn. "The back stalls over there." He waved his hand around the barn aisle. "Create a kill pit right here. They don't see us. They shift back, and we take them down."

"Kind of risky," Sage remarked, now feeling tense. "What if they're already in one of those areas? They could still get the drop on us."

"If we leave the barn where it's safe," Jackson reminded her, "we give up any advantage we might have."

"Let them escape, and they still can get the drop on us," Lance informed her.

"I say we do it," Dean announced, then indicated the ladder. "I'll take the bird's eye view."

"I got the right side," Lance informed them before heading to the end stall on the right.

"We'll take left," Jackson remarked to Sage and indicated the nearby stall. "On five." Once everyone was in place, Jackson started the countdown for his brothers. "Five, four, three, two, one--"

Sage held her breath, then released the time spell. Jackson kept his shotgun aimed at the aisle while his hidden brothers did the same. They heard Dean yell from the loft along with gunfire. Kennedy appeared in the barn aisle, having shifted from some smaller creature. Lance and Jackson aimed their weapons at her and simultaneously fired. Kennedy saw them, gasped, and transformed into an insect.

"Sage, freeze it!" Jackson shouted as he darted into the aisle from the stall.

Sage cried out with fear and concern while attempting to stop time, but nothing happened. She ran to the stall door and saw Dean falling backward from the hayloft. Sage screamed and held her hand out. Everything froze. She stared at the frozen scene around her while her heart pounded as she breathed heavily. Sage quickly darted into the barn aisle and looked up at Dean, frozen mid-fall. She placed her hand on Jackson's shoulder, freeing him from the time freeze. He quickly looked around, then looked up at his brother, frozen in a free fall.

"Son-of-a-bitch!"

Jackson handed Sage his shotgun and then hurried further down the aisle. He looked in the area where he had last seen Kennedy, but she wasn't there. There also weren't any visible insects in the general area that he could see. He again looked up at his brother, frozen while hurling backward from the loft. Jackson positioned himself and held his arms out while attempting to find the perfect spot.

"Okay," Jackson announced to her. "I'm in position."

"No," Sage informed him with concern. "You can't break his fall that way. He's going to hit with all the force he originally had. You could be badly injured while breaking his fall."

"We can't just leave him up there," Jackson interjected while looking at her.

"Do you have a blanket or a tarp?" Sage asked.

While Jackson found a large blanket in the tack room, Sage unfroze Lance. All three of them held the blanket in two hands. Then, when they were ready, Sage unfroze time. Dean continued to scream as he fell hard into the blanket they held. His weight and force from the fall nearly took all three to the ground, but he landed safely. Dean looked around with some disorientation while Jackson, Lance, and Sage looked around the barn for Kennedy and whoever had jumped Dean in the loft.

"What the hell just happened?" Dean cried out while scrambling to his feet, then looked up to the loft. "Fucking Leigh jumped me in the hayloft!"

Creed, Grace, and Toby appeared in the barn doorway, where they stopped and looked around.

"What happened?" Grace asked with surprise. "Where did the horses go?"

"Nice of you to finally join us," Dean scoffed at the three.

"Finally?" Toby asked with surprise. "We were two seconds behind you."

"Sage was manipulating time again," Jackson informed them while looking around for any sign of the female shifters. "They were here, but now they could be anywhere."

"We should go back to the house," Creed insisted.

"We're not safe there," Dean cried out, becoming animated. "We're not safe anywhere!"

"I'd feel safer in the house," Toby muttered.

"Stick together," Jackson ordered. "Stay close to one another. They can't sneak up on us as easily, and we can outnumber them."

All seven hurried from the barn and headed for the house.

CHAPTER 57

O nce they entered the house, Dean shut and locked the door behind them, not that it made any difference, but it made him feel better. They again gathered in the living room while keeping watch over their surroundings.

"This is pointless," Grace insisted while raking her fingers through her hair. "If they can come at us from something as tiny as a gnat, we'll never see them coming."

"I'm open to suggestions," Jackson snarled back at Sage's mother.

"The time freeze spell nearly worked," Sage insisted.

"Nearly worked?" Dean demanded. "I just about fell to my death from the hayloft."

"But you didn't," Jackson snapped at his brother.

"If I can manage to freeze time fast enough, they'll be frozen in some form big enough to see and kill them," Sage announced.

"We need more spells," Toby remarked.

"Got any?" Creed asked with a curious look.

"To my knowledge, there aren't any spells to stop or deter a shifter," Lance informed them.

"What about a spell to ward off insects?" Dean remarked.

"Be serious," Lance scoffed while glaring at his brother.

"I am being serious," Dean snarled back. "They make bug repellant. Why not a spell for repelling bugs?"

Jackson groaned, placed his arms around Sage's neck, and held her against him. "I'm pretty sure this is what hell feels like," he muttered.

Sage placed her arms around his waist and rested her head on his chest. "Don't worry," she announced with a sigh. "I'm sure it's going to get worse."

§

An hour later, it was after eight o'clock, and the world outside was nearly dark except for the light from the full, strawberry moon. The captive men and women had rearranged the furniture in the living room toward the center so they could sit with their backs to one another and watch the room. Unfortunately, they were playing by the shifters' rules, which meant their stalkers had the upper hand and could wait them out until they were all exhausted. The seven knew they'd have to eventually take turns napping in order to keep an eye on their surroundings. No one had said much during the last hour as they mostly just listened to every creak within the house. Toby seemed to be the only one who heard a strange clunk and looked around.

"Did anyone else hear that?" Toby asked.

Everyone now listened for whatever it was Toby thought she heard.

Grace suddenly sat upright and looked around. "I smell smoke," she gasped.

Everyone leaped from their seats and headed for the living room doorway. They saw smoke wafting from the dining room alongside the kitchen just down the hall.

"They're making their move," Jackson shouted as he hurried for the kitchen. "Stay together!"

Everyone kept up with Jackson. He grabbed a fire extinguisher from the hall closet on their way through. Creed nudged Toby and indicated the kitchen. The two broke off from the group and ran into the kitchen for another fire extinguisher. Lance and Dean ripped down the curtains from the hall window and ran into the dining room with Jackson. While Jackson attempted to fight the flames with the fire extinguisher, Lance and Dean beat the flames with the curtains. Sage and Grace remained vigilant and watched the men's backs, but the hallway was rapidly filling with smoke. Creed and Toby appeared in the dining room from the kitchen entrance, and Creed used his fire extinguisher on the flames from their end. They were able to put out the fire between the four men, but there was now smoke everywhere, making it difficult to see much.

Jackson motioned for Creed and Toby to go around the other way and meet them in the hall as everyone now coughed from the smoke. Sage turned toward her mother while both kept their eyes on the smoke-filled hallway. Grace's eyes suddenly widened, and she cast her hands toward Sage.

"Down!" Grace cried out.

Sage gasped and attempted to duck as her mother launched a blue fireball past her, but she wasn't fast enough. Something cold and hard struck Sage on her head just near her temple as a blue fireball whizzed past her. The intense surge of pain to Sage's head rippled down her back and into her legs. For a moment, Sage could only hear her own heart beating despite her mother screaming while casting balls of blue light past her. Sage saw Jackson slide across the floor to catch her as she collapsed, and everything went dark.

§

Sage stared at the darkness surrounding her, where she remained on the hall floor. Everything was eerily silent, and it frightened her. She could somehow feel the presence of others and movement all around her, yet she didn't hear or see anything. Little Tobias appeared from the darkness and stared at her aunt, who lay on the cold, hardwood floor.

"Aunt Sage," Tobias gasped with fear showing on her face and became animated. "Get up!"

Sage could barely move and attempted to focus on her little niece. Her body felt unusually heavy and cold.

"Get up!" Tobias now screamed almost hysterically. "Get up!"

Sage could see the panicked look in her niece's eyes as she continued to scream while tears streaked her little face.

"Older Uncle Jackson can help you," Tobias cried out, unable to control her emotions. "I'll send you to him."

Sage knew Tobias was going to send her into the future back to fifty-year-old Jackson. She couldn't let her do it. No more time jumping.

"No," Sage panted and managed to lift herself onto her hip while gasping, now short of breath. Everything seemed to hurt at once. "No, I've got this."

"Please, Aunt Sage," Tobias sobbed in anguish. "Let me send you away!"

"No," Sage again insisted and now sat up. "I need to wake up."

§

Sage fought to open her eyes and looked around the smoke-filled hallway from her lying position on the floor. The ringing in her ears was so loud that she couldn't hear anything else. Her mother's angry screams were inaudible as she cast blue fireballs across the hallway at something behind Sage. Sage could feel Jackson's knee practically in her back as he crouched over her, remaining against her while firing his shotgun. That she could barely hear the shotgun blast was almost concerning.

She watched helplessly as Dean stumbled down the hallway while fighting something resembling a werewolf struggling for control of the shotgun in his hands. Lance rode the creature's back with a knife in his hand and repeatedly plunged it into the creature's shoulder, which seemed to have little effect. A second werewolf lunged for Creed, who fired several rounds from his handgun while pushing Toby back into the kitchen and out of the creature's path. As the ringing in Sage's ears subsided, the loudness of Jackson's shotgun was almost deafening. Sage weakly pulled herself up to her hands and knees.

"Sage," Jackson cried out while remaining close to her on the floor. "Stay down!"

Sage didn't listen and continued onto her hands and knees. A third werewolf suddenly vanished and appeared behind Grace.

"Behind you," Jackson yelled to Grace while repositioning his shotgun.

Grace cried out and threw herself to the floor just as the creature's claws swiped at her. Jackson fired the shotgun, but the werewolf again vanished, obviously changing into an insect to avoid being hit. Sage sat back on her feet just in time to see the werewolf appear behind Jackson. Grace saw it from her crouched position on the floor and screamed a warning to him. Jackson spun as the creature slashed for his throat. Sage saw the creature's sharp claws about to strike Jackson. She cried out in anger while raising her hand. A massive ball of blue fire shot from her hand and struck the creature sending it flying backward and crashing into the smoke-filled dining room. Grace and Jackson were momentarily stunned, then looked at Sage on the floor, panting in agony and exhaustion.

"Well, son-of-a-bitch," Jackson announced almost matter-of-factly.

Grace ran for Sage on the floor while Jackson bolted for the dining room. He stood in the open doorway a moment and looked around.

"He's gone," Jackson announced, then hurried back for Sage and helped her to her feet. "We need to get her patched up before he recovers and comes back." Jackson attempted to hold Sage upright and stared into her eyes. "Can you stop time?"

Sage held her breath a moment, then shook her head. "No," she gasped.

"They knew," Grace cried out while helping Jackson guide Sage to the hall bathroom. "They knew she was the one doing something and needed to stop her."

Jackson got Sage into the bathroom and sat her on the closed toilet seat lid. "I need to help the others," he informed Grace, then indicated Sage. "See if you can stop the bleeding. Keep her awake."

Grace quickly straightened and stared at Jackson with a look of horror. "You can't go out there alone!"

"My brothers and your daughter could be in danger," Jackson informed her. "I have to go after them."

Grace groaned in frustration as Jackson ran from the bathroom, slamming the door behind him. Sage drew several deep breaths, then looked at her mother and turned angry.

"Freeze it," Sage ordered.

Grace looked at her daughter with some surprise. "What?" she gasped.

"The wound," Sage announced firmly and indicated her bleeding head. "Freeze the wound."

Grace appeared somewhat concerned. "It's going to sting like a bastard."

"Do it!"

Her mother held her breath, then raised her hand to Sage's head. A blue stream of light traveled from her hand to her daughter's wound. Sage suddenly cried out in pain and gripped the sink alongside her. Grace held back her sobs and continued to apply treatment. When Grace lowered her hand, Sage just about collapsed against the sink while panting heavily.

"Are you okay?" Grace asked with concern in her voice.

Sage gasped several times, then nodded and pulled herself to her feet. "Let's go."

"Are you--?"

Sage stumbled past her mother and for the closed bathroom door. Grace drew a deep breath and followed her from the bathroom.

CHAPTER 58

Dean and Lance ran across the driveway and into the well-lit barn with no sign of the werewolf chasing them. Dean shut and latched the door, although that obviously wouldn't matter once the shifter changed into an insect.

"Okay," Dean announced while breathing heavily as he eyed his brother and then nodded. "You were right about it being a shifter."

"We need to come up with a plan fast," Lance informed him. "Because it's going to be inside any minute now if it isn't already."

"I have a plan," Dean informed his brother.

"You do?"

"Yeah, don't die, and kill the fucker," Dean insisted.

Lance hesitated and then looked around the barn. "Isn't this where Tobias said I died?"

Dean glanced around the barn a moment, then looked back at his brother and nodded. "Yeah, I think so."

"Great," Lance muttered.

The men turned their backs to each other while holding their weapons and scanned the area surrounding them. Despite the lights brightening the barn, it was still unusually eerie and silent.

"Why do you look scared, Dean?" Leigh was heard from somewhere within the barn. Her tone was playful and almost sultry.

Both men scanned the area, attempting to zero in on her location. It sounded as if it came from the loft.

"She can only sound like Leigh while in human form," Lance whispered to Dean.

"Okay, got it," Dean muttered and scanned the hayloft above.

"You know how I feel about you," Leigh continued, her voice now coming from the far left back stalls.

Both men remained still with their backs to each other and looked in that direction.

"You said she had to be in human form in order to sound like Leigh," Dean scoffed under his breath.

"She can change to an insect and move around," Lance reminded him. "But she has to be in human form when she's talking."

"I won't hurt you, Dean," Leigh insisted, now speaking from the stalls near the back to the right. "I chose you, remember? I won't let my children hurt you."

"Children?" Dean gasped while scanning the area for any sign of Leigh. "What children?"

"You know them as Paul and Kennedy," Leigh informed him, her voice again coming from the loft but now closer to them.

"How can they be her children?" Dean muttered to his brother.

"They live a long time," Lance reminded his brother. "And she can shift younger or older. Male or female. Animal or human."

"Yeah, I got that part," Dean muttered while scanning the loft, although neither couldn't see much of it from their position. "If you really care about me, you wouldn't hurt my family and friends either."

"We feed off their power," Leigh responded from the lower-left stalls, causing both men to turn and look for her. "It's how we survive."

"No, it's how you remain immortal," Lance informed her while looking around. "You *choose* to kill for immortality. You don't *have* to kill."

"Killing you and your brothers was never part of the plan," Leigh informed him from the right side of the barn.

Both looked to the right.

"We don't want to hurt you," Leigh continued from the loft.

Both looked to the loft.

"Just give us the girls," Leigh announced from the left of the barn, forcing them to again turn with their weapons aimed. "Give us the girls, and we'll leave you and your brothers alone." Her voice continued from the right side of the barn. "Three of them for the three of us." They heard her voice from the loft. "I still want you, and Kennedy wants to be with Creed. It'll all work out." Her voice then came from the left side of the barn. "Just give us the girls."

Dean eyed Lance and raised his brows in question.

Lance's eyes widened in horror. "Are you even considering it?" he gasped.

Dean looked around the barn. "What about the kid?" he asked.

"Too young," Leigh informed him from the right side of the barn. There was a pause as her voice then came from the loft. "We have no interest in her."

Dean moved along the aisle while Lance kept his back to him, although Lance was now somewhat concerned about his brother's motives.

"So I can keep her as my daughter?" Dean asked as he cautiously moved along the aisle with Lance's back to his.

"If you wish it," Leigh replied from the left side of the barn.

Dean listened to the sound of Leigh's beating heart getting louder. He suddenly bolted for the nearby stall on the right with his weapon aimed. Leigh, in human form, was standing in the stall and appeared almost horrified when she saw him. She sneered and swiftly transformed. Dean fired his weapon as she changed into a fly. The bullet struck the insect. Leigh returned to her human form while gasping and clutching her bleeding abdomen. Despite that it was only a 9mm caliber bullet, her entire mid-section was torn through, leaving a huge hole in her body, revealing the damage done while she was in a smaller form. Leigh gasped as she stared at the large hole torn through her. Blood seeped from her mouth as she shifted her gaze, staring at Dean with horror in her eyes.

"No deal," Dean informed her without emotion, then aimed his gun at her head and pulled the trigger.

The second bullet struck her directly between the eyes. Her head snapped back, and she immediately collapsed to the floor. Lance stared at the dead woman, then looked back at his brother.

"You were following her heartbeat, weren't you?" Lance asked.

"And the pattern," Dean informed him. "She moved up, left, right each time." He smiled at his brother with some humor. "She always complained that I never listened when she talked. I'm glad I finally listened for a change."

"Yeah, well," Lance announced. "You're still a dick."

"And I can live with that."

CHAPTER 59

Jackson clutched the shotgun in his hands as he walked along the driveway, heading toward the barn. The barn door was closed, but the light was on. He cautiously made his way toward the barn and then saw a man and a woman running along the fence line, heading toward the woods.

"Creed," Jackson gasped softly.

There was a gunshot from the barn. Jackson raised his shotgun and continued toward the closed barn door when he heard a second gunshot from the same location. Shadows seemed to be moving all around him, forcing him to stop and again scan the area. He heard creaking on the porch behind him and spun with the shotgun aimed. Sage and Grace now stood on the porch and looked around as well. He motioned for them to stay there, then turned and resumed his course for the barn.

§

Creed and Toby ran along the fence line toward the woods while looking up to the sky behind them. The hawk flew after them and was gaining ground. They continued toward the woods, where two horses stood watching them.

"She's gaining on us," Toby cried out.

Creed pointed up ahead where Raven and Karma stood near the woods' edge. "We need to make it to the woods," he yelled back. "She'll need to shift to pursue us."

"I don't see how that's any better," Toby shouted back.

Raven and Karma saw them approaching and spooked, bolting around each other in a tight circle. Creed and Toby ran past the horses and into the woods. Toby eyed the frightened horses and now appeared alarmed. As she followed Creed into the woods, they slowed and turned. Creed was now armed with a hunting knife while Toby grabbed a thick branch.

"This isn't good," Toby insisted while both looked around. "This is where Tobias saw you and my mother dead. Only now I'm with you instead."

"Tobias also said you could save me," Creed reminded her as they watched the woods and the pasture just beyond the tree line where the nervous horses watched them.

The hawk landed just outside the woods and immediately changed into Kennedy. She wore a sly grin on her face while watching them.

"There's no way out of this, Creed," Kennedy remarked while maintaining her smile. "You have no place to run and no place to hide." She then indicated his knife. "And that little knife isn't going to save you."

Both horses stared at Kennedy with fear and snorted, although they didn't run from her. Kennedy slyly eyed the horses and approached Karma with her hand out. Karma snorted but appeared a little more trusting than Raven. Kennedy affectionately pet the horse while moving closer to the mare. As the horse relaxed, claws appeared from Kennedy's fingertips, and she smiled with sharp fangs in her mouth. She turned toward the mare while digging her claws into the horse's neck close to her mane. The mare squealed as the claws sank into her neck, and she attempted to pull away. Kennedy clung to her neck with her claws, holding her in place as she lunged for the horse's throat with her fangs. There was a loud, ear-piercing squeal, but it didn't come from Karma.

Kennedy turned her head and saw Raven rearing in front of her with his front hooves wildly thrashing and his ears pinned back. Before Kennedy could react, the horse's hooves struck her shoulder. She was driven to the ground by the hard strike. Kennedy rolled and sprang back to her feet, changing into a mountain lion. She roared at Raven while exposing sharp fangs and prepared to pounce, but Raven had already spun his back end to her. His rear hoof struck the mountain lion in the face, rolling it across the ground. Although somewhat dazed by the hit, the mountain lion sprang back to its feet. Before it could even react, Raven's back end was once again in front of it, and the hoof again kicked back, striking the mountain lion squarely in the chest.

The mountain lion was thrown several feet and lay motionless a moment. Raven snorted loudly, ears pinned, and pranced back and forth in front of Karma while slinging his angry head at the mountain lion. As the mountain lion slowly moved to its feet, Raven again lunged for it with his mouth open and teeth bared. The demon-possessed horse was nothing short of frightening. The mountain lion cowered a moment.

"Raven, back!" Creed cried out.

The horse bolted away as Creed ran for the injured mountain lion with his dagger above his head, prepared to strike. The mountain lion changed into a grizzly bear and turned its back to Creed. Creed's knife struck the thick hide on its backside, only minimally slicing its thick skin. The grizzly took off across the pasture, needing to recover from the damage done by the horse. Toby ran for Creed and stood just behind him while watching the running bear.

"She'll be back," Creed informed Toby, then took her hand. "We need to get back to the house before she recovers from that head kick."

Toby looked back at the two horses. Raven nuzzled Karma, then sniffed the claw puncture wounds on her neck that barely bled. Creed pulled on Toby's hand.

"She'll be fine," he insisted. "We need to go."

Toby nodded and ran with Creed back to the house.

§

Jackson was now only a few feet from the barn when the sound of a horse squealing in the distance caught his attention. He looked away from the barn toward the distant pasture. His love for his horses would be his downfall. He heard the squeal again. Jackson gritted his teeth and then looked back to the barn. When he saw something move alongside him, Jackson spun just in time to see a blue fireball strike the barn not far from him. He jumped back in surprise and saw a mouse scurry away. Jackson aimed his shotgun and squeezed the trigger. The shotgun blast exploded the ground alongside the mouse. The mouse suddenly changed into a bird and took flight. Another blue fireball struck the barn just near the bird but missed.

Jackson took a step back and then looked at the porch where Grace stood with a blue fireball between her hands, prepared to fire while Sage searched the sky. It was just dark enough that she couldn't see much. Jackson heard something snarl beyond the barn. He took two quick steps past the barn and aimed his shotgun into the paddock. Something large ran past the far side of the paddock but kept going. Jackson continued to scan the area and then looked back to the porch, where Sage and Grace continued to study the surrounding area as well. Paul suddenly appeared behind Grace.

"Grace!" Jackson shouted while raising the shotgun, but he was too late.

Paul grabbed Grace around the neck from behind and placed a decorative dagger to her throat. "I never did like you," he snarled and was about to slit her throat.

A blue light engulfed the dagger while Paul struggled to keep the knife to Grace's throat. Paul's eyes shifted to Sage, only a few feet away. Sage's eyes were fixated on him as the blue light expelled from her fingertips.

"You!" Paul snarled in anger while fighting to maintain control of the dagger. "I guess I didn't hit you on the head hard enough."

Jackson ran across the yard with his shotgun, attempting to get a clean shot. While Paul fought Sage's magical spell for control over the knife, Grace produced her own blue light in her left hand. She sneered and flung her hand and the light backward, striking him in the groin with it. Paul cried out, releasing the dagger and Grace as he was knocked backward from the blow. The dagger flew across the yard, narrowly missing Jackson, who threw himself to the ground with a startled cry. The dagger became embedded in the ground not far from Jackson's head. Grace leaped to the porch floor, giving Sage an unobstructed shot. Sage coiled back in anger and shot a large stream of blue light at Paul. Paul gasped and vanished. The blue light struck the porch railing and nearly obliterated it. Jackson pulled himself to his feet, and all three looked around.

Paul reappeared alongside Jackson, punched him in the face, and snatched the shotgun from him. Grace and Sage both turned before he could use the shotgun and fired blue fireballs at him. Paul again vanished, dropping the shotgun. Within her subconscious, Sage heard Tobias scream.

"Tobias!" Sage gasped and looked around.

"What is it?" Grace cried out with a look of horror on her face.

"Something's happened," Sage gasped in response. "I need to check on her."

Paul suddenly tackled Sage over the porch railing and into the shrubs. Sage launched a blue fireball at him, but he again disappeared.

"Take care of him," Grace shouted to her daughter. "I'll get Tobias!"

Jackson ran for Sage and just about pulled her from the shrubs. They turned their backs to each other and looked around.

CHAPTER 60

Grace ran through the house and for the basement stairs with reckless abandon. She thundered down the stairs, not even attempting to be quiet about it. As she bolted through the basement, she could see the wine cellar door was open, and she could hear something pounding on the solid steel gun vault door. Grace slowed her approach and peered into the wine cellar. Tobias's muffled screams could be heard on the other side of the steel door as a large werewolf creature with a long, bleeding gash on its back pounded on the door, successfully denting the steel. It was entirely possible it could break into the armory. Grace sneered and stepped into the wine cellar doorway.

"Get away from my granddaughter!"

As the werewolf turned, Grace shot a blue fireball at it, hitting it hard enough that it was thrown backward. As the light hit it, the creature attempted to shift, resulting in flashes of several different creatures as well as Kennedy. The powerful ball of light prevented her from shifting. Grace cried out and cast another fireball before Kennedy could recover and change. Kennedy again shifted into several creatures while enduring the agonizing pain, attempting to take any form that would shatter the spell.

Tobias's muffled screams beyond the steel door turned to concern. "Grandma," she was barely heard through the door. "Don't die, Grandma!"

Despite that Tobias had possibly seen her grandmother's demise, Grace continued her angry assault on the shifter Kennedy, casting one ball of energy after another while screaming profanities.

"You will *not* terrorize my family!" Grace screamed as Kennedy continued to writhe in agony while attempting to shift. "Leave them alone!"

"Grandma, no!" Tobias was heard screaming beyond the steel door. "Behind you!"

Before Grace could even understand Tobias's warning, Paul suddenly appeared behind Grace with sharp claws against her neck. Grace cried out and turned just in time to keep the claws from ripping into her throat. His claws, instead, tore into her shoulder. Grace cried out in anguish and fell to her knees while clutching her bleeding shoulder.

"Grandma!" came Tobias's shrill scream.

The sound of the vault door opening from the inside was enough to horrify the injured woman. "Tobias, no!" Grace screamed, knowing the child had willingly opened the door.

Despite that Paul was in a position to kill her, Grace concentrated all her effort on the recovering shifter, Kennedy, who was closest to the vault door. She cast a blue fireball at Kennedy in a last effort to save her granddaughter despite that it meant certain death for herself. As the blue fireball hit Kennedy, Paul grabbed Grace's throat from behind, sinking his claws into her flesh. Instead of Tobias, Grace saw Wolfram step out of the vault with a stone-cold look on his face. He sneered and cast his left hand toward Grace, catching Paul's claws with blue streams of light and stopping them from digging into her neck. He then cast his right hand behind him, slamming Kennedy roughly into the wall. The werewolf creature fought the blue light that kept his claws from digging further into Grace's neck.

Without lowering his left hand or releasing the light projecting from his fingertips, Wolfram slowly approached Grace and the werewolf Paul, locking eyes with the creature while showing no emotion. Wolfram suddenly sneered and closed his left hand into a tight fist. There was a loud crunching sound as Paul's claws were seemingly crushed as he screamed in agony. The werewolf Paul released Grace and vanished. Grace fell to her knees while gasping in pain as she clutched the four bleeding gashes on her shoulder. She looked up at the warlock standing over her.

"Wolfram," she gasped, obviously not believing her eyes. "How?"

"My granddaughter time surfed into the past and asked me to help her," Wolfram replied, then offered a tiny smile as he lowered himself to the floor before her. He gently removed Grace's hand from her wound. "She brought me back with her."

Grace panted while staring at the warlock she hadn't seen in twenty-three years. As he placed his hand over the four gashes on her shoulder, Grace gasped in agony and then cried out while he froze her bleeding wounds. When he pulled his hand away, she just about collapsed to the floor. The werewolf Kennedy now stood behind Wolfram with her claws coiled back, prepared to slash him where he kneeled. Werewolf Kennedy snarled in anger, alerting them to her presence. Wolfram spun with surprise to see the werewolf behind him and shielded himself while coiling back with his hand, a blue flame appearing in his palm.

"You will *not* terrorize my family," Tobias's young angry voice was heard snarling behind Kennedy.

As the werewolf Kennedy turned, Wolfram and Grace saw Tobias just outside the vault within the wine cellar. She had a blue fireball the size of a basketball in her hands close to her chest. The look in the child's eyes was cold and menacing. Without even moving, the fireball was launched from her hands like a cannonball. It struck the werewolf with such power and force, it threw the creature against the far wine rack with a crash and held it inches off the floor. Kennedy snarled and writhed in agony as the energy held her against the wine rack. The massive balls of light shot from Tobias's small hands like torpedoes, striking the creature rapidly and with tremendous force. The entire wine rack behind the creature was crushed from the pressure while the blue light held Kennedy immobile against the wall, each ball of light compounding against the last. The werewolf transformed back into Kennedy's human form as she screamed in agony.

Wolfram and Grace stared in silent shock at what they were witnessing. Tobias kept her eyes locked on Kennedy while keeping her pinned against the wall with a force field of blue light from her left hand. Tobias then raised her right hand without showing any emotion and snapped her fingers. The blue light holding Kennedy to the wall suddenly crushed her against the cinderblock, seemingly snapping every bone in her body at once. Kennedy cried out as her body exploded against the wall like a bug on a windshield. Wolfram and Grace appeared almost horrified, then looked back at Tobias. The little girl gasped and fell to her knees. Grace pulled away from Wolfram and bolted for her granddaughter. She pulled her into her arms and sobbed softly.

"I'm sorry, Grandma," Tobias whispered while clinging to her grandmother. "She was going to hurt Grandpa. Don't be mad at me."

"I'm not," Grace whispered while cuddling her. "Not even a little."

CHAPTER 61

Sage and Jackson looked around outside the front of the house, waiting for Paul to reappear, but he seemed to have vanished for now. Dean and Lance appeared from the barn just in time to meet up with Creed and Toby, who ran all the way from the woods' edge. All four nervously looked around while approaching Sage and Jackson closer to the house.

"Kennedy got away," Creed informed Jackson. "Raven got a piece of her, though. She was injured pretty badly."

"We totally iced Leigh in the barn," Dean informed his brothers a little too proudly. "She's toast."

"Where's Mom?" Toby asked with concern while looking around.

"She went to check on Tobias," Sage informed her sister, then fidgeted. "We should probably check on her. Something had Tobias upset, and she contacted me."

"I'll go," Toby announced with concern.

"Not alone," Jackson snapped back.

"I'll stay with her," Creed insisted.

Toby and Creed hurried into the house while the remaining four continued to scan the area.

"I'd love to think we scared them off," Jackson muttered, "but that's probably wishful thinking."

"We should go inside," Sage suggested while rubbing her sore temple.

Jackson turned toward her with a sympathetic look and checked her head injury. He then met her gaze and offered a tiny smile.

"How are you feeling?" he asked timidly.

"I've felt better," she informed him before considering the comment. "Although, I've felt worse too."

"I should get you some ice for your head," Jackson remarked, then looked at his brothers. "We'll hole up in the kitchen a few hours. Regroup there. Get some ice for Sage and some coffee for the rest of us."

"Or something stronger," Dean muttered.

"You can have something stronger when the last two are dead," Jackson informed him in a stern tone.

All four cautiously headed for the porch, with Lance and Dean bringing up the rear while keeping watch behind them. Jackson opened the door for Sage, allowing her to enter first. As soon as Sage passed through the doorway, she was yanked inside, and the door slammed shut behind her in Jackson's face. Sage cried out with surprise as she was grabbed by the throat and slammed against the door to keep the guys out. Jackson was already kicking the door, attempting to open it while yelling for her. Sage stared into Paul's eyes as he held his clawed left hand close to her face. He snarled at her, revealing sharp fangs. She could feel something was wrong with his right hand that held her throat. There weren't any claws, and his fingers felt somehow stubby and sticky.

"Your friends killed my family," he snarled close to her face. "I'll come back for the rest of your family later, but you? I need your energy now."

Paul lunged for her neck with his teeth as the door thumped harshly against her back from Jackson on the other side. Sage cried out with surprise, then anger. Paul's teeth were close to her neck when he suddenly cried out in agony. He attempted to take a step back and saw Sage's hand several inches from his crotch while a blue light attached itself to his man parts. Paul continued to howl in pain while clutching his stubby fingers against her throat and attempting to coil back with his clawed hand. Sage gritted her teeth and groaned loudly as the blue light attached to his crotch intensified. As his claws attempted to reach her neck, Sage sent another wave of blue energy from her free hand, catching his claws and held them back.

Paul attempted to shift into something more powerful to defeat her, but the pain she was causing him between his legs was hampering his ability. Sage watched him while remaining focused as his face and body attempted to morph. She was horrified when she briefly saw Leo, but it spiked her anger and gave her greater power. He continued to scream while enduring the pain, fighting her, and attempting to shift. He attempted to resume his werewolf form but couldn't manage it. The door again thumped against Sage's back, breaking her concentration and her hold. As his claws came at her face, Sage saw flashes of older Jackson, her niece, and her father. Their voices were now stuck in her mind.

"Do you think, maybe, this will be us in twenty years? That maybe this future will one day be our reality?"

"I have a daughter who can time surf. You must have unlimited power."

"You can fix it, though, right, Aunt Sage? You said you could fix it."

"I've only ever been in love twice in my life, Jackson. Both times, it's been with you."

Sage caught Paul's clawed hand with a stream of blue light and locked eyes with him. He could see the rage building within her emerald green eyes that now somehow seemed to turn ice blue.

"You took my family from me once," she snarled. "You will *never* do it again."

The energy from both her hands increased, and she threw Paul across the hall and onto the staircase. He was consumed by the blue fire that now seemed to pin him to the stairs. Sage's eyes were now glowing blue as she stepped away from the door.

The door was immediately thrown open, and Jackson lunged in the foyer just in time to witness Sage's wrath. Sage held Paul down with one hand that was shooting light and coiled back with her other hand. When she cast her hand at him, the energy practically filled the room and rumbled the entire house. As the second light hit Paul, who was already writhing on the stairs, he burst into a large blue flame. Although it didn't burn him, he screamed in terror and agony. His entire body suddenly crumbled within the light and turned to dust.

Sage released her hold and watched the blue, glowing dust, which was once Paul, glisten through the air and sprinkle across the staircase. Jackson, Dean, and Lance watched with matching looks of horror as the glowing blue dust settled. Sage breathed heavily and stared at the staircase a moment, then uncertainly looked at Jackson's stunned expression. He finally turned, met her gaze, and drew a slightly shaken breath.

"I hope you don't expect me to clean that mess," Jackson informed her.

Sage let out an exhausted breath, smiled, and just about collapsed into his arms. Jackson held her against him and affectionately kissed the top of her head.

"Uh, who's that?" Lance asked, getting their attention.

Jackson and Sage looked down the hall and saw Wolfram carrying Tobias, who happily clung to him. Grace and Toby walked on either side of him while Creed brought up the rear.

"Wolfram!" Sage cried out in surprise and pulled away from Jackson.

"Wolfram?" Lance, Dean, and Jackson all gasped in unison.

Sage hurried down the hall and paused before her father. "How--?"

Wolfram smiled when he saw her, then cuddled his granddaughter in his arms. "Tobias was insistent that I come for a visit."

Sage cocked her head and appeared concerned. "But if you go back to your own timeline, everything you did gets erased," she reminded him.

Wolfram drew a deep breath while maintaining his smile. "You're right," he replied, then chuckled. "I guess I have to stay."

Grace's smile suddenly increased to something somewhat devilish and almost sinister. "Oh, really?" she asked.

Wolfram cast a look at Grace and returned the grin. Toby and Sage both rolled their eyes and groaned. Wolfram then cast his gaze upon Jackson, who just about backed up a step out of reflex.

"And who's this?" Wolfram asked Sage while sizing up Jackson.

"That's Sage's boyfriend," Grace announced with a devious smirk while eyeing Jackson.

There was a tense moment as Jackson waited for the hammer to drop from the woman who despised him and his kind.

Grace maintained her grin and patted Wolfram's arm. "He's a nice young man," she announced, then looked back at Jackson and smiled. "I think you'll like him."

CHAPTER 62

The following spring. Toby held her cellphone and recorded Dean leading Tobias around the paddock on the large chubby pony.

"Faster, Uncle Dean," Tobias cried out.

Dean laughed and ran alongside the pony, making it jog with the little girl on its back. Once Toby stopped recording her daughter on the pony, Creed placed his arms around Toby's waist from behind and held her in a warm embrace.

"Careful," Creed warned while gently caressing Toby's baby bump. "If she becomes too good of a rider, Jackson will want her out working the cattle."

"Fat chance," Toby announced while warmly caressing his hands on her.

"Daddy," Tobias cried out, catching Creed's attention. "Look, I'm a cowgirl."

"Yes, you are, sweetheart," Creed happily called back, then glared at his brother running alongside the pony and gave him a stern look. "Not so fast, Dean!"

Dean and Tobias both responded with frowns. "Oh--"

Sage leaned on the fence at the nearby pasture not far from the first paddock while Jackson held her from behind and rested his head on her shoulder. Both watched Karma and her little black colt enjoying the second paddock together. Raven had his large black head over the pasture fence and snickered at the mare and his colt. When the colt ventured too close to the fence where the stallion stood, Karma circled around her baby, pinned her ears at Raven, and led the colt away. Raven stomped his hoof, clearly annoyed.

Jackson chuckled while warmly nuzzling Sage's body with his from behind. "Karma is definitely in charge," he announced.

"I almost feel bad for Raven," Sage remarked while grinning as she played with Jackson's wedding band while he caressed her abdomen.

"Give it three to six months," Jackson informed her, then smiled slyly. "She'll be begging for his attention again."

"Building an entire army of Ravens?" she teased.

"No," Jackson replied while nuzzling her. "Just one more. One little Raven or Karma for my witchy wife."

Sage turned her head and met his gaze, his face close to hers. "One for me?" she asked while smiling proudly.

"Only the best for you," he replied.

Sage placed her hand on his face and warmly kissed his lips. Jackson eagerly returned the kiss, then spun her in his arms and pulled her against him. As he moved in for a more passionate kiss, Lance approached them from the house.

"Sage, your mother called," Lance announced, interrupting their kiss.

Jackson groaned and threw his head back. "I swear; she knows and interrupts us on purpose."

Lance ignored his brother. "She and your father are back from their European trip," he informed Sage. "They plan on stopping by for the weekend before heading to Australia."

"Australia?" Sage asked Lance with some surprise, then shook her head. "They don't ever rest. I don't think they've been home more than two weeks since Toby plucked him from the past."

"I wonder how many bottles of wine they're bringing this time. We're going to need more space in the wine cellar,"

Jackson remarked while shaking his head. "I can't believe they've single-handedly replaced all the bottles that broke when Tobias threw her little tantrum."

"Tantrum?" Sage remarked as she pulled away from him to meet his gaze. "Is that what we're calling what happened in the wine cellar?"

"She hasn't done anything remotely close to that since," Jackson reminded her. "She needs to spend a little more time with Grandpa Wolfram and learn to control her emotions so she doesn't level the house when she hits puberty."

"I'm just glad my sister's powers are pretty much restored after all that time Paul had spent draining them," Sage remarked.

"All that couples time with Creed hasn't been hurting either," Jackson added with a snicker. "Creed's powers are peaking nicely as well."

Lance rolled his eyes in disgust. "It's not fair," he muttered. "Dean and I don't get any powers."

Jackson grinned and held his hand up, revealing a softball-sized ball of blue light. "You need to find yourself a young, pretty, single witch," he announced, then spun the blue ball of light on his fingertip like a basketball.

"Stop showing off," Sage scolded Jackson while hiding her smile. "Save it for the bedroom."

Lance groaned while rolling his eyes. "And I'm out of here," he muttered. "I won't be home for dinner. I have that council meeting tonight."

Jackson made the ball of light disappear and then eyed his brother. "Swearing in the new sheriff?" he asked.

Lance looked back while grinning. "Yeah, and she's really hot," he replied.

"Don't stay out too late," Jackson announced as Lance headed back to the house. "It's a school night!"

Lance half-assed waved to him, although he might have given him the middle finger. "Yes, Dad!"

Jackson groaned and shook his head. "Damned kids," he muttered, then grinned and pulled Sage into his arms, holding her against him. "How about that picnic lunch?"

"Ready when you are," Sage announced cheerfully.

Jackson kissed her warmly but quickly on the lips, then pulled away and met her gaze. "You grab the wine, and I'll saddle the horses." He kissed her again and then headed for the barn.

Sage was about to head to the house when she heard Tobias's voice echoing in her head.

"Aunt Sage," the little girl announced in the confines of Sage's mind.

"Yes, dear?" Sage replied and glanced across the ranch to the paddock where Tobias happily rode the pony led by her Uncle Dean.

Tobias looked across the paddock, met her Aunt Sage's gaze, and smiled. "I saw Uncle Dean's future wife," she announced telepathically to her aunt. "Her car will break down alongside the road tonight just as it gets dark."

"You know what to do," Sage replied with her mind.

Sage and Tobias exchanged smiles and then went about their business. As Sage headed for the house, Tobias looked at her Uncle Dean leading the pony.

"Uncle Dean," Tobias announced.

He looked back at her and smiled. "Yes, sweetheart," Dean asked.

"Can we go out for ice cream tonight?"

"Of course, we can go for ice cream," Dean replied cheerfully. "I love ice cream."

THE END

Other books by Holly Copella!
Reviews left on Amazon are appreciated!

"The Battle for Andrea Maria"

A cruise ship attack turns six survivors into overnight celebrities after they take credit for the heroic act of a stowaway who died saving them.

The cruise is just what Jess needed--a bit of harmless fun far from her daily grind. But what begins as a relaxing vacation turns into a desperate fight for her life when terrorists take over the ship and start piling up bodies. Teaming up with a mysterious stowaway, Jess attempts to send out a distress call but knows they cannot wait for help to come. If she or the few remaining passengers have any hope for survival, Jess must act now. The papers dub it "The Battle for *Andrea Maria*," but to Jess it is the moment she fought side-by-side with her enigmatic Romeo, saving the ship--and losing him. She thinks the story ends there, but really, the nightmare is just beginning...

"Insanely Deadly"

When the dead return to life, it's up to an admiral's daughter and a mildly insane, former war hero to save their small town.

Jetta Cross, a Navy Admiral's daughter, is tasked with keeping her father's comrade, a former war hero turned town crazy, grounded in the real world. Capt. John Hunter is still fighting the war in his head, where imaginary dead people are part of his world. When a viral outbreak brings about a zombie uprising, Hunter is left to his own devices. He must resume his role as a one-man commando unit in order to destroy the ravenous undead. With Hunter still fighting his own inner demons as well as the undead, the townspeople fear their zombie neighbors may not be the only threat. Stranded at the island's luxurious resort with a handful of workers, Jetta is forced to live up to her father's reputation and take charge of the deteriorating situation at the hotel. She must wage her own war against the infected before the government declares her hometown a total loss.

"Deadly Institution"

A town recluse suspected of killing his wife teams up with a young woman in order to stop a killer.

After being accused of murdering his wife, Konrad Churchill turns his back on the town that once adored him. Ten years later, he still holds his grudge and the title of the most feared man in town. With the reopening of the burned mental institution, where his wife had died, former employees are now murdered one-by-one, throwing suspicion back on Churchill. A young local reporter, Jacey, is forced to reveal her long-time friendship with the infamous recluse in order to clear his name not only in the recent murders but to exonerate him in the death of his wife as well. Will Jacey's relationship with Churchill invite the killer closer to her? Or is the killer already in her life?

"Death Displacement"

A grief-stricken man travels back in time to seek revenge on the woman who murdered his girlfriend but inadvertently falls in love with her.

Kane is about to marry the woman he loves. His life is perfect. A few weeks before the wedding, a vindictive woman from his girlfriend's past mysteriously arrives and kills her. He learns of a traumatic accident that happened five years earlier, which triggers Riley's hatred for his girlfriend. Distraught over his girlfriend's death, Kane uses an antique time machine to travel into the past in order to find and destroy the woman responsible. When he runs into Riley's younger self, he realizes she's not the monster she later becomes, and he can't bring himself to destroy her. With a little help from his oddball friend from the past, they formulate a plan to prevent the accident that sends Riley down her destructive path. Kane's plan backfires when he falls for the younger Riley. His new tortured existence is further complicated when future Riley, his girlfriend's killer, shows up with her own devious agenda that doesn't include him. Will he be able to stop the time ripple, which ultimately ends with his girlfriend's death? Or will future Riley take him out of the timeline forever--

"Dead Village"

After strange happenings isolate a small resort town from the rest of the world, nearly one hundred residents seek refuge at the closed hotel. Only eight survive the night. And that's just the beginning...

One day after the entire population of Fox Ridge Village disappears, a car wreck forces several unsuspecting crash victims to seek help at the closed summer hotel. Within the hotel, they discover the grisly aftermath of a brutal slaughter. Crash victims Vander and Devon, a reluctant clairvoyant, team up to solve the riddle of the "haunted hotel" and the mass hysteria plaguing the remaining survivors. By the time they discover the hotel's secret, they're already drawn into the hysteria. As the body count continues to climb, it's a race to isolate the source and bring everyone back to reality before they kill one another. Will Devon be able to communicate with the traumatized spirits before their fate becomes her own?

"Town Darling"

After surviving a brutal attack that claims the lives of those she loves, a young woman seeks revenge on a corrupt town.

Going back home is never easy, but for Casey, it means returning to her corrupt hometown where she barely survived a brutal attack. Accompanied by two family friends, she seeks justice for the night that destroyed her life. Her physical scars are nothing compared to her emotional ones, forcing the local sheriff to believe that the town darling is back for revenge. As the conspiracy for her revenge appears to be leading up to the coveted town fair, the sheriff is determined to stop her from fulfilling her vengeful scheme...but guilt over his role on that fateful night continues to haunt him. Will his desperate need for Casey's forgiveness be his undoing? Or will Casey's desire for revenge destroy them both?

"Basement Dwellers"

A viral outbreak at a hospital leaves a mortician, sheriff, and coroner fighting for their lives against a horde of undead and the CDC.

After a massive car wreck leaves several survivors in critical condition at the local hospital, a surgeon uses experimental drugs on his critical patients and accidentally causes a zombie outbreak. When local mortician, Lexx, receives an infected corpse as her client, she becomes stranded in the hospital basement during CDC quarantine along with the local sheriff and the coroner. The infamous surgeon struggles to find a cure for his infectious blunder by using the other survivors as test subjects. Meanwhile, Lexx and the sheriff attempt to locate his missing sister, who's stranded somewhere in the battle zone that once was the emergency room. It's a race against time and the ravenous undead. Can they survive the undead before CDC sanitizes the hospital of all infection?

"Misfits, Inc."

A seemingly ordinary, young woman meets four misfits who claim she has given them supernatural powers.

While on a business trip to a remote island paradise, a bored secretary, Hailey, has her world turned upside down when her path collides with a psychic freak, Skyler. He attempts to convince her that they had met in his dreams, and she had chosen him as one of her four mystic warriors. After Skyler foresees a woman's death, they discover an unidentified creature has killed one of the guests. They are joined by a lounge pianist and a rich playboy, who also claim they had met her in their dreams. If Skyler's prophecies are genuine, the evil entity controlling the ravenous creatures needs to destroy Hailey to ensure its survival. Reluctantly accepting her fate, Hailey has to locate the last and most powerful of her chosen warriors, The Guardian. Their fate is in doubt when The Guardian turns out to be a self-absorbed, former cat burglar with a bad attitude. Can Hailey turn her company of misfits into an elite team of mystic warriors? Or will The Guardian's secret agenda destroy them all?

"Deadly Institution 2"

When blackmail turns into murder, a young woman finds herself caught in the killer's crosshairs.

The small town of Stony Ridge is no stranger to scandal and persecution of the innocent. When a brutal killing shakes the town's prestigious country club, Jacey McMurray seeks help from a self-proclaimed vigilante, Konrad Churchill. As her professional and personal worlds collide, Jacey fears the stress of the country club killings have finally taken their toll on Churchill. Can a stressed out vigilante stop the killer before he strikes again?

"Witness Protection"
Also available in audiobook!

After witnessing an execution, a resourceful young woman attempts to disappear while being pursued by a hitman and a handsome federal agent.

A helicopter pilot, Jackie Remus, reluctantly agrees to go on a date with one of her clients, but her date is unexpectedly cut short when she witnesses a man being murdered. After narrowly escaping with her life, she is placed into protective custody. When the safe house is breached, Jackie makes a daring escape from both the hired killers and the handsome FBI agent, who wants to return her to protective custody. With a little help from her sly and crafty friend, Monroe, Jackie is convinced she can disappear until the trial. While on her journey to meet with her friend, she solicits help from a few shady but lovable characters along the way. Although she manages to stay one-step ahead of the hired killers, the federal agent remains in hot pursuit. Will Jackie reach Monroe before she's captured by the FBI and returned to protective custody? Or will the hired killers silence her first?

"Unconditional"

A young woman puts her life on hold to care for an unstable, highly skilled combat soldier, who believes someone is trying to kill him.

A botched military coup leaves a team of elite fighters injured with one clinging to life in a coma. When Harlan wakes from his coma, he's left with no memory of his past life. His commander's daughter, Indy, takes it upon herself to care for the fallen war hero. She's challenged with more than just his physical care as she combats with not only his memory loss but also his newly found desire for her. His infatuation with her becomes the least of her worries when he sinks back into his role of a combat soldier. Believing his life is in danger, his fighting skills surface, turning him into an unpredictable and dangerous man. Will his memory return to him before Indy is forced to commit him? Or will he finally find his nemesis, "the coyote", and possibly claim the life of an innocent person?

"The Pen Pal"

In order to save her friend, she must enter the mind of a serial killer.

When her best friend is abducted, no one believes Jolynn saw it in a psychic vision. With nowhere to turn, Jolynn reluctantly joins Agent Harris Slade and his team on their hunt for a sadistic serial killer known only as "The Pen Pal". Finally confronted with the killer, Jolynn realizes she must enter the mind of the psychopath in order to stop the brutal killings. But when her vision reveals a particularly disturbing death, can Jolynn sacrifice her lover for her friend?

"Witness Protection 2"
The Return of Whiskey Tango Foxtrot

Believing she holds the clue to millions in missing laundered money, a young woman is placed into the protective care of a former Navy SEAL team.

Feeling sorry for her recently separated co-worker, Leeann invites Wiley to join her and her friends on their night out. Little does she know that finding her co-worker murdered is just the beginning of her nightmare. Leeann unknowingly holds the key to fifty million dollars in potentially laundered mob money. With hired killers pursuing her, the FBI places her into a different kind of protective custody. Former Navy SEAL team Whiskey Tango Foxtrot reunites to keep Leeann alive at their secret hideaway. What should be an easy assignment takes an unscheduled turn when secrets, lies, and betrayal threaten to derail their mission. Is the team prepared for a war on their own doorstep? Will Leeann's misguided trust endanger the lives of those sent to protect her?

"Witness Protection 3"
Alpha Mike Foxtrot

A helicopter pilot risks her life to help a team of retired Navy SEALs rescue two girls from a killer.

When former Navy SEAL team Whiskey Tango Foxtrot asks for a simple favor, Jackie reluctantly offers her air-taxi services. What could go wrong? What begins as a search and rescue for two girls turns into a fight for survival against a heavily armed drug cartel. Wanted by the law with the cartel in hot pursuit and their home base breached, the team is forced to call in a favor from a questionable ally. Unfortunately, their new safe house isn't what it seems. Without knowing who the real enemy is, can Jackie and the team save their young witnesses from the hands of a killer?

"Already Dead"
Supernatural Collection

From the already dead to the undead. Three supernatural tales of "things that go bump in the night".

"Bloodletting" - A vampire themed resort allows guests to *participate* in their Bloodletting Ritual to celebrate the island's legendary vampires.

"Reaper of Souls" - A young woman must outwit an evil sorcerer in order to save her brother or become one of his minions forever.

"Already Dead" - When Flight 220 crashes, ten passengers make it to an isolated island, but only one man lives to tell the lie.

"Witness Protection 4"
O-Dark-Hundred

A simple assignment turns deadly when a retired Navy SEAL team uncovers a plot to kill a notorious mob boss.

When Whiskey Tango Foxtrot embarks on a simple stalking case, they're not prepared for a trip to a private island paradise owned by an infamous mobster. With one of their own suffering from traumatic head injuries, the team is left scrambling to decide what is real or imagined. The situation escalates even further when they uncover an assassination plot where everyone is a suspect. Now targets themselves, can the team survive their trip to paradise?

"Witness Protection 5"
Outside the Wire

After suffering several casualties on their last assignment, a retired Navy SEAL team discovers their misery is just beginning.

When Whiskey Tango Foxtrot returns home after suffering a devastating loss, they're hit with even more bad news regarding the rest of their team. Their grief is cut short when they discover their names are all on the same hit list. Hunted by relentless assassins, the scattered team must decide whether to remain safely hidden or find the man who put the price on their heads. Against the wishes of her teammates, Jackie strikes out on her own in order to save a friend who wants her dead. In a kill or be killed situation, will Jackie's emotions finally betray her?

"The Murder of Emily Fisher"

After finding their favorite teacher murdered, the lives of two teenage girls are forever changed.

Everyone loved Emily Fisher. While walking home one afternoon, two teenage girls, Sidney and Trisha, stumble upon a gruesome murder scene. The brutal murder of Emily Fisher, a young, attractive schoolteacher, shocks the small town of **Marilina**. After graduation, Sidney moves far away from the memories of the small town while Trisha retreats deeper into denial. Eight years after the murder, Sidney receives a desperate call from her childhood friend, forcing her to return home. Trisha believes Emily's killer was falsely accused and she manages to turn the entire town against her while attempting to prove it. When Trisha receives a death threat, Sidney realizes there may be some credibility to her friend's wild accusations. Is Trisha's mental breakdown a result of childhood trauma? Or is the real killer actually attempting to silence her? In order to save her friend, Sidney must answer the eight-year-old question. Who murdered Emily Fisher?

"Once Upon a Disaster"

A young homicide detective finds herself at the mercy of a hitman in the aftermath of an earthquake

While investigating the murder of a hitman, Detective Jade Wesson pursues a lead connecting the dead man to a break-in at a computer programming company. She's drawn into the world of nightclub owner and front man for the mob, Cody Riley. Her investigation keeps pointing to Cody's right-hand man and possible hitman, Vahn Lott. Despite her efforts to keep her investigation on track, Vahn has plans of his own for the attractive detective. When an unprecedented earthquake rocks their east coast town, Jade must put her life in Vahn's hands if she wants to survive. Can she trust a man who might be the killer she's hunting?

"Awaken the Dead"

A grieving innkeeper struggles to keep her haunted hotel out of foreclosure.

After losing her parents in a suspicious boating accident, Harley Brandon is determined to keep the family hotel out of foreclosure. Unfortunately, the hotel ghosts have other plans. Built with tainted money, the century old Horizon Hotel thrives on a tradition of murder, scandal, and suicide. As the paranormal activity increases to alarming levels, Harley discovers the truth about the hotel and its residents. Can Harley save her friends from the hotel's frightening hidden secrets?

"Castle Bloodshed"
Murder Collection

From a deadly island paradise to haunted castles. Three novella length tales of murder, mystery, and malicious intent.

"Castle Bloodshed" – A tour of Wesley Castle turns into a fight for survival as six stranded tourists discover the haunting secrets within the castle walls. A mystery writer teams up with an uptight butler in order stop a killer who may already be dead. Novella length paranormal murder mystery.

"Fleshies" – Is Uncle Rutger crazy? Five years ago, four business partners died within their newly purchased, fixer-upper castle. Their bodies were never found. The surviving partner, Rutger, claims a demon keeps him as its slave. Rutger's nephew schemes to save his uncle by sacrificing the lives of a group of stranded motorists and a high-profile novelist. Novella length supernatural murder mystery.

"Demon Island" – A group of strangers are invited to a remote island for the reading of a will. The guests soon discover they were brought to the island to be executed one-by-one. It's up to a private detective and a tenacious young woman to solve the murders and find a way to escape paradise. Novella length murder mystery.

"Brighton Island"

When a psychic visits a haunted island mansion, he inadvertently awakens the ghosts' tortured souls.

Something's not right with Simon. When Jacklyn brings her eccentric friend to her uncle's island mansion, she didn't expect him to slip into psychic overload. As Simon attempts to solve a decade-old, double homicide, Jacklyn is confronted with the possibility that she could be next to join the mansion ghosts. When they find themselves stranded on the secluded island, her Uncle Hyland wages his own war to save them from a flesh and blood killer. Will her uncle's "shock and awe" military tactics save them or get them killed? Can Simon bring peace to the tortured souls or unexpectedly join them?

"A.L.F. Resort"

A fantasy vacation turns into a nightmare when the resort's artificial life forms are compromised.

Welcome to A.L.F. Resort where you can live out your fantasies with safe, state-of-the-art artificial life form robots! When a young journalist and a photographer are sent to A.L.F. Resort to do a story for their magazine, Shay and Becka believe they've hit the jackpot of all work-cations. The engineers pull out all the stops to make their fantasies memorable. Unfortunately, the newly designed A.L.F., the Gen X, is smarter than his programming and creates havoc within Shay's fantasy. A computer malfunction removes their safety inhibitors and the A.L.F.s play out their own hostile fantasies. Zombies, bikers, and mobsters run amuck, turning fantasies into nightmares. Shay gets more of a story than she anticipates, but will she survive long enough to write it?

"Jungle Princess"

While stranded on a prison island, a young woman discovers a creature of "unknown" origin.

After their cruise ship sinks, Alex and two of her shipmates are stranded on a deserted, tropical island. Unfortunately, the castaways soon realize they're not alone. They discover an abandoned prison with over two dozen inmates living on the island's south side. While avoiding the prison on the far side of the island, Alex discovers a strange but loveable creature of unknown origin. When one of her fellow castaways is in trouble, Alex reluctantly seeks help from the prisoners. After the brutal murder of several inmates, their questions surrounding the abandoned prison are about to be answered. What really killed over one hundred prisoners? And is it still out there?

"Murder in Wax"

A series of brutal murders plague a quiet farming community when beautiful women audition for the same acting job.

While all the young women in town are fighting over a once-in-a-lifetime acting opportunity, Devon Vincent is excited about her new job at the local wax museum. Although supportive of her friend's acting aspirations, Devon has a hard time understanding the rivalry among the women in town. When the aspiring actresses are brutally murdered one-by-one, Devon fears her friend may be the next victim. Devon finds herself in the middle of a murderous revenge plot that leads back to the wax museum's doorstep and possibly implicates her boss as the killer. Will Devon's newly found feelings for her boss bring a killer closer to her? Or is the killer already in her circle?

"Witness Protection 6"
Alpha Dogs

An easy rescue turns into a wild ride for retired Navy SEAL team Whiskey Tango Foxtrot when everyone wants to kill their client.

It was a simple task. Rescue a young woman from her mob boss father-in-law. Little did Jackie and company realize that rescuing the young woman was the easy part. Keeping her alive would be a massive undertaking, especially when everyone wants a piece of the mafia heiress. The team fights for survival against their toughest adversaries yet. How many innocent people must die in order to save one woman? Can the team survive the ultimate battle between mercenaries and assassins?

"Midnight Requisition"

A series of brutal murders leaves a traumatized young woman on a hunt to find a killer.

When they were just babies, Scorpio and her twin brother, Kane, tragically lost their parents under mysterious circumstances. Refusing to accept his father was dead, Kane set off on a mission to find a man he'd never met. A home invasion gone wrong leaves Scorpio grieving the loss of those she loves. Out of the tragedy of her loss, two fallen heroes are thrust upon her. Scorpio soon realizes someone wants her dead and the killer may already be in her circle. As her entire life unravels in a web of betrayal and lies, can Scorpio trust her new, slightly questionable friends?

"Until Death"

Liars, cheaters, blackmail and murder. It would be a wedding no one would forget.

Despite knowing he's making the biggest mistake of his life, Raina Steele reluctantly attends her father's third wedding. What should have been a boring reception turns into a web of lies, betrayal, and murder. With no one above suspicion, Raina must put aside her feud with the arrogant yet insanely handsome butler in order to catch the killer before he finds his next victim. With a murderer waiting to strike and lives hanging in the balance, the real question remains...the bride is wearing white? Seriously?

"Tainted"

What happens at the Dark Forest Hotel, stays at the Dark Forest Hotel...for all eternity.

What secrets surround Dark Forest Hotel? After her parents die under mysterious circumstances, sixteen-year-old Jeri escapes foster care and seeks refuge at a "closed for the season" hotel. Over the next six years, Jeri graduates from teenage runaway to the hotel's assistant general manager. When she learns a convention is secretly held every year in her absence, she demands answers from her boss, friends, and co-workers. After getting conflicting stories, Jeri sets out to discover the truth. She's suddenly thrown into a horrifying new world where vampires and vicious creatures are craving her virgin blood. After six years of everyone lying to her, is there anyone she can trust?

"Witness Protection 7"
Bravo Foxtrot

An Army deserter on the run brings mayhem to a retired Navy SEAL team when his teenage daughter is caught in a mercenary's cross-hairs.

A weekend of fun turns into a race for survival as Monique and Colleen's surrogate big brother, Bogart, rescues the girls from mercenaries hunting Colleen's Army deserter father. With the girls safely stashed at their Colorado hideaway, trouble brews when the team discovers Colleen's father was framed by his former commander over a stolen, high-tech weapon. In order to clear Colleen's father and bring him home, the team must fight one of their toughest advisories yet...a high-ranking military officer with countless mercenaries and the U.S. military behind him.

"Midnight Requisition 2"
Amateur Night

A brother and sister duo team up to catch a potential kidnapper.

After finally reuniting with her not-so-dead brother, Scorpio and her friends are taunted into helping him with his new case. A wealthy cattle rancher believes someone wants to abduct his daughter, but the team suspects her ex-boyfriend is pulling off an elaborate scheme to win her back. What appears to be a slice of paradise in the Colorado Mountains turns out to be a venomous snake pit filled with lies, lust, betrayal, and murder. Surviving the depraved family becomes the least of the team's worries when a botched kidnapping turns into murder.

"Cemetery Stalkers" Horror Collection

Four tales of horror from flesh eating alien monsters to blood sucking vampires.

"Night Creatures" – When a rescue party becomes stranded on an abandoned cruise ship, they discover the terrifying secret unleashed from the cargo hold. What starts out as a rescue mission rapidly deteriorates into survival as the small group is hunted by a frightening creature with a taste for human flesh. Novella length horror book.

"Ravenous" – After escaping a carjacking in the back woods, a young woman seeks refuge in a mysterious mansion with a terrifying secret. Despite promises of a ride to town in the morning, she's convinced she's being held prisoner by a cult leader. Short paranormal story.

"The Feast" – Five years ago, a killer went on a murderous rampage at the church picnic. Despite eyewitness accounts of a non-human killer, the local law refused to believe the town's citizens. When a group of teenagers stumble upon the contained remains of the killer, they unwittingly set him free to continue his terror upon the small town. Novella length paranormal book.

"Cemetery Stalkers" – When 'The Reaper' stalks a cemetery, death follows. Following a series of bizarre incidents within the cemetery, a young woman fears for the safety of her friend, who lives in the middle of spook central. Short horror story.

"Jumpers"

When a cruise ship is exposed to a deadly virus, the fate of the world rests in the hands of a lounge dancer and a conman.

An infectious outbreak threatens the passengers and crew of the "Queen Anita" and the entire world if the virus makes it back to civilization. Lounge dancer, Maxine, must find a way to prevent the destruction of the world, but in order to do that, she needs to trust a conman with unique insight into the virus.

"Witness Protection 8"
Midnight Requisition

A brother and sister duo finds themselves on an explosive collision course with a team of retired Navy SEALs.

Obsessed with the belief that his father is still alive, Kane Wayland embarks on a foolhardy mission to confront the elusive, former Navy SEAL, Zack Kinsley. Despite heavy protests, Kane's sister, Scorpio, joins him on his quest. The disastrous "reunion" comes with a steep price that none are prepared to pay. With the haunting reality of the botched mission, Midnight Requisition, still looming over each of them, can the two teams pull together in time to prevent another tragedy?

"Midnight Requisition 3"
Circular Run

A brother and sister reopen a hotel with a tainted history only to discover its past refuses to stay dead and buried.

Scorpio and Kane Wayland finally realize their dream of reopening their grandfather's old, cliffside hotel in Maine. With the hotel's checkered past behind it, the relaunch is a dream come true. Unfortunately, history has a habit of repeating itself. When guests mysteriously vanish, the hotel's somewhat seedy clientele are all now suspects. In order to save their hotel, Scorpio and Kane must stop a killer. When your guests are mercenaries, bounty hunters, and mobsters, who can you trust?

"Raven Force"

An inn keeper becomes involved in a game of espionage after picking up a mysterious hitchhiker.

After surviving a nightmare of a date, Maxine Croft didn't think her evening could get any worse...until she nearly hits a stranger on a dark back road. This unprecedented meeting would turn Max's world upside down as she's thrust into a world of murder, corruption, and deception within her own backyard. As she gets in deeper with an elite, special task force, Max inadvertently puts her sisters' lives in danger. Will Max and her sisters become just more "collateral damage" to facilitate the team's mission?

"Witness Protection 9"
S.N.A.F.U.

A notorious mob boss turns to a retired Navy SEAL team to keep his son alive.

They were made an offer they couldn't refuse. When his son is accused of murdering known mobsters throughout Colorado, Giovanni turns to the retired Navy SEAL team of Whiskey Tango Foxtrot to keep his boy alive and prevent a war between the "families". With the mobster's son in the crosshairs of every hitman and bounty hunter on the West Coast, Jackie and the boys need to find Marco and go completely off-grid. But is the team risking their lives to protect a serial killer?

"Midnight Requisition 4"
Charlie Foxtrot

A mob convention at a remote cliffside hotel has murderous consequences.

Hotel owner, Scorpio Wayland, reluctantly books a "mob" convention at her quiet, cliffside resort. What could go wrong? When former mob boss, Salvatore Romano invites friends for a "family" reunion, disaster swiftly follows.

"Witness Protection 10"
Bravo Zulu

It's all hands on deck when the mob declares war on the team and everyone they love.

Whiskey Tango Foxtrot reunites with Midnight Requisition when war is declared by a notorious mobster and his army of highly trained soldiers. After several deadly attacks shake both teams, their skills, loyalties, and limitations are tested in an explosive and bloody rampage that will scar and change their lives forever.

"Pretty Little Dead Things"

Romance, scandal, and an unsolved murder. Welcome to snob central!

After a disastrous evening at the exclusive country club gala, Marley Temple doesn't think her life can get any worse. When someone close to her is murdered, Marley is left devastated. Although everyone else seems to move on after the unsolved homicide, Marley can't let it go. She's suddenly thrust into the inner circle of a wealthy playwright recluse, whose stage actress wife was brutally butchered just two years earlier. Although Marley fears falling for the infamous Devlin Ryker, forming a strange alliance with him brings her closer to solving the perplexing murder. But as she gets closer to learning the truth, the killer gets closer to her. Will Marley discover the killer's identity before she becomes his next victim?

ABOUT THE AUTHOR

Holly Copella has been writing since the age of twelve when her frustration at a book's poor plot drove her to author her own story. Over the last decade, she's written a number of screenplays, some of which she's now adapting into novels. Her fascination with zombies and other darker material lends an edge to her writing, which tends to lean toward horror. As a fan of Agatha Christie, she appreciates the craft of a good plot and the importance of creating significant characters.

Hailing from Pennsylvania, Copella lives in the Endless Mountains on a farm with her new horse, Maverick, and other animals. In addition to writing and reading fiction, she enjoys riding horses and traveling to Las Vegas.

www.ingramcontent.com/pod-product-compliance
Lightning Source LLC
Chambersburg PA
CBHW071636260626
47170CB00001B/129